UNTO CAESAR

UNTO CAESAR

F. A. VOIGT

G·P·PUTNAM'S SONS
NEW YORK
1938

COPYRIGHT, 1938, BY F. A. VOIGT

All rights reserved. This book, or parts thereof, must not be reproduced in any form without permission.

MANUFACTURED IN THE UNITED STATES OF AMERICA
Van Rees Press · New York

To

S. O. LEVINSON

the father of "Outlawry"
with affectionate admiration

CONTENTS

	PAGE
PREFATORY NOTE	XI
CHAPTER I	3

Marxism—The conflict of "opposites"—Marxian dogma a subjective myth—The Marxian goal of Heaven on Earth—The "final and decisive battle"—The ferocity and complacency of the Marxian vision—Marxism and reform—Marxism and the "petit bourgeois"—Fundamental resemblance between Marxism and National Socialism—The debt of National Socialism to Marxism—The two secular religions compared—The "withering away" of the State—Marxian ethics as spurious as Marxian science.

CHAPTER II	45

The attainment of the Millennium—The myth of Marxism and of National Socialism—Their pseudo-philosophical and pseudo-scientific character—Lenin and Hitler, a comparison of their beliefs and methods—Lenin obsessed by the reality of class, Hitler by the reality of race—Lenin a would-be destroyer of, Hitler a corrupter of, religion—Hitler's fundamental doctrine of the "Greater Germany"—His mission to achieve that end—His identification of racial principles with the "will of God"—His attitude towards class—The difference between Marxian and National Socialist economics.

CHAPTER III	66

The contrasted attitudes of Lenin and Hitler towards mankind—The Golden Age and the Heroic Age—The brutality of Marxism and of National Socialism—A comparison with the Cromwellian era—Lenin's and Hitler's ruthlessness of purpose—Hitler's conception of war as permanently desirable—The Brown Terror—Hitler the chief terrorist—The hatreds of Lenin and of Hitler—Their intolerance—The essential kinship and parallel development of the two leaders—The Marxian and National Socialistic view of history—The arrogance of the Marxian myth—Marxism, Fascism, and National Socialism—Hitler's conception of the "German race"—Hitler and Marxism—The development of the National Socialist counter-myth—An estimate of the "greatness" of Marx and Lenin.

CHAPTER IV	100

Mussolini—Where he differs from Lenin and Hitler—Hitler—The significance of *Mein Kampf*—His aspirations, his qualities, and his practical achievements—His special aptitude for the dirty work of revolution—The intensity of his emotions—The triumph of the National Socialist revolution—The nature of Hitler's demagogy—His version of the "communist danger"—The burning of the Reichstag—Anti-Semitism—Hitler's "case" against the Jews—The "Protocols of the Elders of Zion"—The significance of Hitler's hatred of the Jews—The visual intensity of his hatred and its concentrated malignance—The formation of the Jew myth—Hitler's character and peculiar gifts—His physical characteristics—His projection of himself.

CHAPTER V 122

Social Democracy in Germany—Its achievement—The revolution of 1918—The danger of territorial disruption—The Treaty of Versailles and the German Republic—The stand made by the Social Democrats and the Trade Unions—The defeat of Social Democracy—Reasons for this defeat—The part played by the Soviet Union—Communism and National Socialism.

CHAPTER VI 147

The influence of Versailles in the National Socialist revolution—The powerful sense of German unity—German civilization—The foreshadowing of National Socialism—Its background in German history—The territorial settlement at Versailles—Germany's post-Treaty position—The essential aspiration of the Third Realm is the establishment of a Pan-German hegemony—The implications of this aspiration—War?—The case of Austria—The significance of the "Anschluss"—The position of Czechoslovakia and of the Soviet Union—Germany's own position.

CHAPTER VII 175

The Pax Britannica—The limitations of international law—Armaments a condition not of war but of peace—The achievement of the Pax Britannica—The Pax Britannica and the wider responsibility of the British Commonwealth—The way to its achievement—Civilization itself contains the menace of war—The cause of war—The fixing of the responsibility for war—Nations' reasons for entering upon war—The British post-war dream of the establishment of universal peace—Implications and danger of that dream—The Covenant of the League and the doctrine of sanctions—An examination of that doctrine—Its evil inherent—No reason to suppose that a universal system of "sanctions" would abolish war even for a time—How the "sanctionist" system would operate—The position of Great Britain—The doctrine of "sanctions" a modern myth.

CHAPTER VIII 191

England's vulnerability—Her dependence on armed strength—Her widespread interests and responsibilities—A "World Power or nothing"—Her lack of security—The limitation of her power—"Sanctions" against Japan in 1931—And against Italy in 1935—The logical conclusion of the "sanctionist" policy—Possible consequences of that conclusion—The ethics of the right to declare war for a principle—The decision to abandon "sanctions" against Italy—The results of that decision—The rebirth of Pan-Germanism—England's position in the year 1938—The case of Austria—The *casus belli* for England—Aspects of German expansion in Central

CONTENTS

and Eastern Europe—What policy is demanded by English interests?—The Italian problem in relation to the German problem—England and the Mediterranean—The policy of "non-intervention" in Spain—The real nature of that policy—The significance of the Spanish Civil War.

CHAPTER IX 212

The protagonists in Spain—The course of the Spanish Civil War—German intervention—Italian aspirations—Mussolini's position—The position of Russia—Trotsky and Stalin—Stalin's personal despotism—The "new Russia"—Its achievements and its failures—England's interest in the balance of power in the Far East—Her vital influence in world politics—Germany her foremost foreign problem—The Pax Europaica can only come through a political balance between England, France, and Germany—The purpose of British foreign policy—The League of Nations—Its achievement—Its failure to achieve the impossible—What the League should be—Anglo-American co-operation—The ideal foreign policy of England—The triangle: London, Washington, Geneva—Unless England is strong . . .

NOTES 243

INDEX 297

PREFATORY NOTE

THIS book was finished before the middle of February, 1938. Since then, the union of Germany and Austria—the "Anschluss"—has been achieved. In little more than a month the balance of power has been weighted heavily against Great Britain, while the ascendancy of the Germans and Italians in Spain has increased the menace to her communications in the Mediterranean and eastern Atlantic.

On the 24th March, Mr. Neville Chamberlain said in the House of Commons that, while England could not guarantee the independence of Czechoslovakia, a central European war would have consequences that might compel England to fight in defense of her own security. There is no statesman more determined than Mr. Chamberlain to confine the purpose of his foreign policy to the bare defense of British interests, and his words show, more than the words of any other man could show, that the destiny of Great Britain is entwined with the destiny of Europe as a whole.

It would now seem that the danger of precipitating a general European war will deter Hitler from an armed attack on Czechoslovakia. Mr. Chamberlain's warning will have made him doubly alive to that danger, all the more so as the warning is to be followed by an increase, long overdue, in the speed and volume of British rearmament. It would seem that Czechoslovakia will be "masked" like a fortress that cannot be assaulted with impunity. But she will be invested and will be menaced by political and economic pressure from without and by disruption from within. It would seem that Hitler will reduce Hungary to semi-vassalage. He will then be on the Rumanian border and will, by peaceful penetration and various forms of pressure, including the menace of rebellion amongst the large Hungarian and the smaller German minorities, try to achieve an ascendancy over Rumania that would place her rich supplies of raw material, especially oil, at his disposal.

Nor will Poland, the Baltic States, and Russia be able to elude the German challenge.

A month ago it seemed that the Spanish civil war might go on for another year, or even more, and perhaps end inconclusively. But for the first time General Franco and his German and Italian auxiliaries have been able to concentrate enough artillery and bombing squadrons to create the equivalent of a creeping barrage against which the best infantry in the world would be helpless. The Spanish Government and their French and international auxiliaries are far too ill-supplied with artillery and aeroplanes to carry out a counter-concentration.

It may be that, if General Franco wins the war, the German and Italian troops will leave. But the German and Italian political and commercial agents, their military, technical, and administrative experts, their institutes and educational establishments, their subsidized newspapers, their propagandists, their open and secret clubs and societies, will remain. For a long time to come, Spain will be under German and Italian influence.

England and France will be compelled to develop a counter-influence, for even the discreetest ascendancy of any foreign Powers in Spain threatens one of the main arterial systems of the British Commonwealth and of the French Empire.

The end of the civil war is, therefore, not the end of the Spanish problem. When the fighting has ceased, that problem will be reopened in all its historic gravity.

F. A. VOIGT.

London, May, 1938.

UNTO CAESAR

CHAPTER I

Marxism—The conflict of "opposites"—Marxian dogma a subjective myth—The Marxian goal of Heaven on Earth—The "final and decisive battle"—The ferocity and complacency of the Marxian vision—Marxism and reform—Marxism and the "petit bourgeois"—Fundamental resemblance between Marxism and National Socialism—The debt of National Socialism to Marxism—The two secular religions compared—The "withering away" of the State—Marxian ethics as spurious as Marxian science.

LENIN held that every revolutionary movement must have "a revolutionary theory." [1] He held that the Marxian "theory" not only serves a revolutionary purpose as no other theory can, but that it is "true" by every philosophical, scientific, and "objective" test. But if we examine the Marxian "theory," we find it is not a theory at all, or even a hypothesis. It has no philosophical or scientific validity whatever and breaks down under every "objective" test. It is a myth, or, to give modern myths their modern name, an "ideology."

The conglomerate of dogma, doctrine, precept, and exegesis known as "Marxism," professes to reveal not only man's true destiny, but also the way he can—and must—achieve the fulfillment of that destiny in the universal dominion of equality, freedom, justice, and well-being: in the Kingdom of Heaven on Earth.

Marxism claims not only to be true, but to be *the* Truth. It denies any salvation or way of salvation other than revealed by Karl Marx and his friend, Friedrich Engels.

Marxism is, therefore, a religion. But, in so far as it conceives the "perfect state" as being *of this world,* in so far as its Kingdom of Heaven is *on Earth,* it is a *secular* religion.

The supposedly philosophical content of the Marxian myth, or rather the central myth itself, which is known as "dialectical materialism," is represented by Marxists as being a revolutionary advance on the Hegelian "dialectic."

A hypothesis will undergo modification when it is confronted with contrary evidence which may crystallize in a contrary hypothesis. The fusion of contrary hypotheses will produce a theory that will represent an "advance" in human thought. By this "dialectical" process, or fusion of opposites, truths are engendered.

Here we have a familiar process of the reasoning mind. But Hegel went much further. His system is based on the identity of thought and being. Thought and being move forward by the evolution and reconciliation of opposites, or, in other words, by thesis, antithesis, and synthesis. The *Hegelian* "dialectic" is not merely a process of the reasoning mind, but a cosmic process, indeed *the* cosmic process. All history, the history of the universe, and not only of mankind, is God's "dialectical" self-realization. All history comes to an end in the fullness of His self-realization.

But it is very hazardous indeed to detect the cosmic process in the highly complex, fleeting and intangible phenomena of human life. To accept the Hegelian "dialectic" as a philosophical doctrine is one thing—to interpret actual history (including the events of our own day) in terms of this "dialectic" is another.

If we examine categories such as "Feudalism," "Capitalism," or "Communism," we find that they are complex, hard to define, and incapable of being studied "in vacuo."

Marxists treat them as though they were simple, tangible, and clearly recognizable entities, like elements in a test-tube, and subject to unalterable laws of predictable behavior.

When we try to establish "opposite" categories, we at once encounter insuperable difficulties. Peace and War are presumably "opposites." But it is not easy to see how these opposites could fuse to produce a new entity (unless it be the doctrine of "sanctions"). To say that "Capitalism" is the opposite of "Communism" (or "Socialism") is to say something that may have an illustrative value (as emphasizing certain contrasts between an order in which capital is privately owned and one in which capital is publicly owned), but can have no philosophical or scientific validity at all.

Socialism is a *form* of Capitalism. The tendency towards public control and ownership of the means of production was perceptible in Marx's own day. The tendency has gathered momentum since then and there is considerable truth in his prophecy that Socialism is "inevitable." But it is very doubtful whether pure Socialism is the *ultimate* form of Capitalism—indeed it is doubtful if capital *can* have any *ultimate* form. The movement from private capitalism to Socialism may even be reversed, either by violent or by peaceful revolution, by a "proletariat" hungering after private ownership. Something of the kind would now appear to be happening in Russia.

The criteria of the Marxist are almost entirely *subjective*. The "opposite" of what he likes is what he dislikes—that, and very little more. He imagines Communism and Fascism (or its more advanced German form of National Socialism) to be "opposites." A certain color is lent to his view because the two are often, though not always, in actual conflict. But that is no reason for supposing them to be opposites in any philosophical or scientific sense. Indeed, they are much alike, as we shall see later on, though it would be by no means the first time that people are fighting one another in the pursuit of similar aims.

Are there any discernible "opposites" in the phenomenal world? If so, what are they? This is a question the Marxist does not answer. He neither asks nor answers *any* philosophical questions. He is neither a philosopher nor a scientist—he is a *believer*, who retains this much of the Christian heritage that he thinks in terms of good and evil. But instead of holding, as the Christian does, that we are all *under sin*, he identifies evil with "Capitalism," and imagines that if Capitalism is destroyed, evil will perish with it.

No doubt some of the evil in this world has been caused by the private ownership of capital. Socialism would remove certain evils—but like every general system, it has evils of its own. Neither Capitalism nor Socialism are in *themselves* good or evil. A civilized State, even if it retains the private ownership of capital, is preferable to an uncivilized State, even if it is Socialist, and the reverse. Socialism is by no means incompatible with inhuman oppression or, for that matter, with extreme economic inequality. Nor is there any reason to suppose that the Socialist State as such is less warlike than the Capitalist State. If we survey the world today we shall find the highest civilization and the greatest peace and contentment in the western and north-western fringe of Europe and in North America—that is to say, in regions where public and private ownership of capital go hand in hand (though it would be rash to conclude that this circumstance is the *cause* of their relative well-being—the causes certainly lie far deeper).

The attitude of Marxists to Capitalism has something in common with the attitude of the National Socialist to Judaism, though it is less ignoble. The National Socialist regards the Jew as embodying the principle of evil and, therefore, as his own "opposite" (it is highly characteristic of sectarians that *they* are always good while their *opposites* are always evil). Both attitudes may be fortified by a number of objectively discernible facts, but they remain essentially subjective nevertheless. Both engender a personal hatred, not only of the abstractions "Capitalism" and "Judaism," but of the individual Capitalist and the individual Jew, a hatred that often finds expression in gross, calumniatory caricature. There is a very striking resemblance between the bestial creatures who play the part of typical Capitalists in Russian "revolutionary" films, and the Jew, as caricatured in the pages of the infamous anti-Semitic periodical, the *Stürmer*. If we examine the Communist Manifesto, which was drawn up by Marx and Engels in 1848, and became a kind of Marxian Creed, we shall find passages like the following:

"Our bourgeois, not content with having the wives and daughters of the proletariat at their disposal, not to speak of common prostitutes, take the greatest pleasure in seducing each other's wives. Bourgeois marriage is in reality a system of wives in common...."

These words might have been lifted bodily from any of the grosser anti-Semitic leaflets that circulate in Germany, Rumania, or Poland today, if the word "Jewish" had been substituted for "bourgeois." Hitler repeatedly says things of this kind about the Jews in his book *Mein Kampf*, as we shall see later on. The communal ownership of women is a perennial falsehood (like the dum-dum bullet, that re-occurs in every war). The so-called "bourgeois" said exactly the same thing with just as little truth about the "People's Commissars" in the early days of the Russian revolution, these Commissars being credited with luxurious living and the use of "nationalized" women. But the notion that two bewhiskered gentlemen like Marx and Engels, whose own lives were entirely virtuous, should in all solemnity have penned such stuff, would merely be comic did it not afford a glimpse of the ferocity and untruthfulness that are inherent in the secular religions of our day. It also reveals the naïveté of these "philosophers" who see in the "proletarian" a creature as virtuous as themselves, except when "Capitalism" forces him into a life of vice.

The Marxian attitude towards events, persons, situations always *appears* to be highly critical, and Marxism is paraded as the only effective *apparatus criticus* of universal reliability. But so far from being critical, the Marxian attitude is anti-critical. So far from being critical, the genuine Marxist never questions the fundamentals of his "philosophy," although this is exactly what a genuine philosopher must always be doing. The Marxist is a believer and his belief has the anti-critical dogmatism of the sectarian.

Christian dogma is not an *object* of belief (as the Marxist imagines it to be and as his own dogma is), but rather a sign-post, as it were, pointing out the direction across the Wilderness of this World, across the Slough of Despond, across By-Path Meadow, the Deep Pit, and the Grounds of Giant Despair, and over the Delectable Mountains. But it is not more than a sign-post. It is not part of the Christian faith, but a helpful accessory, though by no means without its own dangers, as the history of every Church has abundantly shown. It is agreeable to linger by the sign-post, and whenever it is used as a resting-place, the Pilgrim is tempted to end his journey (for the sign-post may mark a spot as attractive, seemingly, as the Celestial City), and whenever the dogma becomes an object of belief and dogmatism replaces faith, then doubt—the restlessness of spirit that urges the Pilgrim to continue on his Progress—is extinguished and Christianity assumes the character of a secular religion. It thereby ceases to be Christianity.

Marxian dogma proclaims a supposedly "objective" reality, but this reality is a subjective *myth*. So far from being philosophical and scientific, Marxism is mythological and an attack—the first of the great modern attacks—on philosophy and science.

The Marxian "bourgeois," "petit bourgeois," "proletarian," and so on, have some relationship with the real world, just as King Arthur and other legendary figures may have had. But they have been transmuted into denizens of a mythical world governed by the inexorable "dialectic."

Engels, no doubt unwittingly, reveals the character of this transmutation in a very interesting passage:

"This modern materialism," he writes (meaning "dialectical materialism") . . . "is in fact no longer a philosophy, but a simple conception of the world which has to establish its validity and be applied not in a science of sciences standing apart, but within the positive sciences" [by "positive" Engels means pragmatic]. "In this development philosophy, therefore, is sublated," that is, "both abolished and preserved—abolished as regards its form, and preserved as regards its real content." [2]

Quite true. "This modern materialism" is indeed "no longer a philosophy" (it never was one), but "a simple"—a very simple—"conception of the world." This "conception" is not achieved by objective inquiry or by any process of scientific investigation or philosophical reasoning, it is the myth which the Marxist believes to be the "real content" of philosophy.

Hegel, for whom there was no reality independent of mind, regarded the dialectical process as the moving of the Universal Spirit. But, to the Marxist, terms like "the universal spirit" are merely contemptible. He regards anything that is of the *spirit* and any form of transcendentalism as "bourgeois," "reactionary," "counter-revolutionary," and so on. He divides philosophies into "idealistic" and "materialistic," the former being wholly false, the latter having an element of truth which, in the course of evolution, becomes "dialectical materialism," which is *the* Truth.

Being impervious to doubt himself, the Marxist is intolerant of doubt in his fellow-men when he has power over them—indeed he hates and despises the doubter more than the heretic.

Towards none is the Marxist more intolerant than to co-religionists who deviate but slightly from accepted orthodoxy. The feud between rival Marxian sects like the Communists and the Social Democrats has at times been altogether monstrous in its meaningless ferocity. To be a non-Marxist in Russia today is not a positive offense (provided the principles of Marxism are not openly criticized), but to be a Menshevik or, even worse, a Trotskyite is punishable by death or long imprisonment and exile, although

Mensheviks and Trotskyites have more genuine Marxism than Stalin and his associates.

This is a phenomenon familiar enough throughout religious history:

"As a rule in the ancient, the medieval and, to this day, in the post-Reformation Church, down to Pietism and the Enlightment, conflict with Jews, pagans, and atheists was purely incidental, pursued with nothing like the same zeal as that against heretics.... Between Church and heretics they really talked against each other (instead of past each other), *i.e.* absolutely differently about absolutely the same object.... People took opposite sides to the death, which can only happen when brothers are at feud...." [3]

One reason why doctrinal opposition is not tolerated in Russia is, that the Marxian myth has come to be identified with the ruling system, while the doctrinal opposition threatens to weaken the system by disproving that identity and claiming the myth for itself:

"Heresy can only attack the Church on the ground that the latter is not sufficiently, not truly, the Church." [4]

That is precisely what the very limited doctrinal opposition in Russia has tried to do, and there is nothing that could be more infuriating to the ruling bureaucracy. Another reason why opposition is found to be intolerable is, that the disparities between theoretical precept and actual practice have come about under the cumulatively irresistible pressure of the developing political and economic situation. But not only do those who oppose the regime (and it is opposed almost exclusively by Marxists) claim to be true believers, they also endeavor to promote a policy which, because it is orthodox, is ultimately impossible (being eschatological), and therefore dangerous. And it would, if followed, lead to a renewal of the disasters that were brought about during the first few years of the revolution by too rigid an application of orthodox principles. Thus, although political persecution in Russia is essentially religious, it has a practical purpose as well. And whatever may be said about the methods by which Stalin stamps out genuine "Trotskyism" (as distinct from the fictitious "Trotskyism" that is fastened upon innumerable persons merely that they may be discredited and so the more easily destroyed), it is quite certain that if the "Trotskyite" doctrine of the "permanent revolution" were to dominate Russian domestic and foreign policy, the Soviet Union would move from catastrophe to catastrophe.

In Russia, where Marxism has all the coercive instruments of the modern State at its disposal, there is no such thing as philosophy; nor could there be, under the domination of a doctrine which, even if it has become adulterated by all kinds of accretions, especially nationalist accretions, remains intolerant of all criticism touching fundamentals, a doctrine that never questions its own premises, a doctrine claiming to be the Truth, so that every other doctrine is officially stamped—and stamped out—as falsehood.

The Soviet Union has not produced, because it cannot tolerate, a single work of philosophical value. And this is true not only of original philosophical writing—which has grown scarce everywhere—but even of philosophical criticism. There are not, and cannot be, any philosophical thinkers in Russia, or, if there are, they must keep their thoughts in total obscurity. In no case can they have a public, either at home or abroad. What Russian thought there is today can exist only beyond the frontiers of the Soviet Union—Berdyaeff, who has made interesting contributions to the religious thought of our day, and Lossky, a philosopher of very high order, cannot even live in the Soviet Union, still less can they publish their works there.

What is called "philosophy" in Russia is not, and cannot be, philosophy at all. It is a kind of imitative and Talmudistic exegesis of original Marxian literature. A narrow fanaticism invariably marks this pseudo-philosophy and is combined with an insolently mocking attitude towards everything of a truly critical or philosophical nature.

Marxian political writers and orators often make a parade of so-called "self-criticism" (sometimes referred to as "Leninist self-criticism") when they survey the past and when "mistakes" are "admitted." This "self-criticism" is not criticism at all, but a form of self-righteousness, a pharisaical public display of pseudo-revivalist heart-searching.

Their imperviousness to doubt goes hand in hand with a servile acceptance of even the most platitudinous utterances of Marx and his successors.

Anthony Jenkinson, visiting Russia in 1557, wrote:

"All their churches are full of images, unto which people, when they assemble, doe bowe and knocke their heads that some will have knobbes upon their foreheads with knocking, as great as egges." [5]

There has been no change. The "images" are the teaching of Karl Marx, the writings and the mummified corpse of Lenin, and the speeches and portraits of Stalin. The "knobbes" are "ideological"—but none the less real for that reason.

The corpus of contemporary Russian "philosophy" is a monument of pragmatic ignorance.[6] For the "thinkers" of the Union the work of St. Thomas of Aquinas, Spinoza, Kant, and Pascal, either has no existence at all, or is an object of derision, while the majestic edifice erected by Hegel has no validity except as the footstool Karl Marx used for a while and then kicked aside.

In the pragmatic sciences the Russian achievement is comparable with that of other modern States; but speculative science, no more possible without the constant questioning of its conceptual foundations than philosophy, has to work under impossible restrictions in Russia.

Science everywhere is in a state of confusion largely because of the decline in metaphysical speculation (very few modern scientists are trained metaphysicians), but in Russia the metaphysical background cannot even exist. Even pragmatic biological research is, in Russia, invaded by Marxian subjectivism which, for example, makes the theory of "mutations" seem attractive because it provides a biological analogy to violent revolution; evolution (as expounded by Darwin), being a gradual process, smells of the "petite bourgeoisie," of Social Democracy (or of "Macdonaldism").[7]

If we consider the profoundly religious and metaphysical character of the greatest philosophers and of many great scientific thinkers, and if we consider that for the Marxist this character *as such* is the object of implacable hostility, and, when he is in power, of physical extermination, we are bound to admit that Marxism is at war with the noblest faculties of the human mind.

Marxism is a denial of all but pragmatic thought. The Marxist as such does not and cannot think at all in a higher sense, and we find, even amongst writers with some little claim to be thinkers, the arrogance and superficiality so characteristic of all Marxian literature if they themselves have any affinities with Marxism. Nearly all contemporary English thought that is perceptibly "Left" has been touched by the Marxian blight.

We shall see later on that National Socialist "thought" is similarly subjective and at least equally a spreader of intellectual servility and corruption.[8]

For the Marxist there is no such thing as pure knowledge. Only the pragmatic, only the "thought" that can be translated into political action (not merely into behavior—it is never the purpose of Marxian teaching to make men *good*), only the science that is ultimately *useful*, has any validity for the Marxist or is tolerated when he is in control.

Much has been done for the spread of elementary education in the Soviet Union—but higher education has ceased to exist.[9] Under the oppressive rule of the Tsars there was vast illiteracy, but there was also a marvelous efflorescence of speculative thought, knowledge, and letters that met with widespread and enlightened appreciation. Nothing like it exists, or can exist, as long as Marxism, or even the spurious Marxism that has become the Russian State religion, continues to dominate the Union.

Secular Messianism, or the expectation of the Millennium in this world; secular chiliasm, or the hope of Heaven on Earth, are characteristic of Marxism, of modern "ideologies" as a whole, and of the contemporary spiritual and material Crisis. The modern myths and the gods that inhabit the world of modern mythology are not embodiments of natural forces, are not symbolical creations of man's poetic genius, but projections of those messianic and chiliastic hopes with which modern man endeavors to smother his essential despair.

According to Marxian mythology, the Millennium is the result of an immutable and universal process or law "discovered" by Marx (as though it were a natural law) and clothed in pseudo-Hegelian language. In no sense is the Marxian doctrine "realistic." It is crudely idealistic, but is also pervaded by a kind of animism, seeing that it attributes purposive behavior to the material world. It sees that behavior in the "dialectical" movement of the economic situation. It deduces phenomena from a fundamental phenomenon which it declares to be economic. All things other than economics—art, science, ethics, philosophy, religion—are epiphenomena.

The "dialectic" works through the centuries, bringing opposites together and producing new unities which, in their turn, find their opposites. These Marxian opposites and unities are mythical and subjective, though they bear the names of complex categories belonging to the phenomenal world.

They are never the simple universals in terms of which a "dialectic" would alone be philosophically defensible.

But the "dialectical" process does not go on forever. There is a time when it stops, and, strangely enough, that time is near—not as near, perhaps, as it seemed when the Bolsheviks seized power in 1917 or when the German revolution broke out in 1918—but quite near nevertheless.

Entire civilizations—Egypt, Babylon, Greece, and Rome—have risen and fallen. All that has happened in the past is but a preparation and a transition. Nothing has ever existed of its own right. Nothing ever achieved by man has any intrinsic value whatever. All is a means to an end—and that end is soon. Marx and Engels—and even Lenin—thought the end would be so soon that, had they been right, it would have come years ago, and the Kingdom of Heaven would be with us now.

In all Marxian literature no evidence is given for the reality of the "dialectic" process. The process is simply assumed. Adoratsky, one of the more recent exponents of Marxism, finds one sentence quite enough to indicate the whole of the process as a law of biological evolution:

"The development of the animal kingdom also proceeds by contradictions and the conflict of opposites (the struggle for existence, pro-creation by sex, etc.)." [10]

The existence of the "dialectic" is a dogma, and no evidence is deemed necessary beyond a few illustrations for the sake of the uninitiated (the initiated know all about it and need no illustrations). Nor is there even an attempt to define terms. The Marxist leaves us wholly unenlightened as to what he means by "opposites." We are left unenlightened as to *why* the "dialectical" process should ever come to an end. But come to an end it does, and in the following manner:

The "bourgeoisie" confront their "opposites," the "proletariat," in the capitalist world. Between these "opposites" there are clashes that lead to a final clash—and being final, it must, apparently, be the biggest and noisiest of all (Marxists outdo one another in depicting the blood and thunder of their apocalypse). But for some unrevealed reason the habitual fusion does not take place. "Bourgeoisie" and "proletariat" do not mingle to form a new class. The "proletariat" triumphs—sooner or later—and the "bourgoisie" disappears altogether. "Capitalism" collapses, and is replaced by its "opposite," "Communism."

The "bourgeoisie" does not vanish all at once, and there is a danger that it may retrieve its defeat, so the "proletarian dictatorship" is established to insure the transformation of the Capitalist into the Communist order (if the "bourgeoisie" persist in their disobedience to the dialectical process, it may be necessary to shoot a few, just to make sure that the inevitable is really inevitable). When the "bourgeoisie" has been destroyed (or "liquidated," as Marxists so feelingly call it), the State as such becomes superfluous. As the State is but the instrument of class-coercion (according to Marxian teaching) there will be no more need for it when there is only one class left. So it simply "withers away."

History comes to an end. "Opposites" refuse to face one another any more. The "dialectic" has done its work. We are not told why the wheels of the cosmic process should ever come to a stop, but stopped they have, and forever. And oppression, poverty, wars, injustice, crime—all belong to the past.

Lest it be supposed that we are merely caricaturing the Marxian myth, we shall now try to present it in greater detail, with illustrations from the works of leading Marxists. We shall also try to examine some of the more important implications of the myth.

Lenin believed in the objective reality of the Millennium. He was at least a true believer (in which he resembles Hitler) and did not attribute a purely transcendental character to his master's teaching, or regard Marxism as no more than an *apparatus criticus*. The "classless state" was not a transcendental conception to Lenin, not a Utopia that can never be achieved in this world. The Kingdom of Heaven on Earth was, to Lenin, a new human order, a complete breach with human history, or rather, the end of history as commonly understood, a Millennium that not only *will* come, but *must* come. Without this Millennium Marxism had no meaning. Without it life itself had no meaning to Lenin. So far from being utopian in his eyes, it was the supreme, concrete reality, a reality that had not been invented by Marx, but had been "discovered" by him. "There is," Lenin wrote, "no trace of utopianism in Marx in the sense of inventing or imagining a 'new society.' No, he studies as a process of natural history the *birth* of a new society *from* the old." [11]

So sure were Marx and Lenin that Communism was inevitable ("inevitable" is one of their favorite words) that they gave very little thought to its intrinsic nature. Their vision is an empty one, for it was held not with poetic, philosophical, or religious, but doctrinaire intensity. Their work does not contain any suggestions with regard to the laws or institutions of the New Order, the economic system, the family, education, philosophy, art, and science. The realism of the great utopians—of Plato, Sir Thomas More, and Jonathan Swift [12]—is wholly lacking.

Marx and Lenin seem to have held that as all virtue resides in the proletariat, and as evil is identical with Capitalism, the inevitable Communist order will be inevitably perfect, so that all speculation about its detailed character is superfluous. Once it is established, all will *inevitably* be well, as long as the "bourgeoisie" are prevented from re-emerging. The Millennium is a fact, a "scientific" and "objective" fact, a "mathematical certainty" (a frequent Marxian phrase), so why bother about details?

The State, according to Christian belief, exists because of sin. It is, of course, true that a sinless society would be a structureless and classless society. The Garden of Eden and the Kingdom of Heaven are both structureless.[13] What is *not* true is that sin is "capitalistic" and virtue "proletarian," and that there *can* be a sinless society in this world.

Like all chiliasts, Marx and Lenin believed that the Kingdom of God is not only coming, but is actually at hand. All other periods in human history seemed unreal to them compared with their own period, not because it was their own, but because it was, to them, the *final* period, the period of imminent consummation. The Marxian present, the period of "decisive struggle," is real only because of what is to follow. After thousands of years, according to the Communist Manifesto, "man is *at last* compelled to face with his sober sense his *real* conditions of life and his relations with his kind."[14] Apparently "conditions of life" in ancient Greece and Rome were "unreal," and the "sober sense" of Pericles and Julius Caesar was superfluous.

There is, of course, a certain discrepancy between the belief in an "inevitable" Millennium produced by an unalterable dialectical process, and the determination to bring it about by action. In his preface to Marx's *Letters to Kugelmann*,[15] Lenin says that *"above everything else"* Karl Marx "put the fact that the working class heroically, self-sacrificingly, and taking the initiative itself *makes* world history." What becomes of the "inevitability" of the classless state? Or is the "working class" (unlike the "bourgeoisie") *inevitably* heroic, *inevitably* self-sacrificing, and *inevitably* full of initiative?

According to Christian belief, God's Kingdom will come in His appointed time, and the only preparation for it is in obedience to His will. The Marxist holds that although inevitable, the moment for opening the "decisive struggle" must be chosen by the "proletariat" itself, or by its leaders, and that if the moment is unpropitious, or if the struggle is ill-conducted, the Millennium will be postponed. But if the chance can be missed once, what certainty is there that it will not be missed a second, or a third time, or an indefinite number of times?

Marx and Lenin assume the imminence and inevitability of the Millennium without the slightest critical inquiry, without any doubt or question, and without producing any evidence whatever. Yet they make a great show of being "scientific" and "objective," and spit venom at all who doubt or disagree. In this, as in so many other things, they resemble Hitler, as we shall see later on. And in their malignance and ferocity they foreshadow the Red Terror, just as Hitler in his book *Mein Kampf* foreshadows the Brown Terror.[16]

In the Communist Manifesto, the collapse of the "bourgeoisie" and the victory of the "proletariat" are proclaimed as "equally inevitable." The German "bourgeois revolution" of 1848 (which was then imminent) is proclaimed as "but the prelude to an immediately following proletarian revolution." This prophecy was "immediately" falsified, for the rising of '48 was "immediately" followed by "bourgeois" reaction.

Close on ninety years have passed and the German "proletarian revolution" is further off than ever.

In his "Anti-Dühring" Engels declares that "the point" at which the "division into classes" will "be swept away by the full development of the modern productive forces" has "now been reached"—"now" being the year 1877![17]

Lenin seems to have been quite undisturbed by the obstinate refusal of history to do what Marx and Engels told it to do. He was, if anything, more cocksure than they. In 1917 he wrote that "the existence of revolutionary and proletarian masses within all the European states is a fact; the maturing and inevitability of the world-wide Socialist revolution is beyond doubt." [18]

By the summer of 1920 the Bavarian and Hungarian Soviet Republics had collapsed. The German revolution was over and had, despite the defeat of the Kappist counter-revolution, failed to produce a Proletarian Dictatorship, or anything like it. Colossal blunders had been committed by the "proletarian masses" and their leaders. Nevertheless Lenin still thought the "bourgeoisie" so stupid that it would make the inevitable more inevitable. "The bourgeoisie," Lenin declared at the Second Congress of the Communist International in 1920, "behaves like an arrogant brigand who has lost his head, but commits blunder after blunder, thus making the position more acute and hastening his own doom." [19]

Defeat in Hungary and Bavaria and the failure of the "proletarian revolution" to prevail in Germany and even to begin in France and England, convinced Lenin that final victory, though as certain as ever, would take a little time. In that same year of 1920 he wrote that "the next step" is to "seek out the forms of transition or approach to the proletarian revolution"—the "proletarian vanguard" had been "ideologically won over," but "from this first step" it was "still a long way to victory." [20]

Years passed, and it became more and more evident that even "this first step" had not been taken in the principal "capitalist" countries. But confident prophesying went on. Lenin died in 1924 and was succeeded by Stalin. In 1928 the Communist International held its Sixth Congress and drew up a new program which was really a re-statement and amplification of the original Communist Manifesto. But this new program showed that even eighty years of eventful history had failed to make any impression on the Marxian mind. "Capitalism," so the authors of the new program announced with their customary arrogance, "must inevitably fall beneath the weight of its own contradictions ... the capitalist system as a whole is approaching its final collapse. The dictatorship of finance capital is perishing to give way to the dictatorship of the proletariat." [21]

Today—another ten years after (and ninety after the Communist Manifesto)—the "dictatorship of the proletariat" exists nowhere, not even in Russia.

Throughout the writings of Marx, Lenin and their successors, the revolution is constantly referred to as the "final struggle," or the "final and decisive battle." [22] The words "final" and "decisive" always have a chiliastic significance in these contexts. It is not as though one of the many campaigns of history was to be decided, but *all* campaigns, *all* history (history, to the Marxist, is but the sequence of campaigns in the universal class war). The "final and decisive battle" is the end of history, the end of the social order as we know it, and the beginning of the Millennium.

There is throughout Marxist literature hardly any question of any fundamental continuity between the world as it is and the Communist world of the future.[23] There is no such thing as ordered progress towards the Millennium— it cannot come by evolution, it cannot be brought by reform, or by any peaceful means. It can only come catastrophically. It is an apocalypse—an *absolute rupture,* not only with the immediate past, but with *all* history, with *all* human society as we know it.

The mere suggestion that it could come peacefully is condemned as heretical. The "inevitably" catastrophic nature of the "final decision" leaves the Marxist quite unperturbed. He is indifferent to human suffering and does not care in the least whether a hundred or a hundred million perish. On the contrary, he grows expansive in the contemplation of the wars and upheavals that are needed to engender the Millennium. There is something crudely barbarous in the truculent Marxian vision of the "final and decisive battle," something like the Ragnarök of Norse mythology or the wreckage of the world amid blood and flame in the semi-pagan Muspilli. But the Marxian vision lacks the poetic grandeur of its ancient predecessors. These have a symbolic meaning, whereas the literal-minded Marxist really believes that the projections of his sectarian mind have "objective reality," that the apocalypse will actually happen, and happen soon (though not so soon as he once believed) and with "mathematical certainty."

The Marxian vision is monstrous by reason of its ferocity and complete lack of moral and poetic depth and grandeur. With supreme complacency, the Marxist asks, no, orders mankind to pay an unimaginably dreadful price for his narrow and colorless Heaven. That Heaven *must* come and mankind *must* pay the price—war after war, at home and abroad, a mutual rending asunder of whole nations and classes, ruin, hunger, disease, and the collapse of all civilized life, a long and (as the chiliastic vision fails to materialize) an ever-lengthening epoch of sorrow and desolation in which the years 1914-18 were but an episode.

The Great War, which, contrary to Marxian prophecy, did not engender the universal Proletarian Revolution, was not enough—not *nearly* enough, despite the ten million dead. The Marxist would have us pass through all that and more, over and over again.

What guarantee is there that another World War and further revolutions and counter-revolutions, strikes, armed risings, civil wars, massacres, "purges" will at last establish the Marxian Heaven on Earth? What if in ten years' time another stricken generation is still waiting and, in fifty years, we are again told that there will have to be more slaughter, ruin, and famine, and the Millennium seems as far off as ever?

To these questions the Marxist dare not and cannot give an answer.

If there are any who suspect that in asking them, we do him an injustice or that they caricature his real beliefs, let them study the program from which we have already quoted, the program adopted by the Congress of the Communist International in 1928.

According to this program: [24]

"A period of revolutionary transformation during which 'capitalist society' changes into 'communist society' ... of proletarian struggles with defeats as well as victories [this is 1928—not 1848, or even 1918] ... of continuous general crises in capitalistic relationships ... of proletarian civil wars against the bourgeoisie; a period of national wars and colonial rebellions ... which ... are constituent parts of the world proletarian revolution ... a period in which capitalist and socialist economic and social systems exist side by side in 'peaceful relationships' [25] as well as any armed conflicts ... a period of wars of imperialist States against Soviet States; a period in which the ties between the Soviet States and the colonial peoples become more and more closely established, etc. ... every ... proletarian victory, however, broadens the basis of world revolution and consequently still further intensifies the general crisis of capitalism, thus the capitalist system as a whole reaches the point of its final collapse...." [26]

The Marxist feels no regret in contemplating prospects so inhuman. On the contrary, he is happy in his sectarian belief that they are "objectively" inevitable, and is resentful when they are questioned or deplored. He is, by temperament and conviction, opposed to peace, reform, and all compromise and moderation. Marx and Lenin sometimes counseled moderation, but only for immediate tactical reasons. Like Hitler, they were uncompromising extremists in every ultimate sense and believed reform to be essentially dangerous. The word "reformism" plays a leading part in the rich vocabulary of Marxian vituperation. Marx and Lenin could not be wholly blind to the fact that wage earners demanded *immediate* improvements in their lot, however small, and that even the bargaining that would lead to no more than a paltry compromise had its educative value.

But the Marxist is only willing to make concessions in so far as they will save him and his doctrines from being condemned to complete initial impotence. Reform, however sweeping or radical, cannot achieve the Millennium—even the cumulative effect of centuries of reform will not achieve it. There *must* be armed revolution, the "opposites" are incapable of peaceful or gradual fusion ("gradualism" is another term of Marxian vituperation), they can only fuse in the fire of battle. No reason is ever given by the Marxist why opposites cannot unite peacefully. His sectarian spirit is nothing if not warlike. He is obsessed by revolutionary militarism and can see nothing in history save a succession of class wars. According to the Communist Manifesto "the history of all hitherto-existing society is the history of class struggles." He is suspicious of every peaceful achievement and will only condone it on the strict understanding that it is, at best, provisional, and will not be prejudicial to violence in the end. The Marxist is profoundly hostile to non-violence and pacifism in all its forms—we shall see, later on, how closely he resembles the National Socialist in this respect. He is obsessed by the fear that reform, so far from hastening on the Millennium, may postpone it by substituting for achievements obtainable only by violence the illusion of achievement by non-violence.

The reformer as such is, according to the Marxist, a dangerous person in any case and, in all likelihood, a rogue, a "traitor" to the working class, or a "lackey of the bourgeoisie," especially if he is a humanitarian and shrinks from bloodshed; his real purpose is not reform, but counter-revolution, and his humanitarian ideals are a cunning device to save the capitalist order and to avert the Millennium.

There are none the Marxist hates and despises more than those who, in the Communist Manifesto, are denounced as "economists, philanthropists, humanitarian improvers of the condition of the working class, organizers of charity, members of societies for the prevention of cruelty to animals, temperance fanatics, hole-and-corner reformers of every imaginable kind."

Marx, curiously enough, made an exception in favor of England—there alone, he believed, was revolution possible without violence. On the 12th of April 1871 he wrote to Kugelmann, with reference to a passage in his "18th Brumaire," that the bureaucratic and military apparatus of the State must not be *transferred* from the "bourgeoisie" to the "proletariat," but that it must be destroyed ("broken up"). This, so he wrote, "is the pre-condition of any real people's revolution *on the continent*." This passage has worried Marxists, for they desire violent revolution in England more than anywhere else. They dream of London as the vortex of the world-revolution and central scene of their bloodshot apocalypse.

But Lenin explained that when Marx wrote, England had no "military machine" and not much of a bureaucracy, so that there was no powerful "ready-made state machinery" to break up. An English revolution could, therefore, be peaceful. But "today, in 1917," England, like America, is "in the dirty, bloody morass of military bureaucratic institutions" and there can be no "real people's revolution" without the "break up" of the ready-made state machinery," that is to say, without violence.[27]

The Marxian anxiety lest England might be spared the bloodshed and ruin of violent revolution has therefore been relieved.

For years after the Great War it did not matter if "workers" attempted revolution even in the most unfavorable circumstances, for, according to the Communist Manifesto, they had "nothing to lose but their chains." But the consequences of the many abortive risings that followed the war were so frightful that Marxism would have been swept out of existence by angry workmen everywhere, had Marxists persisted in encouraging them.

It is untrue that workmen have "nothing to lose but their chains." It was nearer the truth in Marx's day, but since then there has been an immense improvement in the lot of the working class, especially in the most advanced "Capitalist" countries.

It is true that reforms have been brought about by fear of the working class, by the threat of direct action and even by direct action itself. It is also true that many great reformers were moved by a religious or secular humanitarian conviction and not by fear.[28] But the love of one's neighbor as such is a conception wholly alien to the Marxian mentality.

Perhaps the most enduring general reforms have been achieved through a mixture of interested and disinterested motives. A labor movement can achieve little and may lose much by force. It can achieve much by peaceful means, but, perhaps, not unless it is prepared to use force as the *ultima ratio*. And the threat of revolution is often more effective than revolution itself that may involve all in common ruin, though even the threat of revolution may defeat its own purpose by precipitating counter-revolution. Rights that have been won after a struggle often have more permanence than rights that have merely been conferred. It was one of the weaknesses of the German labor movement and, indeed, of the Weimar Republic, that more rights were conferred on the German working class and the German people by patronizing statesmanship or by circumstance, than were achieved after a struggle whether on the part of courageous individuals or of the multitude or both. The patronizing attitude of Bismarck and of the German industrialists (who, for all their patronage, were, as a rule, harder men than their English colleagues) and the teaching of Karl Marx, which is so inimical to free initiative, and, by its overemphasis on revolution, so productive of counter-revolution —these together, arrogant patronage and revolutionary arrogance, helped to engender the patronizing, revolutionary and, at the same time, counter-revolutionary, "authoritarian" despotism of Hitler.

Believing as he does in force and determined to secure nothing by peaceful means that can be secured by violence, the Marxist lives in hope of wars and crises that will so unbalance the social order and so loosen the restraint imposed by law and custom, that violence can achieve a maximum breadth and intensity. The situation then arises which the Marxist terms "revolutionary." It is the situation he desires because he believes that only then is the "final and decisive battle possible." To Lenin—as to Hitler—the Great War was *welcome* [29] because it promised to fulfill the revolutionary dream. There was once a memorable prophecy which had bitten deep into the Marxian consciousness:

> "But we must not forget that there is a sixth power in Europe which at a definite moment will establish its domination over the other five so-called 'Great Powers' and make every one of them tremble. This power is revolution.... At the required signal, the sixth greatest European power will come forth in shining armature, sword in hand.... That signal will be the coming European War." [30]

Lenin, with characteristic ruthlessness, was afraid, not that the Great War would last too long, but that it might not last long enough.

Marx and Lenin and their followers did not recognize the fundamental importance of reform and of peaceful achievement and compromise. They believed that minorities can achieve little or nothing except by becoming majorities. They vastly overrated the power of the "proletariat." They underrated the dangers of violent revolution that may involve all in common ruin. They vastly underrated the power of the "bourgeoisie," above all of the "petite bourgeoisie," for which they had such contempt. And, in their obdurate messianism, they failed to recognize that in this world there can be no "decisive" or "final" battle.

Events, at first, only confirmed the illusions of the Marxists. Reform and peaceful achievement had meant little under Tsarist despotism (though more than Marxists try to make out). The Russian "aristocracy" were weak and amenable to violence. The "petite bourgeoisie" were weaker still and largely made up of poorly paid, ignorant officials (it is only now, long after the revolution, that Russia can be said to have a powerful "bourgeoisie" at all, a "bourgeoisie" that is almost exclusively bureaucratic and military). Russian industrial workmen had been in a state of ferment for a generation. Two unsuccessful wars, the Far Eastern War and the Great War, were decisive in promoting the collapse of the Tsarist system and the triumph of the revolution. The appalling inhumanity of Marxian teaching harmonized with the profound barbarism that existed side by side with the refinement and urbanity of Tsarist Russia. Marxian messianism had the strongest possible appeal in a land of extravagant messianic faiths. Marxian godlessness attracted a people always inclined to pass from extreme mystical devotion to crude mockery of religion.[31] The very arrogance of Marxian dogma, an arrogance raised to a mental despotism by Lenin, promoted its domination amongst a people who, although given to violence (and therefore attracted by the glorification of violence), were by nature servile.

Marx was realistic enough to know that between "exploiter" and "exploited" there are those who are neither or both. But in his German passion for ostensibly scientific classification and in his terrible—and often grandiose—hatred of the poverty he saw all around him, in his dramatic sense for contrast, and in his pseudo-Hegelian obsession with the conflict of "opposites," he immensely underrated the power and resources of the middle class, of what he called the "petite bourgeoisie." Indeed he and all his followers not only underrated the middle class, but denied it every function, purpose, or utility, and, looking upon it with hatred, distrust, and never-concealed contempt, vowed it to total extinction. No expression of the Marxian vocabulary is more derisive than "petit bourgeois," "Kleinbürger," "kleiner Mann," or "little man," [32] denoting the "small shopkeeper" or other humble persons of the "lower middle" class.

For the "little man" the Marxist feels far greater hatred than for the "capitalist." The "little man" is worse than "counter-revolutionary." He is *unrevolutionary,* and to be unrevolutionary is, in the eyes of the Marxist, to be a kind of leper. Marxists are habitually contemptuous of the "petit bourgeois mind" as not a mind at all, but something reptilian, something infinitely mean and ignominious.

That the "bourgeoisie" and "petite bourgeoisie," who carried out some of the greatest revolutions in history, might do so again, never seems to have occurred to Marx or Lenin, or if it did occur, it was thrust to the back of their minds by their ever-triumphant subjectivity. It never occurs to the Marxist that the "little man" may be a very big man—or, if it does occur, he will deny sociological significance to this inconvenient phenomenon.

It is certainly true that we have since the war seen a vast impoverishment of the middle class throughout Central Europe, but this impoverishment has been neither constant nor universal—it has not been the result of an inexorable "dialectic." No nation, class, society, religion, civilization, is immune from the uncertainties of this world. There is no evidence of any cosmic process that condemns the "proletariat" to ever-increasing poverty and "depresses" the middle class and thereby makes it swell the ranks of the "revolutionary proletariat."

The impoverishment of the German middle class in particular was contemplated with the utmost satisfaction by Communist observers, who saw therein hope of the so long delayed German "proletarian" revolution [33]—and, therefore, an important step towards world revolution. Nothing was watched with more pleasure in the Russian sociological laboratory than the decline in the happiness and well-being of the German middle class.

The chief source of these radiant hopes was the following passage in Karl Marx's *Capital:*

"While there is a progressive diminution in the number of the capitalist magnates, there occurs a corresponding increase in the mass of poverty, enslavement, degeneration, and exploitation; but at the same time there is a steady intensification of the wrath of the working class—a class which grows ever more numerous, and is disciplined, unified, and organized by the very mechanism of the capitalist method of production which has flourished with it and under it. The centralization of the means of production and the socialization of labor reach a point when they prove incompatible with their capitalist husk. This bursts asunder. The knell of private property sounds. The expropriators are expropriated." [34]

The middle class, so the Marxist theorists argue with importunate reiteration, are made to merge with the "proletariat" by an inexorable economic law. The "bourgeois," losing all he has, and assuming proletarian chains, comes to share the "proletarian" state of having nothing but chains to lose. This is the essential qualification of all who, with rising "wrath," advance to fight "the decisive battle." The "bourgeois" simultaneously undergoes a mystical metamorphosis. His mind and character change with his economic condition—he sheds his "bourgeois" or "petit bourgeois" mentality and acquires a "proletarian" mentality. In other words, he becomes a "proletarian." When the "dialectical" process has gone far enough, he and his fellow-proletarians —that is to say, all save a few "capitalists"—make up the vast, revolutionized, and irresistible majority of the people and carry that process to its consummation. The "husk" of the capitalist order "bursts asunder" apocalyptically. The Kingdom of Heaven is established on Earth.

But experience has shown—and some little insight into human nature might have shown from the beginning—that the "bourgeois" and even the "petit bourgeois" has a soul of his own, and that, powerful as the influence of environment may be (and the economic order is only a part of the human environment), it is by no means all-powerful. The "bourgeois" is quite unimpressed by the Marxian "dialectic" process. In fact, he does not believe in it. He has no intention whatever of becoming a "proletarian." Even if war, defeat, revolution, inflation, deflation, and crisis on crisis reduce his income until it is less than that of the skilled workman, he continues to reject the "proletarian" status. The dialectic may rob him of his money—but it will not rob him of his personality.

In one respect the Marxist is right. The "petit bourgeois" is revolutionized. But he has his own ideas about revolution. He becomes a revolutionary—not as a "proletarian," not even on the side of the "proletariat," not in fulfillment of the dialectical process, not in the manner so prophetically announced by Marx and Lenin, but in defiance of their teaching; not to destroy the capitalist order, but to transform it; not to establish a transitional dictatorship in which the State will "wither away," but one in which the State will be re-established with greater solidity than before, a State armed with terrible coercive power, a State that will send Marxists to prison, concentration camps, or to execution, and will replace the Marxian myth by a kindred myth of its own.

Why should not the "petit bourgeois" be a revolutionary

in his own way? Why should he share the Marxian faith in the inevitability of the Millennium? He may, after all, have read a book or two, he may have observed the absence of any serious philosophical or scientific thought in the works of Marxian so-called "thinkers." And if it comes to sham religion, sham philosophy, and sham science, he can produce all these just as well, if not better, than the Marxist can.

The Marxist, in his sectarian narrowness, cannot conceive of non-Marxian revolution. Marxism is to him *the* doctrine of *the* revolution, to him there is not, and cannot be, a revolutionary movement without the Marxian "theory." But the "little man" has, to the derision, at first, then to the indignation, then to the horror of the whole Marxian world, developed his own "theory" of revolution, his own myth— a myth as untenable philosophically as the Marxian myth, but more modern and more serviceable. The "little man" has organized, has armed, and has attacked with ruthless revolutionary ardor and with immense political and military skill.

In Germany the most powerful Communist Party outside Russia has collapsed like a paper bag (without even a bang) at the first onset. The greatest labor movement outside England—and one impregnated with Marxist ideas—has been destroyed almost overnight.

And the "little man" has made himself absolute master of the greatest military power that ever existed.

He threatens the world with war and spreads fear through the Soviet Union. He forces rearmament upon all. He has already produced radical changes in the whole international order and will produce many more. He has compelled the Marxists to accept every compromise which, only a short while before, they denounced as treacherous and contemptible, compromise with the "bourgeoisie," with the "petit bourgeois," with "bourgeois liberalism," and even with conservative and religious movements, and—supreme humiliation, imposed by bitter need and mortal danger—with "moderates," with Social Democrats (so recently condemned as allies of "Fascism," as promoters of imperialism and as betrayers of the working class).[35] Also with "the robber League of Nations" (or "Imperialist League of Nations"), with nationalism, with imperialism generally, with rearmament and even with religion (the "opium of the people").[36] And all this through fear of the "petit bourgeois," of the "little man" who, self-established in lonely and terrible power, holds the prodigious German heritage in his hands and controls the destiny of the most formidable nation on the European mainland.

The "little man" has driven the Soviet Union (a "sixth of the world's surface," as Communists never tire of telling us) into ever closer co-operation with that same League of Nations (the "main purpose of which is to retard the inevitable growth of the revolutionary crisis and to strangle the Soviet Republic by war or blockade").[37] He has compelled Stalin to hand out bouquets to the once so abominated British Empire.[38] He is carrying revolutionary ferment into neighboring countries with a skill, a resourcefulness, and a determination far beyond anything the Soviet Union was ever able to achieve. He has discarded his "bourgeois respectability" and shakes the foundations of the religious, political, and economic order.

We have referred to Marxism and National Socialism as secular religions. They are not opposites, but are fundamentally akin, in a religious as well as in a secular sense. Both are messianic and socialistic. Both reject the Christian knowledge that all are under sin and both see in good and evil principles of class or race. Both are despotic in their methods and their mentality. Both have enthroned the modern Caesar, collective man, the implacable enemy of the individual soul. Both would render unto this Caesar the things which are God's. Both would make man master of his own destiny, establish the Kingdom of Heaven in this world. Neither will hear of any Kingdom that is not of this world.

Both have been anticipated with dread by philosophers. Solovieff's "Anti-Christ" conquers and unites the world, solves the problem of poverty and unemployment, and establishes peace amongst the nations—and yet he is Anti-Christ and, therefore, wears the signature of doom. Nietzsche, a far deeper thinker than Karl Marx, prophetically saw in socialism "the younger brother of almost obsolete despotism," having aspirations that "are reactionary in the deepest sense," and striving for the "downright destruction of the individual, who is regarded as an unjustified luxury of nature to be improved so as to become a serviceable organ of the collectivity." [39]

Marxism became a kind of mass-madness through the spectacular success of the Russian revolution.

It is not evident that the revolution would have failed if Marx had never lived and Marxism had never been thought of (according to his followers, even, the "dialectical process" was not invented, but was *discovered*, by Marx, and its consummation was "inevitable" in any case and not made so by the publication of the Communist Manifesto and *Capital*).

But the Russian revolution was an event of such an awe-inspiring character that it appeared like the coming of the Marxian apocalypse itself. It seemed to be the practical, irrefutable proof that Marxism was *the* Truth.

For twenty years the Russian people have been agonizingly stretched and bloodily mutilated to fit the Procrustean bed of the Marxian "theory." The attempt to impose Marxism has been abandoned. The theory itself remains sacrosanct, but those who would still put it into practice are shot, imprisoned, or exiled. The Soviet Union is a despotism working through a secret police and a subservient bureaucracy. This alone is the denial of a doctrine essential to Marxism, namely, the "withering away" of the State. So far from "withering away," the Russian State has greater coercive powers than any other in the world.

Marxism would be a phenomenon of little more than historical interest, seeing that it has failed even in its principal stronghold, were it not so closely akin to National Socialism. National Socialism would have been inconceivable without Marxism. To understand contemporary secular religions, it is necessary to understand Marxism, which was the first of these religions to achieve a widespread domination over the souls of men. Only when we have examined Marxism can we proceed to examine National Socialism. And we shall understand the greatest man of action amongst National Socialists, namely Hitler, much better if we study him side by side with Lenin, the greatest man of action amongst the Marxists.

The apparent success of Marxism in Russia gave this religion a tremendous impetus throughout the world. The Millennium was revealed in blood and flame to millions of awe-struck men and women. Without this revelation, Marxism would have become little more than a popular "Weltanschauung" without a deep influence on the actions of its followers, a tendency rather, or a bias, such as it has been amongst the Social Democratic movements of Europe. But the apocalypse, that seemed to be the fulfillment of Marxian prophecy, was decisive in establishing the domination of the visionary chiliastic essence of Marxian doctrine over the minds of millions of believers throughout the world.

National Socialism had a success equally spectacular in Germany. All that Hitler and his associates had preached suddenly *came true*. By the pragmatic test National Socialism is as *true* as Marxism. In 1933 the seeming truth of National Socialism had a burning vividness like some fiery text written apocalyptically with infallible import across the heavens. To see was to believe.

The reason why National Socialism has proved so much more powerful than Marxism whenever the two have met in conflict is that National Socialism is more modern and has a superior technique.

Marxism is a child of eighteenth-century "enlightenment." It is a religion of the mind rather than of the emotions. Although anti-philosophical, indeed anti-critical, its main instrument is the reason, but operating within extremely narrow limits and on an irrational foundation. The Marxist is accessible to logical argument as long as it does not affect his premises. His mythical world remains sacrosanct—but within that world a narrow reason and a limited realism prevail. The National Socialist rejects the sovereignty of the mind, even within the mythological limits, and enthrones brutish instinct. The Marxist—always within the same limits—is for an urban and rational outlook, the National Socialist is for "blood and soil."

Despite his ultimate amorality, which shows itself in truculence and untruthfulness, the Communist has a stern, though narrow, puritanical ethic. He is ruthless, but not by nature brutish. The terror is for him a means to an end. The National Socialist, on the other hand, has a strong tendency towards brutishness—he is often a terrorist without reference to the end he wishes to attain.

Lenin's writings are full of a cold, inhuman truculence. Hitler's book, *Mein Kampf,* and his many speeches are full of vengeful malignance. Hitler is the fulfillment of Robert Herrick's terrible apprehension:

> "Nothing can be more loathsome than to see,
> Power joined with nature's cruelty."

In the course of the Bolshevik revolution, power and nature's cruelty did conjoin, but the Brown Terror that began even before the burning of the Reichstag in 1933, although the number of its victims was very small compared with the number of those who perished in the Red Terror, was peculiarly bestial and vengeful, nor was it in any sense a counter-terror, as the Red Terror originally was (though it is so no longer).

The Red Terror that followed the Russian revolution is incomparably the greatest of modern times—only the Terror now raging in Russia under Stalin can be compared with it. Russia has never been without a Terror. In modern Germany at least, the terror is something new. Germans can at least imagine a State, and even a powerful State, without a terror, whereas the Russians cannot. But in no case will terrorism cease either in Russia or in Germany until the secular religiosity, of which it is an instrument, begins to vanish. Modern secular religion is by nature terroristic.

The belief in the possibility of the Kingdom of Heaven on Earth is akin to the passion for "planning," and, like most other plans—only more so—the Kingdom will not "work." It *cannot* work because the Kingdom of Heaven and this world are in irreconcilable contradiction. The barrier between them is Death. That barrier cannot be passed by any man, not even by a Lenin, or a Hitler. Secular religion does not, because it cannot, see its own essential contradiction, for if it did it would destroy itself. It sees the contradiction, not in itself but in "the opposition," in "sabotage," in "wrecking activities," in "traitors" and "agents of foreign powers," in the "backwardness of the people," in Judaism, Bolshevism, Capitalism, and so on.

Lenin shared Rousseau's optimism with regard to human nature. He recognized the existence of evil, but attributed it to the capitalist system and, as he was unshakably convinced that the capitalist system and all evil with it were doomed, his optimism was fundamental.

To him, as to Marx and Engels, the "worker" or the "proletarian" was the Noble Savage who originally lived in a condition of simple innocence.[40] In the course of its evolution, according to Engels, society "is cleft into irreconcilable antagonisms which it has to dispel." A power "apparently standing above society becomes necessary" to "moderate the conflict" and "keep it within the bounds of order."[41] That power is the State. According to Lenin, the State arises when "class antagonisms cannot be objectively reconciled." It exists only "where there are class antagonisms and the class struggle."[42] Struggles between class and families, or between interests or individuals, the ideas and religions that divide man from man, or the variety and restlessness of man, his desires, his passions, his wrong-doing, yes, and his right-doing also, and the sinfulness that is common to all and is certainly manifested in class struggles, but in a thousand other ways as well —all these are nothing, they, according to Lenin, do not demand the organization and the structure, the strong framework, and the coercive powers that make up the State. The State exists *only* when class is in conflict with class, and if it were not for the State, we should all be living in a happy condition of natural innocence.

The State, according to Lenin, is the instrument with which the ruling class has established and perpetuates its domination. It is "an organ of *oppression* of one class by another"[43]—that *and nothing more*. The very existence of the State "proves" that "class antagonisms are irreconcilable." If "class antagonisms" are eliminated by the "dictatorship of the proletariat" and the "destruction of the bourgeoisie," then the State simply "withers away."[44]

To Hegel, the State is "the reality of the moral idea" and "the image and reality of reason" (both phrases are contemptuously referred to by Marx and Engels).

According to Marxian teaching man is by nature good. "Capitalism" alone is evil. The "capitalist" may be a nice, kindly person (though he is never represented as such in

Marxist propaganda—in Russian films and caricatures he is always made to appear vicious and bestial). But he is an oppressor and exploiter simply because he *is* a capitalist. He is wicked by a kind of predestination. The inexorable dialectic condemns him to inevitable, essential wickedness. He exercises a kind of satanic dominion and the instrument of that dominion is the State.

What Marx and Lenin call State is really not State as such, but Dictatorship.

The State is the condition of all organized society. Peace between classes, whether the peace is one of balance, or whether it stabilizes the ascendancy of one class, is certainly a function of the State, but only one of many functions.

When the struggle between classes has become revolutionary, the victor will not, at first, re-establish the State that was menaced or overthrown, but a dictatorship. That dictatorship may either perpetuate the victory of one side by transforming the open war into a silent and secret war, or it may be a transition from war to peace, in which case it will "wither away." But a dictatorship always usurps the function of the State, not because it is coercive (the State, too, is coercive), but because it is *exclusively* coercive, seeing that the purpose of the dictatorship is coercion and nothing else. The contrary of what Lenin wrote is true—the State "proves" that "class antagonisms" *can* be reconciled, not that they are "irreconcilable." When they are "irreconcilable," the State is usurped by the dictatorship. When the State fails in the presence of faction, the dictatorship takes its place.

The State has repressive power, but is not a "special repressive force" as every dictatorship is. Engels and Lenin remove all doubt that what they mean by State is really dictatorship, when Engels defines the State as a *"special* repressive force" and Lenin calls this definition "splendid and extremely profound." [45]

Like all the utopian and chiliastic elements of the Marxist

myth, the "withering away" of the State is presented as though it were an objective fact. It is to the Marxist an actual process by which the capitalist order is transformed into the Communist order. Lenin wrote that there is "no shadow of an attempt on Marx's part to conjure up a Utopia," for "he treats the subject of Communism as a naturalist would treat the development of, say, a new biological species if he knew that such and such was its origin and such and such the direction in which it changed." [46] But whereas Darwin expounded a working—and by now rather badly shaken—hypothesis with modesty, with a vast array of detailed evidence and illustration, and with respect for contrary opinion, Marx and Lenin propound their doctrines with dogmatic arrogance, without the slightest attempt to produce any evidence, and with hatred and derision for all who dare to disagree. If biology were what Marx and Lenin thought it was, it would not be a science at all—any more than Marxism is.

Lenin's complete incapacity for philosophical and scientific thought is revealed again and again throughout his writings, especially in that naïvely vulgar fabrication, his *Materialism and Empirio-Criticism*.[47]

It is doubtful whether history is a science. In any case it is not an exact science. No exact science is possible without the constant repetition of phenomena and without the possibility of multifarious experimentation. The "naturalist"—as the natural scientist used to be called—has at his disposal an immense wealth of verifiable data; he must be equipped to verify them and he must be able to add to them. He can investigate the problems of heredity and the development if not of "new biological species," at least of variations and "sports" and of new combinations of characteristics through successive generations of infusoria, frogs, mice, and guinea-pigs. But even so, biological hypotheses have none of the certainty Lenin imagined them to have. Lenin's conception of science is that of the half-educated—he regards as certain everything that he can label "scientific." Indeed, he constantly uses the words "scientific," "objective," and "certain" as though they were synonymous. The skepticism of the scientific mind and the uncertainty of all human knowledge are entirely foreign to this bigoted sectarian.

No serious "naturalist" would predict the future development of any "biological species." But it is precisely of the future that Marx and Lenin wrote. Their writings have little significance except as prophecy. They claim to study revolution, and produce what they imagine to be a scientific theory which is not a theory at all, but a myth. They only had one major revolution (the French) and a small number of minor revolutions as the object of their supposedly scientific inquiries (Lenin's teaching was mature even before the Russian revolution of 1905). So that their claim to scientific certainty, which would have been fantastic even if they had a hundred revolutions at their disposal, is merely a piece of naïve dogmatism, which only shows that this supposed science is but the instrument of their sectarian religiosity.

Lenin declares that the theory of Marx is the "objective truth," all other theories leading to "confusion and falsehood." [48]

For thousands of years life went on, whole civilizations rose and fell, great teachers and philosophers, Aristotle, Plato, Pascal, Kant, Hegel, lived and died and illuminated the world with their truths, but not until Karl Marx arrived was *the* Truth made known. "At best, pre-Marxist sociology and historiography gave an accumulation of new facts collected at random, and a description of separate ideas of the historical process"; until Marx came, "the alternation between periods of revolution and reaction, peace and war, stagnation and rapid progress and decline" were wholly mysterious—the facts may have been known, but only since Marx expounded his doctrine do we possess "a clue which enables us to discover the reign of law in this seeming labyrinth and chaos." [49]

Marxism is eschatology without God. It demands unquestioning faith in the coming of the Kingdom of Heaven on Earth and imposes a dogmatic atheism. The Marxist is not even allowed to be an agnostic. Lenin wrote that "from the standpoint of life" (what is *Life's* standpoint?) "practice ought to be the first and fundamental criterion of knowledge... this criterion is sufficiently definite to wage a bitter struggle with all varieties of idealism and agnosticism." [50]

Agnosticism is forbidden because it presupposes an unknowable. But for Marx, Engels, and Lenin and their followers nothing is unknowable, there are no mysteries, and doubt is a form of vacillation, cowardice, or treachery. All is clear, all is certain, all is inevitable—Marxism, and Marxism alone, is *the* Truth about all there ever was, is, or ever will be.

Lenin is incapable of any deeper skepticism and, therefore, of serious speculative thought. Whatever he professes to know —philosophy, science, religion, history, ethics, sociology, politics, economics and what not—he knows it with *absolute* certainty. Marx and Engels have the same mental arrogance (though Marx was not quite so superficial). Even in their prophecies they are cocksure—whatever they say will happen, will "inevitably happen," will happen as an "objective fact," and everybody who thinks it will not is a rogue, a fool, or a traitor.

In August 1917, during the Russian revolution itself, Lenin, for the first time, showed traces of a certain diffidence. He insisted more than ever that there must be a transition from Capitalism to Communism. "The first fact," he wrote, "that has been established with complete exactness by the whole theory of development, by science as a whole... is that historically there must undoubtedly be a special stage or epoch of *transition* from capitalism to communism." [51]

Only the transition might take some time. A little of the cocksureness has gone. The State may take its time about "withering away," and Lenin is compelled to admit "the protracted nature of this process" [52] and its dependence upon the rapidity of the development of the higher phase of Communism; leaving quite open the lengths of time or the concrete forms of "withering away," since material for the solution of such questions is *not available* [53]—an unwonted display of modesty on Lenin's part, for he was not, as a rule, discouraged from making the most confident assertions merely through lack of "material." But where is the "material" upon which he and other Marxists founded their conviction that the State will "wither away"? We shall search Marxist literature in vain for this "material."

Nevertheless the ultimate conviction remains absolutely unshaken, material or no material. While admitting that the State may take some time to wither, Lenin still maintains that the withering is "inevitable." [54]

This "withering away" is inherent in the Marxian conception of the State as a "special repressive force." When the withering is complete, there will "no longer be any real political power." [55] Only then does it become "possible to speak of freedom." "Freed from capitalist slavery, from the untold horrors, savageries, absurdities and infamies of capitalist exploitation, people will gradually become accustomed to the elementary rules of social life—they will become accustomed to observing them without force, without compulsion, without subordination" and "without the special apparatus which is called the State" ... "we see around us millions of times how readily people get accustomed to observing the necessary rules of life in common if there is no exploitation, if there is nothing that causes indignation, that calls forth protest and revolt and has to be suppressed." [56] Here we have the Marxian identification of capitalism with evil.

Marxian ethics are as spurious as Marxian science. The Good, like the True, is what promotes revolution. The "proletariat" is the only "thoroughly revolutionary" class.[57] The revolution is sacred and the revolutionary is alone virtuous. There are no absolute and no transcendental ethical standards. There is only one morality that matters, the one that "represents the future," that alone "contains the maximum of durable elements"—the "proletarian morality." All morality hitherto was "class morality"—"all former moral theories are the product in the last analysis of the economic stage which society had reached at that particular epoch." [58]

The "Proletarian Revolution" is therefore the triumph of good over evil. But more than this: the revolution is also the conquest over the forces of nature—"the laws of his [man's] own social activity which have hitherto confronted him as external, dominating laws of nature, will then be applied by man with complete understanding, and hence will be dominated by man." [59] With *complete* understanding! In other words, the revolution will establish not only the reign of absolute justice, but also of absolute knowledge and wisdom.

It also establishes the reign of material and spiritual freedom and well-being, for it "guarantees" an "existence" that is not only "sufficient," but grows "richer from day to day" as well as "the complete unrestricted development and exercise of physical and mental faculties. It is humanity's leap from the realm of necessity into the realm of freedom." [60] The Kingdom of Heaven has been established on Earth.

"And they shall beat their swords into plowshares, and their spears into pruning-hooks: nation shall not lift up sword against nation, neither shall they learn war any more.... The wolf also shall dwell with the lamb, and the leopard shall lie down with the kid, and the calf and the young lion and the fatling together; and a little child shall lead them.

"And the cow and the bear shall feed; their young ones shall lie down together: and the lion shall eat straw like the ox." [61]

CHAPTER II

The attainment of the Millennium—The myth of Marxism and of National Socialism—Their pseudo-philosophical and pseudo-scientific character—Lenin and Hitler, a comparison of their beliefs and methods—Lenin obsessed by the reality of class, Hitler by the reality of race—Lenin a would-be destroyer of, Hitler a corrupter of, religion—Hitler's fundamental doctrine of the "Greater Germany"—His mission to achieve that end—His identification of racial principles with the "will of God"—His attitude towards class—The difference between Marxian and National Socialist economics.

THE Millennium of modern secular eschatology has nothing in common with the past or the present—or with history, for *its* beginning is the *end* of history. But history cannot end, save with the annihilation of mankind. There can be no Millennium save in the doom of all. That is why the Millennium is unattainable in this world, for no matter how alluring it is made to appear with the help of pseudo-religious, pseudo-philosophical, pseudo-scientific mythology; no matter how ruthless the extermination of all heresy: the suicidal nature of every secular eschatology will be made manifest in time, and men will cry "Halt" before the edge of doom is reached. The present will assert itself once more and peace will be concluded with the past. And the name of that peace is "Tradition."

Every transcendental eschatology proclaims the end of this world. But secular eschatology is always caught in its own contradiction. It projects into the *past* a vision of what *never was*, it conceives what *is* in terms of what is *not*, and the *future* in terms of what can *never* be. The remoter past becomes a mystical or mythical Age of Innocence, a Golden or a Heroic Age, an age of Primitive Communism or of resplendent manly Virtue. The future is the Classless Society, Eternal Peace, or Salvation by Race—the Kingdom of Heaven on Earth. The present is always the Fall.

For the Marxist, the Fall is progressive, a Fall ever more precipitous. The wheels of the dialectic began to move (no one knows what started their motion), they grind out man's ever darkening fate, through the slavery of the ancient world, through the oppression of feudalism, and through the worse oppression of Capitalism, until utter and intolerable darkness suddenly engenders liberating apocalyptic light. Universal revolution, destroying the cosmic machinery, gives freedom from the wrong and sorrow of Capitalism and, completing the cycle, brings back the Age of Innocence and Gold.

The National Socialist does at least offer an explanation of the Fall—it was brought about by an act of disobedience to the Principle of Race, to a defection from the Immaculacy of the Elect who, when shorn of their Immaculacy, are like Samson shorn of his hair. Only by war, revolution, sacrifice, and the ruthless extirpation of the race-polluters, only by the overthrow of their temples, only by the rallying of all the Immaculate can the Heroic Age of Primeval Virtue be re-established.

All revolutions that have been attempted or have been carried out by the action of the multitude are inspired by a myth, and a collective faith, even if only by one as simple as

"When Adam delved and Eve span,
Who was then the gentleman?"

The Racial Principle, which is the central doctrine of National Socialism, has as little philosophic or scientific validity as the Dialectical Materialism of the Marxists. But the mythological character of the two religions is concealed from their followers (who would be followers no longer if concealment came to an end) by the pseudo-philosophical and pseudo-scientific husk. The Marxist really believes that Marxism is "scientific." The National Socialist really believes that the Racial Principle has something to do with serious biology.

For the Marxist, the Marxian myth (or "theory" as he calls it) is not true because it can stand objective tests, but because it can resist them; not because it will explain reality, but because it can be imposed on reality.

Hitler, who has fewer illusions about mankind than Marx or Lenin, declares (and has frequently shown in practice) that the most impudent and extravagant falsehoods will be accepted as truths if they are proclaimed with sufficient force and conviction:

"There is always a certain element of credibility in the magnitude of a lie, because the broad masses of a nation are more readily corrupt than consciously and deliberately evil, so that, in the primitive simplicity of their souls, they fall victims more easily to a big lie than to a small one, seeing that they themselves sometimes tell small lies, but will be too ashamed to tell unduly big ones." [1]

Whenever a big lie is told and repeated sufficiently often, there is a widespread tendency to believe that there must be "something in it." And so "the new Russia," "the new Italy," "the new Germany," are each made to appear either like a Heaven or a Hell. What is said about them by their friends or foes is not only untrue of *these* countries, but of *all* countries, indeed of any conceivable human society. But as Hitler himself has declared in one of his self-revelatory phrases, propaganda can make Hell seem like Heaven and Heaven seem like Hell.[2]

The chief requirement of a revolutionary myth is that it should initiate and sustain direct, collective action. The test of its truth is success. Objective tests are brushed aside by the revolutionary when they seem most inexorable to the philosopher or the scientist, that is to say, when they challenge the theory itself. Marxists and National Socialists employ scientific phrases, not because they are scientific, but because we live in an age of popular science and of scientific superstition, an age in which science is credited with powers more magical and supernatural than any dreamt of in ages of magic or of faith.

The clearness and apparent precision of Lenin's writings and the sweeping, incisive character of his generalizations, give a false sense of scientific accuracy and intellectual power. The flame of his hatred burns so white that it seems the flame of cold, objective reason. His confused, narrow, and superficial thought is thereby concealed, and he is revered as a "scientific thinker" and a promoter of science, whereas the Marxian myth is an attack on science, philosophy, and pure knowledge, an attack that enormously augments its popular appeal. Lenin and Hitler have a good deal in common. It is doubtful whether Lenin knew the work of those who prepared the way for National Socialism—Lagarde, for example, or Lueger, or Schoenerer. He seems to have had no perception at all of the mystical and romantic element in the German character. In his insistence on Class as the essential historical reality, he did not recognize that the Nation could have any permanence. To him, class alone was permanent. The "proletarian" is eternal and universal—he is, according to Lenin, the same everywhere, and his triumph in the world revolution will merge all nations in one universal brotherhood.

Lenin was obsessed by the reality of class, Hitler by the reality of race and of the nation. Lenin contemplated a time when all wars would come to an end. But his immediate purpose was served by war, even by international war which leads to class war which, in its turn, culminates in the "decisive battle." Hitler contemplates the end of class war—but not of international war. For Lenin, war is a means of uniting the international proletariat, for Hitler of uniting the nation.

Foreign war may tear a nation asunder, especially when it is unsuccessful. Russia was torn after the war of 1905, Russia and the Central Powers were torn after the Great

War. But international war may also engender a greater unity, especially if it is successful. The war of 1870 consolidated the unity of the non-Austrian Germans. Lenin wanted international war and defeat, because he wanted the unity of the working class. Hitler wants international war and victory, because he wants the unity of the nation, or rather the racial unity that will establish the greater national unity of all the German-speaking peoples.

Lenin called international wars "Imperialistic." Hitler calls class war "Bolshevism." Both had a gift for reducing complex phenomena to simple terms, terms that are often misnomers, but none the less effective. Both are prodigiously superficial. The deceptive clearness of Lenin's mind and the iron strength of his will recall Horne Tooke, of whom Coleridge said: "He had that clearness which is founded on shallowness. He doubted nothing; and therefore gave you all that he himself knew or meant with greater completeness. ... He left upon me the impression of being a keen, iron man." [3]

Lenin often had a realistic insight into political situations and could measure the forces in conflict with the eye of a strategist. He had a keen apprehension of impending crises. Whenever the crisis came, he showed himself a very shrewd politician. But he was in no sense a thinker, and throughout his work there is not one original idea, not one deep thought. Hitler, although never profound, is not so uniformly superficial as Lenin. But he can be more portentous—he has a genius for portentous platitudes. He was a man of the people in a way Lenin never was, and lived amongst them understanding them as Lenin never did, although he was always a lonely man. He has, what Lenin lacked, at least some sense of the incomprehensible, of the mysterious. There is a good deal of pseudo-science in *Mein Kampf* and a good deal of nonsense about race and heredity, but Hitler is not usually so arrogant in his parade of "scientific method" and of "objectivity" as Lenin was. He sometimes felt what Lenin never seemed to feel, namely, the limitations of science. Some of his greatness as a demagogue—and Hitler is the greatest demagogue of modern times—lies in his ability to sense the muddled aspirations, the obscure worries of the soul, and the deep discontent of the modern European, especially the German, and to give them simple, lapidary expression. For millions of men and women, especially youthful men and women, Hitler's words are revelation and liberation—the dividing line between two epochs, an old and a new, a dead world and a living. He has inaugurated the Kingdom of Heaven on Earth, and all other Kingdoms, whether of this world or of another, are as nothing by comparison.

Lenin is a rationalist within the narrow confines of the irrational Marxian myth. Hitler's mind is more intuitive. He has a sense, quite foreign to Lenin, of the dark, demoniac forces that move masses of men. For Lenin, religion is something unreal that can be explained out of existence. Hitler sees in religion a very formidable power, but useful to his purpose. Lenin is an open foe of Christianity, but so great is his contempt for all religions (Christianity included), that he thinks they will simply disappear as men and women become "enlightened" and thereby become Marxists. Hitler would inject his doctrines of race and nationhood into the Christian religion and so deprive it of its transcendental, eschatological character (without which, it is not Christianity at all) and, making it secular, harness it to his purpose.

Lenin is a would-be destroyer of religion, Hitler a corrupter of religion. The National Socialist attack, accepting as it does much of liberal theology and natural religion, is far more dangerous to Christianity than the godlessness of Marxism. Lenin would destroy the altar or at least promote its decay. Hitler would preserve the altar while replacing the Cross of Christ by the Swastika.

According to Engels, "all religion ... is nothing but the fantastic reflection in men's minds of those external forces which control their daily life, a reflection in which the terrestrial forces assume the form of supernatural forces." [4] God is to Engels "the extraneous force of the capitalist mode of production."[5] God will, therefore, "vanish" when that "mode of production" vanishes, and "the religious reflection will disappear for the simple reason that there will be nothing left to reflect."[6]

Marx argued that "the religious reflex of the real world can, in any case, only then finally vanish when the practical relations of everyday life offer to man none but perfectly intelligible and reasonable relations with regard to his fellow-men and nature."[7]

The problems that awed and preoccupied the greatest minds are contemptuously brushed aside by Marx. The mysteries of birth, life, and death are neither problematic nor mysterious to the Marxist. Does he really imagine that they are all so "simple" and that they will *ever* be "perfectly intelligible and reasonable"? Does he really suppose that man can *ever* have "perfectly intelligible and reasonable relations" with Nature's wonder-world?

Can it be that Marx *never* experienced awe or humility in the presence of infinite time and endless space? Was death to him nothing but physical decomposition? Did he really consider the immortal soul no more than a fiction that will disappear with the disappearance of capitalism? Is the Hereafter but a falsehood, told to divert the proletariat from the class struggle? Is a crown in Heaven only meant as an inexpensive compensation for low wages on earth?

It is hard to believe that Marx, who had a certain prophetic grandeur, was never awed in the presence of the ultimate realities, that he was without the spiritual humility he could have found amongst the "proletarians" whom he so misjudged. But it would seem that the hard arrogance of the

Marxian secular religion is deadly to the deeper subtler stirrings of the soul, crushing more ruthlessly than the narrowest sectarian Christianity crushed the free, brave doubts and questionings of the scientific and philosophical reason.[8]

Nowhere is it so evident that the Marxist is a man of blind faith as in his attitude towards religion. Marx, Engels, Lenin, and their followers, seem never to have been deeply troubled by doubt. They were incapable of the remorseless criticism of fundamentals without which Christianity is inconceivable.

For Lenin "religion" (the "opium of the people") and "religious prejudices" were one.[9] "Religious beliefs" were a form of "ignorance and benightedness,"[10] "a kind of spiritual intoxicant, in which the slaves of capital drown their humanity, and blunt their desire for a decent human existence."[11]

And yet religion was not, according to Lenin, quite as dangerous as it might seem to be. Indeed, it was nothing but a "fog" that could be dispersed by "purely intellectual weapons."[12]

Lenin, usually so intolerant, appears relatively tolerant here—he does not believe in stamping religion out by force, but in hastening on its natural end by peaceful persuasion.

These words reveal the degree of his contempt rather than of his tolerance. Religion is to him so obviously false and despicable that he cannot conceive of its survival after the reasons for its existence have been demonstrated, reasons which to him are "scientific," "objective," and, in any case, perfectly simple. "Even today"—in 1905—"the class-conscious worker, brought up in the environment of the big factory and enlightened by town life, rejects religious prejudices with contempt."[13]

The Marxian program, he continues, is "entirely based on scientific—to be more precise—on materialist philosophy." But the "actual historical and economic roots of religion must be explained." By explained, Lenin means "explained away." The fraud only has to be exposed, and no one will believe it any longer.

"The proletarians" who "still cling to the remnants of old prejudices" must not be rebuffed, for they may be useful to the revolutionary movement, and it would be foolish to turn them away merely because of a few of these "remnants" which will rapidly disappear in any case. Religion is but "medieval mustiness" made up "of opinions and dreams that are of third-rate importance," and are "being steadily relegated to the rubbish heap by the normal course of economic development."[14]

All this was written in 1905. Thirty years later, when Marxism had become the official religion of Russia, when it had kept the Russian people in spiritual and material subjection for more than fifteen years, and had endeavored by prodigious propaganda (reinforced by a ruthless terror) to "explain" the "actual historic and economic roots of religion" in schools, in the press, at public meetings, in countless books and pamphlets, in numerous anti-religious museums, and had excluded not only the clergy, but even church-goers from all administrative posts and from the teaching profession, had suppressed all religious literature, and sent many priests and nuns to death, to prison, exile, or concentration camps, and had ostensibly brought about that "economic development" which would "inevitably" make "religious prejudice" disappear in any case—after all this, and much more, Sir Bernard Pares could write of his visit to a church in Moscow on Christmas Eve, 1935:

> "Everybody stands in a Russian church and we were packed as close as sardines.... The service lasted two hours. The singing was beautiful, and, I felt, more fervent than any I have before heard in Russia. I also noticed that three times the congregation itself was able to join in the singing and did so with great devotion.... I have mentioned that I saw everywhere in Moscow a look of purpose on practically all faces; nowhere was this

stronger than with the worshipers of that Christmas Eve. So far from a congregation of old and withered persons, both sexes and literally all ages were here equally represented, and it was a crowd in which it was impossible to think of the word class.... As we came out, the priests were beginning to go through the whole service again and there was a crowd equally large trying to make its way in." [15]

It is when Lenin sees religion associated with genius that his contempt for it turns into malignant hatred. In his attack on Tolstoi, he denounces religion as "one of the most corrupt things existing in the world."[16] He objects to Tolstoi's proposal that priests who are merely officials of the church should be replaced by "priests of moral conviction." He finds religion much more hateful when it is sincere than when it is insincere. Those who profess it because they gain by it, or because it relieves their "imaginary fears," may be contemptible, but they are much less dangerous than those who *really* believe. In his attack on Gorki's so-called "god-seeking" inclinations, he wrote that "a Catholic priest who violates a young girl" is *"much less* dangerous than are priests who do not wear surplices... the first type of priest can be *easily* exposed, condemned, and driven out—but the second cannot be driven out so simply."[17]

Lenin repudiates the religious or, indeed, any transcendental sanction of morality: "Our morality is wholly subordinated to the class struggle of the proletariat"—the struggle "to set up *heaven on earth.*"[18]

In these memorable words Marxism is exposed as an amoral secular eschatology by Lenin himself. Here is his justification of evil. Only what serves the purpose of the "proletarian revolution" is moral—every falsehood, all treachery and bloodshed are right if they advance the cause of those who would establish, as he himself calls it, Heaven on Earth. There is no wickedness, save hostility towards the revolution —and the sincere opponent is worse than the insincere opponent. The capitalist who merely makes money is not as big a rogue as the one who believes in the capitalist system.

These words of Lenin's recall the whole amorality of the Russian revolution [19] and of the international Communist movement—its mendacity and its cruelty, its foul abuse of all honest dissidence. We shall see later on that National Socialism is similarly amoral. To the founders and leaders of the modern secular religions, and to their followers there are no transcendental, absolute or ultimate values. Truth and justice are a means, not an end, the law an instrument for the preservation of the State, but the State never an instrument for the maintenance of law.

No wonder that Marx, Lenin, Stalin, Mussolini, and Hitler, while claiming to make their people free, equal, prosperous, and strong, have never shown the slightest wish to make them righteous. They have all "omitted the weightier matters of the law—judgment, mercy, and faith."[20]

And they have failed to make their people either free or equal or prosperous. Perhaps they have made them strong, and precisely therein lies their greatest danger, for their strength, precariously founded on armed idolatry, threatens to engulf them all. It is as though some implacable Destiny, deaf to their constant assurances of peaceful purpose, had placed them under an irresistible compulsion to bring disaster upon one another and upon us all.

Lenin was too shrewd a political tactician not to show circumspection even in dealing with the purveyors of "opium" and "medieval mustiness." In any case, he believed their end to be certain, and was convinced it would come all the more quickly if they were gently helped on the way to extinction and not goaded into an effort to avert the inevitable.

Lenin regarded Marxism as "incomplete and inconsistent" without atheism.[21] Hitler regards National Socialism as incomplete and inconsistent without a belief in God. To Lenin, "belief in God is *always* reactionary."[22] To Hitler, belief in God is part of revolutionary faith, though it must be subordinated to belief in race and nationhood.

While Marxism professes to be "scientific" and "objective," National Socialism makes no such pretensions. Hitler, who repudiates objectivity as something vicious, is often more objective than Lenin.

In *Mein Kampf* he says bitter things about the "objectivity" of the Germans. He denounces "the curse of our objectivity" that "corrupts the hearts of our children—we Germans one and all have to suffer under it most grievously."[23] He complains that the German is objective in his attitude towards his own people "as well as to everything else." He attacks the Roman Catholic Church because it tends to make its followers "subjective" with regard to their own countries. He considers Protestantism "better" in this respect, but complains that the Protestant also grows neglectful of his country whenever national interests do not harmonize with Protestant tradition.[24]

But for religion as such he professes reverence. He even places it above party and above the State, and declares that no one with the slightest knowledge of the evolution of religious beliefs and doctrines could imagine that a religious reformation will ever be brought about by political means. Of those who have used religion as the "instrument" of their "political transactions" he says that they are "rascals without any conscience."[25]

But what he denounces is exactly what he is and does himself.

He argues, rightly, of course—and herein he is more just than Lenin, who preferred the sinful to the virtuous priest—that there are rascals everywhere and that if they misuse religion for their own ends religion cannot be held responsible (whereas for Lenin, religion *itself* is the supreme rascality). According to Hitler the purpose of the political rascal, of "the parliamentary ne'er-do-well and pickpocket," is served by blaming religion and so justifying his own double dealing. The "lying rascal" who makes religion appear responsible for his own "personal depravity" thereby hopes to show the world "how right his own conduct really was," and how "the salvation of religion and of the church is the exclusive achievement of his own garrulity."[26]

This is exactly what Hitler is and does himself, as we shall see later on (*Mein Kampf* is of the highest interest as a piece of self-portraiture).

The "lying rascal's fellow-men," so he continues, "who are as stupid as they are forgetful, then fail to recognize, or they forget, the true originator of the whole strife even if only by reason of the great uproar, so that the scoundrel has really achieved his aim."

This is exactly what has happened in the German religious conflict. Hitler himself is the "true originator" of that conflict in its present open form, though the German people fail to recognize or have forgotten it.

Above party, above the State, and above the Christian religion, Hitler places his own secular religion of blood and soil, of race and nationhood, and it is above all "by political means" that he is trying to bring about a "reformation" that will establish his secular religion in the place of Christianity, although the outward forms of Christianity may be preserved. It is his secular teaching alone that Hitler regards as true religion, and in his formidable endeavor to impose it on the German people, even at the cost of arousing the biggest religious conflict known in Europe since the Reformation, Hitler proposes to be a savior of religion, although the success of his effort would mean the de-Christianization of Germany.

Hitler seems to contradict his own practice when he says that "political parties have nothing to do with religious problems," and that the "political leader must regard the religious doctrine and institutions of his country as inviolable."[27] But the contradiction is only apparent, for throughout his book

—indeed throughout his life—Hitler differentiates between *his* party and *all* other parties, between *his* politics and *all* other politics, very much as the Marxist differentiates between *Marxism* and *all* other "Weltanschauungen," between the *Communist* movement and *all* other political movements. Hitler declares that the politician who wishes to interfere with religion has no business to be a politician at all, but ought to be a reformer "if he has the making of one." This is precisely what Hitler is himself—a reformer. And what is happening in Germany today is a political and religious reformation, only its politics are religious, its religion is political, while both are secular and anti-Christian.[28]

To Hitler the National Socialist Party is *the* Party or *the* Movement. And the Party and the Movement *are* Germany —indeed, more than this, they are all that Germany stands for, as well. They are the German nation, the German character, the German national genius. They are Germany and German nationhood—das "Deutschtum" and "das Deutsche." In Germany nothing has a right to exist outside the Movement, nothing has any right to call itself German if it is not of the Movement. And this is true even of religion. Only in so far as Christianity is in the service of the Party or of the Movement is it allowed to exist.

Although Hitler speaks of religion with reverence, the problem of sin does not exist for him any more than it did for Lenin. There is nothing in *Mein Kampf,* or in his recorded utterances, that reveals any awareness of a reality beyond that of this world. He is convinced that men are stupid—but not that they are "under sin."

Lenin repudiates religion with contempt—Hitler lays robber and sacrilegious, even if outwardly reverential, hands upon it. It was clear that when the Marxian belief in the "inevitable" disappearance of religion turned out to be false, the persecution of religion by his followers would begin. But although Christianity is persecuted in Russia, it is not being corrupted.[29] There is in Russia a clear issue, an either-or. This cannot last—with the growth of nationalism in Russia it is certain that, as religion has not been destroyed, and is, indeed, reviving, there will be an attempt at compromise in which nationalism will invite religious sanction. The hour of greatest danger to the Christian Church in Russia is yet to come.

In Germany that hour was brought about by Hitler in the first year of his Chancellorship.

The "Godless" in the Soviet Union may have a powerful organization with a huge membership and a comic paper (the *Bezbozhnik*), they may enjoy official patronage, they may insult and deride, but they do not invade the church, they do not turn out the priest to don his robes themselves, they do not inject their own godless superstition into the preaching, into the ritual, into the hymnology.[30] They do not erect their own symbol above the altar. But this is exactly what is happening in Germany. There the church itself and the inmost sanctuaries of the individual soul are threatened with invasion. In Russia, Christians may be persecuted, but Christianity is left alone. In Germany, it is Christianity *as such*, the Word of God *itself*, which is being assaulted.[31]

In Russia, the dominion of the Hammer and Sickle does not extend to the altar. In Germany, the Swastika is being erected above the altar. In *Mein Kampf* Hitler attacks both Protestants and Roman Catholics as being indifferent to the "systematic" pollution of "Aryan" blood and, especially, the blood of "our inexperienced blonde and youthful girls... those noble and unique creatures"—by those "blood parasites," the Jews. He complains bitterly that the two Christian Churches, instead of fighting against this evil, fight one another, when it is their duty not only "always to be talking outwardly of God's will, but to do God's will and not to let God's work be desecrated."[32]

Hitler is contemptuous of religious differences, not because he believes in a fundamental Christian unity, in the *Una Sancta*. Indeed he is opposed to such a unity because it would be *international*. He is really quite indifferent to Christian teaching as such. What matters to him is not the ultimate or the transcendental, but "whether Aryan man be preserved or die out."[33] He is not at all clear on the subject of race. His "science" is as unscientific as Lenin's.[34] By "race" he means breed or stock. Men of the same race are to him a kind of blood-brotherhood. His conception of nationality is racial and tribal. Men of the same breed, stock, or blood-brotherhood, form one tribe that may inhabit regions separated by political frontiers. The nation, as he conceives it, is a racial homogeneous blood-brotherhood with frontiers separating it from other nations. Frontiers that separate men of the same brotherhood from one another are unnatural, indeed they are an outrage and must be removed.[35] This is Hitler's fundamental political doctrine. The Germans are to Hitler not merely the population of the present Reich, but also the Austrians, the Sudetic Germans of Czechoslovakia, the Germans in Danzig and Memel, the German minority in Poland, indeed, all the German-speaking inhabitants of the world. Ethnologically the Germans are an inextricable mixture of races, but to Hitler they are all "Aryans" who must be united in one brotherhood. This brotherhood is the "Greater Germany," and to achieve it is the principal object of Hitler's foreign policy—indeed, it is the main purpose of the National Socialist Revolution.

This, the doctrine of race and nationhood, is the main content of the Hitlerite myth. It is the essential National Socialist "Weltanschauung" or "theory" (to use the Marxian jargon). To Hitler, a man of Aryan blood is the embodiment of natural virtue just as the proletariat is to the Marxist. The evil in the world is the product of racial mixture or pollution. Hitler conceives his mission as being prophetic and religious. His mission is to purify the German "blood-brotherhood" of every "non-Aryan"—especially Semitic—strain, to unite it within the frontiers of "Greater Germany," and establish it in an armed ascendancy with colonial possessions and dependencies stretching across Europe as far as the Black Sea and the Caucasus. The "superior" race—the "Herrenrasse"—must not only be master in its own realm, its superiority demands that it be master over "inferior" races or strains and subject them to exploitation. This is its duty both towards itself and towards mankind. In this mission, this duty, this endeavor, lies the principal purpose of the German revolution of 1933. That revolution (like the great French and Russian revolutions) is *not* a purely domestic affair, but a matter of universal concern. All Europe, indeed the world, and not least the British Commonwealth, will pay heavily for failure to see that this is so.

Hitler is not so explicitly chiliastic as Lenin, nor has he Lenin's naïve faith in the goodness of man as such. Nevertheless chiliasm underlies his vision of the German "blood-brotherhood" which will shed essential evil by being purged of alien racial strains and will embody in its own domination the domination of all manly and resplendent virtues.

Hitler rejects the Christian conception of sin just as the Marxists do. His whole teaching implies disbelief in the sinfulness of *all* men. The elect, the men and women of Aryan race, who will form the future blood-brotherhood are *not* under sin. They are not merely men and women with *special* virtues, they are the repositories of virtue *itself*. The Aryan, like the Proletarian, is sinless.

Hitler rejects the Christian doctrine of salvation—to him there is no Heaven except through race, just as there is none to Marx and Lenin except through class. To Marx and Lenin the Kingdom of Heaven on Earth is the universal dominion of the proletariat, to Hitler of the Aryan race.

The fulfillment of Marxian and National Socialist eschatology, of their chiliastic mythological vision, is in *this* world.[36]

Marxism and National Socialism are incompatible with Christianity. They have much in common with one another, but they have nothing in common with Christianity. There cannot be peace between Christianity and any State—but between Christianity and the Marxist or National Socialist State there cannot even be that armistice which is the only relationship between Church and State that is not a corruption of either.

Christianity is never safe, but where there is one atom of Marxism or National Socialism left, Christianity is in mortal danger—and so are Marxism and National Socialism wherever there is one atom of Christianity left.

Marx and Lenin knew this, so does Hitler. But there are many Christians who do not.

Hitler often speaks of God and Providence, but never as of something awe-inspiring or inscrutable, never as the *wholly other* or as the *mysterium tremendum*. There is for him neither a God of Love, nor of Forgiveness, nor even of Wrath.

"God's will once gave men their form, their being, their capacities. Whoever destroys His work thereby declares war against the Lord's creation, against the divine order." The meaning of this important passage is not very clear at first sight. But it is made clear when Hitler, as we have seen, accuses the Christian Churches of waging "war against the Lord's creation" by neglecting the racial principle, by remaining passive while the "Aryan race is polluted," or "bastardized," as he calls it, by the admixture of alien races, especially of the Jewish race.[37]

To him, the Will of God is the racial principle in action. Its purpose is that final purity without which the domination of the "Aryan blood-brotherhood" is impossible.

Hitler regards himself as God's instrument for the fulfillment of that purpose. His hatred of the Jews is a *religious* hatred, a hatred of what is, to him, the embodiment of evil. Their elimination is "the will of God": "I believe that I am today acting in accordance with the purposes of the Almighty Creator. In keeping the Jew at bay, I am fighting for the work of the Lord."[38]

The persecution of the Jews in Germany is, therefore, a *religious* persecution. But it is one from which the Jews cannot escape by baptism or any form of conversion, for the religious principle, in the name of which the Jews are persecuted, is *racial,* so that there is, for the Jew, no escape, no mercy, no expiation (as there could be in the Middle Ages), for no one can alter his ancestry. The Jew can never be one of the elect and is forever expelled from any association with them.

That socialism is an advanced form of capitalism was recognized by Lenin himself, when he said that "socialism is nothing but State capitalist monopoly." It is true that this monopoly is "made to benefit the whole people"—and "by this token it *ceases* to be capitalist monopoly"—but not to be capitalistic.[39] By "State capitalist monopoly" Lenin meant the financial monopoly of the proletarian dictatorship (what happens to it when the State has "withered away" he does not explain). By "capitalist monopoly" he means financial power concentrated in the hands of the "capitalists" as a privileged class.

With all this Hitler would agree, except that he would say "fellow-countrymen" ("Volksgenossen") instead of "proletariat," and by "Volksgenossen" he would mean all fellow-countrymen and not the "proletariat" only.

In the sense that he is hostile to "capitalists" as a ruling or privileged class, Hitler is as "anti-capitalistic" as Marx or Lenin are. He is a man of the people, as Marx and Lenin were not; he fought in the war as a common soldier, and spent years of obscurity working at various trades. He worked with his hands and his wits for a living, and amid men and women of all sorts, as Marx and Lenin never did. He had outgrown his youth before he became the professional revolutionary Marx and Lenin always were. He had an experience of the life which most of mankind have to live, an experience denied to Marx or Lenin. He no more dismissed the reality of class as hateful and unreal than he dismissed religion as hateful and unreal. He knew, what Marx and Lenin did not know, that both are with us always. He had a keen sense of the difference between skilled and unskilled workmen, between peasant and artisan, between the lower, middle, and upper classes. His greatness as a demagogue lies largely in his sense of class and in the skill of his appeal to each class in turn. But he also has, what Marx and Lenin never had, the awareness of the human—and inhuman—constant that runs through all classes. He is hostile to class privilege. He is an egalitarian, like Marx and Lenin, but he would, while preserving class-differences, oppose the domination of one class by another. Every class-war is an attempt by one class to dominate another. The principle of class-war is not one of equality but of inequality. And in his opposition to the class-war Hitler is relentless. To him it is incompatible with national unity, a criminal attempt by fellow-countrymen to prevail over fellow-countrymen, a violation of the sacred blood-brotherhood, and therefore the supreme infamy—and therefore essentially Jewish.

What Lenin and Hitler object to in Capitalism is the exploitation of the individual by the Capitalist. Hitler saw the essential principle of exploitation in usurious interest and unearned income.[40] Hitler was no economist as Marx was. There is no counterpart in National Socialism to the immense economic research and often incisive, though confused, thinking of Marxian economists. National Socialists are less influenced by the classical English economists than Marx was, and tend to consider economic science as such with hostility, though in their hostility there is a good deal of cunning as well as a vulgar romanticism. National Socialist conceptions of interest and usury are to be found throughout Socialist literature,[41] but they are primitive compared with the elaborate (though untenable) Marxian theory of surplus value.

Marxian and National Socialist economics have this in common—both are directed against exploitation. But there is this difference. Marx and Lenin opposed the exploitation of man by man, Hitler opposes the exploitation of fellow-countrymen by fellow-countrymen.[42]

CHAPTER III

The contrasted attitudes of Lenin and Hitler towards mankind—The Golden Age and the Heroic Age—The brutality of Marxism and of National Socialism—A comparison with the Cromwellian era—Lenin's and Hitler's ruthlessness of purpose—Hitler's conception of war as permanently desirable—The Brown Terror—Hitler the chief terrorist—The hatreds of Lenin and of Hitler—Their intolerance—The essential kinship and parallel development of the two leaders—The Marxian and National Socialistic view of history—The arrogance of the Marxian myth—Marxism, Fascism, and National Socialism—Hitler's conception of the "German race"—Hitler and Marxism—The development of the National Socialist counter-myth—An estimate of the "greatness" of Marx and Lenin.

ACCORDING to Engels, the only "real" and "historical right" is "the right to revolution."[1] Whatever promotes revolution, therefore, is *right,* and whatever hinders revolution is *wrong.* Successful revolution is the only *ultimate* sanction of morality. It did not occur to Marx and Engels that the "bourgeois" revolutions of the past were by no means over. They regarded the "proletariat" as the only "revolutionary" class. To the proletarian, according to the Communist Manifesto, "law, morality, religion, are ... so many bourgeois prejudices." The only good, therefore, is what is good for the proletarian revolution—the only evil is what is bad for that revolution.[2]

Hitler's conception of good and evil is analogous. National Socialists do not tire of repeating that "what is right is what serves the interests of the German nation."[3] Hitler identifies the racial principles with the "will of God," as we have seen. Nothing matters to him except race.[4] Throughout his book, throughout his innumerable speeches, and pervading all his actions, is the fanatical belief that whatever will promote *his* revolution and establish the blood-brotherhood of the Greater Germany is *right,* and that this revolution is the only ultimate sanction of morality.

Man, in his weakness and his strength, his nobility and his sinfulness, his pride, his diffidence, and his immense variety, means nothing to Lenin and Hitler, but exists only as a "bourgeois" or a "proletarian," a "capitalist," an "Aryan" or a "non-Aryan." Lenin and Hitler have no use for human beings as such, for man "that great and true Amphibium whose nature is disposed to live, not only like other creatures in divers elements, but in divided and distingushed worlds."[5]

They have no use for anything, save for the sinless, all-embracing class, or the sinless, all-dominating race. That the individual has any rights of his own, even the right to live, has no meaning at all to Lenin and Hitler.

Hitler despises all men save the few chosen—the "highest men," the men of "leadership," of "personality."[6] He is particularly contemptuous of the Germans. Many Germans of genius—Goethe, Hölderlin, Nietzsche—have uttered bitter words against their fellow-countrymen. But all German demagogues have been filled with real or assumed admiration for the masses to whom they have addressed themselves—Hitler alone excepted.

He, by far the greatest and most successful of German demagogues, himself no German but an Austrian—despises the Germans, and makes no effort to conceal his contempt.

Lenin, with the optimism inherited from the eighteenth century, believed the masses to be good. Hitler does not regard them as evil, but merely simple and gullible—and the German masses particularly so.

He divides the readers of newspapers into those "who believe everything they read," "those who no longer believe anything," and those "who critically examine what they read and judge accordingly." "The first group," he adds, "consists of the great mass of the people."[7]

Of both the German "bourgeoisie" and "proletariat" he writes that "they, for the most part, stumble towards their doom by reason of their cowardice combined with indolence and stupidity"[8] under the leadership of the Jew (much as Hitler hates the Jews, indeed no hatred could be so terrible as his, he endows them with superhuman power—if what he says about them were true, they would be the mightiest race of men on earth).

He is bitter because the garrulity of the Germans makes it impossible to build up a secret organization of any size. And it is sometimes with contempt and sometimes with despair that he refers to the Germans in phrases like "the stupid herd of our sheepishly docile people."[9]

The difference between the Marxian and National Socialist attitudes towards mankind is inherent in the two myths. The Marxian myth is of a universal Golden Age in which class, nation, and State will vanish. That Golden Age would be the universal reign of stupidity if the masses really were what Hitler thinks they are. The National Socialist myth is of a Heroic Age, in which men of masterful personality will lead hierarchically organized but racially homogeneous communities. Pre-eminent amongst these communities will be those of "Aryan" race, who will have dominion over the mass of mankind. Such a myth presupposes extreme docility and willingness to be led.

An overweening confidence in the progress and in the transforming power of science, and a prodigious human arrogance in the presence of nature and of the eternal, have endowed the Marxian and National Socialist myths with a peculiar, truculent crudity. The sages of old would have found words of mockery, had they foreseen that after two or three thousand years the fantasies of the poetic and philosophic imagination would cease to refresh and irradiate the human spirit, and that man in his arrogance, while boastfully professing to destroy the bright and consoling prospect of the impossible, would burden himself with the tedious and truculent projections of narrowed, sectarian minds, and so bring it crashing down in warfare, terrorism, and a darkening of the spirit:

"The Visions of Eternity by reason of narrowed perceptions,
Are become weak visions of time and space, fixed into furrows of Death." [10]

Lenin and Hitler are quite unashamed in their constant advocacy of ruthlessness, of the bloodiest wars and upheavals. Throughout all Marxian and National Socialist literature there is not a trace of pity, magnanimity, forgiveness, or of any generous feeling, not one word of respect for honor or for righteousness—not one trace of toleration, not the slightest appreciation for a foe who might be brave, or even right in his own way.

The Cromwellian era was one of terrible violence, but it was humane and magnanimous compared with the revolutionary eras inaugurated by Lenin and Hitler. If there was ever a man of courage and determination it was Cromwell. But again and again he has words that are incomparably superior for nobility and depth to anything that Lenin and Hitler ever wrote, words that could never be uttered under the sign of the Hammer and Sickle or of the Swastika: "No one rises so high as he who knows not whither he is going [11] ... what we gain in a free way is better than twice so much in a forced, and will be more truly ours and our posterities'." [12]

Hitler, with his vaunted "somnambulist certainty" [13] and Lenin with his "inevitability," and his hatred and contempt for non-violence, would not even have tolerated words like these, still less have uttered them. Cromwell's last prayer belongs to a world inconceivably remote from theirs—remote and more exalted:

"Lord, though I am a miserable and wretched creature, I am in covenant with Thee through Grace. And I may, and I will, come to Thee for Thy people. Thou hast made me, though very unworthy, a mean instrument to do them some good and Thee service.... Lord, however Thou do dispose of me, continue and go on to do good for them. Give them consistency of judgment, one heart and mutual love; and go on to deliver them, and with the work of reformation; and make the name of Christ glorious in the world. Teach them who look too much upon Thy instruments, to depend more upon Thyself.... And pardon the folly of this short prayer: Even for Jesus Christ's sake. And give us a good night if it be Thy pleasure. Amen."

To say that such words can be regarded as belonging to a past age and impossible in our own, is merely to condemn our own age.

Lenin and Hitler and their followers are as brutal and truculent in their language as in their actions—they are never so serious or so sincere as when they reveal their truculent minds.[14]

We have seen how the Communist Resolution of 1928 complacently foretells an era of wars and upheavals compared with which the Great War was a triviality. Lenin describes the "dictatorship of the proletariat" that will establish the classless society as "the most ruthless war waged by the new class ... against the bourgeoisie." How remote from the notion that "what we gain in a free way is better than twice so much in a forced"! The Communist, like the National Socialist, must know that most of the blood they mean to shed —and have shed—is innocent blood. But they are completely indifferent to the shedding of blood, whether guilty or innocent. The sanctity of human life is to them a piece of religious sentimentality—a conception that is dangerous as well as contemptible. Never for a moment do they feel the slightest misgiving over the essential horror of their own messianic vision. Even if the ultimate good, as they conceive it, were certain to come, it would not justify the immeasurable sacrifice. And it is quite certain that it will *never* come.

Political terrorism is by no means a modern phenomenon. It took dreadful forms under the Caesars.[15] The method of the "purge," as carried out by Hitler and his fellow-butchers on the 30th of June 1934, is nowhere described with such profound insight as by Plato.[16] Terrorism is one of the most frightful afflictions that can visit mankind. It has a horror peculiar to itself and one greater even than the horror of war.

Karl Marx, so far from deprecating the excesses (which, as he knew, accompanied violent revolution) or urging restraint, incited his followers to terrorism even beyond what he considered "necessary" to quell counter-revolution:

> "The workers ... must try as much as ever possible to counteract all bourgeois attempts at appeasement, and compel the democrats to put their present terrorist phrases into practice. They must act in such a manner that revolutionary excitement does not at once subside after the victory.... Far from opposing so-called excesses and making examples of hated individuals or public buildings to which hateful memories are attached by sacrificing them to popular revenge, such deeds must not only be tolerated, but their direction must be taken in hand." [17]

For ruthless purpose there is little to choose between Hitler and Lenin, except that Hitler is rather more brutish. Lenin does anticipate a time when there will be no more wars, whereas Hitler not only looks upon war as a permanent institution (in which he may be right), but as permanently desirable. "Mankind has grown great in eternal fight—mankind will perish in eternal peace."[18] Hitler is more personal in his hatred than Lenin. He does not believe that a system can be destroyed if the men who represent it are not destroyed—and he is for sanguinary vengeance on those who survive the system. To Lenin—as to all Marxists—the spectacle of revolution or civil war is an uplifting spectacle. For its horrors they have no feeling at all. Like Marx and Engels, who were in favor of the Crimean War (and contemptuous of John Bright for his pacifism[19]), in favor, too, at first, of the Franco-German War, Lenin saw the fulfillment of Marxian prophecy in the Great War, and was, as we have seen, fearful lest it might come to a premature end. Hitler's book, *Mein*

Kampf, is pervaded with love and glorification of war. He gloried in the Great War, and rejoiced at its coming: "The struggle in 1914 was, by God, not forced upon the masses, it was desired by the whole people.... To me, those hours [of 1914] came as a deliverance from the petty emotions of youth. Even today I am not ashamed to say that I was overwhelmed with tempestuous enthusiasm and that I thanked Heaven out of the fullness of my heart for the joy of living in such an epoch. A war for freedom had begun, mightier by far than any seen on earth until then."[20]

Lenin, the revolutionary, was against assassinations and "individual terrorism," though Lenin, the despot, used terrorism ruthlessly against all opponents. He would probably have agreed with Hitler's belief that "the first spiritual terrorism entered the much freer ancient world with the arrival of Christianity."[21] He would certainly have agreed with Hitler in believing that "force can only be broken by force and terrorism by terrorism," and that "when certain aims are pursued those who oppose these aims must be destroyed."[22]

Hitler was always in favor of what the Marxists call individual terrorism:

"If a nation languishes under the tyranny of an oppressor who is a man of genius, and if oppression is only made possible by his commanding personality," then "only the republican conscience of guilty little rascals" would regard the assassination of the tyrant "as most revolting." Hitler refers with approval to the glorification of tyrannicide in Schiller's "Wilhelm Tell."[23]

Fearful as the Brown Terror is, it is not as fearful as Hitler would have wished. He demands that "tens of thousands"[23a] of these "criminals" who led the revolution of 1918, must be tried and executed by a "German National Court of Justice." He has a particular fondness for executions. The dignity of justice is nothing to him, and he refuses to have it tempered with mercy. He not only demands that it be severe, but that it be ruthless and barbaric. Treason (Landes- und Volksverrat) he declares "shall, in future, be pursued with barbaric ruthlessness."[24] When he heard the news that the Reichstag was burning, he demanded the *public execution* of the incendiary and his accomplices.[25]

Hitler is one of the principal initiators of the Brown Terror and himself the chief terrorist. He personally superintended the "purge" of the 30th June 1934, when so many of his friends and associates were executed. He is the chief persecutor of the Jews, the leading spirit in the attack on Christianity, and the chief inspirer of the appalling sterilization laws.[26]

Lenin was a prodigious hater, but his hatred has a cold, abstract quality. He constantly breaks out in crude vituperation against abstractions or against persons who are, to him, the embodiments of abstractions. His hatred of "moderates" and of "reformists" is particularly malignant, specially when they are fellow Marxists. Kautsky, a man of some intellectual power and great nobility of character, is pursued with implacable malevolence throughout Lenin's writings. He is a "renegade," he "acts just like a swindler," he and all like him are "miserable Philistines" and "petit bourgeois democrats."[27] Men like Chernoff and Tseretelli are "heroes of rotten philistinism."

It is a favorite trick of Lenin's to put the names of those he hates in the plural so as to damn them and all like them. Or he will add an -ism to their names, and so convert them into types or embodiments of some, to him, odious abstraction. The "Hendersons and Snowdens" are "utterly worthless," "treacherous" and—worst of all—"petit bourgeois."[28]

Nothing is more infamous in Lenin's eyes than "Kautskyism" (he speaks of "the abominableness of social chauvinism and Kautskyism"),[29] but there is also a "Macdonaldism," "Manilovism," "Millerandism," "Longuétism," and so on. Of Kropotkin, one of the most exalted minds of the last generation, he makes "the Messrs. Kropotkin and Co." Throughout his work, everybody who disagreed ever so slightly with the Marxian doctrine (as he saw it) is damned. The list of the damned is enormous and includes almost all who have been prominent in the labor movements of Western and Central Europe.

His hatred of Social Democracy is terrific—it was also one of his most lasting heritages (a heritage that was not abandoned until long after Hitler had crushed the quarreling Marxian sects and they decided, too late, for union). In the Communist International Program of 1928, Social Democracy is denounced as "the mainstay of imperialism," while the whole of the Second International and the Amsterdam Federation of Trade Unions is "the most reliable pillar" of "bourgeois society." The "Austro-Marxism" of the Austrian Social Democrats, who, unlike the German Communists, went down fighting, is "the most dangerous enemy of the proletariat, more dangerous" than all the avowed adherents of predatory social-imperialism. The program also contains a whole bouquet of -isms—Ghandism, Garveyism, Sun-Yat-Senism, and so on—also "Sun-Yat-Senist ideology."

Hitler is animated by similar vituperative malevolence, though his language is more concrete. He denounces the leaders of the German revolution of 1918, who were men of incomparably higher virtue than the leaders of the National Socialist revolution of 1933, as "a heap of climbers... without any conscience," and as "creatures" who "can only be described by words like scoundrel, rascal, ruffian and criminal"... "compared with these traitors every pimp is a man of honour."[30] "The popularity of the German Republic," he declares, "was rooted in a company of pimps, thieves, burglars, deserters, shirkers, etc."[31] The revolution of 1918 was not made "by elements of peace and order," but of "insurrection, robbery and plunder."[32]

What Hitler and his fellow National Socialists think of

their own spiritual kindred, the present rulers of Russia, is very much what is thought about them in return. They are, according to Hitler, "blood-stained, common criminals... the scum of humanity," belonging to a people "who combine bestial cruelty with immeasurable mendacity and think themselves called, today more than ever, to inflict their sanguinary oppression on the whole world"... they are "the representatives of lying, cheating, theft, plunder and robbery." [33]

Hitler fully shares Lenin's hatred of the "bourgeois" and the "petit bourgeois." The "bourgeoisie" ("das Bürgertum") has no "Weltanschauung" (or what the Marxists would call an "ideology").[34] In the revolution, the "cowardly bourgeoisie" was "correctly sized up by Marxism and simply treated as rabble" ("en canaille").[35] "Bourgeois parties are not capable" of "erecting a new and big idea" which, according to Hitler, is essential to successful revolution [36]—which is exactly what Marx and Engels said, namely, that a revolutionary movement requires a "revolutionary theory."

We shall try to show later on that pacifism has a double aspect that makes it dangerous as well as beneficent. But Lenin and Hitler cannot contemplate pacifism of *any* kind without malignant hatred and derision. They remain wholly blind to the humanity that has inspired much modern pacifism. Lenin proclaimed "a ruthless struggle against nauseating, sweet, social pacifist phrases"[37] at a time—1917—when these same siren phrases were being heard by the sailors of the German fleet and produced the first stirrings of the revolution that came a year later, a revolution that may have saved Germany from a worse defeat and Europe from another winter of war. Even if those who uttered these phrases and those who listened to them and passed them on (at the risk of their lives) were mistaken, one can only be nauseated by the concentrated malevolence of the evil, narrow mind that could condemn as "nauseating" the words that were wrung out of men by the torment of war and the intolerable longing for peace. Lenin had no use for pacifism except when the last revolutionary war would be over and the classless society had been established. Hitler declares that "the pacifist, humane idea is perhaps quite good when the highest man has so far conquered and subjugated the world that he is its sole master"—pacifism will then "be incapable of having a harmful influence... therefore, war first and then, perhaps, pacifism."[38] According to Lenin, "whoever wishes a durable and democratic peace must be for civil war."[39]

Hitler's contempt for pacifism is so deep that he believes it to be characteristic not so much of the people he hated most, the Jews, but of those he despised most, the Germans. "If the last German were to perish," he writes, "the last pacifist would perish too, for the rest of the world has hardly been so profoundly deceived by this rubbish, which is contrary to nature and to common sense, as our own people unfortunately have."[40]

Lenin and Hitler are fiercely intolerant while professing to be promoters of freedom. It is true that the maintenance of liberty demands strong government and a stern ethic. The love of freedom is inconceivable without the hatred of her enemies, and the freer a democracy is, the more vigilant and resolute it must be in defense against the internal as well as the external foe.

Milton was one of freedom's grandest champions. Not all he did and wrote was favorable to her cause. But his intolerance was the sinew of his championship. His love of freedom was made strong and fierce by his terrible hatred of tyranny.

The stern quality of Milton's love of freedom is revealed in his conception of the heretical:

"A man may be a hereticke in the truth; and if he believes things only because his Pastor says so, or the Assembly so determine, though his belief be true, yet the very truth he holds becomes his heresy."[41]

These words are the absolute denial of the essential claim advanced by the modern secular religions and by the "totalitarian States." Even if we had not the *Areopagitica* and *Samson Agonistes,* these words alone would place Milton in a world wholly alien and incomprehensible to Lenin and Hitler.

It was through love of freedom that Milton was intolerant in her defense. Lenin and Hitler are haters of freedom and —in so far as they are capable of love at all—they are lovers of intolerance. They want freedom to establish unfreedom. According to Lenin: "Those who are really convinced that they have advanced science, would demand not freedom for the new views to continue side by side with the old, but the substitution of the old views by the new ones."[42]

That, precisely, is what Lenin wanted freedom for—that, and nothing else. The "new views"—the Marxian myth—are not to live "side by side with the old, but to replace them altogether." All men are to be "heretickes" in the Marxian truth.

According to Hitler, a "Weltanschauung" (or what Lenin called a "theory") is intolerant and cannot live as "one party side by side with another." It "imperiously demands that it be fully and exclusively recognized. It also demands the complete transformation of the whole of public life in accordance with its views. It cannot, therefore, tolerate the continued existence of what represents the former state."[43]

These two passages, taken from the writings of Lenin and Hitler, show the essential kinship of the two leaders—leaders in a war of extermination against the freedom of the human spirit, a war that would erect upon the desolation achieved by their victory, the abomination of a pseudo-scientific, pseudo-philosophical, pseudo-religious myth, calling itself a "theory," an "ideology," or a "Weltanschauung."

We have seen how Marxism, while professing to be "scientific" and "objective," is anti-scientific and subjective. For

Hitler science is a means of promoting "national pride." The inventor is never great merely as an inventor, but only if he is also a fellow-countryman.[44] And only they are "fellow-countrymen" who accept National Socialism. Those who do not accept it and have eluded the prisons and concentration camps of the Third Realm and have gone abroad, are "ausgebürgert" or denationalized. They are no longer "fellow-countrymen." They lose not only their nationality, but any eminence they may have in science, art, or letters.[45]

All National Socialist writers are obsessed with race, blood, and nationhood, just as all Marxist writers are obsessed with class and class-warfare. Just as there is no history for the Marxist that is not a history of class-struggle, so there is no history for the National Socialist that is not a history of racial conflicts. Hitler demands that the history of the world be rewritten so that "the racial question" may be "raised to dominating eminence."[46]

Mein Kampf is pervaded by crude pseudo-science just as Marxian writings are. Engels suggests that until men have reached the stage when they collectively control production, in other words, when history has done what Marx told it to do, they are but a transition species between the animal world and a "really human world": "The seizure of the means of production by society puts an end to commodity production and therewith to the domination of the product over the producer. Anarchy in social production is replaced by conscious organization on a planned basis. The struggle for individual existence comes to an end. And at this point, in a certain sense, man finally cuts himself off from the animal world, leaves the conditions of animal existence behind him and enters conditions which are really human."[47]

Neither Lenin nor Hitler ever showed mental progression or development after they had reached an early maturity. Between their earliest and latest writings and speeches there is no essential difference. The Hitler of today is still the

Hitler of *Mein Kampf,* which was written in 1924 and 1926. The Lenin of *Materialism and Empirio-Criticism,* which was written in 1908, is the same as the Lenin of *Left Wing Communism,* written in 1920. There are certain external changes. The later writings and speeches of both are less threadbare and show more practical sense, but the inner man is always the same—without depth, without darkness or light, and without complexity. Neither seems to have wrestled with God, with the world, or with his own soul: dictators, both of them, inwardly and outwardly, rigid, static, intolerant, monomaniacal. Both are entirely unoriginal. Lenin had never got beyond the teaching of his master, Karl Marx. He changed the emphasis—he stressed the "dictatorship of the proletariat" more than Marx and Engels did (they rarely mentioned it, though it is implicit in their "theory.") [48] In Hitler's writings and speeches there is hardly a single idea which is not to be found in earlier Pan-German and anti-Semitic literature—in Lagarde, Schoenerer, Lueger, Jung, Stöcker, Chamberlain, or, for that matter, in Marxian writings and speeches. It is probable that the deep influence Marxism had on Hitler was imparted at public meetings, in discussions, and in the struggle with Social Democrats and Communists, rather than by the study of Marxian literature—though there seems to be little doubt that in the years he passed at Vienna, and perhaps in the few years he lived in Munich, Hitler did a prodigious amount of reading.

Marx was certainly original even if he was no philosopher. The myth he created was not a conglomerate of earlier myths. Hitler said of Marx—with profound, though crooked insight—that he "was really the *one* amongst the millions who, with the sure vision of a prophet, recognized the essential poisons and extracted them so as to use them, like a master of black magic, in concentrated solution for the speedier destruction of the independent existence of free countries upon this earth." [49]

There is truth in this portrait, though, like all Hitler's portraits, it is a caricature and, like them all, it is self-portraiture. If he had said "free individuals" instead of "free countries," the portrait would be even nearer the truth both about Marx and about himself, for Hitler, too, is threatening the "independent existence" of "free countries."

Marx, Lenin, and Hitler are all "masters of black magic"— the black magic of propaganda and mass-suggestion, though Marx never came near the masses save through his apostles. All three were "prophets." "It is not sufficient," Marx wrote, "that the thought should press forward to realization—reality must press forward to the thought."[50] All three were caught in the "Zeitgeist" and reduced its crude emergent forces to simple, prophetic terms.

Marx and Lenin were the prophets of class-war and of class-consciousness. It is, of course, untrue that *all* history is the history of class-struggles—but class-struggles have played a big and often under-rated part in history. Hitler is the prophet of racial war and of the racial consciousness which he identifies with the ideal nation. It is not true that *all* great historical conflicts are racial or national—the conflict between Church and State which is, whether open or latent, perhaps coeval with civilization, is neither one of race or class, though it may be deeply colored by either or by both.

Marx, Lenin, and Hitler are unhistorical, or rather, antihistorical. It is very doubtful whether in their view there is such a thing as "objective history." A "bare record" of so-called "facts" is not history at all. Were Tacitus, Gibbon, Macaulay, Ranke, Mommsen, Burckhardt objective? Yes— and no. The Greeks were the most objective of all peoples— one is again and again compelled to feel mingled admiration and wonder at their sovereign objectivity. But was even Thucydides, whose objectivity seems almost inhuman and quite beyond the reach of the modern historian, altogether "objective"? Was not his profound and powerful intellect deeply impregnated with a religious conception? Is not his history of the Peloponnesian War as much a religious drama as the Agamemnon of Aeschylus? Is not the overweening Hybris revealed by the dialogue between the Athenians and the men of Melos? And does not retributive doom appear in the disaster that ended the expedition to Syracuse, when "fleet and army perished from the earth, nothing was saved, and of the many who went forth few returned home"? [51]

No record could be more "bare" than Thucydides' *History* and more replete with "hard facts"—and yet the sense of implacable fate grows from page to page, and the terrible scene in which Athens in her arrogance pronounced the doom of Melos, foreshadows the inevitable ultimate doom of the Athenians themselves.

Compared with the stern grandeur and the absolute pessimism of the Thucydidian world, the worlds of Lenin and Hitler with their shallow optimism appear mean and shoddy.

Even in Thucydides' *History,* where class-war and many other supposedly modern things [52] receive their due, there is Myth, but not, therefore, untruth. A Destiny—profounder and more inexorable than the crude Marxian dialectic—broods over the whole work, although never revealed in a single word.

All great history is objective—even Macaulay's, despite the crudity of his passionate Liberalism; even Clarendon's, despite his hatred of Cromwell (how noble and, with all its hostility, how fair is his portrait of Cromwell compared with any Marxian portrait of any opponent, compared, for example, with contemporary Russian portraits of Trotsky, whose services to the Russian revolution are incomparably greater than those of Stalin or any other living Russian!).

The truthfulness of all great history arises from the collaboration of the steady, objective mind with the visionary spirit. The sequence of events, circumstances, and conditions unrolled by the narrative, will be brought to vivid life, as it were, by the illumination, from within, of a transcendence (as in Thucydides), of a stern ethic (as in Tacitus), of crystalline enlightenment (as in Gibbon), of tragic wisdom (as in Burckhardt).

The Marxian and National Socialist conception of history is not "historical" at all, nor "scientific," nor "objective." It is sectarian and dictatorial. The myth, the "theory," the "ideology,' or the "Weltanschauung" is imposed upon the past, and "ideological" dictatorship is established, all history being pressed, bludgeoned, and trimmed until it becomes a record of the transition from the primitive state of nature to the apocalypse that inaugurates the Millennium and brings history to an end. Violence is done to the past and to the present. The future, as it emerges, is subjected to the terroristic domination concentrated in the hands of God-Caesar.

All great history is truthful, though no history, however great, can be *the* Truth.

But even Marxism and National Socialism are not *wholly* without truth.

There are so many gradations of wealth, influence, and power in human society that it is impossible to say where the "proletariat" ends and the "bourgeoisie" begins. To divide mankind into "proletariat" and "bourgeoisie" is certainly "unscientific." But in the crude Marxian caricature there is this much truth: similar conditions of wealth or poverty, dependence or domination do tend to produce, though they do not infallibly produce, a common consciousness; and class is, with all the reservations that have to be made, a reality, and that class-consciousness, a tremendous though by no means a constant or an "inevitably" conquering force.

The immense and ever-growing amorphous masses of men and women that were thrown together by the development of machinery and large-scale production acquired—with many exceptions—something like a common character, mentality, and discipline. The optimism of the nineteenth century—

which was more primitive than that of the eighteenth—made the masses, once they had the collective will to which they were predestined by the advance of industrial civilization, the masters of the machine with its seemingly god-like power to give increase such as the world had never known before. The organized masses, with the machine as their formidable and yet docile instrument, appeared, to the Socialist visionary, not only the mightiest, but also the most beneficent of all conquerors. It was assumed that the despotism of the masses would be a benevolent despotism. The last twenty years have shown this assumption to be altogether false—though Plato knew it 2300 years ago.

Through mastery of the machine, labor would be master over the brute forces of nature and over all mankind, for lightning, storm, flood, and disease were being subjugated by scientific invention and, seeing that, without labor, the machine would come to a standstill and large-scale production would cease, labor would have all mankind at its mercy. The "working man" would not only be the mightiest and humanest of conquerors—he would be all-mighty and all-good.

Karl Marx, in whose mind this essential vision had a fierce intensity, gave it a seemingly scientific and philosophical form and content as well as an original structure. We have seen that what Marx and his followers believed to be science and philosophy was neither. His logic is powerful enough, only it proceeds from premises in which truth and falsehood are mixed and only appears unerring because it moves in a world of tractable myth. But it is quite unable to reconcile its inherent self-contradiction, and, indeed, does not try to, but prefers to explode in apocalyptic unreason.

The vision of the early Socialists was not altogether untrue. Organized labor did indeed become a power in the world such as would have astonished many, even amongst those of the "bourgeoisie" (and not the least discerning) who saw in the growth of trade unionism a dangerous, revolutionary force.[53]

The truth that there was in the vision of the early Socialists was made manifest by the growing power of organized labor. But, under the influence of Marxian chiliasm, the vision grew in arrogance, whereas, had it been tempered with Christian skepticism, it would have grown in humility.

Its main weakness came from the expansive optimism of the period, from the belief in the natural goodness of man. It was taken for granted that the working class was not only predestined to omnipotence, but would be omnipotent for good alone. Even this anticipation found a seeming fulfillment in so far as the labor movements developed a high humanitarian ethic. They became a very large part of the conscience of the Western world and were a mighty challenge to predatory imperialism and to the exploitation of man by man.

There was—and still is—amongst workmen, especially skilled workmen, a generous comradeship, a magnanimity, a fundamental decency, and a certain massive wisdom. But the Marxian vision of proletarian omnipotence is an attack on the working class and not merely on the "bourgeoisie," for the workman is as much an *individual* as any other man.

Marx and Lenin were without deeper religiosity. They were even without the mature wisdom that has often been distrustful of power as such. Absolute power has rarely, if ever, been beneficent: "All power corrupts, absolute power corrupts absolutely."[54] Marx and Lenin were obsessed by history and believed that in history they had found a key to the future. Burckhardt, one of the greatest of modern historians, and with a mind deeper and broader than the mind of Marx, held that there was nothing to be learned from history, save a little wisdom. And running right through his historical writings[55] like a *Leitmotif* is the conviction that "power is in itself evil." History is always the evil genius of those who dream of power, and Marx, Lenin, and Hitler were fired by history just as Napoleon was. Nietzsche held that the study of history was responsible for the wars of modern times.[56]

Neither to Marx nor to Lenin was there anything problematic about power—it never seemed to occur to them that power *as such* might be evil. One is again reminded, by contrast, of Cromwell, who had power and used it both well and ill—of his fear and trembling before the Almighty, and of his deep distrust of all human power. Marx, Lenin, and Hitler are without fear and trembling—not because they are bigger men, because they are much smaller men than Cromwell.

It was the very arrogance of the Marxian myth that was its downfall. The Marxian Hybris was followed by a Doom that was all the more frightful because the victims went down —unresisting, ignominious, and pitiful—before the avenger, whose name was Adolph Hitler. It was no accident that there, where the cause of Marxism was strongest, the defeat of organized labor was completest—in Germany, above all, but also in Russia, where despotic power was wielded in the name of Marxism and of the "proletariat," and where Stalin and the Communist Party exercise a domination more akin to that of Hitler and of the German National Socialist Party than to anything other in Europe.

But there, where the influence of Marx has been weak— in England, in the Scandinavian countries, in Holland, Belgium, and France, in the United States—organized labor has achieved, or is achieving, a freedom and an independence, an immense and yet beneficent power. Marxism has led to Fascism and National Socialism because, in all essentials, it *is* Fascism and National Socialism.

Biologists have shown much contempt for Hitler's racial doctrines. There is no such thing as an Aryan race, there is not even a Jewish race. What Daniel Defoe said in his great satire on racial doctrines, in *The True-born Englishman,* is true, *mutatis mutandis,* of all nations. Nevertheless, there is beneath Hitler's pseudo-scientific jargon the reality of racial consciousness, just as beneath the scientific jargon of Marx and Lenin there is the reality of class-consciousness. The "British race" is a term without biological validity—nevertheless, men and women scattered over the entire earth, of diverse ethnological origins, have a common consciousness and a common if multifarious civilization. They are all "British"—to call them the British "race" may be unscientific, but the term denotes an indubitable reality.

It is equally unscientific to speak of the Jewish "race"— but the Jews are nevertheless a collectivity with a religious and cultural heritage, and a common consciousness that is all their own. They are "different" from the rest of mankind —having no frontiers, indeed no mother country, scattered over the world, always subject to persecution in some parts of the world (in most at the moment), and yet persisting tenaciously through the centuries.

What Hitler means by the "Aryan race" is the analogue of what is meant by the "white race" when this term is used to denote a supposedly superior civilization. Those who use the term in this sense are, perhaps, a little vague about the Jews, though Hitler is quite clear about them: his "White," or, as he calls it, "Aryan," race is not only exclusive of the Jews, its supposed characteristics are the antithesis of those that he attributes to the Jews.

The term "white race"—it seems to be going out of fashion now, but was in common use a generation ago—is vague and comprehensive. Those who used it did so with a conviction that there were degrees of "whiteness" and that the English were the whitest of all—the English were, so to speak, an *élite* amongst the "white race." A "white" man was nearly always an Englishman. Such terms were the expressions of a certain mentality that has begun to suffer eclipse in the English-speaking countries. It is the mentality of the conquerer, or would-be conquerer, and, arrogant and narrow as it is, it may be a powerful civilizing agent if counterbalanced by a broad humanity and a Christian ethic.

The term "Aryan race" is used by Hitler with a clear conviction that the German race is an *élite* within the "Aryan race"—indeed, the English almost alone are, in his opinion, comparable with the Germans (many of those Englishmen who use the term "white race" would return the compliment and look upon the German, rather than upon any other foreigner, as equal, or almost equal to the Englishman).

The "German race," according to Hitler and his predecessors and followers, is made up of all German-speaking peoples, totaling about a hundred million. Of these, sixty-four million live in Germany proper and six and a half million in Austria. But the German-speaking peoples spread out beyond the German-Austrian frontiers into all neighboring countries except Holland and Belgium (it is by no means sure that the Dutch and Flemings are not secretly accounted Germans by Hitler).

The "German race" is a reality, just as the British and Jewish "races" are, even if not in any biological sense. Hitler was "unscientific" when he used the word "race" to denote an ethnological conglomerate like the Germans, but the word serves his purpose—a purpose that is being promoted by a powerful "racial" consciousness, or national will, fanatical devotion, and the most formidable army and air force that ever existed.

Hitler spent his childhood and youth amid a confusion of competing, struggling "races." The Balkans were not far off, and within the Dual Monarchy, Czechs, Slovaks, Poles, Hungarians, Croats, Russians, Germans, and so on, struggled and intrigued with one another. To the north was the German Empire which, like the Socialist movement, was growing mighty with the development of capitalist production.

Two powers in pre-war Europe inspired awe because they

were new and spectacular, because they seemed to contain limitless possibilities, because their growth appeared irresistible and their final triumph certain. Their militancy and the very arrogance of their challenge, backed as it was by prodigious organized strength, fascinated while it inspired fear.

These two Powers were German Imperialism and Marxian Socialism. It was they who were the aggressors in the national and social conflicts that began with the Great War. Others shared the responsibility for that conflict, for the situation that made it possible, or even hastened it on. But German Imperialism and Marxian Socialism were the two, the only two *militant* Powers. They were the aggressors.

Frightful as the Great War was, it was *not* a war of extermination. The common civilized heritage was strong enough to give a certain unreality and impermanence to war-time hatred. But the hatred engendered in the class-war has not died away even now.

The principal loser in the Great War, Germany, was spared, although she had been the aggressor. Compared with those who fought in the class-war, the soldiers in the Great War were chivalrous and humane. Wherever Marxism showed itself, it was implacable, and, in Russia, where it triumphed, it waged a war of extermination.

The class-war had been studied by Marx, Engels, and, above all, by Lenin, who was its Schlieffen, thinking day and night in terms of the "decisive battle." He declared open class-war when the Great War between nations began. But it was no merciful Versailles for which he strove, but a merciless Carthage.

The Social Democrats opposed the open class-war in those days because they took their Marxism half-heartedly and shared in the common European heritage—with them, to their eternal honor, country came first, Europe second, and Marxism third. And it was this, above all, that drew upon them the fanatical hatred of Lenin and of all whole-hearted Marxists—a hatred quelled by Hitler, but still smoldering below the surface.

National Socialism and the racial myth existed only in the minds of individuals and a few groups. It was an unco-ordinated movement, lacking a common denominator and a Marx and a Lenin. Nor had it been fired by the Marxian example and urged on to retaliatory aggression by the Marxian attack.

For a time the defeat of Germany destroyed belief in salvation by race, while the sanguinary triumph of Bolshevism in Russia gave Marxism an immense prestige and power. In the eyes of many millions, all that Marx and Lenin had prophesied had *come true*.

But Marxism, instead of being humbled by victory—and by all the woe and ruin that went with victory—was made more obdurate in its arrogance. And this became the chief cause of its catastrophic and ignominious undoing.

The Dual Monarchy, if judged by relative standards, was a very great political achievement in so far as it preserved the peace amongst a large number of rival races or nationalities. It was, perhaps, comparable with British rule in India and had to face external dangers far greater than any that could menace India.

But judged by absolute standards, the Dual Monarchy was indeed "ramshackle" and full of wrong, corruption, and inefficiency. It was no Heaven on Earth—but it was less of a Hell on Earth than most of Europe is today.

Hitler lived in one of those regions of the Dual Monarchy where racial and religious rivalries were fiercest, where across the border, only a few miles off, there was the mighty German Empire which seemed all the Dual Monarchy was not, an Empire predestined to be master of Europe. By nature a visionary and a fanatic, and endowed with a peculiar responsiveness that gave him an almost intolerably vivid perception of racial and national differences, Hitler was predestined above all other men for the part he was to play later on.

We have seen how the Great War filled Hitler with intense joy and how he "thanked Heaven" out of the fullness of his heart.[57] The master race had challenged the world and had opened the gigantic struggle for freedom (like the Marxian proletariat breaking its chains). All that the Pan-German and anti-Semitic sages and prophets had said and written was being fulfilled, the racial myth was *coming true,* the apocalyptic battle had begun, the Kingdom of Heaven was not far off.

But the war ended in the defeat of Germany. She was, according to Pan-German and anti-Semitic belief, overthrown not by her open foes, whom she resisted victoriously for more than four years, but by Satanic Powers. They had established their main stronghold in Russia, and having stabbed the Empire of the Hohenzollerns in the back just when victory was at hand, were threatening the whole world.

To Hitler, obsessed as he was with race and nationhood, the Satanic Powers were international. To him, all that was international was anti-national. All internationalists were heretics in his eyes—or, as he would call them, "traitors" (in post-war Marxian terminology the word "traitor" is also used to denote heretic, milder forms of heresy being called "deviationism.") The satanic, international forces, as he saw them, were twofold—they were Marxian and capitalist. No one is more inclined to be "anti-capitalist" than the "petit bourgeois" or the "little man." Hitler was a "petit bourgeois." He belonged to the lower middle class and passed through all the struggles and hardship which a lonely member of that class may have to endure in times of political and economic crisis. He had, by his reading of Pan-German literature, been indoctrinated with the anti-Semitism which is a form of anti-capitalism.

The enemy was Marxism *and* capitalism, while the agent

of both was the *international* race, homeless, scattered over the earth, calling itself chosen, engaged in banking and brokerage and yet informing the revolution with its spirit and supplying the revolutionary movement with so many of its leaders, above all with its greatest leader and prophet, the Jew, Karl Marx.[58]

The challenge of 1918 would have broken the faith of a man without Hitler's greatness—and without his smallness.[59] Confronted with the prodigious and menacing Marxian myth, the National Socialist counter-myth formed itself afresh in his mind with a terrific intensity, never to leave him for one day, driving him on, a "man possessed," to conquest and revenge.

He learned much from the enemy. The restraining, depth- and breath-giving, doubt-engendering power of Europe's Graeco-Roman heritage and of the Christian religion meant nothing to him. He took over bodily much of the Marxian myth. He became, as it were, both Marx and Lenin—the principal exponent and the principal executor of the militant myth were united in his person. It was almost as though the Marxian dialectic itself were being demonstrated—the two opposites, Nationalism and Socialism, fused into a new unity, National Socialism.

National Socialism is incomparably the greatest revolutionary force in the world today. We shall return to it later on. We shall also examine Hitler's unique personality in more detail. Before doing so, let us say what must be said in any discussion of Marx and Lenin that is not to remain wholly one-sided: something about their greatness.

They, like Hitler, were true conquerors. The greatness of a conqueror cannot be measured by the durability of his achievement. Even if his work end in ruin and nothingness he may yet have been great.

As we have seen, Hitler himself paid Marx the tribute of calling him "a master," though a "master of black magic."

We must wholly reject the verdict that dismisses him as a cantankerous old man whose writings are as dull as they are voluminous, although his writings are often dull and are certainly voluminous.[60] We must also reject the verdict that Lenin was a mere agitator and a promoter of discontent, and that Hitler is no more than an uplifter, a mob orator, and an unscrupulous politician. He is, of course, all of these, but he is more as well.

Marx was not a man of action. He was a poor speaker and inconspicuous as an organizer. He was no philosopher. He was not a profound thinker, not even in a non-metaphysical, unsystematic way as Nietzsche was. Much of his thinking was done for him by his high-minded, generous, intelligent, though superficial, always amateurish friend, Engels. He was certainly no scientist, indeed his mind, as we have seen, was as anti-scientific as it was anti-philosophical.

But he was a great writer and a great personality. His life was one of hardship, deprivation, and exile, brought about by his loyalty to his own messianic faith. His writings are the most formidable indictment ever made of poverty as such. He challenged the arrogance of wealth as none before him had done. He gave poverty an arrogance of its own, setting it up against the arrogance of wealth. His challenge was also a warning—a warning of the judgment that would come upon societies unable or unwilling to make the alleviation of poverty their principal task.

His doctrine was doomed to failure. The bloody and destructive upheavals, for which he and his followers share the responsibility, created far more poverty than they abolished. But his warning was never a bluff—it was wholly serious and prophetic. The Russian revolution was a fulfillment of that warning. Just for once the rich, the mighty and the proud, were struck down—poverty and oppression, sweated labor, low wages, long hours, and all the woe, humiliation, and degradation of the poor, were avenged in a ruinous and sanguinary retributive apocalypse. A judgment and a warning to all and for all time.

The Marxian warning retains its full seriousness and cannot be disproved as Marxian "science" and "philosophy" can be disproved. Extreme poverty amid wealth means the destruction of that wealth, even if it does not mean the end of that poverty. Oceans of blood and tears have been shed in the fulfillment of the Marxian warning—but neither blood nor tears have washed that warning away.

The wrath of Karl Marx was a prophetic wrath and was often clothed in mighty and prophetic words. His voice will never be silenced anywhere throughout the world. It cannot be out-shouted even by the booming, screeching voice of a Hitler. Nor can the Marxian challenge be silenced, even by the prisons and concentration camps of Germany, Italy—and Russia.

His pamphlets on the Paris Commune and the "18th Brumaire" are of small value as contributions to the events they describe and attempt to analyze. But they are masterpieces of polemical and dramatic writing. It was not in vain that Marx was an admirer and a constant reader of Shakespeare. The "18th Brumaire" is Shakespearian in its dramatic presentation and in its incisive analysis of character. In its mighty pulsation and swift and closely articulated movement, there is a grand epic quality. The terrible hatred and prophetic indignation that inspire it, and the awe in the presence of indomitable heroism, give it a mythogenetic truth that cannot be refuted by pointing out many a departure from established fact. Much of it is eternally true and will always help towards an understanding of the struggle for mastery between oppressors and oppressed.

Marx was a great journalist, perhaps the greatest who ever lived. It was an age of great journalists, but none had the mighty fervor and visionary power of Karl Marx, whose contributions to the *New York Tribune* are models of popular political journalism of the most serious kind.

Marx had a rather grim sense of humor—Lenin and Hitler are humorless. Lenin had none of the warmth and plasticity of presentation that make the "18th Brumaire" so memorable. Even in his destructive anger Lenin was colorless and abstract. Marx would dissect a character, a mind, a type, pulling out a leg, then a wing, then another leg, and so on, until the insect lay dismembered at his feet. Lenin would merely add an "-ism" to its name or put it in the plural, and having converted it into an abstraction, smother it in vituperative verbiage.

Lenin's hatred is altogether appalling. But when we consider Lenin, we must not forget *that they hanged his brother*,[61] and there may have been behind his hatred a vengefulness more bitter even than the wrath of Karl Marx. In any case, his brother was fearfully avenged.

Lenin's greatness is not in his writings. He was capable of ruthless political realism whenever his chiliastic vision did not deprive him of his critical faculties. His astuteness often emerges in his writing, and often amid his cold, utopian theorizings he gives shrewd counsels of opportunism and even of moderation.

He was above all a great strategist. He was a kind of revolutionary Schlieffen who thought in terms of class-armies instead of national armies. His whole life was subordinated to the conception of the "decisive battle," the battle that would break the power of the "bourgeoisie" forever and establish the Kingdom of Heaven on Earth.

He was completely optimistic about the "objective inevitability" of that battle. He regarded victory as certain, "scientifically" certain. Everything had, after all, been worked out "scientifically" by Marx and Engels. Marxism could be "proved" just as the theory of gravitation could be proved —and whoever had any doubts on the subject was a fool, a rogue, an obscurantist, a traitor, a lackey of the bourgeoisie, a paid agent, and what not.

The precise time when the "decisive battle" would be fought was never quite sure. Just as a Schlieffen would be conscious of having at his command the most powerful army that ever existed, while being aware that even the mighty cannot afford to make mistakes, that there is a right time and a wrong time for everything, so Lenin, absolutely convinced that the "proletariat" were invincible, realized that mistakes or indecision, or failure to choose the most favorable hour, might mean defeat. But defeat to him meant no more than the postponement of victory. An army in the field can be beaten—and destroyed. The "proletariat" can be beaten but can never be destroyed. To Lenin, the "proletariat" was ultimately invincible and its resources not only inexhaustible, but always augmenting, so that even in defeat it could not but gather strength.

The events of his own day were to him like those of the past manifestations of the inexorable dialectical law which Marx had "discovered." After the Russian revolution he saw that the Communists were making "mistakes" everywhere—but these mistakes were mere deviations, or derailments. The track led with absolute certainty to the field of "decisive battle," and Lenin lectured Communists all over the world, chiding them and yet encouraging them, and leading them on.

The chiliast always tends to the conviction that the Kingdom of Heaven is round the next corner. We have, in our first chapter, tried to show how strong this tendency was in Marx and Lenin.

It constantly made Lenin utter short-term prophecies that were constantly disproved by events. It is easy to multiply examples. He had high hopes of Germany. In April 1917 he wrote that the "German proletariat is the most trustworthy, the most reliable ally of the Russian, of the universal proletarian revolution."[62] He also believed, in common with Marx and Engels, that "the democratic republic was the nearest approach to the dictatorship of the proletariat" because "such a republic—without in the least setting aside the domination of capital, and therefore, the oppression of the masses and the class-struggle—inevitably leads to such an extension, development, unfolding and sharpening of that struggle that, as soon as the possibility arises for satisfying the fundamental interests of the oppressed masses, this possibility is realized inevitably and solely in the dictatorship of the proletariat, in the guidance of these masses by the proletariat."[63]

The falsity of this anticipation was demonstrated in 1933 when not the failures of Marx and Lenin, not the German proletariat, but Hitler, brought the German democratic republic to an end.

In October 1918 Lenin wrote that "the crisis" in Germany . . . will infallibly end with the transference of political power into the hands of the proletariat."[64] In the same month he wrote that "it now grows clear to all that the revolution is inevitable in all belligerent countries."[65] In December 1919 he wrote, "our hopes of world revolution have been *fully confirmed* if we consider them as a whole.[66] But a little doubt as to the immediacy of the Millennium has begun to creep in, for "we have come to the conviction that in advanced countries the revolution is a much slower, much more difficult, and much more complicated affair than could have been assumed."[67]

But it was only the immediacy of the Millennium that was in doubt. Its "inevitability" remained certain.

In 1920 Lenin was even prepared to admit that the "bourgeoisie" might rally after defeat. The "resistance of the bourgeoisie," he wrote, "is increased tenfold by its overthrow, and final victory is impossible without a long, stubborn war of life and death."[68] He still believed that the German Soviet Republic might be established in the near future.[69] The

German Social Democrats were, of course, perpetrating "a series of treacheries" and the Communists were making the blunder of refusing to accept the Treaty of Versailles—Lenin advised them to recognize the Treaty and to endure it, just as Russia had recognized and endured the Treaty of Brest-Litovsk, for "the Soviet Revolution in Germany will strengthen the international Soviet movement," while "the overthrow of the bourgeoisie in any of the large European countries such as Germany" will be all the easier if "the imperialists of France and England are placated and the Treaty of Versailles is recognized"[70] (though, of course, only to be repudiated later on, as indeed it was—but by Hitler).

Although he recognized that the "bourgeoisie" might gather strength in defeat, Lenin's overpowering chiliasm forced him into the compensatory belief that the "bourgeoisie" cannot help making blunders, blunders that will hasten on their "inevitable doom." These blunders are predestined, as are the "betrayals" of their "lackeys," the Labor Leaders and the Social Democrats, for Marxism is not only a secular eschatology, it is also a doctrine of secular predestination. Of Lloyd George, for whom he had great admiration, Lenin wrote that "even the cleverest people amongst the bourgeoisie *cannot avoid* irreparable acts of stupidity. This will bring about their downfall."[71]

Of England, Lenin wrote in 1920, there is "a fresh, broad, powerful, and rapidly-growing Communist movement among the workers which justifies the highest hope."[72] The question in England is not "the kind of struggle that will determine the fate of the proletarian revolution," for "not a single Communist has any doubt on that score"—the revolution is certain, and all that has to be discussed is "the immediate cause that will rouse the proletarian masses, at present dormant, and bring them right up to the revolution."[73]

Seventeen years have passed since Lenin wrote these words and the English "proletarian masses" still appear to be "dormant," and there is only one Communist at Westminster to justify Lenin's "highest" hopes.[74]

Even when Lenin cannot discover any immediate tangible circumstance that promises to fulfill his revolutionary expectations, he is not at a loss—was not, so he asked himself, "the bourgeois French Republic" brought to the verge of civil war by the unexpected Dreyfus case in times less revolutionary than the year 1920?[75]

The revolution is *sure*—even if we cannot see the causes, they are there because they *must* be there. We do not always know how the revolution will come about—but what we do know is that it *will* come about. It is all a question "of vast armies, of an alignment of all the class forces of the given society *for the final and decisive battle.*"[76]

All that Lenin saw at a distance whether in time or space, but saw through the medium of the Marxian myth.[77] It was only when events drew very close upon him that he became a serious politician. By his writings we must judge him a man of hard and narrow disposition, a shoddy thinker and superficial observer, whose doctrinaire arrogance was sometimes mitigated by shrewdness and cunning.

But in planning the "decisive battle" that obsessed him, in his strategy, and in his conduct of the actual operations when the battle was opened, he proved himself a master. Only the battle was not "decisive," because no battle of this world can be decisive in the apocalyptic Marxian sense.

Nevertheless, the "November Revolution" of 1917 was one of the great battles of history. With true strategic genius, Lenin had anticipated the concrete situation, although investing it with a messianic significance which could never be its own. With prodigious intensity, with shrewd human judgment, and with infinite cunning and resource, he helped to shape that situation to his immensely powerful will. He engaged the enemy at the moment most favorable to himself and, amid an utter confusion of opinions, against the counsel of old revolutionaries who were far superior to him in depth and subtlety of intellect, knowledge and education, and with sovereign disregard for unessentials, he unerringly struck the decisive blow in the grand classical manner.

Lenin, who commanded the armies of "the sixth power in Europe" (as Marx called the revolution), was incomparably the greatest strategist of the World War. The "November Revolution" ranks him with the great military commanders of the world—with Cromwell, Marlborough, Frederick the Great, and Schlieffen.

CHAPTER IV

Mussolini—Where he differs from Lenin and Hitler—Hitler—The significance of *Mein Kampf*—His aspirations, his qualities, and his practical achievements—His special aptitude for the dirty work of revolution—The intensity of his emotions—The triumph of the National Socialist revolution—The nature of Hitler's demagogy—His version of the "communist danger"—The burning of the Reichstag—Anti-Semitism—Hitler's "case" against the Jews—The "Protocols of the Elders of Zion"—The significance of Hitler's hatred of the Jews—The visual intensity of his hatred and its concentrated malignance—The formation of the Jew myth—Hitler's character and peculiar gifts—His physical characteristics—His projection of himself.

MUSSOLINI,[1] unlike Hitler, is not doctrinaire or sectarian. He is not "a man possessed," but a kind of modern condottiere, and an opportunist politician, who might have climbed high in any abnormal situation. Deeply influenced by Sorel and, like Sorel, a believer in violence and aware of the immense power of myths over the human mind; endowed with a sure and instinctive understanding of his own people, and with exceptional histrionic gifts, he is one of the ablest of modern rulers and one of the greatest of modern demagogues. His capacity for transforming millions of men and women into a mob, and then dominating that mob with monumental, vulgar masculinity while directing the policy of the nation with cunning statesmanship, is altogether unsurpassed. He is capable of deep and sudden transformations. There can be few political opinions which he has not held at one time or another, though his preference has always been for the violent and the extreme. His past and present utterances are no index of his future actions.

One thing seems certain, that Mussolini is not religious, though he is realistic enough to see in religion a formidable and, possibly, a useful power. In this he is unlike Lenin and Hitler, who are religious to the point of monomania—which is the chief reason why they are fundamentally unchangeable, and why they and all their works are so much of one piece.

Mussolini is an unbeliever. Marx and Lenin were believers. So is Hitler. Marx, Lenin, and Hitler are, therefore, typical of modern secular religion as Mussolini is not.

Hitler is, first and last, a revolutionary—as great a revolutionary as Lenin. And, like Lenin, he was always a revolutionary. Of his boyhood he wrote: "I was a revolutionary even then."[2]

Mein Kampf is a handbook for revolutionaries and contains more practical advice about revolutionary tactics than all Marxian literature put together. It is also a handbook for all demagogues.

It has been underrated as the work of a private individual, written many years ago, and having little relevance to the opinions and actions of the present head of the German State. Much of *Mein Kampf* has been, or is being, translated into reality. The terror, the persecution of the Jews, the religious conflict—all these, and more, are adumbrated in *Mein Kampf*. The objects of German foreign policy, as stated in *Mein Kampf*, remain the objects of German policy today—the union with Austria and the establishment of National Socialist Pan-German hegemony over the European continent.[3]

Some of Hitler's aspirations are incapable of fulfillment because they belong to the realm of myth and eschatology. Others may be thwarted by circumstance (it is, for example, very doubtful indeed whether Germany will destroy the power of France and whether she will ever colonize half European Russia as Hitler demands).[4] Yet even these aspirations exercise a deep influence on the German mind and give German policy a strong bias that may remain concealed for a time, only to show itself in an active and, perhaps, decisive manner at the first favorable opportunity.

Mein Kampf is the principal compendium of political doctrine and precept in the Third Realm.[5] Even if the mythological and messianic elements are abstracted, there remains a new "Realpolitik" in which old revolutionary doctrines (largely of Marxian origin) and old imperialistic doctrines (largely of Pan-German origin) are united. Pan-German revolutionary imperialism informs the policy of the greatest military Power on the European continent and is the most formidable secular force in the contemporary world.

Mein Kampf is an inspiration and an incitement to action for millions of youthful Germans. It has put an end to much discontent that seemed intractable, to many obscure torments of the soul, to seemingly incurable "Weltschmerz." Millions find in *Mein Kampf* and in Hitler, guidance and personal leadership that reduce the world's complexities and despairs to one simple purpose, one simple hope—something to live for, something to die for, something that *is* Germany, the *true* Germany, the "Greater Germany," in a way nothing else in the whole of German history ever was.

Hitler gives that same happiness that Marx and Lenin gave —the happiness of complete abandonment to clear certainty and absolute truth, to the indubitable assurance of final victory, to the delicious and uplifting vision of spiritual and temporal power over "all the kingdoms of the world and the glory of them."[6] It is a happiness so great as to be almost unendurable, a happiness that shines in the face, that makes the body restless for action, that infuses immense resourcefulness and courage. It is also the happiness which is, in the end, brought to the nothingness that gives the eternal answer to the eternal question, "What shall it profit a man if he shall gain the whole world and lose his own soul?"[7]

Mein Kampf carries imperious authority such as no other book does in Europe today—except the Bible (or is the Bible still the exception?). The works of Marx and Lenin are no longer scanned anywhere with the assiduity and enthusiasm with which *Mein Kampf* is scanned in Germany today. The official authoritative status of *Mein Kampf* has been announced again and again.[8]

Hitler is no "puppet dictator." That he is the instrument of "capitalism" or of the "industrial magnates" is Marxian claptrap.[9] He is incomparably the most powerful man in Germany and could have every German industrial magnate beheaded during a single week-end without a perceptible shock to his own power. And as *Mein Kampf* expresses his convictions today, no less than when he wrote it, the study of this book is essential to an understanding of contemporary German affairs.[10]

Hitler is a master of the platitudinous, the commonplace. He is not only *the* Leader, but also *the* common denominator. He has Lenin's gift for the lapidary phrase and all Lenin's grim persistence in hammering that phrase into the public mind until it becomes an organic part of the public conscience. Lenin, although never profound and in no sense a thinker, did have a certain starkness that saved him from vulgarity. But no platitude can be too shallow or too vulgar for Hitler if he believes that it will promote its demagogue purpose. He will not have the slightest hesitation in saying what he knows to be nonsensical or untrue, if to do so will help his cause. And, in the moment of saying it, he will himself believe it to be true. So intense is the fire of his demonic passion that truth and untruth are immediately fused into one burning, molten myth that fills his whole mind.[11]

Hitler often appears shallower and more stupid than he really is. His utterances should not be taken only at their face value, but in relation to their purpose. Nor should they be regarded as proof of insincerity. He is terribly sincere. When he says he wants peace, as he has been saying again and again during the last few years, he is as passionately sincere as he was—and will, perhaps, be again—when he glorifies war.

His practical achievement is prodigious. Although he is without any originality, he is nevertheless unique in so far as he was the principal creator, not of National Socialism, but of the National Socialist Party, the mightiest political organization in Europe. It was chiefly through him that the Party became the common denominator of innumerable tendencies, aspirations, rancors, and beliefs, giving them an iron cohesion such as no other revolutionary movement ever had.

Violent revolution, like war, is dirty work—indeed it is dirtier than war, for it is without any of the chivalry, any of the respect for a brave foe, or any of the humanity towards prisoners that existed in the Great War, but have been altogether lacking in the revolutionary upheavals in Russia, Spain, and elsewhere (the decay of all ethical and humanitarian standards under the influence of modern secular religion will, perhaps, have put an end to chivalry even in wars between nations).

The Marxian attitude towards violent revolution is just as wicked and romantic as the attitude of those who defend and glorify war. The realities of war have done a good deal to silence militarists (at least in western Europe). But the Marxists appear to have learned nothing from the revolutionary catastrophes of the last twenty years, beginning with the Russian revolution and not ending, perhaps, with the Spanish civil war. Marxists still appear to agree with Engels and Lenin that a violent revolution is altogether a noble thing producing "an immense moral and spiritual impulse," and that the belief in the demoralizing effect of force is "a parson's mode of thought, lifeless, insipid, and impotent."[12]

Treitzschke, Bernhardi, or any of the so-called "Prussian militarists" with whom the British public was made familiar in 1914, would have said this about war.

Hitler fully shares this attitude towards armed violence. As we have seen, he gloried in the coming of the Great War and, like Engels, endowed it with apocalyptic significance.

Hitler has a special aptitude for the dirty work of revolution. He is without tolerance, pity, or any generous emotion. He is, as we have seen, dead to the truths of religion. He is dead to all the finer and subtler manifestations of the human spirit. The individual soul is nothing to him.

Lenin's hatred is all the more inhuman because of its abstract quality, but it is this quality which saves it from the unspeakable malignance of Hitler's hatred. There are times when Lenin even came near to showing a certain human greatness in his determination "to spare the lowly and abase the proud" (though his practice when in power was very different). He never hated the weak and humble as such, but to Hitler weakness and humility are in themselves obnoxious and he would ruthlessly exterminate all who have the misfortune to be physically or mentally inadequate or defective.[13]

Hitler has recommended and employed every demagogic trick and every conspiratorial device. There is no perfidy, no falsehood, no piece of cunning of which he is not capable. Lenin did have certain ethical compunctions (at least before he was in power), small and reluctant as they may have been. He *hoped* that priests could be found who would violate young girls, but he did not with deliberate falsity accuse priests of such offenses, merely to arrest, imprison or shoot them, though after he became ruler of Russia his scruples left him; and his successor, Stalin, habitually employs this method.

But Hitler never had any scruples at any time. The very intensity of his emotions, especially the emotions of hatred and vengeful malice, give even his most obvious falsehoods the force of an inner conviction. For example, when he says, as he does in *Mein Kampf,* that the French colored troops were dispatched to the Rhine by the Jews so as to pollute (or "bastardize" as he calls it) the German race,[14] he is saying what, in any calm moment, he must know to be false. But his hatred of the Jew is such as to give his conviction that all things infamous *must* have been caused by the Jews an almost visual intensity. And, as we have seen, he openly repudiates "objectivity"—which is, after all, a repudiation of truthfulness.

Marxists deny that revolution can be "made" and others than proletarians can be revolutionary. Hitler showed that a revolution can be made and that the middle class may become revolutionary. No revolution bigger than a *coup d'état* is possible without the help of circumstance, but whereas Lenin found a revolutionary movement in existence when he began his career as a revolutionary, and whereas one "revolutionary situation" after another arose in Russia that would have arisen even if he had never lived, Hitler and his immediate associates in a few years' time converted a vast multitude of men and women who were in a state of discontent and disarray, but by no means revolutionary, into the most powerful revolutionary force of our time, giving them such a sense of fulfillment when the revolution came that it was widely regarded as a kind of religious phenomenon or apocalypse, Hitler himself becoming the object of an almost religious veneration.

It was in a "revolutionary situation" (as the Marxists would call it) that the National Socialists suffered their severest defeat—in the autumn of the year 1923 when inflation was at its height, when the Ruhr was still occupied by the French, and the break-up of Germany seemed to be at hand. The abortive insurrection (usually known as the "Hitler-Ludendorff Putsch") of the 9th of November collapsed within a few hours. German republican democracy, which was to have been overthrown, grew steadily stronger from that year onwards. Unlike the Russian revolution of 1905 which, although crushed in the end, was at least successful in so far as it was followed by constitutional reform, the German upheaval of 1923 achieved nothing at all.

The National Socialist movement won its principal successes (before its final victory) in the year 1928, a year of economic prosperity and republican and democratic consolidation—the year, too, in which the Social Democrats, who were the main supporters of the Republic and the principal enemy of the National Socialists, won their greatest electoral victory.[15] It was in these years that the movement captured the German countryside, laying the main foundation of its future power by silent revolutionary action in the small towns and villages. It was from this foundation that they advanced to the conquest of urban Germany. That conquest, it is true, was achieved in a period of intense moral and economic crisis, but not of economic or political disintegration. Germany was efficiently governed by decree, though there was a good deal of terroristic violence everywhere. The police, the civil service, and the army were intact. There was nothing comparable with the disintegration of the French and Russian States in 1789 and 1917. Hitler overthrew not a State already decayed, hollowed out and tottering, but one that had all the means of defending itself.

And he overthrew it without the actual use of armed force, although he could not have been successful if he had not held armed force in reserve. At the same time, it is untrue to say that the National Socialist revolution was nonviolent. The movement employed violence and terrorism from the very beginning. Hitler himself is an avowed terrorist and has an essentially terroristic disposition. He is also, as we have seen, an avowed believer in political assassination.[16] The National Socialists and their precursors exterminated half the élite amongst German republican leaders by a close sequence of political murders, nor have they abandoned their terroristic methods since they came into power, as the massacres of the 30th June 1934 and the terroristic practices that go on to the present day abundantly show.[17]

The overthrow of the German Republic was not so much a frontal attack on an already broken enemy, as a swift seizure of power preceded by a systematic revolutionary permeation of the State, a seizure of power from within rather than from without, though clinched by the burning of the Reichstag, which enabled the National Socialists to eliminate the Communists. They no longer needed the presence of the Communists in the Reichstag as allies, but they did need their absence, so that they themselves could have the parliamentary majority which they never achieved in a free election. Using this majority, they transformed the democratic Republic into a "totalitarian" despotism by ostensibly constitutional means, while crushing their opponents with the help of unofficial terrorism.

As an observer Hitler is, if not original, at least direct and realistic. What he says about Marxism is often false and always a caricature, but it contains elements of truth very shrewdly observed.

Like Lenin, he has a talent for coining political slogans. In appealing to mob emotions he stooped lower than Lenin. He had none of Lenin's respect for the common people. "The people," he wrote, "are in their overwhelming majority so feminine in their disposition and their attitude that their thoughts and actions are determined less by sober reflection than by emotions." [18]

Hitler is by no means a commanding intellect or a commanding character. His genius for the commonplace combined with his almost mediumistically sensitive appreciation for waves and currents of public opinion, his burning fervor and his shrewd realism make him the greatest demagogue of modern times (he is also an admirer of demagogy in others).[19] His chapter on propaganda is a masterpiece of demagogic cunning, psychological insight and cold cynicism. There is nothing comparable with it in all Marxian literature.

As we have seen, Hitler holds that big lies are more effective than small ones. His own demagogy is dominated by this conception. His genius for fostering false legends about his opponents and so making them appear monstrous in the eyes of the world is surpassed only by Stalin. By monstrously magnifying the characteristics attributed to his opponents and then reducing their characteristics to a few simple, lapidary slogans, that are repeated year in year out, day after day, hatred will be intensified until it becomes a burning, vehement, contagious emotion that will convert multitudes into mobs animated by the desire for destructive vengeance, mobs fit for the gangster violence and lynch-law that always go with violent revolution.

Oppression under the Tsars was at least a reality. Lenin hardly exaggerated it, and did not need to exaggerate it, although it was mild compared with the oppression that went on under Lenin himself later on. But the National Socialists were never oppressed. Hitler himself was treated with the utmost leniency by the Republic which he attempted to overthrow by armed insurrection in 1923. He was sentenced to imprisonment in a fortress and was able to write his book and receive visitors. Under his own dictatorship, persons suspected even of contemplating opposition are subjected to treatment incomparably more inhuman than anything ever suffered by the National Socialists, who not only contemplated opposition but plotted and accomplished the overthrow of the Republic and murdered many of the republican leaders.

Nevertheless, the falsehood that National Socialists were oppressed is constantly repeated. Something of it "sticks." The falsehood that Hitler saved Germany—and Europe—from the "Communist danger" is also constantly repeated. The German Communists had a big voting strength, but by no means the biggest. Their membership fluctuated between 100,000 and 200,000, and was always much smaller and much less reliable than that of the Social Democrats. The Communists had no arms. What little they had of military organization was altogether pitiable (and known to the police). The German Communists, in fact, were not and never have been serious revolutionaries, and only in so far as they collaborated with the National Socialists for the overthrow of the Republic, was there a "Communist danger" in Germany. They were accessories to that overthrow—in this, and this alone, they were a political danger to the Republic. They were accused, falsely, of setting fire to the Reichstag as the preliminary to a series of terroristic outrages. It was officially declared on behalf of General Goering that the evidence against the Communists had been found and would be made public.[20] It was never published because it did not exist. It is certain that the Communists did not set fire to the Reichstag, but it is not absolutely certain who did, though the circumstantial evidence leaves very little doubt that it was the National Socialists who did it, probably with the connivance of Goering himself.

It is possible that Hitler did not connive at the burning of the Reichstag, but he certainly cannot have believed that the Communists were the incendiaries. This did not in the least prevent him from attributing the outrage to them, just as he is prepared to attribute almost any crime to the Jews, for he really believes crime *as such* to be Jewish, even in the face of all evidence.

Anti-Semitism has always been popular in Germany, especially amongst the lower middle class. It was not injected by Hitler—but it was he who converted popular anti-Semitism into a virulent and lasting epidemic. The Jew has served National Socialism as a kind of domestic foe, a substitute for a foreign foe, over whom victories can be won—easy victories, over the defenseless, but presented as though they were heroic and arduous. The victor has thereby felt the gratifying sense of having risen to heights of heroism when, in reality, he has descended to deepest infamy and cowardice. He parades as the author of meritorious achievement, as the successful champion in the universal war supposedly waged by good against evil, when, in reality, he is more like a rat, infesting humanity's foulest sewer and gnawing with merciless tooth at some stricken and helpless creature that has had the misfortune to fall amongst him and his confederates.

National Socialism, like Marxism, lives on hatred. Hatred, by being concentrated on one object, is intensified.[21] There is no easier method of concentrating hatred than anti-Semitism. The Jew, made to look gross and hideous, becomes the symbol of all that is hateful, of the enemy in the abstract and in the concrete. The Jew of caricature, the Jew with the hooked nose, dark, curly hair and fleshy lips, is made to symbolize evil *as such* in the eyes of the Nazi, just as the capitalist of caricature is made to symbolize evil *as such* in the eyes of the Communist.[22]

The "Jewish problem" is one of the most intractable in the world. It cannot be argued out of existence by saying that there is no such thing as a "Jewish race" and that the Jews are no different from other people. The Jews *are* different from other people—they are mentally *and* physically different. To say so is merely to recognize a very plain reality (it does not imply any disparagement of the Jew). The Jews have a collective conscience (and a very strong one), a civilization of their own, a special sensibility, and a unique religious sense. Their genius is above all religious. In their religion is their true life and their true being. In so far as they have departed from it, they have not averted persecution and have destroyed much of the inner fortitude and deep sense of destiny that can alone make persecution bearable. Eastern Jewry has an intense inner life, a spiritual depth, richness, and beauty, amid unspeakable squalor and deprivation, that are lacking in the Western Jewry. There is amongst the Eastern Jewry still some of that prophetic grandeur which the Western Jewry can never have unless it returns to its religion.[23]

The mere fact that the Jew is different and defenseless, marks him out for persecution. And it is idle to deny that there is often in his manner and appearance something that tends to estrange the non-Jew—something that very easily offends and is all too easily exploited. The virtues of the Jew are largely hidden virtues—his failings are the subject, and not always the illegitimate subject, of common talk. Youthful Jews, who incline towards Marxism, tend to combine shallowness with insolence. And in communities where there is much destitution, overcrowding, and intense economic rivalry, the Jew will, because he is there and because he is different, draw malice, anger, and resentment upon himself. And he will often, with a kind of hard obstinacy, increase and inflame exasperation and give natural mischief-makers, brutes, bullies, or political climbers and demagogues, the excuse for insult and persecution.

The anti-Semite is not really at war with "Judaism," with ideas, principles or qualities that are specifically Jewish. There is a case against the Jews as there is against the English, the Germans and French. But that case is *never* stated, is not even touched, by the anti-Semite.

The untruth of the anti-Semite case is paradoxical, for what the anti-Semite says about the Jew is true only of himself. The case against the Jew as given in *Mein Kampf*, is not a case at all—it is the projection of Hitler's self. In this respect, as in so many others, *Mein Kampf* is a piece of self-revelation.

Nowhere is this so evident as in the attitude of modern anti-Semites, Hitler above all, towards the "protocols of the Elders of Zion." The "Protocols" purported to be the minutes of twenty-four secret meetings held by the "Elders" with the object of establishing a Jewish world domination. They are a crude anti-Semitic forgery, and have been shown to be such beyond any doubt whatever again and again.[24]

They contain the very essence of modern anti-Semitic propaganda. Hitler's attitude to them is highly characteristic. In *Mein Kampf* he declares them genuine because the *Frankfurter Zeitung* (which he despised as being "Jewish"—although it had more non-Jews than Jews on its staff, even in those days) declares they are not. As we have seen, Hitler is indifferent to "objective truth."[25] "It is a matter of complete indifference from what Jewish brain they [the "Protocols"] originate; what does matter, is that they expose the nature and activity of the Jewish people with a precision that is absolutely horrifying."[26]

The "Protocols" represent the Jews and their machinations as being exactly what Hitler thinks they are. The "Protocols" are not a Jewish product at all—they were not even *forged* by a Jew. Anti-Semites, Hitler above all, find in them the projection of their own minds, so vividly and unmistakably that they *must* be true—they are the *subjective* truth, the truth, not about Semitism, but about anti-Semitism.

A few examples will serve as illustration.[27]

According to the "Protocols," "right is might by the laws of nature ... the blind mass of the people cannot be without a leader for one day" and, when authority fails, a "new power replaces the old which has been disintegrated by liberalism."[28]

These words might have been written or spoken by Hitler at any time. Words very much like them will be found in his speech on the origins of the Great War:

"Before God and the world, the stronger always has the right to impose his will"—an interesting sidelight, by the way, on Hitler's religious attitude—"all nature is a mighty struggle between strength and weakness ... states which offend against this elementary law grow rotten." [29]

According to the "Protocols," "a bold man, be he an aristocrat or a son of the people, arises. He overthrows the constitutional order, lays hands on the laws, and transforms the authorities."[30]

These words might occur in any National Socialist biography of Hitler.

According to the "Protocols," the "masses only obey a

strong power that is quite independent of them, a power to which they can look up in blind confidence—they must see in him [the ruler] the embodiment of firm will and inflexible might." [31]

To credit Jewish "Elders" with having come to such conclusions at a secret meeting is an obvious absurdity. But according to Hitler:

"The masses prefer the ruler to the suppliant, and are inwardly more satisfied by a doctrine that tolerates no other beside it, than by the enjoyment of liberal freedom... the masses hardly grow conscious of the indolence of spiritual terrorism any more than of the outrageous abuse of their human liberties... They only see the ruthlessness and brutality of its purposeful utterances [*i.e.* utterances made in conformity with the ruling doctrine] and will always comply in the end." [32]

These words, incidentally, are another of the many examples that show not only the self-revelatory character of *Mein Kampf*, but also show how its precepts have been carried out by Hitler since he came into power.

According to the "Protocols," those who wish to seize power must rouse the countryside and close in on the capital.[33]

This method was followed by Hitler and the National Socialist movement. In *Mein Kampf* he wrote that the German Federal States must be won over first and then be made to take up the struggle against the central power.[34]

It would be easy to multiply examples from the "Protocols" showing how close their spirit is to Hitler's. Indeed, there is hardly an idea in the "Protocols" that is not to be found in *Mein Kampf*.

And, conversely, much of what Hitler says of the Jews in *Mein Kampf* and elsewhere is true of himself and the National Socialist movement. A few examples must suffice here:

He declares the Jew to be without culture of his own.

What the Jew possesses in the form of apparent culture ("Scheinkultur") is, in his hands, mostly damaged goods got from other people.[35]

What the Jew achieves in the realm of art is either mere botching ("Verballhornisierung") or spiritual theft.[36]

"Not because of him [the Jew], but in spite of him will there be any human progress."[37]

"In a short time he [the Jew] begins to twist things so as to make it seem that injustice had only been done to him and not the reverse."[38]

"He [the Jew] judges all knowledge and all evolution in so far as it promotes his nationhood.... He uses all knowledge ... in the service of his race."[39] This is exactly how Hitler himself judges "all knowledge and evolution," as well as right and wrong, namely in so far as they are profitable or unprofitable to German "nationhood" or the Aryan "race." Indeed, this, as we have seen, is one of the essentials of Hitler's.

"He [the Jew] has the impudence to lead the masses himself"[40]—to be a "Fuehrer," in other words.

"The Jew chases every rival off the field.... Whoever has the insight to withstand Jewish blandishments, will have his insight and his defiance broken by terrorism. The consequences of such methods are tremendous."[41] It is precisely in this manner that the opposition, both religious and political, are being broken in the Third Realm. The consequences are certainly "tremendous."

It is not Semitism that calls forth anti-Semitism. The Jew is never an end to the anti-Semite, but always a means to an end. The Jew is never the cause, but always the occasion, of anti-Semitism. The Semitic, so far from being destroyed, is confirmed and perpetuated by the anti-Semitic, both in its weakness and in its strength, in its ignominy and in its glory. Anti-Semitism does not exist to fight the Jew—it fights the Jew to keep itself alive. Hitler *needs* the Jews—"whoever lives by fighting an enemy has an interest in keeping him alive."[42]

Hitler's first conscious encounter with the Jews made him aware of the anti-Semitic myth rather than of the Jews in the concrete. He did not become anti-Semitic through awareness of the Jew—he became aware of the Jew through anti-Semitism. He lived in the peculiarly malignant anti-Semitic tradition of Austrian Pan-Germanism. He had a sense of something hateful and sinister, something that embodied the spirit of evil, a something that he called "Jew," before he had become conscious of the physical existence of Jews.

When he was fourteen or fifteen he would feel "a faint dislike" whenever the word Jew was mentioned.[43] When the *word* was mentioned—not when the object was *seen*. In that one sentence the whole Hitler is revealed. The subjective, emotional conviction existed first—the object, which gives the conviction concentrated intensity and fanatical strength in pursuit of a purpose, was received later on.

No doubt the Jews he met were not at all like their caricature. No doubt he did not at first connect them with the anti-Semitic myth. It was not until he met a Jew who did resemble the caricature that the fateful fusion between his anti-Semitism and the concrete Jew took place in his mind. When he was in Vienna, that is to say, before 1912 (and before he was twenty-three), he "chanced upon an apparition wearing a long caftan and black locks. "My first thought was: Is this a Jew? ... I observed the man surreptitiously but carefully, and the longer I stared at this strange face, and searchingly examined feature on feature, the more was my first question transformed into a second question: Is this also a German?"[44]

From that moment onwards the difference between good and evil was clear to him—the good was German, the evil was Jewish. And it is very significant that his illumination—which was one of the decisive moments in his life—was essentially visual. No Jew had ever done him wrong, he had not lived amongst Jews, he had no knowledge or experience of them, he had no reason either for a personal or a national, or a vicarious grudge when, still a youth, he became the fanatical anti-Semite he has been ever since.

He had, as it were, encountered the principle of evil in the person of a dark, inhumanly alien creature. Later on, he "sometimes felt sick at the smell of these wearers of caftans." Whenever he examined "any ordure or infamy" he was sure to find "at least one Jew" imbedded therein. When extricated "like a maggot from a rotting corpse," the Jew would often be "quite dazzled by the sudden light."[45]

Such words, again, reveal the visual intensity of Hitler's hatred of Jews, as well as its concentrated malignance. Such words may appear too ignoble to be worth serious attention. But they represent, not an attempt at caricature, not an outburst of ill-temper, but a conviction fanatically held by the despotic ruler of the greatest military nation in Europe.

Hitler devoured all the anti-Semitic literature he could get. The myth of the Jews as the principle of evil had taken shape within him—all his subsequent reading and observation only served to give that myth fullness, obduracy, and concentration, just as all Lenin's reading only gave strength and solidity to the Marxian myth that possessed his mind in his early youth, never to leave him.

There was—and is—nothing evil in the world that Hitler does not associate with the Jews. They represent evil in all its forms, both morally and physically. The greatest crime, in his opinion, is the pollution, or "bastardization," as he calls it, of the German race. This is to him "the original sin of this world and the end of a humanity addicted to it."[46] Again and again he insists that this "original sin" is specifically Jewish, that the Jews regard it as their mission in the world to destroy the virtuous and superior races by committing this sin everywhere.

Hitler does not stop at generalities. One example must

suffice, though many could be given, to reveal his capacity for associating *all* forms of evil with the Jews. In a passage on venereal disease, he denounces modern methods of treatment as insufficiently drastic. He refers to "a cure of questionable nature"—meaning salvarsan which, having been invented by a Jew, would of course be "questionable." He demands that the "origin" of syphilitic infection be removed. The "origin," he says, is "the prostitution of love." But he neither explains what he means by this, nor how it is to be removed, and reverts, as usual, to the Jew or Judaism as the origin of this, as of every other, evil, attributing it "to the Judaization of our spiritual life" and "the mammonization of our sexual instincts" (Mammon is for him also a form of Judaism).[47]

Like Marx and Lenin, Hitler is an anti-capitalist. And as "Capitalism" is evil, it is, in Hitler's eyes, Jewish. Anti-Semitism and anti-capitalism frequently go hand in hand —the Pan-German movement before the war and Austria's anti-Semitism were strongly anti-capitalistic. Hitler made them indissoluble in Germany. He succeeded in bringing about a fusion of class hatred and racial hatred, of revolutionary socialism and revolutionary nationalism. The Jew, according to Hitler, is sundered from the "people" and from the nation. He is the object of class hatred as well as of racial hatred. He is the point—the essential point—where the two hatreds are welded. He is the "capitalist," the usurer, money-lender, international banker and financier, embodiment of greed, of Mammon or of capitalist exploitation.

The fusion of the social and national myths amongst people so mighty as the Germans, and the fanatically religious and military character which the twofold myth has assumed, is made all the more formidable through the peculiar gifts and character of the man who is despot over them, of Hitler, the Chancellor, and "Fuehrer."

No one has ever been as near to the German people as he is, no one has ever been able to command such devotion from such multitudes (that there are millions who regard him with hatred and contempt is no proof to the contrary).

Whenever his voice booms out at a public meeting he transports his hearers *and himself* (herein lies his sincerity) into another world and induces a trance-like state (in himself, as in his hearers). His world is dualistic—a world of waking, even if subjective, reality, of shrewd judgment, and sure intuition, and a world of myth which, in terrifying symbol and monstrous caricature, achieves a reality more real than reality itself.

This is Hitler's greatest achievement: that he has, through tremendous intensity of conviction, accompanied by an almost mediumistic intuitiveness, and a hard, peasant cunning, imposed his mythological world, first on a few followers, then on vast multitudes, who in a few years coalesced under the hypnotic contagion of his fervor and his messianic vision; that he kept millions in a state of hot incandescence, so creating a revolutionary movement which, for ardent militancy, for organized strength, and inner cohesion, has never been surpassed.

Compared with this tremendous movement, German Communism appears small and unreal. Like the Jews (who could not help it), the Communists (who could) were useful, indeed necessary to Hitler—and, unlike the Jews, useful to no one else (least of all to the German working class). And, having served him, they were swiftly and easily destroyed (the Jews remain—he needs them still).

Hitler, for all his amorality and opportunism, succeeded without making any fundamental compromise, without changing any of his main opinions. And yet, he is not only a fanatic, not only a "man possessed." He is a master of stage-craft. He has histrionic genius (though he is perhaps not so conscious an actor as Goebbels or Mussolini). He is a stage-manager of the first order. He knows exactly which of his actors is suited to which part, he has a sure insight into their weaknesses, their rivalries, and their ambitions. And although there is much quarreling, friction, hysterics, and wild temper behind the scenes, the play itself will always run smoothly and always hold the fascinated audience afresh. If there is any serious threat of disunity, or the remotest danger that any rival management might possibly arise, Hitler will not hesitate to use the frightful method of the "purge," though after the execution of the only serious rival he ever had, Captain Roehm, and of hundreds who might conceivably have supported Captain Roehm, it may be that no one will ever again aspire to be Hitler's rival.

To say that he is a great man is not to say that he is not a small man. He is small and meanly vengeful in a manner that is as inhuman as his greatness.[48] Few great men can have been so completely without any sort of nobility, candor, or refinement. In all his utterances there is not a word of love or charity. He is, like Bismarck, "a man of blood and iron," but without true manhood or dignity. Bismarck was ruthless but not bloody-minded. Hitler is bloody-minded to a horrifying degree; his book and his speeches are full of ferocious utterances. He has a brutality of language that has no parallel among modern rulers.[49]

He is a very silent man and hardly ever takes part in a conversation. He never argues. But his moody silence will, at times, be broken by long, vehement outbursts, which will be full of cheap, hot-gospelling rhetoric, but may also reveal great political insight and considerable mastery over his subject.

He lives at high tension. He will start up and shout or scream at night and has frequent weeping fits. Any obstacle or any difficulty that may thwart his purpose even for a moment will throw him into a fit of impotent rage or passionate weeping.[50]

He is soft-featured, narrow-shouldered, wide-hipped. The dark eyes shift in timid fashion—until he begins to speak.

Then they are fixed in a penetrating stare, the soft features harden, the effeminate form is rigidly bent as though by some iron stress, the deep voice booms and rages until it becomes half a roar and half a shriek, and the demoniac creature with the black hair and the little black mustache seems like the incarnation of all that is sinister and terrible in man, of all that it has ever said about the Jew. All its life it has cried and raved—"the Jew, the Jew"—or has brooded in moody silence on the Jew and against the Jew. And all the time it has meant "Hitler, Hitler," and has given the name "Jew" to the dreadful projection of itself.

CHAPTER V

Social Democracy in Germany—Its achievement—The revolution of 1918—The danger of territorial disruption—The Treaty of Versailles and the German Republic—The stand made by the Social Democrats and the Trade Unions—The defeat of Social Democracy—Reasons for this defeat—The part played by the Soviet Union—Communism and National Socialism.

THE failure of the German Republic was the failure of German Social Democracy. Although the Social Democrats never had a majority, never dominated the Republic, and never ruled except in coalition, it was they above all who gave the State its specifically republican and democratic character. They fell with the Republic and the Republic fell with them before the combined forces of Muscovite Communism and National Socialism.

Marxism was to the Social Democrats a kind of conventional religion, but not an imperious dogma that must be translated into action as immediate and complete as possible. The strength of the Social Democrat is that he has so little true Marxism—his weakness that he has so much. Having so little, he is capable of pragmatic thought and of practical constructive effort within the framework of a social order which he theoretically opposes and tries to reform rather than destroy. But his acceptance of Marxism as a "theory," a "philosophy," a "Weltanschauung," that explains all social phenomena and throws doubt on all that is not materialistic, condemns him to superficiality.

For religion, the Communist has a contemptuous intolerance, the Social Democrat a contemptuous tolerance. The Social Democrat believes—or believed—that man, or at least the "working man," is by nature good, and that all will be well somehow or other, and that, in any case, the kind of nonsense Hitler talks will never impress "the workers," however much it may appeal to the stupid "bourgeois."[1]

Nevertheless, the German Social Democrats had certain qualities of mind and character that made their achievement very considerable.[2]

That achievement was national rather than social. It is true that the Social Democrats exercised a steady pressure in favor of higher wages, fewer hours, and greater welfare on behalf of German labor. Their influence was greatest in Prussia, where it lasted continuously for nearly fourteen years —until the summer of 1932 when the *coup d'état* of which Von Papen was the chief promoter put an end to it. During that period more houses were built, relatively, for "workers" in Prussia than in Russia, and as much was done for land reclamation as in Italy. The deservedly famous achievement of the Social Democrats in Vienna was more conspicuous because more concentrated and more widely advertised, but the achievement of the Prussian Government was no less admirable—and perhaps financially sounder. Like the social achievements of France, England, Holland, and other highly civilized countries, those of Prussia were never advertised, were never dinned into the ears of the world by an importunate propaganda, like those of Russia, Italy, and the Third Realm.[3]

Nor has the achievement of the Social Democrats been wholly undone in the Third Realm. Much has been destroyed, but much has remained—the National Socialists have respected conditions of labor that were maintained against tremendous difficulties during the Republic, thanks, chiefly, to the tenacity and organized effort of the Social Democrats.

But their main achievement was national, in so far as they, above all others, saved and reconsolidated the unity of the German nation. They carried the work of Bismarck one stage further in circumstances far more difficult than Bismarck ever had to face. And it is this work which Hitler and the National Socialists are completing (and striving to expand) on foundations which would have been destroyed had it not been for the Social Democrats.

Without the Social Democrats and their organized and highly disciplined following, the unity of the German Empire would have perished in 1918.[4]

Defeat, revolution, and the onerous peace terms confronted them with a dilemma as great as ever confronted a political movement that has the responsibilities of power and is resolved to live up to them. What comes first? Party or patriotism? Class or country? The dilemma is rarely absent even in untroubled times, but it has rarely been present in a more urgent and intractable form than it was in the Germany of 1918.

The Social Democrats and the main body of their following (nearly all of whom were industrial workmen) decided that the larger conception and the greater unity should come first. In this decision they were resolute and unflinching, and only the narrowest dogmatism can say that they were wrong.

Having saved their country, they tried to save their doctrine. In this they failed, as they were bound to fail. They saved Germany, but they did not save Socialism. But they did, on the foundation of a renewed national unity, promote the interests of the working class while defending the liberties of all, including the liberty to work for the destruction of that liberty—a blunder resulting, largely, from their Marxian optimism.

For fifteen years they had considerable success. If we ask why did the Republic collapse after fifteen years, we are bound to answer by pointing out not merely the blunder of excessive tolerance that did not curb both the Communist and National Socialist movements and in good time, but a whole series of terrible and ignoble mistakes that were chiefly committed by the Social Democrats.

But when we ask why did the Republic last as long as fifteen years, we are bound to answer with much that lends the German Social Democrats and, above all, their highly civilized following, a certain greatness. Pitiable as their end certainly was, their record as a whole was not without glory —and from German patriots they may proudly claim a debt of everlasting gratitude (a debt that does not look as though it will ever be paid).

The Social Democrats were republican in theory, but it was not their intention to demand a republican form of government in 1918 when, at the approach of total defeat on all fronts and of revolution at home, they insisted on the political reforms that were carried out under Prince Max of Baden. These reforms, that established a constitutional monarchy in October 1918, were the real German revolution— these, and not the disturbances, officially termed "revolution," during the months that followed.

The Social Democrats believed that if a Republic were proclaimed in Berlin, then Bavaria, where royalist sentiment was particularly strong, would secede and German unity would be brought to an end. But when a Republic was proclaimed in Munich, the Bavarian capital, the sacrifice of republican principle was no longer necessary.

Even so, the monarchy could have been saved had it not been for the vacillations of the Kaiser and the inability of his chief advisers to realize what was happening in Germany and in the outside world.[5] By fastening the main responsibility for the war on the Kaiser, the Allied and Associated Powers instilled into the German people the belief that if this brilliant but irascible and flighty person (who, with different advisers, might have been a very good monarch) were eliminated, they would obtain more tolerable peace terms, and that reconciliation between victors and vanquished would be made much easier. The Kaiser was chiefly dethroned by Anglo-American propaganda, and, his son being depicted as only second to himself as a monster of wickedness by that same propaganda, the succession was also made very difficult.

Even so, another candidate could have been found, and the monarchic principle might have been saved, had it not been for the Bavarian Republic and for the thoughtlessness of the Socialist leader Scheidemann (who was not at all thoughtless by nature and far from unintelligent). Scheidemann addressed the crowd from a balcony of the Reichstag on the 9th November and ended his speech with the words "Es lebe die Republik." He did not in the least mean to proclaim the German Republic, but merely to start a cheer for the republican principle which had always been upheld by the Social Democrats in theory, though they were averse to it in practice. The effect of Scheidemann's words was rendered decisive by the widespread hatred which the German working class felt for the Hohenzollerns (who were held, not altogether unjustly, responsible for war and defeat), and by the belief that their removal would make the Allied and Associated Powers incline to leniency. Besides, the abdication of the Kaiser had been expected for days so that there was nothing strange or unexpected in Scheidemann's words. The German Republic had been proclaimed—and the proclamation could no longer be undone.

By promoting the overthrow of the monarchy, the Allied and Associated Powers helped to destroy the political form that was most suited to the genius of the German people. A constitutional monarchy, with the color and ceremonial that are as dear to the Germans as to the English, would have given the German State a certain majesty and fascination that was denied to the Republic, largely by reason of the complete aridity of the Marxian myth (dialectical materialism does not lend itself to picturesquely symbolical representation). It is, of course, possible, indeed likely, that the Hohenzollerns, once re-enthroned, would have attempted more than the recovery of their former power. A restored monarchy meant the menace of reaction and of a new despotism. But it would have been a rallying point for the German conservative movement. It might have transcended the implacable party strife that was the chief weakness of the German parliamentary system. The solution for Germany's internal dissensions might have been found in a popular monarchy, a "Volkskaisertum." Besides, as we shall see later on, the monarchic principle was conducive to decentralization and favorable to that federal spirit which has added such variety, richness, and freedom to German life. The monarchy contained the menace of reaction, but no reaction and no despotism under a restored monarch could have been as tyrannical as the dictatorship established by the National Socialist revolution of 1933.

The revolution of 1918, unlike that of 1933, was not a rebellion against an existing order, but an attempt to save the existing order by liberal reforms and to avert or suppress disorder and anarchy.

The prestige of the German Officer Corps—and with it of the governing class—was destroyed by defeat and by helplessness in defeat. The German naval and military commanders simply lost their heads. The admirals ordered a naval offensive that was to have engaged the British fleet in a last desperate battle. Hindenburg attempted to wreck the negotiations for an armistice. The former project was mutinous, the latter at least an act of indiscipline. The effect of either could only have been to prolong the war, in which case Germany could hardly have secured better terms, but might well have had terms far severer, or no terms at all; she might have been invaded with the permanent loss of the Rhineland and of East Prussia and, perhaps, the secession of Bavaria.

Orders to put to sea and engage the British fleet were given on the 28th October without the knowledge or authority of the German Government which was engaged in negotiations for an armistice as a preliminary to the peace, a peace to save what could still be saved. The offensive was prevented by the crews who drew the fires. These crews are habitually described as mutineers, but it was their superiors who were the real mutineers—the crews saved Germany from worse defeat and Europe from another winter of war. That their action put an end to all discipline in the navy and gave the revolution a powerful impetus is not at all surprising.

On the 24th October, Hindenburg, who with Ludendorff had been pressing for an "immediate armistice," wired to his generals, without the knowledge of the Government, that President Wilson's reply (in which it was bluntly stated that there could be no armistice that would allow Germany to renew the war) "can only be the call to continue resistance," that if resistance were to continue, the Allied and Associated Powers would be "ready for a peace that will secure Germany's future." [6]

Later on, the facts about the defeat of Germany and the revolution were falsified in the legend of the so-called "stab in the back" (the "Dolchstosslegende"), according to which Germany was on the point of winning the war when the revolution stabbed her victorious army and navy in the back and so doomed her to defeat. This legend has been adopted by the National Socialists, above all by Hitler himself, with the addition, of course, that the revolution was a Jewish plot and that Germany owes her downfall in 1918 to the Jews.[7]

The truth is that the revolution, led by men whom Hitler habitually calls the "November criminals," [8] saved Germany from a peace that might have been far more disastrous than the Treaty of Versailles, as well as from anarchy at home—and Europe from another winter of war. Germany and Europe owe these "November criminals" a monument—a true "Völkerdenkmal."

The authority of the German Officer Corps was further weakened by the estrangement between officers and men. A distance has to exist between officers and men in every army, if there is to be any discipline at all. But in the German army the distance was too great—far greater than in the French and British armies. Officers and men lived in different and often antagonistic worlds. Actual ill-treatment of men was rare and has been exaggerated in revolutionary literature. But there was so much injustice and inequality and so few means of obtaining redress, that a deep and widespread sense of injustice began to prevail.

Many officers retained the respect of their men, but confidence in the Officer Corps as a whole was destroyed by defeat, by the lack of loyalty shown by the military and naval commanders towards the Government, and by the absence of comradeship amongst the officers and men in disaster—the result, very largely, of inequality and injustice before disaster came.

Ludendorff and Hindenburg had helped to destroy the prestige of the Reichstag and of the Government by their political intrigues and their interference with the conduct of non-military affairs. And trying to play off the Throne against the Government, they helped to damage the authority of the Throne. There was no other authority left in Germany, nothing that could command obedience and respect, save the authority of the Social Democrats and of the Trade Unions.

Their authority alone could save, and did save, what was left to be saved.

The first serious disorders at home and on the fronts and the waning prestige of the Officer Corps were followed by the emergence of the Workmen's, Soldiers', and Sailors' Committees.[9] These committees were not instruments of social upheaval. It was chiefly they that led the defeated armies back to Germany in perfect order. The disciplined homecoming of the German troops has been much admired. Hindenburg got most of the credit for it—which he accepted, as he accepted all credit that came his way, however undeserved it might be (just as he accepted the credit of the victory of Tannenberg, a victory that would have been won if he had never been born). Much of the credit was due to General Gröner, one of the ablest and most high-principled of all the German commanders, who was responsible for the organization of transport. But without order and discipline within the ranks, the best organized transport would have been useless. And that order and discipline were established and maintained by the freely elected committees—of which many officers were the freely elected chairmen.

By saving the army from becoming a horde, the Workmen's, Soldiers', and Sailors' Committees set a limit to social disruption and civil war. The social disruption and civil war that followed never involved the army as a whole and therefore remained relatively innocuous.

But the danger of territorial disruption remained.

German "particularism" was always associated with the local dynasties. The Bavarian revolution, by overthrowing the chief of the particularist dynasties, the House of Wittelsbach, removed one of the obstacles to centralization, as we have seen. The Republican Government promoted centralization by giving federal law a greater preponderance over the law of the separate federal states [10] and by amalgamating the federal railways and postal service in a homogeneous national system.

There was some "particularist" or separatist sentiment in the mainly Roman Catholic Rhineland. But this sentiment was incompletely expressed in the "Separatist Movement," which was at first led by a Dr. Dorten, a man with a nebulous mind and a purely emotional hostility towards Prussia.[11] But he was not a rogue, as he was made out to be. Later on the movement fell into the hands of rogues and adventurers, though with a sprinkling of genuine idealists of utopian, pacifist, and anti-Prussian tendency. In the background, and only venturing towards the foreground with extreme discretion, was a Roman Catholic movement that embraced many of the higher clergy and some municipal dignitaries in favor of a special federal status for the Rhineland.

But Rhenish separatism and federalism were fatally compromised from the beginning by the clumsy support and encouragement they got from the French army of occupation (in 1923 many of the Separatists were no more than gangsters whom the French had armed, paid, and turned loose on a peaceful population—acts of frightful vengeance were perpetrated against them).[12]

It is impossible to say whether the Rhineland could ever have become an independent or semi-independent Republic. But there was amongst the Rhinelanders a centrifugal tendency far deeper than is generally recognized—it was killed by the French, and with it perished the dream of a Rhineland that would remain German and yet be profoundly western European, a kind of bridge between Germany and France, a bridge where the two civilizations would meet and be forever reconciled. It is doubtful whether that dream will ever come again, but in spite of painful memories, the Rhineland is not anti-French, and cherishes a deep regard for the glories of French civilization.

The Treaty of Versailles was favorable to German unity. The Allied and Associated Powers dropped the distinction between the rulers and ruled in Germany when it no longer served a propagandist purpose.

Had the Allied and Associated Powers made peace not with the "German people" but with the German dynasties, had royalty and the nobility on the Allied side remained in personal and political contact with them, the true foundation of German power, national unity, might have been weakened.

Had the Treaty been more generous, the revival of German militarist nationalism would have come sooner. But the apparent harshness of the Treaty re-enforced German fear of the former enemy and helped to keep militant nationalism in check. Without that fear, it would have made itself master of the Republic long before 1933. Even in the "Kappist" counter-revolution of 1920, the fear of the outside world—which was fear of another defeat—added strength to the resistance with which the Republic and its supporters confronted the "Kappists."

More generous terms would, in all likelihood, have killed the Republic very quickly, for the German Imperial Government and the High Command would have been vindicated by a peace that could have been presented not as a German defeat but as a German victory. Hindenburg and Ludendorff would have appeared as men of profound statesmanship because they had agreed to accept peace on the basis of the Fourteen Points after a series of victories before defeat had become plain to all. The abdication of the Kaiser and the revolution would have seemed foolish and superfluous—the Kaiser would have been recalled by an elated nobility and the revolution would have been crushed by the Officer Corps with an arrogance revived by the prestige and consciousness of victory (and, no doubt, with all the ruthlessness of those who have recovered their courage after having been severely scared).

As we shall try to show later on, the war could only end in a total victory or a total defeat. A draw, or anything less than Versailles, would have been a German victory (indeed, it is becoming doubtful whether even Versailles was not a German victory).

The sense of grievance that expressed itself in acts of fearful savagery (like the Vehmic murders[13] and, later on, the Brown Terror) against fellow Germans and in maudlin complaints, tearfully trumpeted into the ears of an indulgent world, was not produced by the severities of the Treaty so much as by the fact of defeat, a fact which was exacerbated by the terms of the Treaty.

To the German militarist nationalism and, therefore, to the indubitable masters of the German people (and largely to the German people themselves), the supreme injustice was *the defeat itself*. To them the defeat was—and still is—a flaw in the divine order, an anomalous phenomenon that deprives history of its meaning, a cosmic wrong that must be righted. The "November criminals" are hated with so much intensity because they are held responsible for the defeat which rankles much more deeply than the Treaty of Versailles. And it rankles deepest of all in the minds of those who were responsible for that defeat and would undergo a kind of catharsis or redemption if they, or their successors, could retrieve it.

While a more generous treaty would have saved German militarism and have enabled it to resume the war after a few years, a treaty with harsher terms, but attuned not to the horizontal but to the vertical divisions (so to speak) in the German nation, might have given permanence to an enfeeblement which would alone have signified the final defeat of Germany and the final victory of the Allied and Associated Powers. To divide the Hohenzollerns and the other dynasties from the German nation was to strengthen and not to enfeeble the unity of that nation. But to widen the regional differences that went hand in hand with the dynastic principle was to intensify the real weakness of the German nation. Whether the attempt to do so could have succeeded is a matter for speculation, but there was no other way to achieve a loosening of the German national structure and a permanent weakening of Germany. And that way could not have been taken unless the dynastic principle and the special character of Bavaria and the Rhineland had been respected.[14]

The main opposition to such an attempt would have come from German industrial labor and especially from the Social Democrats and the "Free" (or Socialist) Trade Unions.

It was the Social Democratic and Trade Union movements

above all that overcame social, political, and territorial disruption, as we have seen. It was they, above all, who quelled the revolutionary disorders of the year 1919 and the counter-revolution of 1920. And from the beginning they opposed every form of separatism, particularism, and decentralization.

Bavarian particularism had the support of the political Right not only in Bavaria itself, but throughout Germany. It was resolutely opposed by the Social Democrats even in Munich. Rhenish Separatism enjoyed discreet clerical support and was not always opposed by the extreme Right. But it was consistently opposed by the Social Democrats. When, in 1923, the conservative administration of Dr. Jarres considered abandoning the Rhineland to the French, it was from the Social Democrats that the most determined opposition threatened. In the Ruhr, the main resistance to the French occupation came from the working class as a whole and not from the Social Democrats alone, though they and their organized followers were the backbone of the resistance.[15]

The Social Democrats and the Trade Unions had a certain simple decency. They stood above narrow provincialism and the ambitions and intrigues that provincialism stirs up when national disintegration threatens. Against all separatist and secessionist tendencies, they upheld the unity of the working class in a united Germany. And against growing nationalism, militarism, anti-Semitism, and xenophobia, the German Social Democrats upheld the ideal of international brotherhood in a united Europe.

But they were lacking in the stronger political passions, above all in the passion for freedom and for justice to the individual. They found injustice regrettable rather than intolerable. They were, of course, right when they insisted on the need for order and unity, but they saw little beyond order and unity as such. The repression of disorder was carried out with appalling ferocity by troops with the mentality of gangsters led by adventurers who resembled Chinese bandit chieftains—men like Rossbach, Ehrhardt, and others. These troops acted on behalf of Governments in which the Social Democrats preponderated, and of a Republic which had a Social Democrat for President. For the atrocities perpetrated by them, the Social Democrats share a large measure of responsibility.[16]

The Social Democratic organization was rigidly bureaucratic and left little room for personal initiative or leadership. Proportional representation—one of the diseases of the German Republic—helped to destroy contact between leader and led. The Party, while professing to promote democracy, was undemocratic. It had the patient compliance of its immense following, but for the leaders there was little devotion. Of few, if any, of these leaders did German workmen ever say, "He is one of us." There were amongst the Social Democratic leaders men of high intelligence and humanity, men who were clean, honest, and disinterested. Amongst their followers there was a matchless élite: the German skilled workman, in particular, has, at his best, a mature and massive wisdom, a breadth of understanding, a tolerance, an iron courage, a strength of character, and a calm confidence combined with the fundamental pessimism that comes from acquaintance with hardship and poverty.

The failure of the Party, when disaster came, resembled the failure of the German armies in the hour of defeat. There is no better soldier than the German, and no abler commander. The best army may suffer defeat, and it may be that German Republican Democracy *could* not have been saved. Indeed, it sometimes seems a wonder that it held out for fifteen years against so powerful a combination of enemies—against the internal enemy both on the Right and on the extreme Left, an enemy that included almost everybody with financial power; and against the foreign enemy, especially France, with her effort to promote territorial disruption, and Russia, with her effort to promote social disruption. It seems a wonder indeed, just as it seems a wonder that the German armies held out for more than four years against more than half the world.

But defeat need not be the total annihilation of a spirit, of an ideal, of solidarity in combat (whether the combat be military or political), it need not be the end of everything. Nineteen eighteen was the end of Imperial Germany—the Germany that has arisen under the leadership of Hitler is a new Germany and not a restoration of the old. Nineteen thirty-three was the end of the German Republic and of Social Democracy. Neither will ever come back—even if the Third Realm is brought to an end, the Germany that will emerge will be yet another "new Germany," no matter what it will call itself.

The resemblance between the Social Democratic leaders and the old Officer Corps is closer than either would admit, indeed both would indignantly have rejected any suggestion that there could be any resemblance at all. But the resemblance is there nevertheless.

What the 8th August 1918 was to the German armies in the field, the 20th June 1932 was to German Republican Democracy. Among those of the leaders who had understanding, there was no will; and among those who had the will, there was no understanding. And between the leaders and the led there was the abyss.

The 8th August 1918 (described by Ludendorff as Germany's "black day") led to the Republic and Versailles. The 20th June 1932, when the Social Democrats were ejected from their chief stronghold, the Prussian Government, by a *coup d'état,* led to the Third Realm.

But there was this difference. The victorious Allied and Associated Powers and the Social Democrats were merciful. Hitler and his National Socialists were not. Nineteen thirty-three was not a Versailles, it was a Carthage.

Social Democracy not only suffered defeat, it suffered annihilation. On the 20th June 1932 it collapsed within, leaving nothing but an empty shell which Hitler was able to smash completely in the terrorist elections that followed the burning of the Reichstag.

From June 1932 until March 1933, when all was finished, and even the pulverized fragments of the shell were being swept out of existence with the iron broom of the Brown Terror, Social Democratic leaders lived on nothing but vain hope. Every apparent weakening of the foe aroused exaggerated expectations, all kinds of miracles were hoped for, in 1932 as in 1918.[17]

The political freedom maintained by the Republic perished altogether. But freedom won without a struggle by those who enjoy it is easily lost. German liberties were won not by the Germans as much as by the armies of the Allied and Associated Powers. A democracy must have teeth and claws, no less than a dictatorship, though with this difference: in a dictatorship the teeth are permanently bared and the claws always exposed, whereas a democracy must keep them concealed, displaying them only in the hour of extreme necessity. Woe betide a democracy when in that hour its teeth are loose and decayed, its claws blunt, and the spring and the swiftness have gone from the feline motion!

Power would, in any case, have been taken out of the hands of the Social Democrats sooner or later. Their weaknesses grew with age and were even more marked amongst their younger generation than amongst the older—the surest sign that a movement is ageing. What made the downfall of German Republican Democracy so complete was, in the first place, the tremendous military and terroristic organization of the National Socialist movement with its revolutionary impulse and its matchless demagogy and, in the second place, the exclusively destructive power of German Communism.

German Republican Democracy, established by the German revolution of 1918, was ruthlessly and persistently attacked by Russia. Even after it had been crushed by Hitler, these attacks went on. Even then, Muscovite vituperation descended upon the prostrate Social Democrats until, as though appalled by the immediacy of a danger from which the German Republic had sheltered her, she tried to save the remnants of what she had helped to destroy, called off her conspiratorial and defamatory campaign, and everywhere tried to promote a "united front."

The German Communist Party never had a will or spirit of its own.

Its leaders cringed before Lenin or Stalin, before Radek and Zinovieff (joining in the execration when Radek was sentenced to imprisonment and Zinovieff to death), but in Berlin they were as insolent and overbearing as they were abject in Moscow.

It was they who, for the first time in Germany, infused into great multitudes that combination of arrogance and servility, that relationship between cringing slave and ruthless tyrant, that worship (with its undercurrent of loathing) for the master, that harsh, domineering spirit (with its ill-concealed background of contempt) that make up the so-called "Führerprinzip" or "Principle of Leadership," [18] which was converted into such a formidable system by Hitler and his fellow National Socialists, who in this, as in so much else, were all that the Communists were—and much more, and a hundred times as cunning and efficient.

The German Communist Party, like the whole Comintern, was the docile instrument of Russian policy in the world-wide effort to promote two incompatibles—the national interests of Russia and the Marxian universal apocalypse (the former, in the end, always prevailing over the latter).

The state of Germany was inconsistently misjudged in Moscow.[19] At no time was a German Communist revolution possible. Whenever the German situation was "revolutionary" (to use the Marxian jargon), the danger was not one of revolution but of counter-revolution, a danger invariably augmented by the Communists. The Russian Communist leaders and their German "comrades" saw everything through the false medium of their Marxian messianism and anticipated a *successful* Communist revolution until long after the Third Realm had been established.

To the Communist every murmur of discontent is a political opposition. Every strike is a revolutionary challenge to the existing system. Every disorder is a rebellion, every rebellion a revolution—and every revolution *the* Revolution.

The Communists were a danger to the Republic, but a *counter-revolutionary* danger—never a *revolutionary* danger. To Hitler they were a help of decisive importance.

The Communists were instigators of sanguinary and senseless armed risings.[20] They fought against the Republic—not against Hitler. Indeed, they never concealed their determination to destroy the Republic. Their main attack was always directed against the Social Democrats. There was no abuse too foul, no calumny too outrageous, that was not poured, day in day out, upon the Social Democrats in the Communist press and by Communist orators. The narrow malignance of Lenin's fanatical mind, his whole mocking hatred of moderation, of variety, of freedom, truth, and justice, was turned on the German Republic in general and the Social Democrats in particular.

Lenin's associate, Zinovieff, a monster of cowardice and cruelty and a master of hot-gospelling vituperation, split the Independent Socialist Party, which was an honest attempt, led by some of the best minds and noblest characters in the German labor movement, to bridge the widening abyss between Communism and Social Democracy. This was at the Congress of Halle in 1920. It was then that Zinovieff denounced the leaders of the Trade Union International (and with them the Social Democrats) as being worse than counter-revolutionary agents and murderers.[21]

Here was a country weakened by hunger, [22] a prey to social, political, and regional disruption, surrounded by harsh foes, a country striving to fulfill an onerous Treaty, to achieve brotherly reunion with a hostile world, and to develop a more liberal system of government and higher standards of social justice and well-being, a country trying—as few other countries tried—to heal the wounds of war, and not only its own, but mankind's; a country, too, that was conscious as few other countries were of the common civilized heritage. And *there* was a country that had endured even worse, that harbored aspirations even higher and held them with even greater intensity, but was, by reason of its very vastness and remoteness, much safer and much better able to work out its own destiny. Never were two countries more imperiously summoned by their common sufferings in defeat and in revolution, and by all their real and ideal interests, to help one another than the Soviet Union and the German Republic. But the Union, instead of helping, instead of being the one genuine friend, became the most implacable foe. The Allied and Associated Powers occupied the Rhineland. The French and Belgians occupied the Ruhr and stirred up the Separatists. The Poles instigated armed rebellion in Silesia. The Lithuanians took Memel. But Russia, through the instrumentality of the German Communist Party, insinuated her taloned fingers into the body of the Republic, and, tearing at the heart, injured it irreparably.

If we try to think in terms of politics and not of a higher morality, even then, what Russia did was stupid with a gigantic and almost unimaginable stupidity, for she created an enemy for herself, the most formidable enemy, perhaps, she ever had, whereas she could not only have found a friend in the German Republic, but could have created the basis for a lasting association that would have given her a security in Europe such as she never enjoyed before.

There could be no illustration more terrible of the corrupting influence of secular religion, for if Russia had pursued only her most selfish interests (which, in the end, disastrous circumstances compelled her to pursue), if she had not been obsessed by Marxian messianism, if she had not rendered unto Caesar the things which are God's, her relations with Germany, the greatest military power in Europe, would have been altogether different; she would have had nothing to fear in the west and could have augmented her strength in the Far East. Had she done so, the present Sino-Japanese war might never have come about.

Zinovieff's abuse of Social Democracy was only a repetition of the abuse with which the writings of Lenin abound. Later on, when Fascism had begun to show itself, Social Democracy was habitually called "Social Fascism," as though it were a kind of crypto-Fascism, and, through its very deceptiveness, something far worse than the open Fascism of Mussolini. Republican Democracy was treated as a progression along the way to full Fascism. And this, indeed, is what it turned out to be—but only because Communism helped to push it along that way. At times the Communists would talk of Republican Democracy as though it was a hateful nuisance that stood between Communism and Fascism, and prevented the Communists from attacking and destroying the Fascists. Let Social Democracy itself be destroyed, let it collapse with the collapsing "capitalist system" and let Fascism show itself—the Communist International would then come face to face with Fascism ("the last hope of the perishing Capitalist Order") and annihilate it in the final apocalyptic battle that would establish the Kingdom of Heaven on Earth.

And yet, the Communists did not shrink from direct overtures to the extreme, counter-revolutionary Right.

In 1923 the German Communist Party, acting as usual under the inspiration of Moscow, declared themselves in favor of "National Bolshevism." But "National Bolshevism" is nothing other than "National Socialism": "Strongly to emphasize the nation," wrote the *Rote Fahne* (the chief organ of the Party), "is a revolutionary deed." [23] These words might have been uttered by Hitler himself (that Communism retains this tendency to compound with the foe is shown by the recent appeal of the Italian Communists for union with the Fascists).[24]

Never did the German Communists recognize any virtue of any kind in any Social Democrat. It is impossible to find a single generous reference throughout Communist literature to any of the Social Democratic or Trade Union leaders (save, perhaps, to a few who were on the extreme Left). But under the banner of "National Bolshevism" bouquets were handed out to men like Schlageter, a member of a secret counter-revolutionary organization, who was shot by the French for "sabotage" in the Ruhr. He was a completely undistinguished and unscrupulous adventurer who, when tried, betrayed all his accomplices. He and Horst Wessel, a pimp who was killed in a fight over a prostitute, are the two national heroes of the Third Realm, and objects of almost religious veneration by the National Socialists (streets have been named, statues have been erected, and a whole literature has been written in their honor).[25]

But the *Rote Fahne* wrote: [26] "Schlageter, the brave soldier of the counter-revolution, deserves to be revered in manly honor by us soldiers of the revolution." Karl Radek, who was the chief Muscovite emissary to Berlin, made a speech (which was reproduced in the *Rote Fahne*) full of the kind of bad poetry that fills columns of the National Socialist *Voelkische Beobachter*, the *Angriff*, and the *Schwarze Corps* today: "Only when Germany's cause is her people's cause, only when Germany's cause is upheld in the struggle for the rights of the German people, will that cause win active friends for the German people. If the people's cause is made the nation's cause, the nation's cause becomes the people's cause. This is what the Communist Party, this is what the Communist International has got to say in front of Schlageter's grave!" [27]

There was no limit to the abasement the German Communists were willing to undergo at Muscovite bidding. Incomparably the greatest figure of the German revolution was that lonely, profound, humane, and passionate writer and orator, Rosa Luxembourg, one of the greatest women who ever lived. Her associate was Karl Liebknecht, very much her inferior in critical intelligence, but a man of unselfish, single purpose. They were both foully murdered by members of the counter-revolutionary organizations and deeply mourned by the German working-class. But the *Rote Fahne* wrote, when National Bolshevism was the order of the Russian day, "we shall even work together with those who murdered Liebknecht and Rosa Luxembourg if they will join our ranks." [28] The very language of Communism and National Socialism is often identical—and is becoming more and more so. Recent leading articles in the *Pravda* and *Isvestia* show an attitude and a phraseology that is indistinguishable from that of the *Voelkische Beobachter*. The servility to Stalin only differs from the servility to Hitler in being more cringing, more oriental.

The indirect help given by the German Communists to the National Socialists and their precursors was of decisive importance in destroying Republican Democracy. The Communists, obsequious to Muscovite guidance, rejected Parliament as an institution. They treated it as a sham which helped to make "capitalism" acceptable by concealing its nudity with liberal phrases about equality, freedom, and justice.

The German Reichstag never had any pride as a parliament, it never even had a collective consciousness. During the war it constantly allowed itself to be insulted and bullied by the High Command, and it accepted as Chancellor that creature of Ludendorff and Hindenburg, the wretched

Michaelis. After the revolution the Reichstag was often paralyzed by the indiscipline, the insolence, and the deliberate obstruction of its own members, especially those of the extreme Left and Right. Again and again, the Reichstag showed a majority that was hostile to Parliament as such and determined to make it unworkable as an institution.

The national Socialists were just as hostile as the Communists to the Parliamentary system, but their hostile tactics were much more methodical, disciplined, realistic. The National Socialists knew what they were doing, the Communists did not. In March 1933, when the Communists were beginning to realize whither their own policy had led them, they would have voted with the Republican parties, thus depriving National Socialists and the Nationalists, who were then in alliance with them, of the majority. But as their services were no longer needed, they were swiftly annihilated with the help of the Brown Terror.

In Moscow there was no understanding at all for German affairs. Even an intelligent observer like Karl Radek did not penetrate below the surface. Muscovite domination was like a scythe which swept over the heads of the German Communist movement again and again, cutting off every head that rose above the others.[29] In this way the stature of the German Communist movement was steadily reduced—it became a party of pygmies led by pygmies. Whenever a German Communist showed any critical intelligence or independence of character he at once became suspect in Moscow—and suspicion was followed by a verdict of exclusion from the party on some hair-splitting point of Marxian dogma.

The Communists carried Muscovite disruption into German politics and Muscovite barbarism into German civilization. The brutality of their language and of their actions, their constant incitements to violence, their savage joy over every sanguinary deed committed in Russia,[30] their own armed risings, their conspiracies and their outrages were as senseless as they were appalling.[31]

The counter-revolutionaries with whom they wanted to ally themselves, were far worse and committed a long series of foul murders for which the Republic never exacted retribution. But they, and their successors, the National Socialists, were in deadly earnest, which the Communists never were. Indeed, the Communists were not revolutionaries at all. In Republican Germany it was only the counter-revolution that showed revolutionary ardor and revolutionary skill. The Communists were never more than amateur revolutionaries. They were not even a *German* party, as the National Socialists were, but a *Russian* party (though made up of Germans) and under Russian tutelage and control—a party as un-German and as alien to Germany as they were un-revolutionary and estranged from everything that had anything to do with revolution.

They despised reform. They did not have a single piece of major legislation to their credit. Had they been good revolutionaries, they might have had some excuse for being bad reformers. Had they been good reformers, they might have had some excuse for being bad revolutionaries. But they were neither good reformers nor good revolutionaries.

When the day of the "decisive battle" came, there was no battle at all. The Communists, no less than the Social Democrats, were swept out of existence at the first open onset. They were arrested, imprisoned, sent to concentration camps, or driven into hiding or exile. And that was the end of them, an end as ignominious as any in history. A few individuals endured the frightful barbarities of the Brown Terror with an almost superhuman fortitude, and tried, with immense courage and resource, to organize a secret political opposition. But they were unable to retrieve the total defeat of a party—the most powerful Communist Party outside Russia—

which had, by its combined arrogance and obsequiousness, its stupidity, its amorality, its crude violence, and the sectarian narrowness of its doctrine, brought annihilation upon itself and disaster upon its followers.

CHAPTER VI

The influence of Versailles in the National Socialist Revolution—The powerful sense of German unity—German civilization—The foreshadowing of National Socialism—Its background in German history—The territorial settlement at Versailles—Germany's post-Treaty position—The essential aspiration of the Third Realm is the establishment of a Pan-American hegemony—The implications of this aspiration—War?—The case of Austria—The significance of the "Anschluss"—The position of Czechoslovakia and of the Soviet Union—Germany's own position.

ONLY the shallowest understanding will see in the National Socialist Revolution "the result of Versailles." That revolution is the nightmare of German genius come true. In the history of the Third Realm, Versailles is but an incident and the Great War but an episode.

Versailles might have been better and it might have been much worse. Some conquerors have been more generous than were the Allied and Associated Powers, but most have been far less so. There is meanness in the Treaty but there is magnanimity as well. There is much that is realistic and much that is politically unsound.

It is always difficult to say what would have happened if something else had not happened. Versailles postponed the German nationalist revival. A more lenient treaty could not have done so. A severer treaty might have postponed the revival a little longer, but even that is doubtful—the "National Bolshevism" which showed itself in 1923 was stimulated by outrages like the occupation of the Ruhr and the encouragement given to the Rhenish "Separatists." Had these outrages continued, it is possible that "National Bolshevism" would have grown into a movement embracing the entire German people, a revolutionary movement of national and social "liberation" from the "chains of Versailles" and of "Capitalism," a movement resembling the National Socialism of today except in so far as it would have been pro-Russian instead of anti-Russian (and therefore perhaps even more dangerous).

Only if German unity had been destroyed could Versailles have been more than an incident and the war more than an episode. Ought the destruction of German unity to have been the principal aim of the Allied and Associated Powers? It would have been a difficult, perhaps an unattainable, aim. France and England would have been compelled to make the permanent subjection of the Germans their permanent policy. France aspired to such a policy, but had not the strength to carry it out, even with the help of her central and eastern European allies. The occupation of the Ruhr and the help given to the "Separatists" were but half-hearted efforts. France did all in her power to obtain the help of England in perpetuating the defeat of Germany, but that help could never be given. Only a nation united by a fierce ideal or revolutionary myth, a nation fired by imperialist ambition, and prepared to face a whole epoch of wars and to take fearful risks—only such a nation could have undertaken such a task. France and England could not, least of all England. That her strategic frontier should be along the German western border is sufficiently grievous. It is necessary because the Narrow Seas *are* narrow, and possible because that frontier is also the strategic frontier of France. Two friendly nations can have the same strategic frontier—two unfriendly nations cannot, unless one is so small and weak that it can be kept in permanent subjection.

To achieve the permanent elimination of the German menace, it would have been necessary to treat Germany as she treated eastern Europe in 1917 and as she proposes to treat eastern and central Europe in future. Not Versailles, but Brest-Litovsk have been the model, not the Covenant of the League of Nations, but *Mein Kampf*. The mentality that could conceive or follow such models did not, and does not, exist in western Europe as it does in Germany. Nor would the western European nations, after enduring the abominations of the Great War, have submitted to further sacrifices—with the prospect of further wars—such as the German nation now (half willingly and half unwillingly) accept.

To achieve the permanent disunion of Germany, it would have been necessary to establish a permanent domination over her—and also to maintain peace and order amongst her people, to promote their well-being and to undertake their defense (even the most ruthless conqueror must do *something* for the conquered if his conquest is to last).

As matter of *practical politics,* the "German problem" (which is the problem of Pan-Germanism and its menace to the peace of the world) was insoluble. And it remains insoluble, for German unity, which could not be destroyed in more than four years of war with the sacrifice of about ten million lives, remains indestructible in peace-time. France and England have to live with Germany in the same Europe, whether they like it or not.

It is no accident that a land more divided in the past than any other, and more deeply aware of the disaster of division, whether social, political, or religious, should have acquired a sense of unity so powerful as to be a fierce obsession.

Each of the two great movements of modern Germany, socialism and nationalism, was in itself dominated by the same powerful sense.

The Third Realm has been established through the fusion of the two. Both have undergone changes in the process—the socialism of Hitler is different from that of Marx, of the Social Democrats, and of the Communists. His nationalism is different from that of Schoenerer and Treitschke. But the difference is not in the essentials.

Marxian socialism as well as nationalism imply the domination of the collective mind, the collective soul, the collective will. The "collective man" is their Caesar to whom they render all. The reign of this Caesar has been dreaded by German genius more than by any other, for Germany is not only a land of secular religion, it is also the land of the Reformation, and nowhere has the absolute necessity of the *twofold* rendering—unto God and unto Caesar—been more deeply apprehended, and the calamity of the *onefold* rendering more deeply feared.

Even the Third Realm with its fanatical determination to impose absolute spiritual unity has been unable to bring this Crisis to an end, or even to drive it underground—as the intractable German religious conflict, perhaps the central event of our time, has revealed to a but half-comprehending world.

No modern nation has had men of greater genius than Germany. First in philosophy, easily first in music, second to none in science, high in art and letters, her civilization is an organic part of our modern civilization as a whole.

But in no other country has there been so profound an antithesis between the man of genius and his fellow-countrymen. Goethe's life was one of aloofness from all popular movements, and nothing could have been more distasteful to him than secular religion in any form, despite his hatred of Christian religion. He loved liberty, but feared her priests.[1] He warned the Germans against preferring nationalism to freedom,[2] and unlike the Marxists, who believe that only the "proletarian" is revolutionary, Goethe, with deeper insight, perceived that in Germany at least the revolutionary class is the *middle* class, as Hitler was to show a hundred years after Goethe died.[3]

In famous and wonderful words, Hölderlin reveals his appalling prevision of the Germany that was to emerge more than a hundred years later. He saw a people "made barbarous by industry and science and *even by religion*"—a prophecy that must have been almost unintelligible in his day when secular religion had not become a power, modern industry was not yet born, and popular science had hardly begun.[4]

The Austrian, Grillparzer, wrote prophetically, "The path of the newer education leads from humanity, *through* nationality, *to* bestiality." [5]

Nietzsche saw the growth of militant nationalism after the war of 1870 (which he regarded as a defeat for German civilization) and of Marxian socialism (we have referred to his view of the essentially despotic character of socialism). His brother-in-law, Foerster, was a narrow and truculent anti-Semite agitator. Nietzsche not only loathed anti-Semitism as very dangerous, but as odious in itself. Wherever there is nationalism, he wrote, there "the Jews are led to the slaughter as scapegoats for all possible public and private evils.... Every nation, every individual, even, has unpleasant, indeed dangerous, characteristics, and it is cruel to demand of the Jew that he be the one exception." [6] *How* cruel is shown by the beatings, expropriations, humiliations, and other wrongs inflicted on the Jews in Germany today. It is astonishing how, long before Versailles, long before the Great War, before Hitler was born, even, Nietzsche foresaw the significance of the popular leader with Hitler's special qualifications. Whenever a man of great mental poverty or exhaustion, he wrote, "appeared on the scene with gestures of the greatest activity and energy," a man in whom "degeneracy determines an excess of spiritual and nervous electrical discharge," such a man was mistaken for one of mental plenitude—"he inspired fear... the fanatic, the man possessed, the religious epileptic, all eccentrics, have been regarded as the highest types of power, as divine." [7]

Whole recipes for Hitler's achievements are to be found in Nietzsche's writings. For example: "In all circumstances get them [the masses] something that is very agreeable, or put it into their heads that this or that might be very agreeable, and then give it to them. But not at once, not on any account—fight for it with the greatest expenditure of effort, or seem to fight for it. The masses must have the impression that a mighty, indeed invincible, will-power is there—at least it must seem to be there...." And the man with the strong will (or of seeming strong will) must have "all the qualities of the masses, for they will then be all the less ashamed of him and he all the more popular—let him, therefore, be violent, envious, an exploiter, let him be an intriguer, a flatterer, a crank, let him be puffed up, indeed, let him be everything according to circumstance." [8]

Nietzsche's contemporaries, Burckhardt and the Protestant theologian, Overbeck, shared the apprehensions of German genius. Burckhardt's mistrust of power as something intrinsically evil was deepened by the militant nationalism that was growing in Germany.[9] Overbeck foresaw "a downright rebirth of superstition in which the whole of our modern education may yet find its grave." [10]

The pessimism of these warnings lies in their prophetic character. They are warnings of what is to come, not of what can be averted.

German prophetic genius was moved not by hatred, but by love of country. Even Heine and Büchner, who were Jewish émigrés, loved their country. So did the revolutionary Büchner. So does Thomas Mann, the greatest German writer of our day.

Such men cannot be compared with the small men of the literary coteries that flourished under the Republic and, cultivating a false cosmopolitanism, made a mock of everything German (such coteries have their counterpart in England now).[11]

The German Crisis was maturing rapidly before 1914. Except in so far as the National Socialist Revolution was deeply affected by the influence and impact of the Russian Revolution, the Third Realm might almost have grown directly out of the Empire of the Hohenzollerns, as though there had been no Great War and no Versailles in between. William II, with his demagogic leanings [12] and his belief in his divine mission, was a faint anticipation of Hitler. The restraint, the dignity and the silent strength of the Prussian heritage were being replaced by what came to be known in England as "Prussianism," but was closer akin to National Socialism than to anything that existed in the old Prussia. There was an ominous outbreak of national arrogance masquerading as "national humiliation" over the Agadir crisis of 1911. It was accompanied by intensified anti-Semitism. Marxian socialism was achieving an arrogant militancy and, with its disciplined battalions of workmen and its general staff of theoreticians, it was preparing to challenge the social order, just as the German Officer Corps was preparing to challenge the international order. The double phenomena of militant socialism and militant nationalism did not exist anywhere else in such force and magnitude as in Germany. Bismarck was the last of the great Prussians. The traditions associated with great names like Stein, Hardenberg, Scharnhorst, Gneisenau, Schlieffen, and Moltke were forgotten (even the famous "Schlieffen Plan" was botched when it came to the point, and the younger Moltke, with his belief in occult forces and his distrust in himself, was all that his father was not). The dismissal of Bismarck by the youthful Emperor William was of more importance in the genesis of the Third Realm than Versailles. The national and the social myths were ripening into secular religion. In no other country were the national and social myths so arrogant in promising the Kingdom of Heaven on Earth as in the Germany of the Hohenzollerns.

The two myths lived in relentless rivalry. Either saw in itself the promise of the Kingdom of Heaven and the threat of the Kingdom of Hell in the other. The hope of either was the dread of the other. On hope and dread they grew more fiercely militant. They lived on one another and could not live without one another.

The Russian Revolution established what seemed to some the Kingdom of Heaven and to others the Kingdom of Hell (and to how few a Kingdom of this World!). It inspired apocalyptic hopes and fears that intensified the fervor of the two myths, inciting them to an ever greater effort to overwhelm one another. In overwhelming one another they fused in the fierce collectivity that has established the Third Realm. National Socialism, the secular religion that bears the name of both, is a kind of modern Islam established on the strong foundation of German unity. What Burckhardt said of the Turks is true of the National Socialists:

"Their fanaticism operates as a political and military power in the service of the whole... every year [of theirs] is a religious war." [13]

There was much in Versailles that was incompatible with the professed ideals of the Allied and Associated Powers, but it was by no means uninfluenced by these ideals. No other treaty ever liberated so many millions of human beings from alien domination. The original terms of Versailles were certainly incapable of fulfillment, but they were modified in course of time, partly under pressure of political and economic realities, and partly because the hatred and distrust of the victors for the vanquished ebbed away, especially in England and the United States.

Versailles deprived Germany of one-tenth of her population and one-thirteenth of her territory, but this loss included Alsace-Lorraine, which she had forcibly annexed in 1871, and was mainly French in language and sentiment. Versailles confirmed the newly-achieved freedom of the Poles from German rule by the Poles, a rule they seem to have hated no less than the more barbarous Russian domination (perhaps because it was more efficient). But German and Pole are so intermingled in eastern Europe that a frontier line cleanly separating one from the other is impossible. And even an ideal ethnological frontier would be a very imperfect economic frontier. Danzig is almost entirely German in language and sentiment, but with a market that is mainly Polish. The inhabitants of the Polish "Corridor" (the provinces of Poznan and Pomorze) are mainly Polish, although there is a considerable German population in the cities. Broadly speaking, the poorer inhabitants of the frontier regions are with mixed populations Polish and Roman Catholic, the wealthier inhabitants German and Protestant, though there are many exceptions to this rule. Amongst many of the eastern European peasantry the sense of nationhood hardly exists and their main loyalties are religious and narrowly local.

There is strong feeling against the Polish "Corridor" in Germany because it severs the German province of East Prussia from the rest of Germany. In economic terms the separation is not serious, for most of the trade between East Prussia and the rest of Germany was always sea-borne and, in any case, there are arrangements by which the "Corridor" ceases to be an impediment to overland goods traffic.[14] Since the National Socialist Revolution, anti-Polish propaganda has ceased and, for the time being, little is said or written against the "Corridor" in Germany.

The Upper Silesians are Silesian, rather than German or Polish. The Roman Catholic workmen and peasants, who speak a Polish dialect, have had to endure much at the hands of a highly efficient but domineering and unimaginative Prussian Protestant bureaucracy. In the plebiscite of 1921 about a third of the electorate voted for incorporation in the Polish Republic. But all Upper Silesia was an organic part of the German economic system. A complicated series of agreements embodied in the "Geneva Convention" preserved Upper Silesia from economic disruption for a period of fifteen years (which have now expired). It was an unsatisfactory settlement, but it would have been difficult to suggest a better one. It placed several large towns with big pro-German majorities under Polish and, therefore, alien rule. But as these towns were ethnological enclaves, there was nothing else to be done. The plebiscite itself was calamitous (as most plebiscites are) and was followed by an atrocious civil war.[15]

The territorial settlement made at Versailles will not endure unless Germany is weakened by some internal or external disaster. A strong Germany will revive the ancient feud between German and Slav along the eastern borderlands. If there is an open conflict, the initial successes will, in all likelihood, be won by Germany, though it may be that the Slavs, even if they lose their independence, will never be subjugated, for they have a genius for conspiracy, resourcefulness, and courage, and tenacious historical memories that make them consider every national struggle in terms not of years, but of generations, or even centuries. It may be that the Germans will, under all outward successes and acquisitions of territory, be creating new dangers and new sources of weakness for themselves. The struggle between Slav and Teuton is not over, nor will it be over even when German power extends to the Urals.

The eastern European settlement was politically unsound, but the differences of opinion amongst the Allied and Associated Powers and the demands of the liberated nations made it very difficult to impose a better settlement.

The liberated nations took armed possession of coveted territory. They could not have been dislodged without fighting. A peace that would have been "just" by absolute standards would have been impossible without renewed warfare.

The financial clauses of the Peace Treaty were robbed of their devastating character by their absurdity, though they did great harm in so far as they led, indirectly, to the occupation of the Ruhr. On the whole, Germany was able to borrow what she had to pay in reparations. And reparations lasted about as long as the borrowed money lasted.

The clauses containing the demand for the trial and punishment of the so-called "war criminals" were rooted in the idealism of the victorious Powers. The demand itself was mainly pharisaical. It was, of course, a political blunder and was never seriously enforced. A few "war criminals" were tried at Leipzig but were either acquitted or were, if sentenced, allowed to escape.

The occupation of the Rhineland and the unilateral disarmament of Germany were reasonable precautions. The military clauses were interpreted with such leniency that the troops of the victorious Powers were withdrawn from the Rhineland long before the specified term, and Germany was able to rearm without any serious opposition from her former enemies.

The essence of the matter is that Versailles left her potentially by far the greatest single military Power in Europe. Compared with Brest-Litovsk, Versailles appears magnanimous. Under the Versailles Treaty Germany had to undergo provisional eclipse as a Great Power, but Brest-Litovsk condemned Russia to dismemberment and extinction as a Great Power.

Russia was dismembered in such a way that, if the Treaty had stood, she would have lost most of her industries as well as her richest agricultural region, the Ukraine (which included her Georgian oil supplies and her Black Sea ports). The Baltic would have become a "German lake" and along the eastern shores of the Baltic there would have been a series of vassal States, under German tutelage and hostile to Russia.

European Russia's richest resources would have been exploited to the advantage of Germany and many millions of her people would have come under German tutelage. Russia herself would have ceased to be a European Power at all and would have become a crippled and mainly Asiatic State, with

Germany and the German dependencies always able to paralyze her at the least sign of revolt.[16] Her weakness would have been such that she would probably have lost Sakhalin and the Maritime Province to the Japanese.

Germany's own defeat at the hands of the Western Powers saved Russia and the Russian Revolution.[17]

English statesmanship realized that no settlement can be permanent. While leaving Germany with the foundations of her power intact, it concentrated on the establishment of a "collective system" to replace the "Armed Peace" that ended in the war of 1914. The attempt failed, and was bound to fail, but it was made with enough realism and circumspection to be of some service in maintaining the European equilibrium for at least nineteen years and to reduce the general European tension. That this tension is growing once more is not the result of Versailles and of the post-war policy of the Western Powers, but of German recovery, the revival of Pan-Germanism, and the spread of secular religion.

The defeat of Germany in the Great War was, therefore, imperfect or transitory. Germany is not only determined to undo the consequences of that defeat, but to be more than she was in 1914. Like his Pan-German predecessors, Hitler regards Germany's pre-war frontiers as ethnologically, politically, economically, and strategically inadequate.[18] He vehemently complains that the Peace that ended the last war was unjust, but proposes a peace immensely unjuster to end the next war—and before the next war has begun.

National Socialist policy is not a *back to* the Germany of 1914, but a *forward from* that Germany. To Hitler, the Germans number not sixty-seven million but a hundred million.[19] In *Mein Kampf* he writes that the territorial expansion needed to achieve even the Germany of 1914 is not possible without a war: "About this there ought to be clearness, namely, that the recovery of lost regions does not come about by solemn invocations of the good God above ('des lieben Herrgotts'), or by pious hopes based on a League of Nations, but by force of arms." [20] Hitler himself, therefore, regards the last war as no more than an incident and the present peace an interval between two wars.

Just as the Third Realm is determined to disestablish Versailles, it is determined to re-establish Brest-Litovsk and carry out the dismemberment of Russia and the colonial exploitation of her richest European territories. The Third Realm is also bent on the destruction of France as a Great Power. All these aims are bluntly proclaimed by Hitler.[21]

The Third Realm is determined on the establishment of a Pan-German Empire which will exercise a military, political, and economic hegemony over the European continent. This Empire is to have dependencies of a semi-colonial nature in the East. It may, or may not have, overseas possessions, but its will is to count in *every* continent. It is to be a World Power, or, in Hitler's words, "a World Power or nothing." [22]

All these aspirations existed in pre-war Imperial Germany, but they did not dominate German foreign policy. The Empire of the Hohenzollerns strove, with energy, though not with fanaticism, to increase its influence throughout the entire world (its "Weltgeltung"). But the establishment of a Pan-Germany was not, and could not be, an object of its foreign policy, for "Pan-Germany" would have meant the dissolution of the Dual Monarchy and the end of Austria as an independent State (if for no other reason). Nor was the Empire of the Hohenzollerns bent on semi-colonial expansion in eastern Europe. The Polish Republic did not exist, Germany and Russia were contiguous, and an attack on Russia, impossible now (save with Polish consent), was possible then. But to those responsible for the conduct of German foreign policy then, a war of conquest against Russia, such as Hitler demands in *Mein Kampf,* would have seemed fantastic.

But the *ideals* and *aspirations* that are expressed in *Mein Kampf* and dominate German foreign policy now existed in pre-war Germany. The Pan-German League was a small but energetic body with cravings that have been taken over by Hitler. Hitler's anti-Russian policy is made to appear as though it were not anti-Russian at all, but anti-Bolshevik. "Bolshevism" did not exist in those days, but the same policy was recommended by precursors of Hitler many years before the war—by Albrecht Wirth for example:

"A continental extension of German soil and of German peasantry, whose labor and efficiency tower high above the slothful dullness of the Muzhik, is a sure safeguard against the flood of our enemies, and a sure foundation for our rising power. We must resume the colonizing policy of the Ottos, of the Siebenburg Saxons, of the Teutonic Order, and of the first Kings of Prussia. The German Volga peasants and the increase of German commercial activity in the whole Russian economic system have already made a beginning in this respect." [23]

This is almost exactly Hitler's own program of eastward imperialistic expansion (even the present German method of economic penetration and of collaboration with the German minorities is implied in Worth's demand).

Austria and the Austrian Pan-Germans always tended to be anti-Russian rather than anti-Polish. Prussia was deeply influenced by the Bismarckian heritage and tended to be pro-Russian and, therefore, anti-Polish. The principal enemy, as seen from Vienna, was in Moscow. As seen from Berlin, he was in Paris. Hitler has taken over the anti-Russian tradition of Austria, adding, characteristically enough, the anti-Russian heritage of pre-war Socialism and Liberalism which saw in Russia the stronghold of tyranny in Europe. The despotism of the White Tsars has been replaced by the despotism of Stalin, the Red Tsar. Russia today, as before the Russian Revolution, is by far the most tyrannically governed country in Europe, and there is far more tyranny in Europe now than there was then. Hitler has, with prodigious demagogic effect, combined the whole anti-Russian tradition of the Dual Monarchy with those German dreams of expansion, that took various forms, from romantic enthusiasm over the achievements of the Teutonic Order to professional schemes for the dismemberment and colonization of Russia. He has also intensified the belief that there is "not enough room" [24] in Germany, and has given that belief a purpose by holding out the prospect of vast territorial acquisitions in the East. He has also given his anti-Russian policy the aspect of a crusade against tyranny and an inferior civilization, so that youthful Germans dream of entering Russia as conqueror and liberator.

Hitler has revived Prussian gallophobia (Republican Germany remained gallophile, despite the provocations she had to endure at the hands of the French). Every Power is Germany's "natural ally," Hitler declared, and "no sacrifice" can be called "unspeakable" if the result is "the mere possibility of overthrowing the Power that hates us most grimly," that is to say, France.[25]

Bismarck was resolutely pro-Russian because he dreaded what, in the end, came about—the alliance between Russia and France, and the "war on two fronts." He was just as resolutely set against any policy that might antagonize England (had he not been dismissed by the Emperor William II, or had his warnings been heeded, there would, in all likelihood, have been no Great War).[26] Prussia, under Bismarck's guidance, was always prepared to assist Russia in crushing Polish freedom—the Poles have never had an enemy more implacable than Bismarck and, to the present day, they have a far greater distrust of German conservatives than of the National Socialists.

The Poles were crushed between a Germany and a Russia who were friendly to one another. Today they are in danger of being crushed between a Germany and a Russia who are hostile to one another. Germany cannot attack Russia without at least the passive help of Poland. This help will not be given willingly, for it might convert Poland into a battlefield. If German troops pass through Poland, the Poles must fear that they will not leave again, or that they will at least remain in permanent occupation of all Germany's former eastern territories. If Russian troops invade Poland, the Poles must fear that if they are not driven out, they will remain in occupation of the eastern regions where there is a poverty-stricken and oppressed White Russian and Ukrainian population (not to speak of the impetus which Polish Communism—at present stronger as a mood than as a movement—might receive).

A German attack on Russia through the Baltic and the Baltic States would be very difficult in any case, but would also require the passive consent, at least, of Poland, for a hostile or even a doubtfully neutral Poland would be a deadly menace to the long German lines of communication and to the extended German right flank.

A German-Polish war against Russia could only come about if Poland were forced into it by Germany. It might be successful at first. But the final success would be Germany's. Poland would be occupied by German troops. The peace terms would—in case of victory—be dictated by Germany (in case of defeat they would be dictated by Russia). The conquered territories would be chiefly held and colonized by Germans. Poland herself would become a German dependency.

With her long, open frontiers and her inferiority in population and material resources, Poland cannot hope to be as strong as either Russia or Germany (assuming that neither is weakened by disaster at home and abroad). The principal object of her foreign policy is to maintain the *balance* between Russia and Germany. Only by a powerfully armed neutrality from which she would emerge if the balance were threatened can she hope to survive as an independent nation. Her strength will always have to be greater than the *difference* between the strengths of her two great neighbors. As that difference may be considerable, Poland is condemned to carry a heavy burden of armaments. But unless she is strong she is doomed.

By being strong she makes a German-Russian war impossible—and thereby reduces the chances of a general European war. A strong Poland must always make Germany hesitate before venturing on a conflict with the Western Powers. A strong Poland is therefore essential to the maintenance of the present European order.

A German-Russian understanding is not likely under Hitler and Stalin. But it is not impossible. The two systems resemble one another much more closely than either resembles the systems that prevail in western Europe. The term "National Socialist" fits them both, and it would be easy for Hitler to argue, if he wished to, that Russia is no longer "communistic" (it is perhaps significant that he always refers to "Bolshevik Russia" now, and never merely to Russia).

A genuine German-Russian understanding would give Russia absolute security in Europe and therefore a great access of strength in the Far East. It would leave Germany neutral in a war between Russia and Japan, and Russia neutral in a war between Germany and the Western Powers. Russia must always be interested in maintaining the "neutral belt" between herself and Germany, but it is inconceivable that Germany, if she remains a Great Power at all, will forgo *all* eastward expansion. If she cannot expand at the expense of Russia she will try to expand at the expense of Poland. Indeed, Poland is in *permanent* danger of suffering territorial loss (for Germany will always wish to recover the territories she ceded to Poland in 1918). It may be that Poland will again be menaced with partition. And the partition of Poland will be as baneful to the Europe of the future as it was to the Europe of the past.[27]

The National Socialist Pan-German hegemony which is

the essential aspiration of the Third Realm, an aspiration that dominates German foreign policy, would be the end of Austrian independence in any form, the dismemberment and vassalage (if not worse) of Czechoslovakia, the dismemberment and semi-vassalage *at least* of Poland and German tutelage over Baltic States and perhaps even over Rumania. The dismemberment and colonization of European Russia, though so passionately demanded by Hitler, is not *essential* to that hegemony. It may come about if Poland and Russia are weak, but the hegemony may be achieved without even a German-Russian conflict.

With Austria absorbed and Czechoslovakia and Poland reduced to the status of German dependencies, the essentials of the Pan-German hegemony will have been achieved, and the next, but not the last, act in the terrific drama of Germany's rise from a European to a World Power will have been played.

Militant Pan-Germanism *alone* threatens Europe with a general war. The "Italian danger" is not comparable with the German, for it exists *only* on the margin of insecurity created by German rearmament.

The "German problem" cannot be solved *either* by the drastic method of "encirclement," that is to say, by an anti-German alliance (least of all by an alliance with Russia), or by "concessions" by the Western Powers in the form of overseas colonies,[28] loans, a "free hand in the East," and what not. Either course would tend to bring on rather than avert a general European war—the former because Germany would strike, and "preventively" (as she did in 1914) *because* she was being "encircled," and the latter because she would interpret every concession as a sign of a weakness that would tempt her to strike at the Western Powers first.

Although appearances and logic point towards another European war, that war is uncertain even beyond the uncertainty of all things political. Can Germany get what she wants without a war? Not all or even most of it—but *some* of it. She does not in the least shrink from war *as such,* but she does not want defeat. And almost any war that begins anywhere in the eastern hemisphere may become general, so that there is no telling whether war begun in circumstances favorable to the aggressor may not, in the end, expose him to defeat by a superior coalition. The hazards of war, and the effects even of victory, on the internal situation of the most stable country may be such that even those who love war (and they are not confined to Germany, as the widespread pleasure taken in the Spanish war has shown) will not lightly incur those hazards, even if the initial prospects may seem very favorable. An excessively mechanistic view is too often taken: the Third Realm (with Italy as a satellite) is represented as being an inevitably expanding imperialism, while the rest of Europe is presented as rigidly static. From this it is deduced that war *must* come.

But, just as the most ambitious person even when endowed with a powerful will and helped by vast material resources, never gets more than *something* of what he wants (and many get nothing), so the Third Realm, although animated by a determined militancy and disposing of immense resources, cannot gain all the things it is set on achieving. And might lose all, for another German defeat is more likely to be another Carthage than another Versailles.

Perhaps the German danger does not lie so much in an immediate threat to the peace of Europe as in the spirit which is being infused into the oncoming generation of Germans. The corruption of the young by a barbarous secular religion, the suppression of freedom and of every humane and generous impulse, the arrogant ascendancy of the "collective man," the dominion of the mediocre, the hatred of individual genius, of refinement, balance, and mercy—all these things threaten to destroy a great civilization in the heart of Europe, and are therefore a menace to European civilization as a whole.

If we consider what the National Socialists are, and if we consider that they closely resemble both Fascists and Communists, and if we consider that the greater part of Europe is under the domination of National Socialists, Fascists, or Communists, and that even western Europe is not uncontaminated, we cannot but anticipate evils of which war is only one, even if we remain skeptical about the likelihood of another European war.

National Socialism, like all secular religions, is anti-political. Germany, Italy, and Russia have no internal politics—though it does not follow that Germans, Italians, and Russians may not be astute politicians. National Socialism is, above all, warlike. National Socialists conceive of politics, both domestic and foreign, as a form of war. They employ warlike methods when they *can,* and peaceful methods only when they *must*. To them (as to the Communists) war is not an instrument of policy, policy is an instrument of war (whether international or social). To the National Socialists and to the Communists war is sacred, whether it be war between nations or between classes, while peace is profane. Both National Socialists and Communists are outwardly warlike when it is not inopportune to be so, and are seemingly peaceful when to be so is opportune—but inwardly they are always warlike, and think always and in everything (in politics, art, science, philosophy, and what not) in terms of aggression, of strategy, of tactics, of "fronts," of trenches, of maneuver, of ultimate victory and of a "peace" that is always a "dictated" peace and always merciless. They seek "friendly relations" with foreign Powers whom they inwardly hate or despise, if these powers are strong or likely to be useful, while they are intolerably overbearing to such Powers as are weak and not useful. The Communists, when frightened, take refuge in the skirts of much-despised Liberals, or make peaceful overtures to the churches (dispensaries of "opium for the people") or even to labor parties or trade unions ("worse than Fascists"), and proclaim "United Fronts" not to promote any general cause but to save themselves from annihilation.

To the National Socialists the warrior is the ideal man, just as the "fighter on the barricades" is to the militant Communist. To the National Socialist, peace is a means of preparing for war, just as to the Communist social peace is the means of preparing for class-war. Peace, in itself, has no meaning to either, save as a "preventive peace." And to both the love of peace as such is a form of treachery or treason (to the "race" or the nation, or to the "workers"). When such beings have made themselves masters over whole nations, over the great German nation above all, it is only natural that all those who love peace and their own country and the common civilized heritage should feel the darkest apprehensions. But if we think—as we must constantly think—in terms of practical politics, we are not compelled to accept the inevitability of war, even if we must be aware that the question of peace and war is once more the question of the day—and of many days and years to come.

The most immediate object of German foreign policy is the union with Austria—the "Anschluss." The Union is a vital necessity, not in any material sense, but in the sense again and again emphasized by Hitler himself in *Mein Kampf* (he opens the book with the assertion that the Union must come whether it is economically advantageous or not).

To Hitler, the Union is, together with the persecution of the Jews, a sacred mission, *his* mission above all, and assigned specially to him by Providence. To him, Germany *with* the Jews and *without* Austria is a mockery, an empty shell. His life, and all he lives for with the concentrated passion of a religious monomaniac, is totality and homogeneity —and to him the supreme homogeneous, racial totality is the Pan-German National Socialist "Aryan" (and therefore non-

Jewish) State, which may be more than Austro-Germany, but cannot be less (without more it will be incomplete—but with less it will not be at all).

If, contrary to reasonable expectation and the fanatical resolve of Hitler himself (with all the resources of the greatest military Power in Europe at his disposal), the Union with Austria cannot be achieved, then the National Socialist Revolution will have suffered a defeat so decisive that its whole content will be imperiled. It is doubtful whether Hitler could survive as "Fuehrer." Even if he continued to hold office as Chancellor, he would be a broken man. The terrible burning passion would be extinguished. The fanatical will would undergo dissolution. He would himself become an empty shell—an amiable person, perhaps, talking confused abstractions (with an Austrian accent), with his mind wandering amongst Bavarian highlands (from where the lost realm of Austria can be surveyed). He would, perhaps, be regarded as the savior of his country still, as the chief promoter of "national unity" in time of crisis and threatening chaos. But he would no longer be Hitler (he might even relent in his persecution of the Jews), nor would Germany any longer be the Germany of the National Socialist Revolution.

The Union of Germany and Austria would be one of the great events of European history, and Hitler, as its chief author, would take a permanent seat amongst the immortals. But it would also be a human tragedy. Most Austrians do not want it and would only accept it under duress, though some, moved by a sense of Austro-German brotherhood, desire it ardently and not ignobly.

Much of the brightness has gone out of Austrian civilization. There is a weariness of spirit like a gray dust over the land, while a peculiarly sinister form of clerical reaction is creeping over Austrian life. And yet that civilization, with its lightness and elegance, even amid poverty; with its inner freedom that persists, even though dimmed and feeble;

with its ultimate cheerfulness, despite the appalling calamities endured by the Austrian people (calamities far worse than those that have afflicted the Germans but endured with far greater courage and dignity by the Austrians)—that civilization, or some of it, is still there, awaiting its hardest ordeal, its absorption into Pan-Germany.

The presence of many Jews in Austria would alone make the Union a human tragedy—but a human tragedy does not make a political problem.

Germany, in control of Austria, places Czechoslovakia in a hopeless strategic position. Czechoslovakia lies across the path of German south-eastward expansion—a path that is again, as it was before the war, conceived as extending to Baghdad. Czechoslovakia has a large German-speaking minority, the Sudetic Germans. If the Third Realm has its way, the question will be not whether the Sudetic Germans get Home Rule in the Czech State, but whether the Czechs get Home Rule in the Pan-German Empire.

Germany, with Austria absorbed, and with Czechoslovakia dismembered or reduced to vassalage, has a broad base from which she can achieve an economic, political and *religious* domination over central and south-eastern Europe and impinge on the northern Italian plain and, through Trieste, on the Mediterranean.

The Pan-German Empire, uniting Hitler's 100,000,000 Germans in a homogeneous nation under a central government and with vassal or dependent States to the east and south-east, would impinge upon the Soviet Union. If the Union were weak enough, German penetration—with or without war—would begin. It is conceivable that even without a rupture of diplomatic relations Russia would become a field for German capital and enterprise. Russia has undergone every kind of German invasion except military invasion. She accepted German bureaucracy under Peter the Great, she invited German peasants who established prosperous farmsteads and villages along the Volga, and she accepted the despotism of a German idea when she accepted Marxism. It is even conceivable that Russia, if she is weak and her Government unstable, will *solicit* German help, and that German administrators, engineers, financiers and merchants will carry the preponderant influence of the Pan-German Empire to the Urals, and to the Caucasus and the oil-fields of Baku.

The Slavs are more formidable as subject nations than as independent nations. It is easier to crush them than to keep them crushed. The Czechs have succeeded in establishing a strong, well-balanced and well co-ordinated social and political order (their weakness is exclusively strategic). The Yugoslavs are in a state of latent revolution, the Poles of latent anarchy. Neither nation has succeeded in maintaining that balance between homogeneity and variety without which no nation can have inner strength. In both there is a perilous rift between the governing and the governed. The Yugoslavs and the Poles love freedom more fiercely than the Germans do, but they have been less successful than the Germans in establishing national unity and leadership.

Both Hitler and Stalin are popular. The Third Realm and the Soviet Union are not as undemocratic as they are commonly alleged to be. No government can express *the* will of the people, for no people in the world have any *one* will (except, perhaps, in time of war). But the German State is strong both in the multitude and devotion of its supporters amongst the people. Free elections are impossible in Germany, for the terror is an organic part of the system. But the Government is not founded on terrorism alone—terrorism ensures the margin of safety which it requires. The foundations of every government expand, contract, and fluctuate, and it is against excessive shrinkage or dissolution that the terror is meant to be a safeguard. Hitler and his associates are the political constant in Germany, and in so far as their policy and their aspirations are the nearest possible approach to the common denominator of the many desires, aspirations, opinions of the German people, Germany (like Russia) is not wholly undemocratic as the Greeks would have understood the term—and they had no illusions about the danger of despotism inherent in democracy.[29]

There is in Germany today no serious political opposition. The German working class are under a despotism that is all the more appalling because it is felt—acutely, tragically felt —by the critical, the intelligent, the morally and physically courageous. That it is "popular" increases, instead of diminishing its frightfulness. It is all the more oppressive because workmen, living as they do in close contact with one another and working together in mines and factories, are much more easily invigilated (largely by fellow-workmen) than merchants, shopkeepers, farmers, and so on. The mighty organization built up by German industrial labor has proved a weakness in defeat. It has been taken over bodily and transformed by the new German State and, from being the means by which German workmen aspired to domination, it has become the net in which they are now inextricably entangled.

There is in Germany a widespread desire for freedom (freedom is never so loved as when it is lost). But it is accompanied by a fear of anarchy, for few would, after the experience of the post-war years, want another upheaval, another outbreak of terrorism, and all the strain and anxiety of another "transition period"—a transition to no one knows what.

Even against war there is little opposition in Germany (and that little, fatalistic and ineffective), while in favor of war there is not only the militancy of National Socialism, but also the growing hope, widespread amongst all who endure social or national oppression, that war is, in the end, the only liberator.

War promotes national unity—unless it lasts too long, when

it tends to precipitate disunity. Germany is at war in imagination even now, and German unity is cemented by a warlike atmosphere (the terror strikes, above all, at supposed "traitors"—it derives much of its ferocity from the conception of all political dissent as connivance with the enemy, whether the enemy be the Jews, "Communism," or foreign Powers).

Every Slav nation would unite in war—but unity that only comes with the outbreak of war comes too late (by their treatment of their minorities the Poles [30] have created an additional source of great weakness in war time).

The hazards of a warlike atmosphere resemble those of war itself. A dictatorship *must* have success, or the *appearance* of success, especially when it is popular, like the German. Indeed the Germans, more than any other nation, need victory. The Slavs have lived on defeat in the past and will do so again. They grow strong on defeat—the Germans grow strong only on victory. Always in the background of the National Socialist movement, and now, in the days of its triumph no less than in the days of its struggle for power, there is the phantom of inner collapse, of the sudden wilting, the calling of a great bluff (that is not altogether bluff).

The German reoccupation of the Rhineland eliminated the distinction between the victors and the vanquished of the Great War. It brought the immense armed preponderance of the Western Powers to an end and divided western from central and eastern Europe.

The German North Sea coast is invulnerable. The approaches are so difficult that to lay mines, to remove buoys, and to extinguish lights, is enough to make them secure. With shore batteries and her small but formidable fleet, Germany can prevent any long-range bombardment of her ports.

By reoccupying the Rhineland, Germany has extended her belt of invulnerability from the North Sea to the Alps. In the eternal competition between defensive and offensive weapons, the former, it would seem, are gaining the upper hand [81]; surface craft are conquering submarine, and the ground the air. Against the rifle, the machine-gun, the anti-tank and anti-aircraft gun, supplemented by ground artillery and aircraft, an even vastly superior weight of metal can, it would seem, achieve little while the air-arm is losing the character of a decisive weapon (if it ever had that character).

Along her western frontier Germany has constructed a deep system of defenses which, if not absolutely impregnable (which perhaps no defenses are), could not be taken without fearful losses—without a series of battles that would, within the first few weeks, be like the Somme, Passchendaele and the Chemin des Dames all in one. In the west, therefore, Germany would seem to be invulnerable, on land, on the sea, and in the air; nor could she, because of the Alps in the south and the difficult sea approaches in the north, be outflanked.

The advantages of the defensive over the offensive, increased by a favorable terrain in the west, are decreased by the long and open frontier and the vast expanse of level ground in the east. Interior lines make it possible for Germany to carry out rapid concentrations of superior forces against foes who are unlikely to achieve complete co-operation and are compelled to hold immensely long fronts without being able to concentrate rapidly and heavily on any sector.

The chances of war—if it comes—are therefore strategically favorable to Germany.

But they remain chances. The superiority of the defensive over the offensive is not certain and may not be permanent. And no nation can be sure of its internal strength, especially under despotic rule. Nowhere is it certain that the "home front" will stand a war, least of all a long war. No General Staff can wholly trust its own instrument. And if the German "home front" collapses, it seems very unlikely that any of the leading National Socialists (including Hitler himself) would escape massacre—the devotion felt for them would vanish or would be transformed into a hatred that would merge with the deep and widespread hatred felt for them even now. The internal weakness of Germany may well be far greater than that of the Western Powers—her present rulers, at least, would seem to think so, for they think in terms of a "home front" which may have to be held by *troops* (the "Black Shirts" or "SS" are a powerful armed force, meant, principally, to quell disorder or revolt *at home* in time of war).

CHAPTER VII

The Pax Britannica—The limitations of international law—Armaments a condition not of war but of peace—The achievement of the Pax Britannica—The Pax Britannica and the wider responsibility of the British Commonwealth—The way to its achievement—Civilization itself contains the menace of war—The cause of war—The fixing of the responsibility for war—Nations' reasons for entering upon war—The British post-war dream of the establishment of universal peace—Implications and danger of that dream—The Covenant of the League and the doctrine of sanctions—An examination of that doctrine—Its evil inherent—No reason to suppose that a universal system of "sanctions" would abolish war even for a time—How the "sanctionist" system would operate—The position of Great Britain—The doctrine of "sanctions" a modern myth.

THE love of peace is inseparable from the determination to defend it. The Pax Romana came to an end because it was too weakly defended against external and internal enemies. The Pax Britannica will come to an end if the determination to defend it weakens.

To oppose this determination, or to be without it, may be pacifism, but not love of peace. The Pax Britannica is more majestic than even the Pax Romana was. It has given peace and liberty to a quarter of the world. Many varied civilizations, a multitude of peoples from the most primitive to the most advanced, many different economic and political systems, and almost all the great religions are kept at peace with one another in the Commonwealth.[1]

International treaties and covenants cannot by themselves keep the peace. International law is not a condition of peace —peace is a condition of international law. Municipal law can help to diminish social injustice and so promote a condition unfavorable to class-war, but it cannot prevent class-war. International law can help to promote a condition unfavorable to international wars, but it cannot prevent war between nations. To legislate against war between nations is as vain as to legislate against revolution. Laws against revolution are a threat of class-war and are themselves, therefore, revolutionary. International laws against war are themselves threats of war.

International peace, like social peace, is an order, and there can be no order without compulsion. Armies, navies, and air forces are the condition not of war but of peace. War would be possible without them—peace would not. If they were spirited out of existence, the international order would dissolve in anarchy, for the general equilibrium would be destroyed. The power of the countries with large populations would increase, while the power of those with small populations would diminish. Areas of high civilization and prosperity which are now armed in self-defense, would be exposed to invasion, and there would be a series of migrations, of "Völkerwanderungen" which, in Europe, would take a westward course. The advantage would be with those who are the most numerous and barbaric. There is no reason to suppose that the incursions of barbaric hordes and the displacement of entire populations would be any less frightful than in the days of Genghis Khan, Tamerlane, and Attila, even if the only weapons left to mankind were sticks and stones.

The State, and the terrible coercive powers at its disposal, are the conditions not, as Marx and Lenin thought, of social war, but of social peace. Without them there would be social anarchy (it is in anarchy alone, and never in any kind of order, that the State "withers away").

Only if man were free from sin would the total renunciation of all coercive powers be possible. The State is necessary because of sin. Marx and Lenin believed that the State would "wither away" with the suppression of capitalism, because they identified capitalism with sin. Absolute pacifism is the denial of sin's reality. To practice non-resistance to evil is to promote the dominion of Satan.

The greatest extension of international, social, and religious peace ever achieved has been achieved within the British Commonwealth. Throughout a quarter of the world the satanic forces that engender war and revolution are curbed, thanks to the Pax Britannica, with which a beneficent Providence has associated the Pax Americana and the Pax Gallica.

The Pax Europaica is one of those ideals that transcend practical statesmanship, which is necessarily short-sighted and bent on the fulfillment of immediate tasks. Excessively farsighted statesmanship may be very dangerous,[2] and to pursue an international ideal by political means is to invite a general catastrophe.

The Pax Europaica would certainly be in the interest of the British Commonwealth, but to enforce it is beyond the power of the Commonwealth (we often forget that the greatest power—even the power of the Commonwealth—is limited). England is under the absolute necessity of defending western Europe because that defense is self-defense. That necessity imposes a terrible burden and is attended by fearful dangers. The burden and the dangers must be borne, but to augment them in the pursuit of an ideal that is, in any case, unattainable in so short a time as one generation, would be madness. The Pax Britannica would be shaken and, perhaps, fall to pieces, British vital interests would suffer profound and perhaps irretrievable injury, and the ideal would certainly not be achieved but would, in all likelihood, be buried forever in the general ruin.

The Pax Europaica cannot be achieved by political means alone, or even principally by political means. It can only come through the rebirth of the European consciousness in the heritage that has come down to us from Athens, Rome, and Jerusalem.

That heritage is incompatible with secular religion. Marxism and National Socialism are denials of the free inquiring mind, of law, and of transcendent truth. Both are at war with the European consciousness. Against that consciousness

Marxism is waging *class-war,* National Socialism is waging *national* war, and both are waging *religious* war.

Only when secular religion has been overcome can there be a rebirth of the European consciousness. Only then can there be a Pax Europaica.

To love peace, it is not enough to believe that war is wrong. There is no good in war—war, whether between nations, classes or religions, is the supreme manifestation of collective evil.[3] None of the arguments of militarists or of revolutionaries are true. It is not true that war "produces" heroism, self-sacrifice, and comradeship, or that violent revolution "releases" these qualities. War is not only evil in itself, it is immensely destructive of mercy, justice and truth. War is far worse than the catastrophes of nature—famine, flood, earthquake, and epidemics (these do not produce virtues either, though, like war, they may provide opportunities for the display of virtues less conspicuously displayed, though no less active, in time of peace). War is worse than such catastrophes, for they are outward, while war not only has more than their outward destructiveness, but is an active evil, a horror, and a corruption of the soul.

To love peace, it is not even enough to hate war.[4] Love of peace is not a negative but a positive emotion. But it cannot exist without the awareness of war. The intrinsic miracle of peace cannot be apprehended without a deep sense of the dangers against which it must always be defended—always, because the enemy is not merely the armed, foreign foe, not merely the ever-vigilant foe at home, but also the foe within ourselves.

Peace is a state both of equilibrium and of harmonious evolution. It is not the passive but the active principle of civilized life. Without it civilization is inconceivable. Love of peace is love of civilization, of one's neighbor, of country, all in one.

The true lover of peace will be more concerned with peace

in the concrete than in the abstract; with defending his and his country's peace, rather than with chimerical schemes for extending peace beyond the limits of the possible. He will always reflect whether its extension beyond the frontiers of his own country will be an extension not of peace, but of war. Even a seemingly small extension of peace may be dangerous, as the extension of the Pax Britannica to western Europe is. Inherent in universal peace is the menace of universal war—"indivisible peace" is "indivisible war."[5]

A nation when attacked always will defend itself if defense has any chance of success (and sometimes when it has none), but the problem of peace and war cannot be stated only in terms of armed defense.

A peace-loving nation like the English may have to fight even when they are not the object of a direct, armed attack. A vital interest is one which a nation must defend by force of arms if no other defense is adequate. A Government who are not prepared to make war in defense of the vital interests of their country are faithless to their trust—it would be in the vital interest of their country to sweep them out of existence.

The sacrifice of a vital interest can never be conducive to peace. It means the permanent weakening of the nation—and, therefore, a permanent menace to its peace.

The utmost that can be reasonably expected of a civilized nation is that it shall not go to war save in self-defense (which includes the defense of its vital interests). Many wars have arisen out of the conflict of interests that are not vital, and many out of conflicts that have no relation with any interest at all. This has always been so, and there is no evidence that it will not always remain so.[6]

Civilization *itself* contains the menace of war. The higher a civilization is, the greater the danger that it will turn into its opposite. The Greeks were not less civilized than we are. It is untrue that the Germans, who now menace the world with war and live under a barbaric despotism, are less civilized than the English, the French, and the Americans. There is something terrible about civilization *as such*—the more beautiful it is, the more hideous its caricature (and all civilization is in permanent danger of becoming its own caricature). Sin, concealed under urbane manners or repressed by noble conventions (or rendered diffuse by the lack of them), will surge up and achieve a frightful collective ascendancy, and, parading as a kind of super-virtue, will overthrow justice, confuse and debase ethical and esthetic standards, and, denying God, render unto Caesar the things that are God's. It is then that war comes into its own, irrespective of national interests (that wars are often altogether senseless does not make it easier, but more difficult, to avert them).

We sometimes know the immediate causes of this or that war, but we do not know the cause of war as such—indeed, that men, not driven by absolute necessity, should kill one another must always remain an insoluble mystery. There have been wars of pure aggression,[7] but often there is no telling who the aggressor is. There is no unanimity, even amongst objective historians, as to the causes of the Great War. To define the aggressor is often impossible even when all the facts are known, when all the documents are accessible, when those chiefly responsible for policy can be questioned, when events can be surveyed dispassionately from a distance that is neither too great nor too small. To define the aggressor in advance and in general terms will always be impossible, though several States with a common vital interest may help to maintain *their* peace by defining the specific circumstances in which *they* would treat the action of any other State as aggressive. But, in actual fact, the designated aggressor may not be the aggressor at all by any objective test. In a formal sense every preventive war is a war of aggression—but a preventive war may nevertheless be a necessity, and, although taking the form of aggression, it may serve a purely defensive purpose.

Not one of the many suggested definitions of the aggressor exclude, and, indeed, no conceivable definition could include, the possibility that the Power designated as the aggressor under the definition may itself be the victim of aggression in any but a formal sense, and may itself have acted under the inexorable necessity of self-defense.

A nation's existence may be threatened without actual war, and it may *have* to wage preventive war. For example, if Great Britain had failed to rearm or if she were to withdraw into complete isolation, France and her allies, Poland and Czechoslovakia—and perhaps Russia, Yugoslavia and Rumania—would be compelled at least to consider going to war preventively before the completion of German rearmament could menace their existence as independent States. The question of preventive war against Germany cannot have been ignored altogether in Paris, Warsaw and Prague,[8] but the rearmament of Great Britain and her close association with France, have operated, and continue to operate, as a deterrent not only on Germany, but also on France and her allies.

If the causes of so many past wars are in dispute, how can we know the causes of future wars? Many a war will be transformed from one of aggression into one of defense while it is being waged.[9]

The Allied Powers certainly did not begin the Great War to make the world "safe for democracy" or to "defend the rights of small nations," or "to end war." Yet each of these motives acquired a certain reality as the war went on. The comparatively lenient treatment of Germany at Versailles (lenient, that is to say, considering the fearful character of the war and the obvious potential strength of Germany even in defeat) was at least partly the result of the idealism that influenced the war aims of England and, above all, of the

United States (the French, who had endured invasion for the second time within living memory and knew that the bare existence of Germany exposed them to further invasions, were less inclined to be idealistic).

The satanic character of war and the dark irrational forces that will often make a war fought on behalf of an exalted ideal more merciless than a war fought for some base material advantage, mock all schemes for establishing universal peace. Some of our poets have had a deeper insight into the causes of war and a more imaginative realism than the promoters of such schemes. We ought to know that:

> "... when nations set them to lay waste,
> Their neighbors' heritage by foot and horse,
> And hack their pleasant plains in festering seams,
> They may again—not warely, or from taste,
> But tickled mad by some daemonic force." [10]

Nothing is easier than to declare the indubitable iniquities of war, nothing is easier than to declare the disparity—and some disparity is always inevitable—between the real and professed views of the belligerents, between the declarations with which they enter a war and the terms on which they bring it to an end. But beneath such declarations there lurks the danger of self-righteousness and of blindness to the reality of sin. War does not show the guilt of politicians, diplomats, generals, and armament firms alone, or of abstractions such as "capitalism" or "imperialism." It does not show that people are good and their rulers bad. It reveals the sinfulness of man in the most terrifying manner, and if the utopian pacifist or conscientious objector imagines he is superior to his fellow-men and that he cannot go to war because to do so might stain the whiteness of his soul, he is guilty of arrogance and self-deception in so far as he claims exemption not only from the duty of defending his own country but also from the consequences of the Fall.

Whoever lives as member of a collectivity (and who does

not?) and accepts the State (who could do otherwise?) with all its terrible instruments of coercion and intimidation (amongst which the gallows are not, perhaps, the worst, for to many a quick death will be far preferable to lifelong loss of liberty), whoever enjoys the protection, the order, the peace, and the freedom that are maintained with the help of these fearful instruments, cannot consistently or in common honor refuse to do his share when the collectivity is compelled to fight for its existence.

It is conceivable that a genuine patriot may desire the defeat of his own country if defeat means the frustration of a war undertaken not in the interests of country but of faction, or in fulfillment of a tyrant's irresponsible wishes. But when war threatens the security, the general welfare, or the independence of a nation, then there is no alternative—defeat has to be averted, no matter by whose fault the war may have begun.

Some contempt has been poured on the phrase "right or wrong, my country," but the phrase implies love of truth as well as love of country. That it should have received currency in England is a high tribute to the English character. Can we imagine the youthful Russian of today, the National Socialist, or the Fascist admitting for one moment that his country might conceivably be wrong?

To know that their country may be wrong, and yet to take part in its defense when its independence is endangered, will be the attitude of all who still love truth and country if the threatening judgment of another European war descends upon our generation.

To the English, war, until 1914, was something that happened abroad (as revolution is still). The Great War was new to their experience. But to the French and Germans it was nothing new—war is something with which they have reckoned in the past and must reckon with in the future, much as the Jews must reckon with persecution. To the French and the Germans, war is part of a tragic national destiny—just as persecution is to the Jews.

To none did the Great War seem more monstrous, iniquitous, and irrational than to the English. To them it was not in the nature of things, as it was to the French and Germans. To the English it was a terrible and abnormal irruption into their peace, the Pax Britannica. And nowhere has the belief that war can and must be abolished been so fervent as in England.

The modern effort to establish universal peace is perhaps for this reason mainly an English effort. After the armistice, the English experienced a prodigious revulsion against war. But they also felt an island security that could no longer be menaced, seeing that the German fleet had been destroyed. Their pacifism acquired a messianic character—they were less concerned with saving their fellow-countrymen than with saving all mankind from war. Their own security made them more accessible than any other nations to utopian dreams of universal peace—and blinder to the danger inherent in such utopian dreams.

The revulsion against war immensely increased the volume and influence of the political "Left." Men of letters, attracted by the facility with which utopian dreams of international peace can be popularized, took to politics or to political writing, under the illusion that such dreams are the substance of politics.

Pacifism was at first a profoundly humanitarian revolt of the outraged conscience against war and hatred between nations. It had a noble literature, beginning with the marvelous poetry of Wilfred Owen and Isaac Rosenberg.[11] But it became a political and literary fashion. It was exploited for vote-catching, first by the "Left" and then by the "Right." Peace was no longer a precious heritage, hard won and hard to preserve, even within its greatest stronghold, the British Commonwealth. It became a messianic abstraction to be imposed upon the entire world by every known form of coercion from economic and financial boycott to actual warfare.

Monstrous proposals, like the proposal to create an international air force that would emerge—from some Alpine stronghold, presumably—and bomb the cities of the alleged aggressor, found a considerable following in the post-war years. Such inhuman phantasmagoria had an affinity with the secular religions of the European continent. Indeed, English militant pacifism had something in common with the Marxian dreams of a universal realm of peace, justice, and wellbeing. As we have seen, the Kingdom of Heaven on Earth is inseparable from its own opposite. It can only come about by violence. It contains a contradiction that was irremediably established by the Fall.[12]

The threat of universal war as a means of establishing universal peace is a peculiarly English conception that has crystallized in the doctrine of "sanctions." [13] This doctrine is analogous to the doctrine of the proletarian dictatorship which would establish social peace by making class-war permanent and universal. "Sanctions" are the counterpart of the revolutionary terror—the purpose of either is peace, but the effect of both is the consolidation, through war or the threat of war (whether between classes or nations), of power in the hands of those who hold it.

The Covenant of the League embodies the doctrine only in a diluted form. Had this not been so, the League could hardly have survived the Far Eastern conflict of 1931, and perhaps not even the "Corfu incident" of 1923. But even in its diluted form the doctrine, so far from strengthening the League, is the main source of its weakness.

We shall return to the League of Nations in a later chapter. Let us, meanwhile, examine the doctrine of "sanctions" more closely. We have touched on the difficulty—indeed, the impossibility—of defining the aggressor.

The purpose of ordinary warfare is to defeat the armed

forces of the enemy. It is urged in defense of "sanctions" that they are unwarlike. Before there is any resort to arms, a general boycott (as prescribed by Article 16 of the Covenant) is attempted. There is economic and financial pressure and a rupture of commercial and political relations (a method applied, though incompletely, in the abortive attempt to avert the Italian conquest of Abyssinia).

The armed forces of the enemy are to be spared as long as possible, while trade (including the trade of the "sanctionist" Powers with their victim) is to be ruined and the civilian population is to endure shortage, perhaps even hunger. The soldiers shall not be exposed to any danger until the old men, the women, and children have suffered.

A Power resisting the pressure of "sanctions" can keep its armed forces intact, or use them to suppress rebellion amongst a population made desperate by hunger. A despotism will always be better able than a free country to resist "sanctions."

To erect the "punishment of the aggressor" into a general system would be to concentrate immense power into a few hands and establish an abominable and universal tyranny. In nothing is the evil inherent in universal systems of enforced morality more evident than in the doctrine of "sanctions." It was against such systems that Karl Barth uttered one of his great warnings:

"That men should, as a matter of course, claim to possess a higher right over their fellow-men, that they should, as a matter of course, dare to regulate and predetermine almost all their conduct, that those who put forward such a manifestly fraudulent claim should be crowned with a halo of real power and should be capable of requiring obedience and sacrifice as though they had been invested with the authority of God, that the Many should conspire to speak as though they were the One, that a minority or a majority—even the supreme democratic majority of all against one—should assume that they are the community, that a quite fortuitous conduct or arrangement should be regarded as superior to the solid organization of the struggle for existence and should proclaim itself to be the peace which all men yearn after and which all should respect; this whole pseudo-transcendence of an altogether immanent order is the wound that is inflicted by every existing government—even by the best— upon those who are most delicately conscious of what is good and right. The more successfully the good and the right assume concrete form, the more they become evil and wrong—*summum jus, summa injuria.* Supposing the right were to take the form of theocracy, supposing, that is to say, superior spiritual attainment were concreted into an ideal Church and all the peoples of the earth were to put their trust in it; if, for example, the Church of Calvin were to be reformed and broadened out to be the League of Nations—this doing of the supreme right would then become the supreme wrong-doing. This theocratic dream comes abruptly to an end when we discover that it is the Devil who approaches Jesus and offers Him all the kingdoms of this world. It ends also with Dostoevsky's picture of the Grand Inquisitor. Men have no right to possess objective right over other men. And so, the more they surround themselves with objectivity, the greater is the wrong they inflict upon others." [14]

But let us examine the doctrine of "sanctions" as a *practical* means of preventing war by the coercion of all warmakers. Even if "sanctions" operate with a maximum of injustice to individuals, even if the suffering they inflict falls more heavily on the weak and helpless than the suffering inflicted by actual warfare, will not the evil they do be trivial compared with the supreme evil of war itself? Will not all the woe, the deprivation, and the injustice be worth while if war is abolished forever?

There is no reason to suppose that a universal system of "sanctions" would abolish war even for a time. One evil would be replaced by a greater evil. Private wars would be abolished—only world wars would be allowed. Local or private wars would be abolished—world wars would replace them. Such a universal system would be a more grievous burden on its own spiritual home, England, than on any other country. Indeed, the very existence of England as a

Great Power within the Commonwealth is incompatible with this doctrine.

Other Powers might perceive—and indeed have perceived—a certain protection for themselves in "sanctionist" systems (such as the "Geneva Protocol"), because an act of aggression committed against them or in their vicinity would be quelled by a world-wide coalition with little danger or sacrifice to themselves, whereas an act of aggression, committed far away, would concern them little, by reason of their inability to take part in collective action overseas or far away. For example, Russia, if attacked by, say, Germany, would, under a universal system of "sanctions," count on the active support of the British Commonwealth, support that might save her from defeat at little cost to herself and at frightful cost to the Commonwealth. The British air force could operate against western Germany and the navy against the German trade routes of the North Sea and Baltic coasts. But if Germany were to attack England, Russia would be unable to give effective help. Italy could strike at Russia by denying the Mediterranean to Russian trade. Russia cannot strike at Italy unaided.

Italy and France have little effective power in the Far East, Japan has none in the Baltic, Germany none in the Middle East, and so on. But England, with vital interests throughout the world, with all the high seas as her frontier, and with a reach extending all over the globe, has effective power everywhere. She would have to take an active part in almost all "sanctionist" wars, including those that would in no way touch her vital interests. All other Powers—including even the other Naval Powers whose reach, in the absence of distant naval bases, does not, like England's, extend over the whole globe—could take an active part in only a few "sanctionist" wars and a major part only in such as were being waged in their own vicinity. Whatever hypothetic conflict we examine, we shall nearly always find that the burden of "sanctions" would be least in the vital interest of England while demanding from her the greatest sacrifice.

A universal system of "sanctions" could always be defied by one Power or another. The coercion of Russia will always be difficult, no matter how numerous her foes. But if England were to be the victim of "sanctionist" pressure, her defeat would be swift and certain.

Vulnerable everywhere and dependent for bare subsistence on supplies from across the sea, she would be altogether at the mercy of any world-wide hostile coalition. Such a coalition could reduce her to surrender merely by putting an end to her foreign trade.[15] Russia might hold out indefinitely against a universal boycott, Germany could hold out for many months or years (she would increase her sources of supply by pushing her fronts far into Poland, Russia, or Rumania as she did in the Great War). England could hold out only for a few weeks.

A universal system of "sanctions" could never equitably distribute the burden of maintaining the world's peace. Such a system would never make universal disarmament possible. On the contrary, it demands a colossal increase in armaments. And England, in particular, would have to rearm far more heavily than she is rearming now (so heavily, indeed, that she would have to accept a far lower standard of national well-being, and perhaps have to establish some form of War Communism). Other Powers would have to arm against their neighbors—England against the world. She is now undertaking limited and regional commitments in defense of her vital interests, whereas under a universal system of "sanctions" she would undertake unlimited commitments to defend interests not her own.

A universal system of "sanctions" would menace the British Commonwealth with disruption. Nor would the "aggressor" be quelled. On the contrary, "sanctions," if enforced against any Great Power, would leave the victors so weakened that, although one aggressor may have been stricken, all the would-be aggressors in the world would have their long-desired opportunity (while the stricken aggressor would prepare for vengeance). Under a universal system of "sanctions," not peace but Caesar and Attila would prevail. The doctrine of "sanctions" is an attempt to satisfy the human craving to establish the Kingdom of Heaven on Earth. It is one of the great modern myths, like Marxism and National Socialism, in which modern man, aspiring to that Heaven, threatens to convert that Earth into a Hell. *Summum jus, summa injuria!*

CHAPTER VIII

England's vulnerability—Her dependence on armed strength—Her widespread interests and responsibilities—A "World Power or nothing"—Her lack of security—The limitation of her power—"Sanctions" against Japan in 1931—And against Italy in 1935—The logical conclusion of the "sanctionist" policy—Possible consequences of that conclusion—The ethics of the right to declare war for a principle—The decision to abandon "sanctions" against Italy—The results of that decision—The rebirth of Pan-Germanism—England's position in the year 1938—The case of Austria—The *casus belli* for England—Aspects of German expansion in Central and Eastern Europe—What policy is demanded by English interests?—The Italian problem in relation to the German problem—England and the Mediterranean—The policy of "non-intervention" in Spain—The real nature of that policy—The significance of the Spanish Civil War.

ENGLAND is the only Great Power exposed to the permanent danger of total and *permanent* defeat in war.

The United States have absolute security. They are exposed neither to blockade, nor invasion, nor attack from the air. Not one of their vital interests can be menaced. Unless their whole fleet engages in some rash enterprise far from its bases, they are safe from major defeat. And even major defeat would not expose them to conquest by a foreign foe. The United States can never be less than a Great Power.

France, Germany, and Russia can be defeated. They can be deprived of territory. But they will always *exist*. If they are dismembered, they will, in time, recover their national unity. If they are submerged as Great Powers, they will re-emerge. They are vulnerable but indestructible. They can never be less than potential Great Powers.

Of all the Great Powers, England is the most vulnerable. On her armed strength depend her own *existence*—and the existence of others.

She can never share the enviable state of the small countries on the north-western fringe of Europe. Without her, these countries would be threatened with extinction. If it were not for the British command of the sea, Holland would be absorbed by Germany, and her colonial empire would be at the mercy of Japan. It is very doubtful whether Denmark would exist at all if she were not situated on the fringe of the Pax Britannica. Norway and Sweden have a certain security in their remoteness—but the security of Norway, at least, is made doubly secure because England could not tolerate an alien conquest or penetration that would give a foreign navy the use of the Norwegian coast.

Belgium cannot exist as an independent nation without England and France. It is not even sure that Swiss independance would survive if the Swiss had not the French for neighbors and the French had not the English for allies.

Whatever is left of freedom and of the Graeco-Roman heritage in Europe now, it cannot survive without a strong England in association with a strong France.

More, even than this: wherever, amid the collapse of higher civilization in Europe, there are stirrings of a rebirth, wherever in Germany and Italy men and women aspire to restore the justice and balance, and the freedom of the religious conscience and of the inquiring spirit—there the hope is in England and in France.

England is not merely a Great Power—she is the only World Power. The United States, Japan, Russia, Germany, Italy, and France are Great Powers in one continent or in two, and Minor Powers in a third, but England is a Great Power in *all* continents and on *all* seas.[1]

Hitler's "World Power or nothing"[2] is not true of Germany. She can be a Great Power without being a World Power. She can be neither a Great Power nor a World Power and yet be something (she was neither when she was a Republic).

"World Power or nothing" is true of England alone. She cannot exist without overseas markets and investments. She is dependent on precariously established economic and political adjustments all over the world. She is more sensitive than any other country to events in the remotest regions. She is more vulnerable than any other because she is vulnerable *everywhere*. She can be destroyed without actual warfare—by boycott, by economic "sanctions," or even by protection.

If she were to sacrifice her vital interest in any one continent, the least that would follow would be the dissolution or partial dissolution of the Commonwealth. This in itself would be a disaster. If it were followed by conflict between the members of the Commonwealth and the end of the Pax Britannica, it would be the greatest disaster suffered by mankind since the collapse of the Pax Romana.

Of all Powers, England has the longest lines of communication, lines so exposed that she has to exercise permanent vigilance in their defense. And on these lines she is dependent, not only for greatness, but for existence.

No other Power could be reduced to unconditional surrender by the loss of a single battle.[3] Had the German fleet been destroyed off Jutland, the course of the Great War would not have been affected. Had the British fleet been destroyed, Germany might have won the war. She would have made herself master of Europe, and England would have ceased, irretrievably, to be not only a Great Power but a Power of any sort.

The war created new States and destroyed none. Even if France had been defeated, she would have continued to exist —in narrower frontiers, no doubt, but she would still have been France, and Paris would still have been Paris. But if England had been defeated London would no longer be London.

Russia, Germany, and France can be invaded and their capitals can be occupied. But they always remain—today with less territory, tomorrow with more. As long as she holds the command of the sea England cannot be invaded, for she is more than ever an island.[4] But she can be reduced to unconditional surrender without the presence of a single foreign soldier on her soil. Moscow, Berlin, or Paris can be bombed or bombarded into capitulation, but a shell exploding in the hold of any ship with a cargo of grain bound for any English port, is deadlier than a bomb exploding in a London street. And even if the Commonwealth fall apart, Canada, Australia, and South Africa can go on living. England cannot.

Other Powers are only in immediate danger when their frontiers are menaced. Their vigilance is a border vigilance, their armies essentially border patrols. If their frontiers are secure, then they have security.

But England has no frontiers and no security, for her frontiers are the high seas of the whole world and she can be menaced anywhere throughout the world. Japan is an island as England is, but Japan's *security* lies in the length of her overseas communications, whereas England's *insecurity* lies in the length of her communications. The distance, that weakens the reach of British naval power, is Japan's strength. There is no one to challenge Japan in her home waters— England can always be challenged in her home waters. England alone of the Great Powers never had security, and never can have. Her downfall is her end—an end more fearful than any defeat that came upon any country in the Great War.

The least secure of the Great Powers, and with more potential enemies than any other, England is *always* on the edge of doom. Her whole foreign policy is, or ought to be, a cautious, balanced walking on that edge. She cannot with impunity side-step or take long strides, though she may be compelled to react with the utmost force and rapidity of concentration to any violent disequilibrium. Her people have achieved what no others except the Romans have achieved. Nothing compels her to run any risks abroad, except the immediate dangers of a greater risk. And she will always try to mediate and conciliate, for there is no crisis, no danger, anywhere in the world which may not set in motion a series of events which will, in the end, become a danger to herself.

To Italy it matters little if there is a war in the Far East—indeed, she can hope for greater naval strength in the Mediterranean as a result of a British naval concentration at Singapore. To Germany it matters little if there is a conflict in the Mediterranean, for if a British fleet is engaged or immobilized between Gibraltar and the Suez Canal and a French army has to be vigilant on the Italian (and, possibly, the Spanish) frontier, she will be all the stronger in the North Sea and all the more able to parry any attempt to restrain her from having her will in central and eastern Europe. To Russia, a war between Germany and the Western Powers means the weakening of Germany and, therefore, greater security in Europe (and, therefore, greater security in the Far East). But for England, war anywhere is an immediate or ultimate danger.

English power, however great, is always limited. No matter how strong she is, she can never achieve a security such as the United States enjoys. She *cannot* be *too* strong, and she must always have at least one Great Power for a friend on the Continent, and must in all circumstances have for a friend the United States (as indeed she can, if she does not try to convert that friendship into an alliance, or expect the United States to take risks and make sacrifices equal to hers in defending interests that are much more hers than theirs).

Every order, whether social or international, is a precarious and ever-shifting balance of forces. The strength of England lies mainly in her ability to preserve the balance.

Her power has to be omnipresent, because it may, at any time, have to be concentrated at one end of the world, without prejudice to any eventual concentration at the other end. She must be able to act decisively—and perhaps simultaneously—in the North Sea, in the Low Countries, in the Mediterranean, and in the Far East, while preserving the peace in the Near East and in India, a combined task no other Power has to face or ever had to face—not even ancient Rome, for there was then no menace from the air, the Roman command of the sea was unchallengeable after the defeat of Carthage, and only the legions had a task comparable with that of the British army today.

England's policy must always be empirical. Her reluctance to bind herself in advance, or to make decisions with regard to hypothetical contingencies, has been confirmed by long experience. That reluctance was weakened by the illusions of the post-war period when a false sense of security made her a prey to utopian pacifism.

We have, in a previous chapter, tried to examine the doctrine of "sanctions" and to show that England, the principal exponent in theory and practice of that doctrine, is most endangered by it. After a prodigious rearmament she is hardly strong enough to defend the Pax Britannica. She could take a leading part in the enforcement of peace all over the world (even when her own vital interests are not menaced), only if *all* her moral and material resources were subordinated to one purpose—war. She would have to accept Ludendorff's doctrine of the "totalitarian war."[5] Her own free institutions and her relationship with the rest of the Commonwealth would make it impossible for her to bear this burden, even if her people were determined to bear it (which they will never be). And they would bear it in vain, for no Great Power other than England has any permanent interest in a universal system for the enforcement of peace.

Had the coercion of Japan been attempted in 1931 the consequence might well have been a Japanese victory. Despite Mr. Stimson's assurances, the co-operation of the United States was far from certain, and, even if the United States had co-operated, "economic sanctions" would have been very incomplete, seeing that France, Italy, and a number of other

Powers had no wish to take part in the coercion of a formidable Power with whom they had no quarrel.

The Singapore base had been neglected, there was no possibility of defending Shanghai or even Hong-Kong, and the immense distances, that determine naval strategy in the Pacific, excluded Anglo-American operations against the Japanese fleet.

Ineffective "sanctions" would have given Japan the victory. Had "sanctions" but begun to take effect, Japan would certainly have replied by an offensive on land, on the sea, and in the air. The *chances* of victory would have been with her (like Mussolini later on, she would perhaps have preferred to go down gloriously before a numerically superior armed coalition, than have surrendered ingloriously to slow economic strangulation). And in any case, no victory, whether for her or her enemies, would have been possible without death and wounds, and a ruin and dislocation that would have widened and deepened the universal economic crisis that was growing sufficiently disastrous even without a Far Eastern war.

England rightly shrank from an enterprise that might, at the worst, have destroyed her as a Far Eastern Power and left her with a crippled fleet.

In 1935 she attempted what she had refrained from attempting in 1931.

By going to war with Abyssinia, a fellow-member, Italy violated the Covenant of the League. The coercion of Italy, unlike the coercion of Japan, was physically possible, for not only were more than fifty Powers, led by England, prepared to co-operate against her, she was also within easy striking distance (as Japan was not).

The British Government were fully aware that utopian pacifism had a strong hold on the public.[6] There was a widespread sense of outrage over a war of indubitable aggression waged by a powerful State with modern weapons against a weak, unorganized, and almost unarmed people. The sense of outrage was inflamed by the gross truculence of Mussolini's speeches, and by his personal appearance as presented to the public view in frequent caricature and photograph— the scowling eyes, and the massive protruding jaw, and the arrogant posturing.[7] Many of those who supported the "sanctionist" policy of the British Government were inspired by a generous indignation and a resolve to see international law vindicated just for once.

England had no direct quarrel with Italy, whose conquest of Abyssinia menaced no vital British interest. Nor had the other fifty Powers that took part in "sanctions" a direct or material interest in the conflict. France, who had, after a long and difficult diplomatic effort, eased the tension that had for years existed between herself and Italy, felt a profound reluctance to break with a neighbor, a newly found friend, and a potential ally, over a colonial war which, before the existence of the Covenant, would have called for no interference of any kind. But France was neither able nor willing to antagonize England. She therefore took part in "sanctions," while using all her influence to keep them as innocuous as possible in the hope that Italy would not be antagonized either. Laval, a man of natural flexibility and astuteness, had to twist and turn. He acquired an international reputation for double-crossing, but at a time when Europe was burdened by principles so exalted and dangerous as those embodied in the Covenant, and when all statesmen, especially English statesmen, showed such a severe preference for the rigid and the perpendicular, there had to be at least one who could assume the serpentine and the horizontal. Laval was almost universally condemned for his wriggling, but he was animated by a love of country and of peace no less deep than any felt by the statesmen of other nations.

The reason why the other members of the League followed the English lead against Italy did not lie in any particular respect for the Covenant or in any vital objection to the Abyssinian war, but in the precedent that was—apparently—being created. The coalition, organized and led by England at Geneva against Italy, might also operate against the next aggressor. In other words, if, when "sanctions" had been successful, Germany were to make the attack which all Europe dreaded (and still dreads), she would not only find all Europe arrayed against her, but would face England at the head of a world-wide alliance. England, in demanding "sanctions" against Italy, placed herself at the head of a continental alliance for perpetuating the European *status quo* by armed force. She thereby placed herself at the head of a potential anti-German coalition.

The coercion of Italy was possible. But was it possible without war? The economic "sanctions" that had been enforced were not a deterrent, but they would have become so if an embargo had been placed on oil (Mussolini left no doubt that he would regard the "oil sanction" as an act of war). Italian communications with Abyssinia could have been severed by the closing of the Suez Canal (a procedure of doubtful legality).

Had the "sanctionist" Powers been resolved to act regardless of the consequences, they could have compelled Italy to capitulate within a very short time. But France and England, at least, could not disregard the consequences. If Mussolini had been placed before the alternative of capitulating gloriously or ingloriously, he might have preferred the former. That is to say, rather than abandon the Abyssinian campaign (which might have meant his downfall at home), he would have attacked the British fleet in the Mediterranean and have endured a kind of Thermopylae at the hands of an immensely superior armed coalition led by the mighty British Empire.

The British fleet, although present in great strength, was in an unfavorable strategic position, the Mediterranean bases having been neglected in so far as they had not been made to keep pace with the expansion of Italian sea-power. The victory of the combined British and French fleets would have been as certain as anything can be in war, but their losses, especially the British losses, might have been heavy ("sanctions" meant, as they must habitually mean, that England had to make the greatest sacrifice in men, material, and money).

It was at the height of the combined effort to coerce Italy that the British Foreign Secretary, Sir Samuel Hoare, made his celebrated speech. The essential passage deserves quotation because it is a masterly statement of everything British foreign policy ought *never* to be:

"In conformity with its precise and explicit obligations, the League stands, and my country stands with it, for the collective maintenance of the Covenant in its entirety, and particularly for *steady and collective resistance to all acts of unprovoked aggression*. The attitude of the British nation in the last few weeks has clearly demonstrated the fact that this is *no variable and unreliable sentiment,* but a *principle of international conduct* to which they and their Government hold with firm, enduring, and universal persistence." [8]

No Government in the world has the right to declare war for a principle. The principles for which nations fight are rarely found to have any objective validity when they are examined in a critical spirit. They are, very often, sentiments and opinions derived from current popular philosophies, shreds of history, and emotions of the moment. Sometimes they will serve to conceal more tangible aims. It will often be found that the true war aims of a power are rational, whereas the "principles" for which the war is ostensibly waged ("principles" put forward to justify it in the eyes of the world) are irrational. The principles for which a war is begun will often change in the course of the war and will rarely be those on which the peace is founded. Even material war aims are often transformed by varying opportunity and circumstance while war is still being waged.

The impact of war produces profound psychological changes amongst all the belligerent peoples. War, especially modern war, releases many hidden forces and may transform whole nations in their outlook and their policies by a rapid sequence of unexpected events. It is therefore idle to talk about "steady and collective resistance to all acts of unprovoked aggression," about "sentiments" that are not "variable" and "principles of international conduct which can be held with firm, enduring, and universal persistence."

To provoke aggression is certainly an outrage, but aggression has to be resisted if it menaces a vital interest, whether it has been provoked or not. National sentiment is often unreliable and may vary with varying conditions—to expect anything else is to expect far too much of human nature.

War (whether masquerading as "sanctionist" or not) is a calamity of such an awful kind, and (even when used by a Great Power to coerce a small one) so uncontrollable an instrument, and so full of uncertainty, that any Government committing a country to war, except to defend the lives and the present and future happiness of its people against a mortal danger, deserves to be swept out of existence.[9]

A very strong Power may, it is true, remonstrate or even exercise pressure when another Power commits iniquities too outrageous to be borne with equanimity by decent human beings (the ever-worsening persecution of the Jews in Europe calls for an icier attitude, at the very least, on the part of the Governments of the still civilized Great Powers towards those Governments that are responsible for the persecution). But no Power, however strong, can reconcile a sense of responsibility towards its own people with any warlike risks incurred for the sake of principle.

Sir Samuel Hoare's claims on behalf of his country were

very soon disproved. It was shown that English resistance to "acts of unprovoked aggression" was by no means "steady," and that this "attitude of the British nation" was by no means a "principle" to which they held "with firm, enduring, and universal persistence."

Mussolini was saved by German rearmament, which was rapidly reducing the margin of safety in Europe (a margin already narrowed beyond the danger-point by the utopian belief in disarmament), and by the potential menace of war in the Far East.

Armaments are relative, not absolute.[10] We have in a previous chapter tried to show that universal disarmament would be the end of every civilized order. The disarmament of one Power is the rearmament of another. Germany was disarmed at the end of the war—the disarmament of France and England would have been equivalent to the rearmament of Germany, who, with the small forces left to her, might have attempted as much against the reduced forces of her former foes as she can with her present augmented forces. That is why disarmament, or even a drastic reduction of armaments, was impossible—it would have ended the armistice of November 1918 and have restarted the war.[11]

England reduced her armaments, if not drastically yet considerably, thereby narrowing her margin of safety, all the more so as Italy was becoming a Great Power in the air and on the sea. That England did not keep well ahead of German rearmament was a mistake that condemned her to political passivity when she was menaced in the Mediterranean (she herself having, by her "sanctionist" policy, called for the menace), in the Far East, and then again in the Mediterranean as a result of the Spanish civil war.

The danger of a Mediterranean war was brought nearer by the pressure of "sanctions." Even if the war had been short and victorious, it would have cost a heavy price in destroyed or damaged ships at a time when the German danger made that price too big to pay. Germany might have used the diversion in the Mediterranean to make herself mistress of central Europe, Japan to make herself mistress of the Far East (the naval base at Singapore had not been completed then, and the Chinese were less formidable than they are now).

In politics it is always necessary to anticipate the worst. When the choice had to be made between war in the Mediterranean or the abandonment of the attempt to coerce Italy, the only course consistent with avoiding the worst (although that worst was but a very remote likelihood) had to be taken.

English prestige was lowered, but although it is desirable that England should be held in high honor throughout the world, there are times when a diminished prestige may have its advantages in so far as it will discourage excessive expectations on the part of others. When the attempt to coerce Italy collapsed, all the Powers that hoped England would fight their future battles for them, were compelled to think in terms of self-help. Even England, passing through the disillusionment which her own policy had brought upon her, shook off many utopian dreams and prepared to meet the tangible dangers that began to threaten her existence.

The attempt to coerce Italy drove her into coalition with Germany, thereby augmenting the strength of Germany (and, therefore, of Japan). Although no attempt was made to coerce Japan in 1931, even the remote menace of "sanctions" (which were demanded by an influential opinion in England) and the neglect of the Singapore base deepened Anglo-Japanese antagonism (nothing is so conducive to foreign enmity as a threatening attitude combined with insufficient armed strength to translate that attitude into action).

The armed preponderance of France and her allies after the Great War gave western Europe and, above all, England, a relatively tranquil period in which utopian pacifism was able to flourish. That period could not last. In Germany, it was not utopian pacifism but the foundation of national unity that was strengthened, and in that foundation the Pan-German movement was reborn. The tranquil post-war period might also have been an opportunity for the small nations of central and eastern Europe to consolidate—but that opportunity was missed. It is, to some extent, being taken now, but now may be too late.[12]

The rearmament of Germany brought the armistice of November 1918 to an end. The first tangible consequence was the rebirth of the Anglo-French alliance. The second was the withdrawal of the British naval reinforcements from the Mediterranean, the victory of Mussolini in the "sanctionist" war, and the collapse of the doctrine of "sanctions."

The year 1938 is certainly one of dangers ahead, but also of dangers avoided and averted. England's armament is still insufficient for her needs. Her failure to rearm in time (a failure that left London exposed to attack from the air) has largely been made good by the accelerated rearmament of the present year. The security of western Europe, menaced by the German reoccupation of the Rhineland, has been partly re-established by the Anglo-French alliance.

Not so the security of central and eastern Europe. The fate of Germany's southern and eastern neighbors can never be a matter of indifference to England. A German attack on France, Belgium, or Holland is a *casus belli* for England, because the eastern frontier of all these Powers are her own strategic frontiers. She has to defend them in sheer self-defense.[13]

The union of Germany and Austria [14] is not a direct menace to the security of England, and is, therefore, not an immediate *casus belli*. Nevertheless, the question of Austrian independence cannot be considered *in vacuo*, as though it were of no more than academic or, at best, a humanitarian interest of England's. To say that the independence of Austria is "not our business" is as unpolitical as to say that we must defend her against aggression in all circumstances.

A change in the international status of Austria would begin a sequence of events that might, by altering the balance of power in Europe, become a matter of vital concern to England. For England to commit herself to the defense of Austria is to commit herself to war with Germany. Such a commitment, undertaken to avert an event merely because it *might*, in the course of years, create a situation dangerous to England, would be political lunacy. But it would be a very big political error to relinquish *all* influence over a sequence of events that might, in the end, threaten a vital interest.

England's general interest is in the national independence of existing States within their present frontiers and, therefore, in the European *status quo*. But that interest is not so vital that she can make *every* change in that status a *casus belli*. Indeed no change in the territorial status anywhere in Europe, except in the west and in the Mediterranean area, can be a *casus belli* for England. But so delicate is the European equilibrium and so far-reaching may the consequences be if it is upset, that *any* territorial change anywhere in Europe may, by involving other Powers (especially France), lead to a situation so full of danger that she must always reserve to herself the possibility of intervening in defense of her vital interests.

Nor is the question purely political. The triumph of the militant, imperialistic Powers would promote the spread of protection and of tied economies. German expansion in central and eastern Europe would extend the area of German "self-sufficiency." Wherever Germany achieves political domination, or even a decisive political and commercial influence, tariffs and systems of quotas, subsidies and of import and export licenses are promoted to the advantage of Germany and to the exclusion of other countries.

Loss of trade in an area so extensive as the prospective

Pan-German Empire and the zones of German ascendancy influence beyond the borders of that Empire would be a very serious matter for England.

German political and commercial ascendancy and influence will be exclusive as long as the Third Realm retains its present nature. Foreign trade will be reserved for Germany and positions of influence for German subjects. The German people as a whole may not be the gainers, for some, at least, of the coveted regions are densely populated and have poor natural resources, so that German wealth per head of population may not increase (or may even diminish).

In the regions where the Third Realm will have established its ascendancy, a privileged class (chiefly—or perhaps exclusively—members of the National Socialist Party) will provide governors, administrators, concessionaires, managers, officials, experts, technicians, and so on. German domination over Slav peoples will leave the poorer vassal population in its poverty and reduce the wealthier amongst the vassal population to poverty, while German newcomers will form a kind of élite or "bourgeoisie," who will be the instruments of an exclusive political and commercial and military tutelage or domination.

The policy demanded by English interests is neither one of intervention nor of aloofness. It is for England to defend commercial and political interests everywhere by severely empirical methods, above all by amicable bargaining and by mediation (accompanied by pressure only when pressure is an absolute necessity), for the purpose of perpetuating the balance of general or local political and commercial forces and interests.

While avoiding direct intervention in the affairs of central and eastern Europe, she must always be able to impinge on the central and eastern European situation, using her influence and her good offices to preserve the *status quo*. A general anti-German policy would be excessively dangerous and costly. Any general coercive system would be fatal to England if it were to dominate her policy. Isolation would be no less fatal. Her path must run clear of a utopian universalism and an equally utopian isolationism.

It is for England to distrust all political abstractions and all utopian systems, to have a *bias* in favor of detachment and isolation and against all alliances, coalitions, and commitments, but to shun doctrinaire isolation, and to conclude alliances, join coalitions, and take on commitments whenever the defense of her vital interests leaves no alternative (the Anglo-French alliance is an absolute necessity for the defense of her supreme interest—her island security).

The "German problem" has been reinforced and made more dangerous by the "Italian problem."

The *material* interests of Italy and England are not in conflict. But Italy—or rather Mussolini—has aspirations which are incompatible with interests vital to the Commonwealth. Both England and Italy are interested in the freedom and security of the Mediterranean. The Italian interest is immediate and absolute. The English interest is ultimate and relative—but nevertheless vital. England could endure the closing of the Mediterranean for a time—but not for a long time. If Italy secures the permanent command of the Mediterranean, she threatens to control the Straits of Gibraltar, from where she can menace the communications between England and the Cape of Good Hope. If she has the command of the Mediterranean, she threatens to achieve an ascendancy in the Near East that could be extended to the Suez Canal and the Red Sea, from where communications between the Cape and India could be menaced. The problem of the Mediterranean is therefore not confined to that sea. It is also a problem of the Atlantic and Indian Oceans and, therefore, a matter of vital concern to the British Commonwealth.

Italy is not strong enough to play the part of a Great Power except in coalition with other Powers. She is dependent on overseas supplies of iron, coal, oil, and other essential commodities. Strategically she is weak, because she can be confined to her home waters and so be cut off from her main sources of supply and from her colonies by the Power that commands the two entrances to the Mediterranean. She is weak even in her home waters, for even a hostile "fleet in being" would be enough to menace her vital communications.

The Italian problem has no independent existence, as we have tried to show. It exists only by virtue of the German problem. It was German rearmament that saved Italy in Abyssinia. It was German rearmament that enabled her to intervene in the Spanish civil war. It is German rearmament that may give a certain reality to Mussolini's dream of an Italian hegemony in the Mediterranean area.

Italy is maneuvering for position—in Spain and in Libya—so that if there is a general European conflict she may raise her value as an ally in German eyes, and as a neutral (or even as an ally) in French and English eyes. With the main armed forces of France and England immobilized by the German menace, Italy could make a bid for the command of the Mediterranean—or, as in the year 1915, obtain concessions from one or the other belligerent, or prospective belligerent, as the price of her support (or at least of her neutrality).

Germany is strong enough to achieve the aims of her foreign policy without allies, though not without neutrals (she cannot fight the whole world). Italy cannot realize her—or rather Mussolini's—aspirations without the help of Germany.

These aspirations stand in the way of a normal relationship between Italy and England. England is compelled to maintain the balance of power in the Mediterranean, to defend the freedom and security of her Mediterranean communications, and yet to miss no opportunity of bringing the tension between herself and Italy to an end. Even if that tension does not grow worse, it remains a source of weakness to England. Even a potential danger in the Mediterranean, even uncertainty as to the Italian attitude in a general conflict, means that ships, airplanes, and men needed for the defense of vital interests elsewhere are immobilized.

At the moment of writing (February 1938) the Spanish civil war is undecided. That any Great Power should establish itself in Spain is incompatible with the freedom and security of the Mediterranean.

The policy known as "non-intervention" is a weak policy. It is not for that reason a mistaken policy. A strong policy is only right when there is adequate strength behind it. Had the rearmament of England been more timely, access to Spain could have been denied to Italy, Germany, and Russia. Had England been strong enough, there would have been no question of outside interference in the Spanish conflict. But the margin of safety was made so narrow by German rearmament, by the delay in English rearmament, and by German-Italian understanding, that there was no alternative to the policy of non-intervention.

To prevent German and Italian clandestine intervention by force would have meant either a direct challenge to both Powers, or an intervention very much more massive than theirs, for they could, with relatively weak forces, not only tip the balance in favor of the "Rebel" faction,[15] but also deny Russia access to the Governmental or "Loyalist" faction, while large French and British forces would be needed both to maintain the balance in Spain itself and to carry out a blockade, or a naval and aerial patrol, that would prevent German and Italian war material from reaching the Rebel ports.

"Non-intervention" is a misnomer. The policy that goes under that name is really one of limited intervention, for Germany and Italy have intervened by supplying the Rebels with men and material, and Russia and France have intervened similarly, though not so massively, on behalf of the Loyalists. England has kept up the appearance of being a non-interventionist Power, indeed a neutral. But by denying belligerents rights to the Rebel faction (and so making it difficult for the Rebel fleet to blockade the Government ports), by defeating the Italian attempt to wage secret submarine warfare against the shipping that supplied the Spanish Government with essential supplies,[16] and by covering the help given to the Spanish Government by France, England impinged on the Spanish situation in a manner that has told heavily—and perhaps decisively—in favor of the Spanish Government. It was the fear that France and England might regard open intervention in Spain as too great a menace to their vital interests, that kept German and Italian intervention within limits, though these limits have been very elastic. A German-Italian blockade of the Loyalist ports, for example, or the landing of an Italian expeditionary force on Loyalist territory would have been quite easy in themselves and would have broken the resistance of the Spanish Government. The sea-power of France and England, though held severely in the background, has until now prevented Germany and Italy from establishing themselves in Spain and destroying the balance of power in the Mediterranean.

But the Spanish civil war has a deeper and wider significance than can be expressed in terms of material interests. It is a tragedy of hair-raising frightfulness. The war itself would have been frightful enough if the Spaniards—a people as cruel as the Russians—had been left to themselves. But, supplied as they have been by foreign Powers with all the destructive weapons of modern warfare, they have made it doubly frightful, shelling and bombing their own cities, their own men, women, and children, or allowing foreign gunners and aviators to do so. And the war itself is not the worst. Its horror has been exceeded by the horror of the massacres. Tens of thousands of helpless people, young and old, have been murdered by the savage partisans of either side.[17] There has been nothing so abominable in Europe since the Russian

Revolution (the resemblance between the Russian and Spanish revolutions and counter-revolutions is very striking in many respects, and not least in the appalling savagery of either).

The Spanish civil war has revealed the spiritual disunity of Europe. It is a terrible foreboding of the fate that menaces Europe as a whole. It is the rehearsal for the European Holy War, the "War of Ideologies," the war dreamt of so ardently by all the followers of modern secular religions, by all the worshipers of Caesar.

Europe, instead of uniting in common pity to stop it, is divided in ardent partisanship to prolong it. This partisanship is shared by innumerable youthful Englishmen. A whole literature has been produced by writers who had been on "the Spanish tour" and had enjoyed the agony of an entire nation. Sides have been taken as in a football match, and enthusiasm has been inflamed rather than cooled by the cruelty of the spectacle.[18]

The Spanish civil war is a manifold warning, a warning that Hitler and Mussolini will do all in their power to injure the vital interests of England if they can do so with impunity [19]; a warning, above all, that the aims of *German* neo-Imperialism are *not* confined to central and eastern Europe, but that they threaten the Pax Britannica; and a warning of what may come upon all Europe. That the Spanish civil war has aroused more enthusiasm than pity and horror, even in England, is a foreboding of the merciless character of the wars, both international and social, of the future. In Spain a whole civilization is being destroyed before our eyes, no matter who, if anyone, remains the victor. That this spectacle should be applauded (as it is being applauded by the partisans of both sides), even in England, is a warning that Caesar's bloodshot stare is fixed, snake-like, even upon England, and has begun to hypnotize the rising generation.

CHAPTER IX

The protagonists in Spain—The course of the Spanish Civil War—German intervention—Italian aspirations—Mussolini's position—The position of Russia—Trotsky and Stalin—Stalin's personal despotism—The "new Russia"—Its achievements and its failures—England's interest in the balance of power in the Far East—Her vital influence in world politics—Germany her foremost foreign problem—The Pax Europaica can only come through a political balance between England, France, and Germany—The purpose of British foreign policy—The League of Nations—Its achievement—Its failure to achieve the impossible—What the League should be—Anglo-American co-operation—The ideal foreign policy of England—The triangle: London, Washington, Geneva—Unless England is strong...

THE Spanish civil war is chiefly a conflict between revolution and counter-revolution. The Spanish Government are commonly referred to as "Red" and denounced as "Bolshevik" by Hitler and Mussolini. It is true that Russia and the Third International have played a leading part in the revolution, though a big part has also been played by the anarchists and anarcho-syndicalists, a species with which Hitler has very little acquaintance (such intense individualism and such distrust of the State in any form is foreign to the German and Austrian mind, though Mussolini, if he ever reviews his own past, may recall the admiration felt for it).[1]

During the year 1937, the Spanish revolutionary process was not only brought to a standstill, but, to some extent, even reversed by the Spanish Government. The domination of the Communists and the manifold utopian experiments of the anarcho-syndicalists came to an end, and the middle class began to re-emerge.

The Government, who had lost all control over the revolution, reasserted their authority. By the end of 1937 they had become very strong. They were able to subordinate everything to administrative and military efficiency, as well as to sound economics and finance.[2] The three chief leaders—

Prieto, Negrin, and General Rojo—were men of sober understanding and dour character, remarkably free from utopian and messianic leanings. The new army was a disciplined and well-officered force of trained and resolute men.

The Government are strong in this sobriety and also in the popular character of the causes for which they stand—the cause of recently achieved (even if diluted) socialism, and the cause of a nationalism that has become more and more pronounced as Russian and Communist influence has diminished, while the counter-revolutionary forces led by General Franco remain in considerable dependence on their German and Italian auxiliaries.[3]

The ostensible purpose of German intervention in Spain is to "crush Bolshevism." Had it been the real purpose, German intervention could have come to an end. Germany's real purpose is very different. Alone, her association with Italy is an advantage to her. A strong and pro-German Italy will weaken France and England in the Mediterranean—and, therefore, in western Europe and the North Sea. Germany is also interested in Spain as a source of raw material needed for her rearmament. She is also interested in securing a foothold in a region that commands the approaches to the western Mediterranean and gives access to northern Africa and to the Atlantic. By intervening in Spain, she has taken the first step beyond her own frontiers on her way to the achievement of World Power, in accordance with Hitler's doctrine of "World Power or nothing."[4]

Even if she can retain no more than a foothold in Spain (with the outcome of the civil war, perhaps, still uncertain), that foothold, however precarious, is bound to immobilize French and British forces in a general conflict, especially if the attitude of Italy remains in doubt. Anything like German-Italian ascendancy in Spain would be a severe embarrassment to England and France in a general conflict.

Italy's permanent vital interests are, as we have seen, with

France and England, but her present aspirations are not. She has much to fear from Germany, for a German ascendancy in central and south-eastern Europe would exclude her own. German pressure, although not taking any hostile form, is, even now, forcing Italy southward. It has, even now, deprived her of the influence she once had in Austria, so that her aspirations are now being confined to the shores of the Mediterranean and Red Seas. Her unalterable dependence on essential supplies coming by routes that can be menaced by other Powers, her economy that has not yet recovered from the strain of "sanctions" (which, though unsuccessful, were not without effect), by the Abyssinian war and the intractable nature of the less than half-conquered territory, by her costly intervention in the Spanish civil war—all these sources of weakness make it impossible for her to realize her aspirations unless the British Commonwealth and France are themselves weakened, either by a conflict with Germany or by internal crises. And it is by no means sure that Italy can herself avoid an internal crisis that might lead to agrarian revolution, to a kind of communism in the towns, and perhaps to sporadic anarchy accompanied by anti-clerical excesses. A complete reversal of her present foreign and domestic policy [5] would in itself be a crisis, but might be necessary to avert a revolution which would bring Mussolini's personal dictatorship to an end. But he is, above all, audacious, and may, like Achitophel, prefer the greatest hazard of all, namely a general conflict, in which the specific Italian crisis would dissolve in the wider conflict and create a demand for the "strong man" who will defend Italy against a hostile world:

"In friendship false, implacable in hate,
Resolved to ruin or rule the State." [6]

But it is no easy matter to start a general conflict. Mussolini may well wish to see it come—he will hardly move towards it. Russian and Italian vital interests are not in conflict. Until the Abyssinian war, Russia and Italy were on excellent terms, indeed there seemed to be more fellow-feeling between them than between most other States.[7] But in 1935 Russia had to choose, or believed she had to choose, between Italy and England. She chose England for the reasons we have tried to give in a previous chapter—England, as leader of the "sanctionist" coalition (or as Russia herself would have called it, of "the indivisible peace"), became a prospective ally against Germany. For Russia the League of Nations either means nothing at all, or it means an alliance with England and France against Germany and Japan.

The Third International was for years Russia's main instrument of aggression against the rest of the world. Its defeat by Chiang Kai-shek was one of the great defeats in the whole of Russian history, which is exceptionally rich in lost battles. In Germany the Third International, although professing to fight against Hitler, helped him in his struggle against the Republic. It thereby transformed a friendly Power, that would have made a European war against Russia impossible, into the formidable and hostile Third Realm, which proposes to wage precisely such a war. Even in a small, weak country like Esthonia, a neighbor and accessible to Russia but remote from any Powers who might come to her help, the Third International suffered crushing defeat,[8] a defeat altogether typical because it was ignominious, because it could have been foreseen, and because the conflict arose not out of the realities of the situation, but on the Marxian abstractions as interpreted by the infallible Muscovite papacy.

Where the Communist parties were not strong enough to instigate armed risings, they contented themselves with disruptive activities within the labor movements. Everywhere, without exception, they galvanized the Right into fiercer energy, while weakening the Left by injecting confusion of purpose and disunity of action. And everywhere they spread Muscovite cynicism and disregard for mercy and truthfulness.

Few Powers can ever have produced so much misery and disaster by interfering with the internal affairs of other countries all over the world as revolutionary Russia and its obsequious instrument, the Third International.

Russia, so far from revolutionizing the world in accordance with Marxian doctrine, became, by her own example and by her policy, a formidable counter-revolutionary force. Wherever revolution began to achieve the smallest success—in Germany, in Austria, in Mexico, and elsewhere—it was immediately subjected to disruptive hostilities, while its leaders were denounced as "reformists," "lackeys of the bourgeoisie," "social Fascists," and so on, by Russia.

All the hatred and fury, all the insults and calumnies, that Hitler has poured upon the Soviet Union are no more than Lenin and his associates (including Stalin, before Hitler had frightened him into respect for the common decencies of international intercourse) poured upon all the civilized countries, and most of all upon England, year after year. But the enmity of Hitler is not impotent—behind it is the greatest military Power in Europe. While it is untrue that Hitler saved Europe, or even Germany, from the danger of Communism (for there never was such a danger, except in so far as the Third International promoted counter-revolution and helped Hitler to victory), it is true that Hitler has compelled Russia to make peace with the rest of the world, peace so extravagant in its humility that in a dozen countries the Communists, under Muscovite tutelage, vie with Conservatives in their veneration for established order (the Third International has become almost fanatical in its support of the Covenant of the League of Nations and the European *status quo*).

Thanks to Hitler, the Spanish revolution was able to count on the support and not (like so many of its predecessors) on the implacable hostility of Russia. For the first time, Russian interference helped both a popular revolution and what was, at least in a formal sense, a constitutional Government.[9]

Russia has an interest in every conflict between Germany and the Western Powers. She lives in fear lest these Powers, England above all, come to terms with Germany. Nothing could suit Russia better than an Anglo-German war. Her conception of the "indivisible peace" is one that conceals the wish to transfer the potential battlefields of Europe from the east to the west. Germany, even if undefeated, would then be weakened for years to come and Russia would have security in Europe.

The Anglo-French policy of "non-intervention" has, until now, not only defeated the German-Italian attempt to secure a foothold in the western Mediterranean, but also the Russian attempt to embroil the Western Powers in a war with Germany.

Within the elastic but nevertheless real limits imposed by "non-intervention," the Soviet Union helped to promote the interests of France and England in Spain. Her intervention contributed heavily—perhaps decisively—towards the freedom and security of the western Mediterranean. For the first time, the revolutionary Russia contributed towards the maintenance of the European order.

Since the Revolution, Russia has stimulated a malignant hatred of England, doing all in her power to injure the interests and prestige of the British Commonwealth throughout the world. But ever since Hitler became the object of her greatest fear, there has been no conflict between her *practical* foreign policy and England's. The rise of Hitler has not eliminated the antagonism between the ultimate aspirations of England and of the Soviet Union, but it has brought this antagonism to an end.

The principal achievement of the Russian Communism is, like that of the German Social Democracy, national. The outside world has associated so-called "Bolshevism" with anarchy and subversion; and, throughout the world, "Bolshevism" has indeed been a force inimical to every liberal and harmonious order. But in Russia it has, despite its destructive and disintegrating tendency, established social and national unity. Through civil war, through foreign intervention, through famine and immense ruin and disruption, Lenin and his associates, and after them Stalin (whom Lenin distrusted profoundly), re-established the unity of a nation vaster, more diverse, and much more a prey to centrifugal forces than Germany. And they not only prevented the State from "withering away," but re-established it in a form more powerful than any that existed before, showing themselves to be better realists than Marxists. They had to sacrifice the western border territories of Russia—Finland, the Baltic States, the eastern regions of Poland, and Bessarabia—because every attempt to recover them would have brought Russia into armed conflict with the western and central European Powers (as the help given by France to Poland in 1920 when the Russian armies reached the outskirts of Warsaw showed). These territories now serve Russia well. With Poland and Rumania, they form a vast "neutral belt," that gives Russia much security against German attack.

Georgia made herself independent of Russia very much as Finland and the Baltic States did. Georgian independence was recognized but not respected by Russia, who had nothing to fear from Turkey (a friendly neighbor), because if she held Georgia, she held one of the great oil supplies of the world.

Russia, therefore, waged what would, in Marxian jargon, be called an "imperialist war," or an "oil war," against Georgia, invading her, overthrowing her Government (in which Social Democrats predominated), and ruthlessly crushing a popular resistance that lasted long after the campaign was over.[10]

Many visitors to Russia have, like Gibbon's philosophers,[11] been disillusioned merely because they found that Russia resembled other countries. By the Marxian standard, the Russian Revolution has certainly failed, as it was bound to fail, because that standard is unattainable by *any* human society. The Russia of today is even further from the Leninist than from the strictly Marxian ideal, for Marx did not stress the "withering away" of the State as Lenin did. In this respect alone the Russia of today is the negation of Lenin's doctrine. Narrow and superficial as Lenin was as a thinker, he had a shrewd human judgment, at least with regard to his collaborators, but even if he did not realize that what he asked of human nature was impossible, he did realize that whatever of his teaching might survive, it would be endangered by Stalin. Marxian teaching is theoretically anti-tyrannical, but Marxian practice is, and always must be, tyrannical, for an abstract system can never be made acceptable to all, but can only be enforced—all attempts to establish the Kingdom of Heaven on Earth must, as we have tried to show in our early chapters, become violent and oppressive as soon as they become serious. The Kingdom of Heaven on Earth is always the Procrustean Bed which can be made to fit mankind only by war, terrorism, the prison, the concentration camp, the firing squad, and the hangman's rope. It is impossible to establish the Kingdom of Heaven on Earth without at the same time establishing the Kingdom of Hell on Earth.

Lenin saw in Stalin a man who was tyrannical by nature and not by reason of the doctrine which Lenin himself did not regard as tyrannical. Lenin knew that Trotsky, for all his faults, was the greater man. Stalin himself recognized Trotsky's services to the Revolution,[12] services that have now been expunged from Russian records with an ingratitude that can have few parallels in history. Lenin's last instructions to the Central Committee of the Russian Communist Party revealed a deep and prophetic disquietude. On the 25th of December 1922 he warned the party against Stalin, who "in becoming Secretary General has concentrated in his hands an immense power, and I am not convinced that he will be able to use it with sufficient prudence." Of Trotsky, Lenin wrote: "He is not only distinguished by the most eminent abilities; he is personally the most able man in the present Central Committee. But he has too much self-assurance and is carried beyond the needful by the purely administrative side of things." On the 4th of January 1923 Lenin wrote: "Stalin is too rough-mannered, and this defect, which is quite tolerable amongst us Communists, becomes intolerable in the function of General Secretary. That is why I propose that the Comrades reflect on the means of replacing Stalin in this post and nominating in his stead a man who, in all respects, is distinguished from Stalin by being superior to him, that is to say, by being more patient, more loyal, more polite, more considerate towards his comrades, less capricious, and so on.

"This may seem a small matter," Lenin continued, "but it may, in view of the relations between Stalin and Trotsky, acquire a decisive importance." [13] It certainly did!

A shallow thinker, ruthless, ambitious, imaginative, a gifted writer, a magical orator, a man of immense energy and powers of organization, impulsive, often witty, irrepressibly romantic, Trotsky is by far the greater man. But his very virtues (rather than his faults) exposed him to defeat at the hands of Stalin, a man of narrow understanding and concentrated malignance, taciturn, a tedious orator, infinitely patient, experienced in slow but sure-maturing conspiracy, mendacious, cunning, calculating, and more ruthless than Lenin and Trotsky put together (monsters of ruthlessness though both of them were), and despising the Russians (Stalin is a Georgian and speaks with a Georgian accent, and his contempt for the Russians recalls the contempt Hitler—an Austrian and speaking with an Austrian accent—feels for the Germans).

The impact of the Russian Revolution, like that of the French, was eastward. No emancipatory influence from Russia radiates through Europe and America. She has long ceased to be the hope of the working classes. She is still as in Tsarist days, the most tyrannically governed of all European countries, although there is far worse tyranny in Europe now than there was before the Great War. "Planning" has not given Russia stability, order, or well-being above so-called "capitalist countries," none of which have been so shaken by economic crises as Russia has. Her early experiments in Communism were such that, great as was the misery of the blockade and of the interventionist war, a greater misery followed. She might be almost self-sufficing—no other Great Power could make itself so independent of general crises as she could. There is not a greater free-trade area in the world, and no other Power has such natural resources. And yet the Russian people were flung from one violent crisis into another. The famine of 1931 was the most frightful European calamity since the Great War (except the great famine of 1921). And it was brought about not by natural causes, but by Marxian politics and economics—and it afflicted one of the richest regions of Russia, the Ukraine, destroying millions of people by starvation.[14]

At the moment of writing (February 1938) Russia is visited by another of her appalling political and economic crises, accompanied by massacres, arrests, and industrial dislocation.

"Planning" is one of the modern superstitions that have been engendered by popular science. Writing of the Russian Five Year Plan,[15] Mr. Julian Huxley declares that "it heralds the birth of a new kind of society, a society which is coherently planned, and has not, like Topsy and the out-of-hand individualisms that constitute our Western nations, 'jest growed.' "

It is precisely the nations that "jest growed" and have not been stretched on the Procrustean rack or suffered the Procrustean mutilation of "planning," that reveal the greatest stability and inner cohesion. "Planning" in Russia has caused immense misery and has always been made to work with the help of executions, jailings, and the other coercive measures (including that atrocious form of "speeding up" known as Stakhanovism) such as no workmen in western Europe or the United States would tolerate. That modern societies require greater control and co-ordination than the societies of old may be true. Some planning there must always be. But the less planning there is, the better. To say of western society that it "jest growed" is as high a compliment as could be paid to any society.

"Planning" has a very powerful appeal as something essentially "scientific," as the application ("for the first time in history") of "scientific" thought and method to human affairs, as the principal instrument for creating a "new society" or a "new civilization." In reality it belongs to the pseudo-scientific myth of the Kingdom of Heaven on Earth.

That Kingdom has, above all, to be new and spectacular. God has been discarded and man, having thrown off his "chains," having freed himself from "capitalism" and from "outworn superstition," has "scientifically planned" and erected the *"new* society" and *"new* civilization." It covers "a sixth of the earth's surface" (as believers proclaim with importunate reiteration) and, year after year, pilgrims visit the Kingdom and return to tell of its glories.

And yet there is little to be said of Russia that is "new" —less perhaps than of most countries. In the perspective of history, the Russian Revolution is seen as an upheaval, differing from its predecessors by reason of its immensity, but, in the end, establishing a new Russia that has reverted to the main characteristics of the old.

All history is tragic, but Russian history is exceptional for the number and violence of revolutionary upheavals, for the long periods of immense passivity, for stagnation alternating with frenzied material progress. Again and again there is a jostling superabundance of every conceivable form of the crudest and sublimest mysticism, of sectarian bigotry and exalted, world-embracing idealism; a prodigious pullulation of cults and superstitions, of every imaginable political and social doctrine (conservative, liberal, reactionary, revolutionary, reformist, anti-Semitic, communistic, nihilistic, Pan-Slav, western, eastern, and what not). The explosive ferment of the Russian world is surrounded by an iron ring of orthodoxy and nationalism. The ring is broken with seismic revolutionary violence, only to be forged afresh in a new orthodoxy and a revived nationalism. Revolution is succeeded by spiritual and material despotism that has no parallel in any other country. The abandonment of religious beliefs is followed by hatred, mockery and persecution of all religion, in the name of the gross materialism in which the religious, political, and social aspirations of man combine so as to be imposed on the once more subjugated, quiescent Russian masses by every imaginable method of ruthless coercion.

In no other country has there been such an alternation of explosive upheaval and of immense passivity or stupor. Even the fluctuating growth of Russian industry expresses not so much the growing material needs of the Russian people as the fluctuations in the national character.

Under Peter the Great, under Catherine II, under Nicholas I, under Alexander III, Russian industry expanded with prodigious momentum, always urged on by the terroristically despotic State in pursuit of a fantastic dream of human bliss but wholly regardless of the cost in human lives and human happiness. And there is always the same arrogance towards the outside world, the same ill-concealed hatred of the foreigner and yet always the dominating presence of foreign ideas (whether it be the enlightenment of the eighteenth century or the Marxism of the nineteenth), and always the aid of imported engineers, experts, soldiers, architects, and so on. Russia has again and again—and long before the Revolution—rivaled the greatest industrial countries in the production of staple commodities. The industrial development of Russia was prodigious under the Romanoffs—it has been resumed with immense energy under Stalin. But real achievement has been concealed and unreal achievement magnified by Russian statistics (for which the Russians have an almost carnal passion). Meaningless percentages are proclaimed to impress the world with the delirious tempo of industrial output. Year in year out material progress is demonstrated by phantasmagoric arrays of uncontrollable figures that are intended to make the industrial output of other countries seem dwarf-like by comparison.

Since the war, the revolution, and the civil wars, and the disastrous experiments in utopian communism—calamities that reduced Russia to unimaginable misery and ruin—there has been progress in material well-being, and the younger generation whose world began with the revolution, whose historical perspective has been falsified by the deliberately distorted presentation of pre-revolutionary and revolutionary history, lives in a world emerging from chaos to order, from penury to relative abundance and hope of greater abundance to come.

But after all the immense sacrifices of the last twenty years, the wars, the fearful massacres, the inner political conflicts, the economic crises of inconceivable violence, the planning, the replanning and the super-planning—after all these, it remains impossible to say whether the Russian "proletariat" in town and country, for whose sake all the effort and sacrifice have ostensibly been made, is any better off in any general sense than it was under the last of the Romanoffs.

The Russian "proletariat" remains, broadly speaking, on the eastern European level, and far worse off, materially and spiritually, than the workmen, peasants, and farm laborers of the west.

Russia has again and again reverted to type (or rediscovered her own soul). The reports of the Elizabethan merchants who visited the court of Ivan the Terrible,[16] ring strangely true at the present day:

> "For as they themselves are very hardly and cruelly dealt with by all their chief majestrates and other superiors, so are they as cruel one towards another, especially over their inferiors and such as are under them. So that the basest and wretchedest Christianoë (as they call him) that stoopeth and croucheth like a dog to the gentleman, and licketh up the dust that lieth at his feet, is an intolerable tyrant where he hath the advantage. By this means the whole country is filled with rapine and murder. They take no account of the life of a man." [17]

The massacres that are now going on in Russia, and the mock trials,[18] serve the double purpose of destroying not only opponents (for there could be few under a terror so efficient and ruthless); not only all rivals, but all potential rivals; not only all those who think differently, but all who might at any time think differently; all who could promote a dissident mood or atmosphere.

Under the ruthless personal despotism of Stalin a sanguinary purge has swept through the officer corps,[19] reducing to subservience a body that might, in time, have exercised considerable political influence. The bureaucracy, and the emergent middle class of party officials, factory managers, foremen, technicians, Marxian journalists, have been similarly oppressed. Between the despot and the vast submerged mass of the Russian people there is no intervening or moderating power. All that is in between has been pulverized by the "purge." The tyrannical character of the socialist State (as foreseen by Nietzsche) and the semi-oriental absolutism of the Russian Tsars over a subservient people, are realized in an immensely concentrated form under the despotism of Stalin.

The permanent Russian passion for orthodoxy has revived in an immensely potent form with the Hammer and Sickle instead of the Cross as its symbol. The revival is accompanied by a renewed nationalism, more centripetal and more intolerant than the old, and by a renewed imperialism.

Russian, like German, Italian, and Japanese nationalism, is militant and imperialistic. But unlike the three other Powers, Russia has vast unexploited territories, so that she is not under the same pressure to expand at the expense of her neighbors (though she has no respect for their independence when she can gain by destroying it). The conquests dreamt of by Hitler, Mussolini, and the Japanese military chiefs, are modest compared with those dreamt of by Lenin and his associates, who aspired to a universal Kingdom, with Moscow as its capital. There cannot be the slightest doubt that if Russia had been strong enough she would have attempted the conquest of the world, not merely by promoting revolution everywhere, but by following revolution up with armed intervention with a view to establishing puppet States, subservient to Moscow but parading as "proletarian dictatorships," in all the countries on her eastern and western borders.

With the vastness of her population and the wealth of her natural resources, Russia might have been master of at least two continents, were it not for the restlessness of her people, their messianism, their inefficiency, and their violent fluctuations from one extreme to another.

The leaders and the admirers of the "new Russia" have only themselves to thank if the Russian achievement is examined more critically than that of other countries. It is they who have set up absolute standards and they cannot, therefore, complain if Russia is judged absolutely. What they claim on behalf of Russia is not true, and never can be true, of *any* human society. In making an impossible claim they condemn themselves to the subterfuge, the evasion, and the disingenuousness that characterizes Communist (no less than Fascist and National Socialist) writings and, indeed, all propaganda which would make "heaven seem hell and hell heaven."

But we must also judge revolutionary Russia by relative

standards and disregard the partisan pretensions made on her behalf. What she is and what she stands for is almost wholly injurious to western civilization. She has spread false standards, cynicism, the grossest superstitions, arrogance, and narrow fanaticism in Europe. But her past and her present reveal not only a land of colossal imposture and terrible wrong and misery, but of spiritual and material achievement. The face of the Soviet Union is much more attractive when seen from the east than when seen from the west.

The achievement of Russian administrators, pioneers, and colonizers is very great indeed. For size and diversity the Soviet Union is second only to the British Commonwealth. The Pax Moscovita has been established, or re-established and reconsolidated, against external attack and internal disruption, from the Black Sea to the Pacific Ocean, from far beyond the Arctic Circle to the Afghan and Persian borders.

The spirit of Yermak and of the other great Russian pioneers and explorers has returned. The Russians of Siberia, a more independent and enterprising race than the Russians of Europe, are rivaling the achievement of the North Americans in an even vaster continent. The Russians are great empire-builders and great colonizers.

As an emancipatory solvent, as a force engendering political and social progress, the Russian revolution has penetrated far and deep amongst the Asiatic peoples. There has been a revival of the eastern and central Asiatic imperialism of the Tsars. Compared with the political systems of Europe, the system established by the Russian revolution is despotic and reactionary, but for Asia the revolution has been the great awakener and modernizer. Although China broke with Russia in 1927, Russian influence and her institutions have had a deep and lasting influence on Chinese life. Turkey and Persia have undergone the same transforming impact, and even India continues to feel it like a tremor beneath the shaken but tenacious and perhaps enduring Pax Britannica.

Whether Russian institutions are better or worse than those of the Asiatic peoples is not the point—the point is that they serve those people in the process of adaptation to changes brought about by the general impact of the western upon the eastern mind, by modern science, industry, and transport, changes that may be good or bad, but make up modern progress and are altogether irresistible.

Like the French revolution the Russian revolution proclaimed internationalism and gave a powerful stimulus to nationalism. Through its internationalism it made all subject and semi-independent races conscious of potential or emergent nationhood.

Along her central Asiatic border she has consolidated her central authority and has imposed a standardized political and economic system. Outer Mongolia, nominally a member of the Chinese Republic, has become a Russian protectorate, and Sinkiang is gradually coming under her tutelage.[20] The Far Eastern imperialism of Russia differs from that of Japan in so far as it is more subtle, more skillful, and more invisible. Her touch, so heavy upon her own people in Europe, is light in the Far East and she has rarely resorted to armed invasion (though it is true that she does not have to overcome organized resistance such as confronts Japan in eastern China, seeing that the regions she is placing under her control are vaster and thinly populated).

Russia has lost the world-wide revolutionary crusade she conducted for years against the Pax Britannica, and, although she still has a deep-seated and perhaps ineradicable instinctive hatred of England, the international situation condemns that hatred to passivity.

She is no longer a menace to the Pax Britannica. The English can afford to wish the Russian people well, to wish that they may recover the depth, the variety, and the brilliance in literature and in thought (and, not least, in religious thought) which they had before the revolution, and that they may achieve some measure of individual freedom.

A weak Russia is not in the interest of the British Commonwealth. The destiny of the Far East depends, above all, on the future of Chinese nationalism. Will it, despite military defeat, prevail against Japan by drawing the Chinese people together in a national unity? Or is Japan destined to be what Rome was to Greece—to exercise a political and administrative domination that will extinguish China as an emergent Great Power, though perhaps saving her revered and ancient civilization for posterity?

England is interested, above all, in the balance of power in the Far East. That balance was destroyed when revolution removed Russia and defeat removed Germany from Far Eastern affairs. The present weakness of Russia and the still embryonic state of Chinese unity give Japan an enormous preponderance. A weak Russia and a disunited China make the balance of power impossible—but it is on this balance that the peace and prosperity of the Far East, and the principle of the open door in China, depend. That balance, even if Russia grows stronger and China more united, is bound to be uneasy because each of the three Powers will feel menaced by the other. The Singapore base enables England to exercise a distant pressure that may contribute towards re-establishing the balance.

England is not only the most vulnerable of all countries. Her downfall would, as we have tried to show, be irretrievable. It would be unalleviated by the charity of her foes, for there would be no charity, seeing that she of all nations is the most hated. For without England, Japan would make herself master of the East Indies (a far richer spoil than Manchuria). Without England, Italy could attempt to achieve mastery of the Mediterranean (while Germany immobilizes or engages the armed forces of France). Without England, Germany would break the power of France and make herself master of all of Europe and gain access to the Atlantic and to Africa.

The hatred which the militant and revolutionary imperialisms feel for England is deepened by envy—envy of her well-being, her balanced social order, her strangely effective political system, her power and, above all, for the Pax Britannica as such. That hatred is further deepened by the awareness that wherever there is opposition to the barbaric despotisms of our day, that opposition sees in England something of what it would like its own country to be some day. Wherever freedom is astir in the bloodshot night of despotism—there England is the distant, shining ideal.

England's most difficult and tragic foreign problem is Germany. England not only stands for all that the Third Realm hates and in the way of all it wants, she is also within striking distance—and is less able to strike than to be struck at, for she is highly vulnerable on the sea and exposed to attack from the air, while Germany is, as we have seen, invulnerable on the sea and far less vulnerable in the air, seeing that she offers a less concentrated target than England does.[21]

If England commands the North Sea she can do no more than put an end to the direct overseas trade between German ports and the outside world. If Germany can successfully challenge her command of the North Sea, she has England at her mercy. But England is not only compelled to remain in command of the North Sea, she also has to maintain the freedom and security of the Atlantic, of the Mediterranean, of the Red Sea, of the Indian Ocean, and of the southern Pacific (a task she shares with France and the United States).

England is, therefore, compelled to have such a naval superiority over the Third Realm that even if she is engaged elsewhere—in the Mediterranean, or in the Far East—she can still be sure of retaining her command of the North Sea. To compensate for her strategic inferiority in the air, she ought to dispose of an air force numerically superior to the air force of the Third Realm. She does not require the command of the air as a matter of life and death as she does of the sea, but she does require security against the bombing of her towns, her dockyards, and her shipping. Anglo-German numerical parity in the air is not good enough, for it is not true parity (only the coefficient of numerical strength and vulnerability is the index of true parity).

True Anglo-German all-round parity would make it impossible for Germany to impose her single will on England or for England to impose her will on Germany. And this is the essential condition of a tolerable political relationship between the two Powers. It will be said that England does not desire to impose her will on Germany, and, indeed, she does not in present circumstances, while there can be no doubt that Germany will, if she can, impose her will on England. But circumstances change, and, even if they did not, Germany would always fear that England would impose her will on her. And in politics whatever is feared, whether real or not, is often identical in effect with what is real.

The German danger is made much more formidable by the peculiar character of the Third Realm, its fervent militancy, its religious imperialism, and its antagonism to the beliefs and aspirations of the English—to their "Weltanschauung." The reality of the danger has been demonstrated, even now, by the intervention of Germany in Spain (an intervention that strikes, and is meant to strike, at one of England's vital interests—her interest in the freedom and security of the Mediterranean and eastern Atlantic), by the German effort to gain a political influence in Portugal (with a similar purpose), by German colonial claims, by the presence of German agents in Palestine,[22] and by the "anti-Comintern Pact." This Pact is an anti-British Pact. Although not an alliance, it expresses the common interest that Germany, Italy, and Japan have, not to strike at Communism, but at the British Commonwealth whenever the absolute weakness or passivity of England make an attack possible.

The Japanese danger, like the Italian, is subordinate to the German. Without Germany, the Italian danger would not exist and the Japanese danger would be excluded from the southern areas of the Far East. But even without Italy and Japan, the German danger, though small, would still be mortal.

Nor is that danger distant. Hitler is at the gates of Vienna, Prague, and Madrid. The fall of Vienna and Prague will weigh the balance of power heavily against England. The fall of Madrid will be a direct menace to her command of the sea. If we consider that any weakening of England in Europe and the western Mediterranean increases the Italian danger in the Near East and the Japanese danger in the Far East, we cannot escape the conclusion that the very existence of the Pax Britannica is challenged.

The principal antithesis in the world today is not between Berlin and Moscow, London or Rome, but between London and Berlin. Without this antithesis, a Pax Europaica or a United Europe would be possible.

The greatest—and perhaps unattainable—political need of Europe today is that a relationship, such as exists between London and Washington, should also exist between London, Paris, *and* Berlin. If England, France, and Germany are united, not in any federation or any centrally directed system, or indeed any system of any kind, but by virtue of a certain fundamental identity of outlook and by a common civilization (no other unity can be real), then *Europe* is united, and the dream of all "good Europeans," the Pax Europaica, will have come true.

The Pax Europaica cannot be achieved by protocols or treaties, by pacts, by alliances, by mutual assistance or by the League of Nations. It can only come about by a spiritual change—in Germany, but also in France and England.

If Germany, France, and England are united, the rest follows—they together would have such an ascendancy in Europe that they would maintain the European peace. They, together, would make European unity, the Pax Europaica.

The problem of the Pax Europaica cannot be a primary object of foreign policy. Foreign policy is, or should be, dominated by the *immediate* demands of the day. To disregard these demands, to neglect the defense of vital interests for the sake of an ideal (for disarmament, the League of Nations, "collective security," international brotherhood, and what not), will never promote European unity but European anarchy, will never establish the Pax Europaica but will make it impossible forever. The Pax Europaica can only come through a political balance between England, France, and Germany, and through an inner harmony between their civilizations.

The European problem can never be solved by any predetermined policy, because no policy can be predetermined, nor can it be solved by any ideal scheme or plan. No solution can be imposed, because the character of the solution (if there is a solution) cannot be known in advance, and may be inscrutable even when it does come (its coming will not be an *event,* but an intangible process).

Politicians and statesmen, members of Parliament, voters and all who make opinion can have and should have a bias in favor of the Pax Europaica, a bias that may even have an influence on policy whenever vital interests allow. But the problem of the Pax Europaica is, above all, *a problem of civilization* and can never be solved or solve itself, without a renewal of the heritage that has come down from Athens, Rome, and Jerusalem.

The *trahison des clercs* is a betrayal of that heritage, an apostasy, an abandonment of religion in favor of secular religion, a rendering unto Caesar of the things which are God's. Even if secular religion has not yet taken *political* form in western Europe, it has eaten deeply into western European civilization. That is the reason why the spiritual change must come in England and in France, as well as in Germany.

The purpose of British foreign policy is, or should be, to promote the well-being, defend the security, and uphold the honor of the British people. Vital interests have to be defended in all circumstances. But beyond the defense of vital interests and without prejudice to them, it should be an object of foreign policy to counteract every warlike trend and to assist in averting situations that may contain the menace of war, for not only is war fearful in itself, but there can, in the modern world, *never* be any certainty that if war begin at one end of the world, it will not spread to the other. But the defense of vital interests must *always* come first.

A true League of Nations is one that is not condemned to become an alliance or an armed coalition. A true League will have no coercive powers of any sort. It will not even have *moral* authority or any sort of authority. A League with coercive powers will always be an arena which the Powers enter "for faction and not for satisfaction," [23] a packed jury, and at least a potential alliance of some Powers against others.

The League of Nations has disappointed its more ardent supporters because, although it has been in existence for almost twenty years, wars still go on. Its failure has helped to obscure its immensely beneficent secondary functions. The League is a universal Ministry of Health. It is helping powerfully to fight the traffic in drugs and women. Its International Labor Office is helping to improve factory legislation all over the world. It has given financial aid to Austria. It has settled 1,400,000 refugees in Greece and has arranged the exchange of Greek, Turkish, and Bulgarian populations. It has supplied advisers and experts to China and other countries in need of them. These, and its other secondary functions, have increased the happiness of many millions of human beings. They alone would justify its continued existence a hundred times over.

The League has failed to achieve the impossible. Its failure might have been much worse if the Covenant had been theoretically perfect. It is precisely the *defects* of the Covenant that have saved the League. The vagueness and elasticity of the Covenant and the loopholes (above all the famous "gap" which utopian pacifists have so misguidedly wanted to close) have made it possible for the Powers on the Council to stretch a point here and there, and to escape from obligations that would have committed them to disastrous coercive action under a more rigid and theoretically perfect system.

There is no universal remedy for war. No League of Nations, indeed no system that man can devise, will remove the causes of war, because these causes are inscrutable. They lie deep in the nature of man, and not in any specific economic or political system (though some systems may be more conducive to wars than others).

England may do much to avert this or that prospective war. By being strong and by having a sound foreign policy she may be able to keep war at a distance. While the League cannot prevent wars, it can, nevertheless, be the instrument of a civilized and pacific diplomacy.

The League should be a kind of clearing-house for all international disputes. It should be a permanent conference of ambassadors, a conference where the policies of the Powers who wish to avert an apparently impending conflict may be collated. It should represent an improved diplomatic technique. A true League will not cease to operate, even when war has broken out. On the contrary, it is of the utmost importance that representatives of precisely those Powers that are at war with one another should continue to meet and probe and discuss the possibility of bringing the war to an end. If the League is to help in promoting the cause of peace, it must do so in war-time no less than in peace-time.

The coercive powers embodied in the Covenant have made it impossible for the United States to become, and for Germany, Italy, and Japan to remain, members of the League. No sovereign States will be members of a society that threatens them with war (even if the war masquerades as "sanctions"), but will endeavor to form a defensive—or even an offensive—society of their own, or a counter-League (the "anti-Comintern Pact" is directed against the League of Nations as well as against the British Commonwealth). Nor will any States remain members if they are to be the object of moral reprobation. In few disputes, if any, is right all on one side and wrong all on the other, and no tribunal devised by man could conceivably be qualified to give a final and universally authoritative decision as between right and wrong in all international conflicts.

It is the strength and inviolable security of the United States that make it possible for them to show an exalted idealism in their conduct of affairs (an idealism made all the more real by the natural generosity of Americans). And yet they are freer than any others of the Great Powers from the desire to impose their ideals on others.

England is less fortunately situated. But thanks to her status as the *only* World Power, thanks to her harmonious relationship with the United States, and thanks to her insular detachment (though her people are among the least insular in the world),[24] she is destined to leadership in a true League of Nations.[25]

In a true League she will always be the principal mediator between nations. And she will be so without risk of creating enemies with whom she has no quarrel of her own, and without injury to her own vital interests, a risk that is inseparable from every universal coercive system.

Universal Anglo-American co-operation is not possible, because the interests of England and the United States are different. To expect the United States to support England in every foreign enterprise, even when they have no direct, or no equal, interest in doing so, merely because London and Washington have similar political "ideals," is as presumptuous as it is unrealistic (it is also most injurious to that genuine Anglo-American harmony, which is infinitely precious to the British Commonwealth). But in a true League of Nations, Anglo-American harmony will show itself not in any close political association, least of all in an alliance, but in a common concern for peace and liberty and in mutual good offices of a practical, day to day, informal nature.

No League of Nations can ever be a substitute for policy. The most efficient League that can be devised will never enable England to dispense with her armed strength and her own diplomacy. League or no League, she is compelled to take her *own* precautions against every threat or potential threat to her vital interests.

The terrible "German problem" cannot be "solved" by this or that action or policy. There is only one practical way of dealing with it (which is not the same thing as "solving" it), namely to take all the naval, military, aerial, and diplomatic precautions needed to avert the dangers which the problem contains.

But a great and civilized Power like England should strive for a margin of security big enough to make a certain *bias* in favor of an *ideal* policy possible, a bias that may never show itself in any specific political action but will inform the manner or spirit of her international conduct.

The ideal foreign policy of England can be symbolized by a triangle.

Inexorable necessity compels her and France to be allies, and all who have the welfare of the Commonwealth at heart, who cherish liberty and the civilized European heritage, may well feel a deep affection for France and be thankful that it is she who is the continental ally. But in the Pax Europaica England's principal contact would not be through Paris, nor through Berlin, but through Geneva, the seat of the true League of Nations. The Pax Europaica would not stand in opposition to the Pax Americana (if it did, England could have nothing to do with it). England's principal contact with the world outside the Commonwealth would be through Washington and through Geneva.

The triangle, therefore, is London, Washington, Geneva. Contact with all capitals, certainly, but above all with Washington and Geneva.

This ideal cannot be forced: "What we gain in a free way is better than twice so much in a forced, and will be more truly ours and our posterities'.... That which you have by force, I look upon as nothing." [26]

This ideal cannot even be actively promoted, it cannot be a tangible object of foreign policy. It is a projection, so to speak, of the European consciousness, a consciousness that hardly even exists, save as a kind of sporadic, floating awareness, a dream, an aspiration, though, perhaps, a premonition.

An ideal is a very dangerous thing, dangerous even to itself, for it tends to become its own negation as soon as it is translated into reality. A national ideal is the most dangerous thing of all, for it presupposes a spiritual homogeneity that can never be achieved, save by force, and, when achieved, can never be maintained, save by the despotism of secular religion. A despotic national ideal will always lead to the worship of Caesar. And it is immaterial if the ideal be true or not. Even its truth will be the truth of those "who changed the truth of God into a lie, and worshiped and served the creature more than the Creator." [27]

In their argument with the men of Melos, the Athenians abandoned their own heritage and denied their own greatest glory—their manifold conceptions of Truth, the pride and humility of the critical inquiring intellect, and their sense of a transcendental ethic and of a *mysterium tremendum* in the universe. To the Melians they proclaimed the doctrine that what serves the cause of Athens is not merely expedient but *right,* making themselves the ultimate arbiters of truth and of right and wrong, just as Marx and Lenin and Hitler have declared that whatever serves the cause of the social or national revolution, or the "proletariat" or of the "Aryan race," is right *as such* and that there are no other criteria of right and wrong.

Just as Athenians claimed the right over the men of Melos, so they claimed dominion over the divine order, arrogantly claiming to violate the eschatological limit that is inexorably set on all human endeavor. Their Hybris was secular religion and was in all essentials the secular religion of our day.

The Athenians had sea-power with all its dangers and its blessings—"how great a thing is sea-power."[28] But, as a sea-power, they were vulnerable, as England is today. Their existence depended on their success in maintaining a balance in their inner and outer world (as well as the freedom and security of their overseas communications). They achieved a glory, never surpassed, in the pursuit not of one ideal, but of many ideals. Their end came because they gave way to the Hybris, because they rendered unto Caesar the things which are God's.

The existence of England depends upon her success in the use of sea-power, in maintaining a balance in her world, and it is the whole world—in pursuing many ideals, and in *never* accepting the domination of *one*.

England is in danger. Her spiritual life is threatened by the Hybris of secular religion. Her material existence is menaced by the greatest military power in the world. Unless she is strong, the Third Realm will be to her as Sparta was to Athens, whose fate will be hers.

England lives under the inexorable necessity of being strong in armed defense:

"And nation was destroyed of nation, and city of city, for God did vex them with all adversity.

"Be ye strong, therefore, and let not your hands be weak: for your work shall be rewarded."[29]

NOTES

ABBREVIATIONS

THE complete works of Marx, Engels, and Lenin are of immense bulk, but convenient editions of their more important writings are available. The *Handbook of Marxism,* published by Gollancz, is very convenient for students of Marxism. It contains the whole of the *Communist Manifesto* of 1848 and the *Communist International Program* of 1928. It also contains several complete essays and pamphlets as well as the more important passages from the writings and speeches of Marx, Engels, Lenin, and Stalin.

A convenient edition of Lenin's shorter works has been published under the title of "Little Lenin Library" (referred to below as LLL) by Martin Lawrence, who have also issued an English edition of Adoratsky's *Dialectical Materialism.* Quotations are referred to these sources whenever possible, for the sake of convenience. Quotations from *Mein Kampf* are from the German edition published in 1935 (when Hitler had been Chancellor for two years). The following abbreviations have been used:

ADM— Adoratsky, *Dialectical Materialism.*
HM— *Handbook of Marxism.*
IPC— *International Press Correspondence.*
LFA— Lenin, *Letters from Afar* (LLL).
LR— *Lenin on Religion* (LLL).
LWC— Lenin, *"Left Wing" Communism* (LLL).
MK— Hitler, *Mein Kampf.*
RF— *Die Rote Fahne.*
SR— Lenin, *State and Revolution* (LLL).
TC— Lenin, *The Threatening Catastrophe* (LLL).
TPR— Lenin, *The Tasks of the Proletariat in Our Revolution* (LLL).
WD— Lenin, *What is to be Done?* (LLL).

NOTES TO CHAPTER I

[1] "Without a revolutionary theory there can be no revolutionary movement." Lenin, *What is to be Done? (HM,* p. 585).

[2] Engels, *Anti-Dühring* (*HM*, pp. 265-6).
[3] Karl Barth, *The Doctrine of the Word of God*, English edition, pp. 34-5.
[4] *ibid.*, p. 35.
[5] Master Anthonie Jenkinson, in Hakluyt's Navigators.
[6] The whole wretchedness of "philosophy" in Russia today is revealed in a useful compendium, *Marxism and Modern Thought*, edited by Ralph Fox. The following passage, which ends an essay by Tiumeneff, will suffice as an example of this "philosophy":

"Bourgeois historians have abolished the law of history, but the law discovered by Marx, the law of development of the capitalist system, continues to work and inevitably leads to the collapse of the capitalist system and the establishment of the classless communist society. Bourgeois historians deny history and historical development, but the mole is digging as never before and historical development is moving with such seven-league strides as it never did in any preceding age of history" (p. 319).

The mole unearthed by Marx and, apparently, sent underground again, after having received instruction in dialectical materialism, seems to be a spirited animal to put in seven-league boots and make such furious subterranean progress.

[7] The "theory of mutations" fits the "ideology of the fighting proletariat" more closely than the Darwinian hypothesis. It is therefore closer to Marxian "truth." Darwinism is suspect as being "reformist." "Marxism and Physics," "Marxism and Biology," and the like, are frequent themes of contemporary Russian "philosophers." To the genuine Marxist, thought has no validity except in so far as it serves the purpose of the revolution. "Philosophy is the realm in which he (Lenin), with the art of a true strategist, dragged his opponent and enemy, step by step, into problems of tactics, there to destroy him mercilessly"— these words are to be found in Troyitzky's "Philosophy in the Service of the Revolution" (*Under the Marxist Banner*, 1924, No. 45). Max Werner, in his interesting and important article "Der Sowjetmarxismus" (*Die Gesellschaft*, 1927, vol. ii.), says Troyitzky regards philosophy as "concentrated politics." But this is true not only of Troyitzky, but of all genuine Marxists.

[8] It is easy to find many fundamental similarities between Marxian and National Socialist writings. The following example could be multiplied indefinitely:

"Culture, in the narrower sense, spiritual creation in literature, art, and science, must give expression and direction to the living substance of nationhood ('Volkstum'), raise that substance to visual consciousness and then react with ennobling, formative power on nationhood in the service of its plenary task." (Ernst Krieck, *National Political Education*, p. 22.)

If the word "nationhood" were to be replaced by "the proletariat," this passage might be written by a Soviet "philosopher."

The recent growth of nationalism in Russia has made the resemblance even closer—there is often an almost complete verbal identity between the more portentous leading articles in the *Pravda* and the *Voelkische Beobachter*.

[9] The study of classical philology was abolished by the Soviet Government in 1928. Professor Semenoff, who, until then, was lecturer in Greek at Rostoff, had to publish his *Greek Language and its Evolution* in England.

[10] *ADM*, p. 27.

[11] *SR*, p. 38 (italics in the original).

[12] Swift seems to me the greatest of English utopian realists. The voyage to the Houyhnhnms embodies the truth that Utopia is impossible amongst men, but only amongst creatures which, like the gentle horses, are free from sin. Its lesson is that the Kingdom of Heaven *cannot* be of this World.

[13] So is the land of the Houyhnhnms.

[14] Italics my own.

[15] Quoted in *ADM*, p. 87 (italics in the original).

[16] Brown from the color of the shirt worn by the S.A. (and by Hitler himself).

[17] *HM*, p. 297.

[18] *TC*, p. 62. At the International Socialist Conference which was held at Berne in February 1919, Lenin declared "let the bourgeoisie rage; let them kill thousands of workers.... The victory of the universal Communist revolution is assured." (Lenin, *Collected Works*, English edition, xvi. p. 36.)

[19] Lenin, *Collected Works*, vol. xxv. (1920, Russian edition).

[20] *LWC*, p. 72.

[21] Program of the Communist International, 1928 (*HM*, p. 972, italics my own.)

[22] *LWC*, p. 73 and elsewhere.

[23] The only exception in Lenin's writings that I can discover is in vol. xvii. (German edition):

"Proletarian *culture* must be an ordered further development of the stock of knowledge which humanity has... developed under the yoke of the Capitalists and of the Landowners" (italics my own).

[24] *HM*, p. 988.

[25] The term "peaceful relationships" is placed between inverted commas in the original as a mark of derision—throughout Marxian literature the word "peaceful" always expresses contempt.

[26] *HM*, p. 989.

[27] Quoted by Lenin in *SR*, pp. 30-1 (italics my own).

[28] Were Owen, Lord Shaftesbury, Samuel Plimsoll, and others nothing but "hole-and-corner reformers" who were animated only by the desire "to secure"—in the words of the Communist Manifesto—"the continued existence of bourgeois society"?

[29] Lenin's opinion of the efforts to bring the war to an end was that "peace guarantees" were identical with "social peace" and "the submission of the proletariat to the bourgeoisie, the calming of the proletariat.... Objectively [sic] who will benefit by this peace slogan? It will certainly not help the propaganda on the ideas of the revolutionary proletariat." (*vide, Letters of Lenin*, English edition, published by Chapman & Hall.) Hitler describes his delight at the outbreak of war in *MK*, p. 177, *vide* also p. 87.

[30] This passage has often been quoted by continental Marxists. Presumably it is by Marx himself, but I have not found it in his own writings.

[31] Kluchevsky describes the mockery of religion that went on under the patronage of Peter the Great, who founded an "Imperial College of Drunkards" which met under "Our All-bawling and All-jesting Patriarch of Moscow" and was made up of twelve "Cardinals" and many "Bishops," "Archimandrites," and "other spiritual dignitaries" (who, in each case, bore nicknames which the conditions of our censorship will not allow me to set down in print). There were "All-jesting Mothers Superior and 'Lady Abbots.' At Shrovetide, 1699, the 'Prince Priest' 'quaffed a health to the assembled guests and bade them go upon their knees to receive his blessing,' then 'crossed' them with tobacco pipes in the same manner that the Church's ministers cross genuine congregations... and, lastly, taking 'pastoral staff' in hand, executed a dance. At this point, a foreign ambassador who had been

watching this scene of folly could endure it no more, but precipitately left the company to continue its mocking derision of the Orthodox Church... but as a rule, foreign observers took the view that the aim of the 'Council' enormities was political, and, possibly, popular—educational... and that the movement was directed politically against the Church." Kluchevsky, *History of Russia* (English edition, vol. iv. pp. 36-7).

[32] Marx and Lenin frequently use the term "philistine" to denote a man of narrow prejudice belonging to the middle class or with a "middle-class mentality." The German word "Spiesser" is often used in this sense. There are not English equivalents, though the terms "suburban" and "Victorian" as used by parlor-Bolsheviks convey something of the meaning contained in "philistine" and "Spiesser." The German expression "der kleine Mann"—the "little man"—is used, though not necessarily with contempt, to denote what Marxists call the "petit bourgeois." (English Marxists often use the term "petty bourgeois," a philological monstrosity.)

[33] Early in 1932 Karl Radek told me that he regarded the Brown Shirts (the "S.A.") as a "reserve" from which Communists would be recruited later on. It was the other way about—the German Communists became a reserve from which the Brown Shirts were recruited by the thousand.

[34] Karl Marx, *Capital*, vol. i. ch. 32.

[35] All these expressions and many more can be found throughout Communist writings as late as 1934 or even 1935, when efforts to form a "united front" between Communists and Socialists began to reduce the violence of Communist vituperation.

[36] Marx calls religion "the opium of the people" in his criticism of Hegel's *Philosophy of Law*. The phrase was abundantly used by Lenin and can be found throughout Marxian literature. It is engraved on a wall opposite the shrine of the Iberian Virgin in Moscow. According to the Communist International Program (*HM*, p. 1009) one of the main tasks of "the cultural revolution" is "the task of systematically and unswervingly combating religion—the opium of the people."

[37] Vituperative references to the League of Nations were common in Stalin's speeches and all Communist literature until Russia joined the League in September 1934. In the Communist International Program of 1928 (*HM*, p. 981) the League is described as existing mainly to "strangle the Soviet Proletarian

Republics by war or blockade." When Russia became a member, the Russian press described the League as capitulating before the Soviet Union.

[38] *vide The Times*, 1st April 1935 (article "from our special correspondent" in Moscow).

[39] Friedrich Nietzsche, *Human all too Human*, i. p. 473.

[40] Engels, *Der Ursprung der Familie, des Privateigentums, und des Staates*, passim.

[41] *ibid.*

[42] *SR*, p. 8 ff. (italics in the original).

[43] Lenin quoting Marx (*SR*, p. 9) (italics in original).

[44] *ibid.*

[45] *ibid.*, p. 16.

[46] *ibid.*, p. 66.

[47] In this work (which was first published in 1909) Lenin, quoting that completely discredited "philosopher" Mach, declares: " 'The problem of science can be split into three parts:

'1. The determination of the connection of presentations. This is psychology.

'2. The discovery of the law of the connections of sensations (perceptions). This is physics.

'3. The clear establishment of the laws of the connections of sensations and presentations. This is psycho-physics.

'This is clear enough.' "

Is it?

[48] Lenin, *Materialism and Empirio-Criticism (HM,* p. 672).

[49] Lenin, *The Teaching of Karl Marx (HM,* pp. 544-5).

[50] Lenin, *Materialism and Empirio-Criticism (HM,* p. 673).

[51] *SR*, p. 67. How can the "whole theory of development" (whatever that may be) establish a fact? How can "science as a whole" establish a fact, especially a "fact" so uncertain as the nature of a future epoch in the history of mankind? And all these "facts" are established with "complete exactness."

[52] *SR*, p. 74.

[53] *ibid.* (italics in original).

[54] *ibid.*

[55] *ibid.*, p. 20.

[56] *ibid.*, p. 69.

[57] *ibid.*, p. 21.

[58] In what sense was the Sermon on the Mount the product of the "economic stage" of Palestine in that "particular epoch"?

UNTO CAESAR

[59] Engels, *Anti-Dühring (HM,* p. 299).
[60] *ibid. (HM,* pp. 298-9).
[61] Isaiah 2:4; 11:6-7, cf. Lenin *(SR,* p. 64): "There will vanish all need for force, for the *subjection* of one man to another, and of one part of the population to another, since people will *grow accustomed* to observing the elementary conditions of social existence *without force* and without subjection" (italics in original).

NOTES TO CHAPTER II

[1] *MK,* p. 252.
[2] *MK,* p. 302.
[3] Coleridge, *Table Talk.*
[4] Engels, *Anti-Dühring (HM,* p. 299).
[5] *ibid. (HM,* p. 301). Was Engels unaware of archaeological evidence showing that religion existed before "the capitalist mode of production"?
[6] *ibid. (HM,* p. 301). The ideas of Marx, Engels, and Lenin on religion are on a level with those of the "girl student" in Dostoevsky's *Possessed:* " 'We know ... that the superstition about God came from thunder and lightning.' The girl student rushed into the fray again, staring at Stavrogin with her eyes almost jumping out of her head. 'It's well known that primitive man, scared by thunder and lightning, make a god of the unseen enemy, feeling this weakness before it.' "
[7] Karl Marx, *Capital,* i. 1 *(HM,* p. 421).
[8] The shallow Marxian philistine, Adoratsky, writes *(ADM,* p. 67): "The creation of phantoms *(e.g.* regarding the power of the dead, demons, god, discarnate powers, etc.) is due to various complex causes, chief of which is the dependence of man on circumstances which enslave him, such as national and social forces, and which appears to him to be external and alien. This also explains various religions and faiths." The Devil it does!
[9] *LR,* p. 12.
[10] *ibid.,* p. 13.
[11] *ibid.,* p. 11.
[12] *ibid.,* p. 13.
[13] *ibid.,* p. 12 and also p. 11. It only remains useful to the employers, teaching them "to be 'charitable' "—(Lenin's contemptuous inverted commas are characteristic)—"thus providing a justification for exploitation"—an atheistic employer would,

presumably, have to find another justification—"and, as it were, a cheap ticket to Heaven"—why not to Hell?

[14] *LR*, p. 15. This naïve belief in the power of reason is characteristic of Lenin's superficially rational but fundamentally irrational mind. Faiths that are "irrational" by Marxian standards have persisted for centuries. But Marx discovered *the* Truth —and in the light of this Truth, all religion, superstition, prejudice, or everything except Marxism, will vanish like night at the approach of day. Marxism itself is so devoid of rational content (despite its "scientific" phraseology) that it is hardly worth refuting (to express it is almost enough). But its eclipse has not come about through the reason. That no serious thinker has been, is, or can be a Marxian counts for nothing. Marxism has been overcome not by reason, but by another form of unreason, not by philosophy or science, but by a rival myth, by National Socialism.

[15] Bernard Pares, *Moscow admits a Critic*.

[16] *LR*, p. 45. If religion is "one of the most corrupt things in the world," how can it be "of third-rate importance"?

[17] *LR*, p. 50 (italics in original). When Lenin was in power, and, even more so, under Stalin, accusations of delinquency were fastened upon dissidents or alleged dissidents, precisely because they could then be *"easily* exposed, condemned, and driven out." It is for this reason that the National Socialists have brought accusations of immorality against Roman Catholic priests—making it so much easier to "drive them out."

[18] *LR*, p. 50 (cf. p. 96) (italics my own).

[19] "So far as I am able to judge, the whole essence of the Russian revolutionary idea lies in the negation of honour" (Karmazinov in Dostoevsky's *Possessed*, vol. ii. p. 26, in the Everyman edition).

[20] Matthew xxiii. p. 23.

[21] *LR*, p. 9.

[22] *"Every* defence or justification of the idea of God ... is a justification of reaction ... the idea of God ... has always bound the oppressed *classes* by faith in the divinity to submission to their oppressors." (*LR*, p. 54, italics in original.)

[23] *MK*, pp. 120, 124.

[24] *ibid.*, p. 123.

[25] *ibid.*, pp. 124, 125.

[26] *ibid.*, p. 125.

[27] *ibid.*, p. 127.

[28] The issue in the German religious conflict is perfectly simple. Hitler and his fellow National Socialists have disobeyed, and have ordered others to disobey, the First Commandment. The religious "opposition" is a call to obedience, that and nothing more (this call to obedience runs through all the marvelous literature, the greatest literature, perhaps, of our day, which emanates from the German "Confessional Church" and those Swiss theologians, like Barth and Brunner, who are in sympathy with it).

[29] In the early years of the Soviet Union an abortive attempt was made to establish the so-called "Living Church." This Church observed Christian forms but was subservient to Communism and the Russian Revolution. It was the exact counterpart of the "German Christian" Church which is subservient to National Socialism and the German Revolution. The "Living Church" held its first Congress at Moscow on the 6th August 1922. The Communist writer, "R.A.," described it as "a movement towards the revolutionary regeneration of the Church, a movement which has for its basis, not new religious doctrine, but the adaptation to a new social order" (*IPC*, 1922, 73, p. 552, English edition). Any National Socialist writer might say much the same about the "German Christian" movement today.

[30] Lenin had great contempt for Lunacharski's pseudo-religiosity and for Maxim Gorki's "God-seeking" and "God-creating" (*LR*, p. 50) which resembles pseudo-religious efforts of men like Rosenberg and Hauer.

[31] The persecution of Christianity has been much more inhuman in Russia than in Germany. But that is not the point— the point is, that in Russia Christianity is persecuted, in Germany it is being persecuted *and* corrupted.

[32] *MK*, p. 630.

[33] *ibid.*, p. 130.

[34] The following is a specimen of Hitler's pseudo-philosophical and pseudo-scientific jargon: "Only in our own day does the significance of the laws of race and racial heredity dawn upon mankind. This clear perception ('Erkenntnis') and conscious taking into consideration will serve as the basis for the coming development." (Speech at Nuremberg, *Deutsche Allgemeine Zeitung*, 3rd Sept. 1933.)

[35] Men of the same blood must inhabit the same country— "Gleiches Blut gehört in ein gemeinsames Reich." (*MK*, p. 1.)

[36] "Heaven on earth," as Lenin himself calls it (*LR*, p. 14).
[37] *MK*, p. 630.
[38] *ibid.*, p. 70. Hitler regards himself as the chosen instrument of Divine Providence: "neither threats nor warnings will deter me from my path. With noctambulist certitude I go the way Providence bids me go." (Speech at Munich, 15th March 1936.)
[39] *TC*, p. 37 (italics in original).
[40] He constantly uses the word "Zinsknechtschaft," a term indicating the state of dependence produced by the necessity of paying interest on borrowed capital.
[41] F. Henderson, for example, says that interest is "loot taken from labour" (*vide* his *Money Power and Human Life*). This is very much what Hitler means by "Zinsknechtschaft."
[42] Russia and Germany have each been subjected to a strong egalitarian impulse under the influence of Marxian and National Socialist ideas. But the contrasts between the two countries, though not between the systems that prevail in them, are so great and the circumstances in which these ideas have operated are so different, that any deductions as to which of them has the greater egalitarian force must remain inconclusive.

Russia is a land of far greater poverty than Germany. Inequality amongst the Russian peasant multitude must be much smaller than amongst the German peasantry, who are prosperous by central and eastern European standards. The inequalities of income between skilled and unskilled labor have grown under both Stalin and Hitler. There must be more wealthy individuals in Germany than in Russia. But it would seem that there is greater inequality between the Communist bureaucracy (who make up the new Russian "bourgeoisie") and the Russian people as a whole than between the National Socialist bureaucracy and the German people as a whole.

NOTES TO CHAPTER III

[1] Engels, *Class Struggles in France* (*HM*, p. 91).
[2] cf. p. 61.
[3] "Recht ist, was dem deutschen Volke nützt, und Unrecht, was ihm schadet." (Hitler, quoted by Frank, the German Minister of Justice, at the Congress of German Jurists at Leipzig, 2nd-4th October 1935.)
[4] "Was nicht Rasse ist, ist Spreu."

[5] Sir Thomas Browne, *Religio Medici*.
[6] *MK*, p. 493.
[7] *ibid.*, p. 262.
[8] *ibid.*, p. 504.
[9] *ibid.*, p. 606.
[10] William Blake, *Jerusalem*.
[11] Gardiner, *Civil War*, iii. 143.
[12] Cromwell, *Letters and Speeches*, iii. 340.
[13] Hitler, speech in the Reichstag.
[14] "Perhaps posterity will believe what the nations of the past endured, but never what they listened to in silence. The sword destroys possessions and murders the body; but the word destroys right and murders the soul." (Ludwig Börne, *Letters from Paris*.)
[15] *vide* Boissier, *L'Opposition sous les Césars*.
[16] Plato, *Republic*, 566 ff.
[17] Karl Marx, Address to the Communist League (*HM*, p. 66).
[18] *MK*, p. 149.
[19] *vide* Karl Marx, *The Near Eastern Question*.
[20] *MK*, p. 176-7.
[21] *ibid.*, p. 507.
[22] *ibid.*, p. 371.
[23] *ibid.*, p. 607.
[23a] "etliche Zehntausend," *ibid.*, p. 611.
[24] Speech in the Reichstag, 23rd March 1933.
[25] *ibid.*
[26] *MK*, p. 29. For the effects of the German "sterilization laws," *vide Manchester Guardian*, 30th May 1936.
[27] *SR*, p. 28.
[28] *LWC*, p. 66.
[29] *ibid.*, p. 15.
[30] *MK*, p. 301.
[31] *ibid.*, p. 584.
[32] *ibid.*, p. 589.
[33] *ibid.*, p. 589. Words like these are constantly written about the Soviet Union in the *Voelkische Beobachter* and the *Angriff*, and about present-day Germany in the *Pravda* and *Isvestia*.
[34] *ibid.*, p. 552.
[35] *ibid.*, p. 590.
[36] *ibid.*, p. 597.
[37] *TPR*, p. 21.
[38] *MK*, p. 315.

[39] Lenin, *Socialism and War* (*HM*, p. 686).
[40] *MK*, p. 315.
[41] Milton, *Areopagitica*.
[42] *WD*, p. 14.
[43] *MK*, p. 506.
[44] *ibid.*, p. 473.
[45] The greatest living German writer, Thomas Mann, is one of these—and he is not a Jew. If Einstein had been "Aryan" and had accepted National Socialism, he would *certainly* be paraded as one of the greatest of German scientists in Germany and would have been personally honored by Hitler.
[46] *MK*, p. 468.
[47] Engels, *Anti-Dühring* (*HM*, p. 298). According to Engels, man is still a transition species. This recalls Herman Gauch who, in his notorious *Mein Grundlagen der Rassenforschung*, argues that the Jews are a transition species between man and the lower animals.
Adoratsky, who is a kind of Russian Gauch, writes with characteristic obsequiousness and mendacity that "Lenin was able to contribute something [what?] to the study of natural phenomena. He gave precise indications [where?] of the nature of the errors of the natural scientists [of all of them?]—who are materialists rather by instinct—and showed wherein they deviated from materialism because of their lack of knowledge of dialectics." (*ADM*, p. 65.)
[48] Marx demands the "Dictatorship of the working class" in his *Class Struggles in France* (*HM*, p. 114). Engels uses the expression "Dictatorship of the Proletariat" in his *Civil War in France* (*HM*, p. 171).
[49] *MK*, p. 420.
[50] "Es genügt nicht, dass der Gedanke zu Verwirklichung drängt, die Wirklichkeit muss sich zum Gedanken drängen." Bishop Lightfoot expressed a similar idea when he said that "ideals are prophecies which work their own fulfilment."
[51] Thucydides, *History*, vii. p. 87.
[52] The following are a few of the political and military phenomena commonly regarded as modern, which occur in Thucydides' *History:* Revolution and counter-revolution (iii. 82; viii. 21, 53-4), Insurrection behind the front (v. 14, 23), atrocities (iv. 47-8; vii. 29-30), Terrorism and political assassination (vi. 54, 59, 60), Sham trials for "wrecking activities" (iii. 70—the Corcyrean

"wreckers" showed far more spirit than their Russian successors have shown), Propaganda (iv. 85), Flame-throwers (iv. 100), The importance of sea-power (i. 143), self-determination (iii. 52).

[53] In *Hard Times,* Dickens described the early trade-union movement much as a modern observer with liberal or labor sympathies would describe the beginnings of a Fascist movement. Dickens, apparently, did not foresee that the trade-union movement would, as it grew, become an organic part of the English social order.

[54] Lord Acton.

[55] Especially his marvelous *Weltgeschichtliche Betrachtungen.*

[56] Nietzsche, *Morgenröte,* p. 180.

[57] *MK,* p. 177.

[58] It is very regrettable from Hitler's point of view that Lenin was not a Jew.

[59] A German official who had long personal contact with Hitler once said to me: "The world will never understand him, for it will never understand how small and mean he is." No doubt this is true—but it is only part of the truth. Lenin also combined *concentrated* smallness with greatness. A fellow-revolutionary who knew him very well once said to me of Lenin: "Er war kein anständiger Mensch" (he was without human decency).

[60] "That dismal, sour-tempered old bore, Karl Marx" (St. John Ervine in the *Observer,* 11th October 1931).

[61] Lenin's brother was a member of the terroristic "Narodovoltze." He was executed in 1891, when Lenin was 21 years old.

[62] *LFA,* p. 47.

[63] *SR,* p. 55. This passage is characteristic of Lenin's muddled thinking. How can the merely "possible" be "inevitable"? Are not the "oppressed masses" and the "proletariat" identical? If so, how can the latter guide the former?

[64] *Isvestia,* 4th October 1916.

[65] *ibid.,* 25th October 1918.

[66] *ibid.,* 7th December 1919 (italics my own).

[67] *ibid.,* 7th December 1919.

[68] *LWC,* p. 9.

[69] *ibid.,* p. 57.

[70] *ibid.,* p. 58.

[71] *LWC,* p. 63 (italics in the original). Why cannot they? And how can unavoidable acts be stupid? In the next sentence Lenin

writes: "But our people may do stupid things (provided they are not very serious and are rectified in time), and yet in the last resort they will prove the victors." What if they *are* serious and are *not* rectified in time? Why, in any case, are the blunders of the "bourgeoisie" unavoidable and irreparable and those of the "proletariat" avoidable and reparable?

[72] *LWC*, p. 58.
[73] *ibid.*, p. 77 (italics my own).
[74] Or have they found their fulfillment in the Left Book Club?
[75] *LWC*, p. 77.
[76] *ibid.*, p. 73 (italics in original).
[77] Examples of the Marxian faith that the Millennium is at hand could be multiplied indefinitely. Here are a few from writings and speeches by others than Lenin:

"The proletarian revolution in Austria and Germany will inevitably call forth a revolution in exhausted France and Italy." (Karl Radek, *Isvestia*, 4th October 1918.)

"We are not prophets or dreamers when we say that when it is finally clear that the German working class have stretched out their hands after power, the following day will see the proletarian barricades erected in the streets of Paris." (Trotsky, *ibid.*)

"The German proletarian revolution is developing normally and quickly and in not too long a time it will reach its final aim—the complete dictatorship of the proletariat." (*Isvestia*, 11th December 1918).

"The hour will strike and events will come that are historically inevitable. There is no power in the world that can save the German bourgeoisie from its fate. No one will snatch the victory from us." (Zinovieff on Germany in 1923, *IPC*, v. p. 34, 1924.)

"In general we have correctly estimated the objective (*sic*) tendencies. We were only wrong in estimating the time factor. At the time of Brest-Litovsk even Vladimir Ilyitch [Lenin] himself was of opinion that the victory of the proletarian revolution in a whole series of advanced European countries would be a matter of two or three months. . . ." (Zinovieff in 1924, at the 13th Conference of the Russian Communist Party.)

"The fateful hour of retribution approaches. Under the waving flag of the Communist International the working peoples of the whole world are preparing, in alliance with the oppressed nations of the East, for the last and decisive battle... for the establishment of a world-union of Socialist Soviet Republics and of the communist order throughout the world." (Resolution submitted by Comrade Stewart of England to the 5th Congress of the Communist International in 1924 and passed unanimously. *IPC,* 74, p. 914.)

"The revolutionizing of the East will give a decisive impulse to the intensification of the revolutionary crisis in the West. Imperialism, harassed on two sides, by a frontal attack and an assault from the rear, will have to recognize that its death sentence has been passed." (Stalin in 1925, *IPC,* v. p. 810.)

NOTES TO CHAPTER IV

[1] Italian "Fascism" is but imperfectly "totalitarian," the chief reason for this being the existence of the Roman Catholic Church. National Socialism is being imposed on the German people as a national religion. The attempt to impose Fascism on the Italian people as a national religion cannot succeed, because Roman Catholicism is already the religion of the Italian people, whereas the German people are divided into Roman Catholics, Protestants, and, latterly, National Socialists. The last Papal Encyclical is a grandiose polemic against secular religion in all its forms (*vide* the official summary in *The Universe,* 2nd April 1937).

Unlike National Socialism, Fascism is not anti-Semitic or specifically "racial."

[2] *MK,* p. 13.

[3] Hitler expressed himself against the acquisition of overseas colonies in *Mein Kampf* (p. 153). He believed that they could only be acquired by war—which meant war with England. He was for an understanding with England and for expansion not overseas but in Europe. He could hardly have dreamt that there would be Englishmen who were quite willing to give up colonial territory that had been won with so much sacrifice in the Great War merely for the asking. The prospect of recovering the former colonies without a fight, of harvesting the prestige which the recovery would engender, and of establishing naval stations and airports in the Atlantic, the Indian Ocean, and the Pacific, naturally produced a change even in Hitler's mind.

[4] *MK*, pp. 742, 755, 757.

[5] The *Third Realm* ("das Dritte Reich") is the dominion inaugurated by the National Socialist Revolution of 1933. The term was, apparently, coined by Möller von der Bruck, a writer of some genius and precursor of the revolution (he committed suicide before it began). The *First Realm* is medieval Germany or the Holy Roman Empire. The *Second Realm* is the Germany of Bismarck and the Hohenzollerns. The Republic either does not count or is a transition stage from the Second to the Third Realm.

[6] Matthew 4:8.

[7] Mark 18:36.

[8] For example, by General Goering in his speech at Breslau (26th October 1935): "We National Socialists know only one fundamental work. It is called *Mein Kampf*, by Adolf Hitler. Nothing else is official" (*vide Voelkischer Beobachter*, 28th October 1935).

[9] Self-styled "anti-Fascists" are incorrigible in their habit of underrating their opponents. It is true that "Fascists" overrate the "anti-Fascists," but it is much less dangerous to overrate than to underrate a foe.

[10] It is a great pity that no complete translation of *Mein Kampf* has appeared in the English language. The only existing English version has been so doctored as to be worthless. The difficulty of publishing a reliable version is one of copyright—it is quite understandable that the National Socialists should *not* want this most important and revealing book to be known in England.

[11] cf. Perkin Warbeck—"Himself (Perkin) with long and continued counterfeiting, and with oft telling a lie, was turned by habit almost into the thing he seemed to be; and from a liar into a believer" (Bacon, *Life of Henry VII*). Only in Hitler the process is more modern in its tempo—indeed it is almost instantaneous.

[12] Lenin, quoting Engels (*SR*, p. 18).

[13] *MK*, p. 29.

[14] *MK*, p. 704.

[15] In the Reichstag elections of the 20th May 1928, the Social Democrats were returned with 182 seats in the Reichstag. The next strongest party were the German Nationalists, with 73 seats, the next strongest were the Centrists (Roman Catholic) with

UNTO CAESAR 259

62. The Communists were returned with 54 (a gain of 9), the National Socialists with 12 (a loss of 2).

[16] *vide* pp. 90, 91.

[17] One of the noblest of German Republican statesmen was Walter Rathenau. He was murdered in 1922. His murderers are honored as national heroes in Germany today.

[18] *MK,* p. 201.

[19] Hitler refers in glowing terms to Mr. Lloyd George and the "pre-eminent political ability of this Englishman" (*MK,* p. 534).

[20] *vide Preussischer Pressedienst,* 1st March (evening edition), 1933.

[21] "Une haine, en se précisant, devient plus forte." (Julien Benda, *La Trahison des Clercs.*")

[22] *vide* pp. 6, 7.

[23] In the ghettos of Warsaw, Vilna, and Lemberg, it is possible to see aged, poverty-stricken Jews with sublime prophetic faces, such are not to be seen amongst the wealthier Jews of Frankfort, London, and New York.

[24] They are referred to as "an impudent forgery" in the *Encyclopaedia Britannica* (*vide* article on "Anti-Semitism"). The completest exposure of the forgery was made by P. H. Graves in *The Times* (16, 17, and 18 August 1921). Graves showed that the "proctocols" had been plagiarized from a book by Maurice Joly, *Dialogue aux enfers entre Machiavel et Montesquieu, ou la politique de Machiavel au XIXe siècle,* which was published in 1864. The meetings of the "Elders" were alleged to have been held at Bale in 1897 and the minutes to have been taken by an agent of the Russian secret police and to have been placed at the disposal of the Russian Ministry of the Interior. These alleged "minutes" or "protocols" were published by the anti-Semitic Russian paper *Znamya* in 1903 and were embodied by the Russian anti-Semite, Sergii Nilus, in the second edition of his book, *The Big in the Small,* which appeared in 1905. Many editions in German and other languages followed and the "protocols" became one of the chief weapons against the Jews. A detailed exposure of the forgery was also made by two legal experts, Professor Baumgarten and C. A. Loosli, at Berne in October 1934, when a group of Swiss "Frontists" were prosecuted for circulating literature conducive to depravity (the "protocols" were amongst this literature). Henry Ford treated the "protocols" as genuine in his book *The International Jew,* but when the

fact that they were forgeries was established he had the decency to retract. But the "protocols" remain part of German anti-Semitic literature—Hitler, Rosenberg, Ludendorff and others who declared them to be genuine have never retracted.

[25] *vide* p. 66.
[26] *MK*, p. 337.
[27] The point has been examined in detail with many illustrations by Alexander Stein in his "Adolf Hitler, Schüler der Weisen von Zion" (published *Graphia*, Karlsbad). We have drawn largely on this valuable study.
[28] *Protokolle der Weisen von Zion*, ed. by Gottfried zur Beck, 8th edition, 1923.
[29] Speech made in 1923 (quoted by Stein).
[30] *Protokolle*, p. 9.
[31] *ibid.*, p. 79.
[32] *MK*, p. 44.
[33] *Protokolle*, p. 56.
[34] *MK*, p. 643.
[35] *MK*, p. 331.
[36] *ibid.*, p. 332.
[37] *ibid.*, p. 332.
[38] *ibid.*, p. 344.
[39] *ibid.*, p. 346; cf. note 3, ch. iii.
[40] *ibid.*, p. 349.
[41] *ibid.*, p. 354.
[42] Nietzsche, *Human all too Human*, p. 531. In the autumn of 1932 a Japanese mission arrived in Berlin to study the National Socialist movement. I asked a member of the mission what he thought of the movement. He replied: "It is magnificent. I wish we could have something like it in Japan, only we can't, because we haven't got any Jews."
[43] *MK*, p. 55.
[44] *ibid.*, p. 56.
[45] *ibid.*, p. 61.
[46] *ibid.*, p. 272.
[47] *ibid.*, p. 269-70.
[48] *vide* note 59, ch. iii.
[49] *Mein Kampf* abounds in truculent utterances. Hitler is constantly speaking of the sword. "Lost territories can only be recovered with the sharpened sword, that is to say, by sanguinary fighting" (*MK*, p. 710); Similar words will be found on pp. 711,

721, 741, 774-5 of *MK*. Brutal threats against whole categories of men also abound. The only kind words Hitler has are for mice *(MK,* p. 239).

[50] One, who was his closest collaborator for many years, told me that Hitler was always like this—that the slightest difficulty or obstacle could make him scream with rage or burst into tears.

NOTES TO CHAPTER V

[1] " 'There is nothing about it that appeals to the intellect; its market will be restricted to the unintelligent, the mentally inferior, the people who do not think.'
'They called that a reason why the cult would not endure. It seems the equivalent of saying:
'There is no money in tinware; there is nothing about it that appeals to the rich; its market will be restricted to the poor.' " (Mark Twain, *Christian Science*.)

[2] To understand the Republican Germany, it is necessary to read *The Fall of the German Republic,* by R. T. Clarke, one of the few masterpieces of contemporary historical writing. It is critical of the Social Democrats but rejects the ignorant and stupid belittlement of Social Democracy which is so fashionable amongst parlor Bolsheviks.

[3] It is high time that an assessment were made of the comparative social achievements of post-war Governments. It would be found that those who have achieved the most are not those who have made the biggest noise.

[4] It has often been asserted not only that Europe as a whole would gain by the weakness or disunion of Germany, but that Germany herself would profit spiritually, seeing that her art, music, science, and philosophy flourished most when she was prostrate and disunited. That may be so, but a powerful working class cannot be expected to sacrifice its own material welfare and that of its children, nor can a great people be expected to forgo its own national unity merely because there is a belief which can never be proved beyond all doubt that the sacrifice will be beneficial to the higher manifestations of the spirit. The social conditions of Germany in Goethe's day were atrocious.

[5] *vide* Mr. Wheeler Bennet's admirable *Hindenburg, the Wooden Titan* for a very interesting account of this period. I

believe it was Bismarck who said that the German monarchy could only be destroyed if it destroyed itself.

[6] The telegram was held up the next day, though not before it had reached some of the generals to whom it had been addressed. Ludendorff had approved of it before it was dispatched, but declared, later on, that he did not know it conflicted with the wishes and the policy of the Government.

The events from the 8th August (which Ludendorff called the "black day" of the war, when "belief in our victory... was finally lost") and the 11th November (when the armistice was signed) are summarized in *Hindenburg* (by F. A. Voigt and Margaret Goldsmith). The chief source of information about the German military, naval, and political collapse in 1918 are the findings of the Commission of Enquiry appointed by the German Constituent Assembly and the Reichstag (a one-volume abridged edition of these findings was published in English translation in 1934 by the Stanford University Press).

[7] According to *MK*, p. 204 ff., the Jews secured control of the German financial and economic system while the German armies were winning the war. By means of strikes and revolutionary propaganda the Jews brought about the collapse of the "home front," thus defeating the German armies from behind and handing Germany over to "the domination of international capital."

These pages in *MK* are amongst the many that show how no falsehood is too gross for Hitler if it will serve to make the Jew appear as the embodiment of evil.

[8] *MK*, p. 611.

[9] "Arbeiter- Matrosen- und Soldatenräte." The German word "Rat" means council or committee like the Russian word "Soviet." Much confusion has been caused by the use of the word "Soviet" to imply something sinister, as though every committee system must be a form of so-called Bolshevism.

[10] Under the Republican Constitution the laws of the central Government overrule the laws passed by Governments of Federal States ("Reichsrecht bricht Landesrecht").

[11] In the autumn of 1921, Dr. Dorten complained to me about the "intolerable centralization" imposed on Germany "by Prussia." He uttered the word "intolerable" as though it expressed physical suffering on his part.

[12] *vide* G. E. R. Gedye's vivid book, *The Revolver Republic*.

¹³ The "Vehme" was a kind of Ku-Klux-Klan that carried out many assassinations in the early days of the Republic.

¹⁴ Jacques Bainville enlarges on this theme in his brilliant *Conséquences politiques de la paix,* but I think he overrates the strength of the dynastic principle bred in Germany.

¹⁵ The idea of abandoning the Rhineland to the French and so throwing the burden of financing it upon them was known as the "Versackungspolitik."

The victory won by "passive resistance" in the Ruhr was a very doubtful one. Nor was it as heroic as it seemed, for the workmen in the Ruhr continued to get their wages when they were on strike against the French.

¹⁶ This is true, above all, of Gustav Noske, the Social Democratic Minister of Defense until April 1920, a man of narrow understanding and ruthless temper, a bureaucrat with a passion for order who, by employing counter-revolutionaries to crush revolution, helped to promote the German counter-revolution.

¹⁷ In the autumn of 1918, Ludendorff clutched at the hope that the epidemic of influenza, then sweeping across the world, would paralyze the Allied and Associated Powers *(vide* the findings of the Commission of Enquiry, referred to in note 6).

The National Socialist movement seemed to be losing ground in the autumn of 1932. Every time its voting strength receded there was a tendency to assume that the tide was turning. Some Social Democrats believed that the Western Powers would not tolerate a revival of German militarism. But it must be admitted that some of the leaders had no illusion—two of them (both well known) admitted to me in June 1932 that a "Fascist dictatorship" would follow.

There was similar disparity of views in the German High Command after the 8th August 1918. Some knew the end had come, though the dull and stupid Hindenburg still believed that Germany could annex the Longwy and Brieuy coal basins. Ludendorff lost his head—for a time he hoped that the French and British would quarrel over the possession of Calais, and that the great influenza epidemic that swept the world in the autumn of that year would weaken the Allied and Associated Powers *(vide* the volumes issued by the Reichstag Commission of Enquiry into the causes of the German collapse).

Some of the younger Social Democrats, as I well remember, had plans for arresting Von Papen, who led the coup d'état in

June 1932, and for distributing weapons belonging to Social Democratic policemen amongst the industrial workmen—plans rather like the projected attack on the British fleet in 1918, though less disloyal.

[18] The "principle of Leadership" was well understood by Swift: "In most Herds there was a Sort of ruling *Yahoo* (as among us there is generally some leading or principal Stag in a Park) who was always more *deformed* in Body, and *mischievous in Disposition,* than any of the rest ... this *Leader* has usually a Favourite *as like himself* as he could get, whose Employment was to *lick his Master's Feet and Posteriors.* ... *This Favorite* is hated by the whole Herd; and therefore to protect himself, keeps always *near the Person of his Leader.* He usually continues in office till a worse can be found; but the very Moment he is discarded, his Successor, at the Head of all the *Yahoos* in that District, Young and Old, Male and Female, come in a Body, and discharge their Excrements upon him from Head to Foot." (*Voyage to the Houyhnhnms,* ch. vii., italics in the original.)

[19] During the many elections of the year 1932, Social Democratic workmen were frequently assaulted by men wearing the Brown Shirt, who had assembled them in previous election campaigns wearing the badge with the Hammer and Sickle.

There was no comparable migration from the ranks of the Social Democrats to the ranks of the Nazis.

In fairness to the Communists it must be stated that their *leaders* have stood the frightful test of the Brown Terror far better than the Social Democratic leaders.

[20] The abortive insurrection of 1921, for example (only one of many). It was led by Max Hoelz, a man of fiery temperament and fanatical conviction who bore a strange resemblance to Hitler, though he was of a much more heroic disposition. I asked Hoelz after he had captured the town of Sangerhausen, "What is the good of it?" He replied, "It's the Hegelian dialectic—pressure engenders counter-pressure."

[21] Of the Trade Union (Socialist) International Zinovieff said in his speech at Halle (*vide* G. Zinovieff, *Die Weltrevolution und die III Kommunistische Internationale.* Rede auf den Parteitag der U.S.P.D. in Halle am 14 Oktober 1920) that it was "the only bulwark of the international bourgeoisie" and a "rope round the neck of the working class," that it was led "by men who have the London and Paris bourses in their waist-coat pockets," that

it was "the sharpest and most dangerous weapon, I would like to add the only effective weapon, which the bourgeoisie has against us today." "All these generals of the civil war, these Orgesch" [the "Orgesch" was a Bavarian counter-revolutionary organization and one of the precursors of the S.A. and S.S.], "these White Guards" [as the Russian counter-revolutionary troops were called] ... "are much less dangerous than the leaders of this so-called trade union international."

Communist literature abounds with such attacks on the Trade Unions, on the Second International, and on all moderate Labor movements throughout the world. These attacks went on long after the Third Realm was established.

These attacks have not ceased even now, despite all the talk about a "United Front." Dimitroff, writing in the Communist *Runa* (11th November 1937), denounces "reformism" and Social Democracy, and quotes Stalin as saying, "It is impossible to make an end of Capitalism if there is no end to Social Democracy in the Labour movement."

[22] In some parts of Germany, in the industrial villages along the Bohemian frontier, for example, it was, even in 1920 and 1921, possible to see children with spidery limbs, "potato bellies," and abnormally large heads, the result of prolonged under-nourishment.

[23] *RF*, 21st June 1923. An article, such as might appear in the *Schwarze Corps* or any of the cheaper and more radical of Nazi papers today, appeared in the *RF* on the 23rd August 1923. The author was Von Henting, an ex-officer: "The honour of the nation, driven off ... by tradesmen, and by politicians who have grown grey in dishonour, will take refuge in the fists of the workers. Germany's honour will not allow her to sell one foot of the soil, either in the west or in the east." The *RF* wrote, in an editorial comment, "We are happy to find ourselves in line with officers of his [Von Henting's] calibre."

[24] The appeal is directed against "the handful of big capitalists," the few "parasites" and "sharks" (pescecani) who are exploiting and oppressing the Italian people. "Only the fraternal union of the Italian people by reconciliation between Fascists and non-Fascists will be able to destroy the power of the sharks and to enforce the fulfilment of the promises made to the masses for many years" (by Mussolini?) "and never kept." It is not conflicting ideals or interests, but "these big magnates of capital,"

who "incite Fascists and anti-Fascists against one another." This appeal is quoted with approval by the Communist *Rundschau* (v. p. 37, 20th August 1936). The *Rundschau* calls it "an important manifesto of the Italian Communist Party."

[25] It is not only the national heroes of the Third Realm who are above suspicion. Thucydides makes the famous blow struck at tyranny by Harmodius and Aristogeiton seem a very crooked affair *(Thuc.* i. p. 20 and vi. p. 54). Gibbon says of St. George: "His employment was mean; he rendered it infamous. He accumulated wealth by the basest art of fraud and corruption" *(Decline and Fall,* xxiii.).

[26] *RF,* 26th June 1923.
[27] *ibid.,* 26th June 1923.
[28] *ibid.,* 18th August 1923.

[29] The first leaders of the German Communist movement, Rosa Luxemburg and Liebknecht, were murdered. Their chief successors were Froelich and Thalheimer, men of some intelligence and strength of principle, who were, for that reason, condemned to political decapitation. The third succession—by one head lower than the second—Brandler, Ruth Fischer, Maslow, and others—were decapitated after a brief interval. In Thaelman Moscow found a man of sufficiently narrow understanding and doglike devotion to be above suspicion (he behaved with great fortitude under abominable treatment in the prisons of the Third Realm).

[30] During the Menshevik trial in March 1931, the *RF* published an article with the headline "Erschiessen! Erschiessen!" ("Shoot them! Shoot them!"). The Mensheviks, who belong to the Second International, are still ferociously persecuted in Russia, while the Communists are clamoring for a "united front" with that same international.

[31] For a very interesting account of Communist outrages in Germany, *vide* W. Zeutschel, *Im Dienste der kommunistischen Terror-Organisation.*

NOTES TO CHAPTER VI

[1] "Heilige Freiheit! Erhabener Trieb des Menschen zum Bessern!
Wahrlich, du konntest dich nicht schlechter mit Priestern versehn!"

(Xenien, 1794-97—these "Xenien" were written in collaboration with Schiller, and there is no telling which is by Goethe and which by Schiller.)

² "Zur Nation euch zu bilden, ihr hoffet es, Deutsche, vergebens;
Bildet, ihr könnt es, dafür freier zu Menschen euch aus."
(ibid.)

³ "Sagt, wo steht in Deutschland der Sansculott? In der Mitte; Unten und oben besitzt jeglicher, was ihm gefällt."
(ibid.)

⁴ Hölderlin, *Hyperion*. (Complete Works. Hellingrath's edition, vol. ii. p. 282 ff., italics my own.)

⁵   "Der Weg der neureren Bildung geht
      Von Humanität
      Durch Nationalität
      Zur Bestialität."

⁶ Nietzsche, *Menschliches Allzumenschliches*, i. 475.
⁷ Nietzsche, *Der Wille zur Macht*, i. 37.
⁸ Nietzsche, *Menschliches Allzumenschliches*, i. 460.

⁹ Burckhardt (1818-97) consoled himself with the thought that "human inequality will be honoured again somewhere. But what will happen to the State and to conceptions of the State in the meantime, the gods only know." (Burckhardt, *Complete Works*, vol. vii. p. 104.)

¹⁰ Overbeck, *Christentum und Kultur*, p. 270. Burckhardt was Swiss. Overbeck was a German-Russian who lived in Switzerland. Both were men of German speech who shared in the German civilized heritage.

¹¹ "The cosmopolitanism which does not spring out of, and blossom upon, the deep-rooted stem of nationality or patriotism, is a spurious and rotten growth." (Coleridge, *Table Talk*.)

The importance of literary clubs, circles, coteries, and cabals is greatly underrated. Their influence on the ripening generation can be profound. They are often embryonic political gangs, societies for mutual advancement and for promoting a spirit of intolerance. Literature (especially political literature), the stage, and the film in Republican Germany did much to prepare the way for the spiritual triumph of National Socialism. Every kind of horror and cruelty was considered fit subject for author and producer.

German taste was coarsened, sensibility was blunted, and cruelty and brutishness were infused into the imagination of the young by Russian "revolutionary" films that encouraged the spirit of intolerance and engendered dreams of bestial vengeance for wrongs never suffered, and by peculiarly sadistic German products. What was done in print, on the stage, and on the screen in those days was translated into reality by the National Socialists. The transition from things imagined to things real is a very easy one, and men, no less than children, will suit action to fantasy. The abominations perpetrated in the German concentration camps were foreshadowed on the German stage—and many who were actors and delighted spectators then, are victims now, their tormentors delighting, as the victims did then, in the spectacle of horror and pain, on the hypocritical pretense that some ethical purpose is being fulfilled.

The insensitiveness and inhumanity in those who set standards of taste and feeling today, accompanied by the spread of literary cabals, may yet be fearfully avenged, in England as it was in Germany.

What Edmund Burke wrote in his *Reflections on the Revolution in France* is as true now as it was then (indeed, his *Reflections* remain, for all their one-sidedness, incomparably the profoundest work ever written about revolution in the English language—a revolutionary book against revolution, as Novalis called it):

"They [the literary cabal] were possessed with a spirit of proselytism in the most fanatical degree; and from thence, by an easy progress, with the spirit of persecution according to their means.... They continued to possess themselves, with great method and perseverance, of all the avenues to literary fame. Many of them indeed stood high in the ranks of literature and science. The world had done them justice; and in favour of general talents forgave the evil tendency of their peculiar principles. This was true liberality; which they returned by endeavouring to confine the reputation of sense, learning, and taste to themselves or their followers.... To those who have observed the spirit of their conduct, it has long been clear that nothing was wanted but the power of carrying the intolerance of the tongue and of the pen into a persecution which would strike at property, liberty, and life.... These writers ... pretended to a great zeal for the poor, for the lower orders, whilst in their satires they rendered hateful, by every exaggeration, the faults of courts, of nobility, and of priesthood.... They served as a link to unite, in favour of one object, obnoxious wealth to restless and desperate poverty."

[12] William II was a very good speaker. His address to the workmen at Essen in 1917 was an able piece of demagogy (*vide* the edition of his speeches in the "Reklam Library").

[13] Burckhardt, *Complete Works,* vol. vii. p. 303.

[14] The "Corridor" touches German sentiment, rather than German material interests. It looks bad (from the German point of view) on the map. Many Germans feel galled or humiliated if, to travel in their own country, they have to pass through another.

I have never been able to discover much strong feeling about the "Corridor" amongst the poorer peasantry of Pomerania and East Prussia, but there is—or has been—much strong feeling amongst the middle and professorial classes, especially in Königsberg. Throughout Germany it was promoted by a well-organized, heavily subsidized, and persistent propaganda.

So little hatred of the Pole is there amongst the German farm laborers that in 1931, when there was some distress amongst the Polish laborers in the "Corridor," the laborers of East Prussia made a collection in aid of the Poles, although their own wages are extremely low (and are, mostly, paid in kind).

[15] Plebiscites may seem to be an ideal method of settling territorial disputes in accordance with the wishes of the inhabitants, but these wishes are rarely so definite (if they exist at all) as to indicate a clear-cut or even a possible frontier-line. The passions aroused are often very violent, which is only natural, for to many the transfer to alien rule means the loss of home and country. To some it may mean freedom from old oppression, to others it may mean new oppression, or exchange of the old for a new one. The Upper Silesian plebiscite of 1921 was preceded by many acts of terrorism, and in the sanguinary insurrection that followed, acts of appalling barbarity were committed on both sides.

The plebiscite by which Denmark recovered territory she had lost by her defeat in 1864, was exceptional in so far as the inhabitants of the German-Danish border-region are highly civilized, their wishes fairly definite, and a frontier-line could be drawn without great injustice to either side.

In the west, Germany also lost the two tiny regions of Eupen and Malmédy. They were transferred to Belgium as the result of a sham referendum. The transfer was simply an act of spoliation —it was deeply, and rightly, resented in Germany.

[16] Hitler declared that whereas the Treaty of Versailles was "inhumanly cruel," the Treaty of Brest-Litovsk was of "downright, unlimited, inhuman cruelty" (*MK*, p. 524). The whole passage is characteristic of Hitler's aptitude for the portentously untrue—also of the German aptitude for tearful self-pity combined with cynical disregard for wrongs endured by others.

[17] The Russian Revolution, saved by the final struggle on the Western Front in 1918, was consolidated by the so-called "Wars of Intervention" which, although they had a counter-revolutionary bias, were not primarily waged to crush the revolution, but to prevent a German-Russian alliance.

At the end of the Great War it was not unreasonable to suppose that Germany might repudiate the peace terms, even after she had signed the Treaty of Versailles. The German Government would not have been in favor of renewing the war, but the danger of counter-revolution had begun to grow. While the National Assembly was meeting at Weimar, members of the former German officer corps were considering the possibility of establishing a front along the River Oder and defying the Western Allies. The German Communists would certainly have been in favor of military collaboration between Germany and Russia (they demanded repudiation of Versailles—Lenin had, at first, advised acceptance, but only so that repudiation should be more certain later on). Even in 1920 after the "Wars of Intervention" were over, Ludendorff, who had authorized the transit of Lenin, Zinovieff, and Radek through the German lines into Russia in 1917, with the object of strengthening the Russian revolutionary movement, wished to offer his services to Russia when she was parrying the Polish attack.

England took certain precautions. She held the Murman Coast and Archangel, fearing lest the White Sea might become a base or refuge for German submarines. She occupied Baku, so that neither the Germans nor the Turks nor the Russians would be able to obtain oil for war against the Western Allies. She seized the fleet of General Denikin (much to his disgust, for he had thought England was his friend) because any Russian fleet in the Black Sea might be a nuisance to the Western Allies and useful to their present or potential enemies, whether Germans, Turks, or Russians.

The fortunes of the Russian civil war being in the balance, England gave support to the Russian factions that seemed least likely to help a defiant Germany and would, perhaps, co-operate in eventual hostilities against such a Germany.

Thus it was that Koltchak as well as Denikin received moral and material support from England, though she, having no great faith in any of the Russian factions, retained a certain control over Denikin's fleet and over the oil fields of Baku. The blockade of Russia was really an extension of the blockade of Germany, for even a non-belligerent Russia might have become a source of supply for a Germany at war once again.

The British effort in Russia was abandoned as soon as the danger of a German-Russian alliance was over, though the French continued to support General Wrangel.

The Russian revolution was, naturally, strengthened by victory not only over the counter-revolution but over the foreign invader. The "Wars of Intervention" intensified the Red Terror. But the counter-revolution within the revolution was brought out all the sooner (every revolution contains a germ of counter-revolution). The suppression of the so-called "Mutiny of Kronstadt" was a decisive counter-revolutionary action carried out by Lenin, Trotsky, and Zinovieff with all the ruthlessness of which they had so often accused Koltchak and Denikin. The Kronstadt sailors were a revolutionary élite—when they were crushed, the last chance that Russia would become a land of relative freedom and humanitarian enlightenment was crushed with them.

[18] *MK*, p. 736 ff.
[19] *ibid.*, p. 688.
[20] *ibid.*, p. 708.
[21] *ibid.*, pp. 726-58.
[22] *ibid.*, p. 742.
[23] Albrecht Wirth—*Volkstum und Weltmacht* (1901), p. 235. Wirth was the type of bellicose professor so common in Germany then as now, who fights terrific wars with his pen. In the same book he delivers himself of the following sentiment: "Now that we have smashed France with blood and iron, it is certainly a matter for satisfaction that we are engaged in crushing England

with our industries" (p. 226). He also claimed Abyssinia for Germany, declaring "this glorious Alpine land to be indispensable" (p. 26).

[24] The novel *Volk ohne Raum* by Grimm did much to popularize the notion that Germany is overpopulated and that the Germans, unlike the English, have not enough "room." There is a widespread belief in Germany that England "owns" the entire Commonwealth and that the English have a quarter of the world as "room" to live in.

[25] *MK*, p. 757. On the same page Hitler calls France "the mortal enemy of our people." What Hitler says about France and the French is a mere repetition of Prussian gallophobe utterances. The poet, Ernst Moritz Arndt, was typical of these gallophobes. In his *Schriften für und an seine lieben Deutschen* (1815), he wrote: "I want the French to be hated not only in this war. I want them to be hated for a long time, for ever.... May this hatred burn as the religion of the German people, as a sacred fury in all hearts, and always keep us in faith, honesty, and courage" (p. 371).

[26] Bismarck's genius for foreign affairs makes the conduct of German foreign policy under William II appear all the more wretched seeing that his example and his many warnings were still so near a memory. The anti-German coalition of 1914 was promoted by the Emperor William and his military and naval advisers. The naval rivalry with England was altogether superfluous—it promoted no German interest. The pharisaical habit of talking in portentous abstracts was no less common in Germany then than it is now. Germans talked about "equality" ("Gleichberechtigung") then as they do now (*vide* E. L. Woodward's masterly *England and the German Navy*, p. 374, footnote). But there is this difference—when Hitler demands "equality," it is with the purpose not merely of enunciating a principle, but of securing something very real, whereas the Emperor and his advisers demanded "equality" without reference to vital interests or to the political consequences. Hitler has demanded "equality" with the Western Powers in armaments on land and in the air, because that is the way to secure armed superiority over the eastern and central European Powers. He has demanded "equality" with regard to overseas possessions, because that is the way to get something for nothing. But he has not demanded "equality" on the sea, for that is the way to antagonize England—a piece of insight

that William II and Von Tirpitz never showed (the recent German naval agreement is an admirable piece of diplomatic empiricism). Germany could have had a fleet adequate for her needs without antagonizing England. She would then have become a greater Power, a greater naval Power, even, than she was in 1914, for power is always relative. If she had also refrained from going through Belgium, she would not have had England amongst her foes. She could have contained the French along her relatively short western frontier and could have won a rapid and decisive victory over the Russians which would have given her that preponderance in eastern Europe to which she still aspires.

The English effort, above all, and the French too, and the Russian largely, was for peace in the years that led up to the Great War. But the chances of peace were spoiled again and again by Germany, not through any desire to precipitate a war, but through pharisaical arrogance, clumsiness, and downright stupidity. It seems to me that English historians, in their desire to seem objective at all costs, are far too lenient in their verdicts on the German diplomacy of that period.

[27] Burke thought that England ought to have supported France in her wish to prevent the partition of Poland in 1773: "But a languor with regard to so remote an interest, and the principles and passions which were then strongly at work at home, were the causes why Great Britain would not give France any encouragement in such an enterprise. At that time, however, and with regard to that object, in my opinion, Great Britain and France had a common interest." (*Thoughts on French Affairs*, 1791.)

[28] If Germany were to recover her former colonies, she would be able to build naval stations or air-bases (or at least provide hiding-places for submarines) on the east or west coasts of Africa and in the Pacific. The danger of commerce-raiding on her part would be greatly increased. Her presence in Tanganyika might even give her the possibility of co-operating with the Italians against Kenya or the Sudan.

Quite apart from strategy, the thought that entire populations should be expelled from the Pax Britannica under which they have now lived for close on twenty years seems to me quite outrageous.

[29] cf. Aristotle, *Politics* (iv. 4), where the resemblance between democracy and tyranny is emphasized. Also Plato, *Republic* (viii.

14 ff.), where the organic connection between democracy, tyranny, and the terror (or "purge") is examined.

[30] The Ukrainians in Poland number several million (according to Polish computation 3,000,000, according to their own 5,000,000). The "pacification" of the Polish Ukraine (Eastern Galicia and Volhynia) in the autumn of 1930 was as inhuman as it was politically stupid. Detachments of Polish police and cavalry went from village to village, arresting peasants, flogging them, and destroying property. Thousands of peasants were so flogged that their buttocks resembled raw masses of pulped flesh. Many had to lie on their bellies for weeks afterwards. Never will the "pacification" be forgotten by the Ukraine, and it is quite natural that they should now look upon Hitler as the coming avenger and deliverer—"surely oppression maketh a wise man mad" (Eccles. 8:7).

[31] The military lessons of the Spanish civil war are of doubtful validity. The front follows the line along which the resistance of the Loyalists, weak, at first, through disorganization and lack of arms, was able to stiffen naturally. Great masses of barren mountain, ravines, sheer cliffs, and rivers favor the defense. Only round Madrid does the terrain favor the offense, but the Loyalists had time to build an elaborate system of trenches and fortified positions. Until the end of 1937, at least, there was little artillery of any kind and almost no heavy artillery, so that there are no barrages as in the Great War. The immense power of the rifle, machine-gun, and anti-tank gun (and, on the side of the Rebels, the modern anti-aircraft gun) has been demonstrated in Spain, but the lack of artillery leaves the demonstration a little inconclusive.

NOTES TO CHAPTER VII

[1] The Congress of Religions held in London in the year 1936 was mainly a congress of the religions of the British Commonwealth, and was yet a congress of the religions of the whole world.

[2] I believe it was Bismarck who said that in politics far-sightedness is much more dangerous than short-sightedness.

[3] "War is always Satanic in origin." (Pope Nicholas I.)

[4] "Peace is not the absence of war, but a virtue engendered by the strength of the soul." (Spinoza.)

"La paix, si jamais elle existe, ne reposera pas sur la crainte de la guerre mais sur l'amour de la paix; elle ne sera pas l'abstention d'un acte, elle sera l'avènement d'un état d'âme." (Benda, *La Trahison des Clercs*.)

5 I believe the term "indivisible peace" was first used by Mr. Eden after his return from Moscow in April 1935. It was subsequently used by the Russian Ambassador in London. To Russia "indivisible peace" means that England must go to war with Germany if Germany attacks Russia—in other words, "indivisible war."

6 I do not say this cannot be changed, I merely say that there is no evidence that it will be.

7 The war between Italy and Abyssinia, for example.

8 It was considered by Marshal Pilsudski in 1933 when the Third Realm was established. But the Poles could not attack Germany without French co-operation.

9 Poland attacked the Soviet Union without any provocation in 1920. But with the defeat of the Polish armies and the invasion of Russia, the war became one of defense. When it began, patriotic Poles would have been justified in opposing it—but later on it became the indubitable duty of every Pole to co-operate in repelling the invader.

10 Thomas Hardy, *Winter Words:* "We are getting to the end."

11 It is characteristic of these two great poets, that their verse is without propaganda or ranting protest. The reality of war is transfused by the poetic imagination and not argued or thought out of existence in facile visions of some Utopia. Wilfred Owen went through a stage of utopian pacifism (*vide* Edmund Blunden's preface to the 1931 edition of the poems), but there is not a trace of it in his greater verse. Rosenberg's *Dead Man's Dump* has something in common with the greatest choruses of Aeschylean tragedy.

12 Perhaps there was never a time when English men of letters talked and wrote as much and knew as little about politics as they do now. Anyone scanning the multitude of books and articles by contemporary writers would, if he had nothing else to go by, conclude that the political genius of the English had evaporated altogether.

The great political writers—Bacon, Swift, Dryden, and Pope— were either *in* politics or lived in close association with those who were responsible for the conduct of affairs. They knew what they were talking or writing about when they touched on the affairs of the nation—or of the world. One is again and again astonished by their political realism and by their complete lack of utopian sentiment. Swift, indeed, is *the* great political realist—his *Conduct of the Allies* is full of profound lessons for the modern student of foreign affairs. There is no book in English more packed with political wisdom than *Gulliver's Travels*, the most formidable attack ever made upon all political Utopias. Bacon in his *Life of Henry VII* showed himself to be the English Machiavelli (with a greater and subtler mind than Machiavelli's). The profound political insight constantly shown by Pope and Dryden seems almost miraculous at the present day. The tremendous intensity of Milton's poetic vision and his deeply messianic nature sometimes overwhelmed his political insight, and it may be that special causes helped—the failure of the Commonwealth, the despair of the post-Cromwellian period, and his great personal afflictions. Nevertheless, even the purely political greatness of Milton (and it is but a small part of his whole greatness) stands immeasurably above that of any English writer living at the present day. What Wordsworth said of him in his sonnet, "Milton thou shouldst be living at this hour," is far nearer the truth now than when it was written, so much nearer as to be prophetic: "England hath need of thee" indeed!

Sir Thomas More was a great political writer and a great visionary. But he knew that his Utopia was Utopia and did not, like the Utopians of today, pretend that it could be brought about by "planning," by "socialism," by the "dictatorship of the proletariat," by "collective action," or by any scheme of "social reconstruction" or "international settlement."

But the writers of the present day are (with the rarest exceptions) wholly divorced from public affairs. This is not in itself an evil, for the dreamer, the visionary, and the ethereal spirit are no less needed than the realist. It was the greatness of the sixteenth and seventeenth centuries that there were men who could be all these things. But the visions of today are either nightmares or tenuous abstractions, and it is with these, not with politics, that would-be political men of letters are chiefly concerned in our own time. When they abandon themselves to plausible utopian schemes or to this or that "ideology" and imagine themselves to be *political,* they are not *political* at all, indeed they are *anti-political,* for such schemes are altogether incompatible with the genius of politics.

Both the English Communists and Fascists are anti-political ideologues. But utopian pacifism continues its affiliation with the Left, especially the extremer Left. It still goes to the making of parlor Bolshevism and has, since Russia joined the League of Nations, been cultivated by those who find that to be sentimental about the Five Year Plan and flippant about English Royalty is a full life, and by those who are engaged in the pleasurable occupation of fouling and feathering their own nests (an occupation varied, from time to time, by visits to Spanish and other battlefields).

Any book, almost, however worthless it may be, stands an excellent chance of success if it is sufficiently anti-English and pro-Russian. The manufacture and marketing of so-called "anti-Fascist" literature has become a profitable racket in England.

[13] The term "sanctions" does not occur in the Covenant of the League of Nations. Under Article 11, "any war or threat of war, whether immediately affecting any of the members of the League or not, is hereby declared a matter of concern to the whole League, and the League shall take *any action that may be deemed wise and effectual to safeguard the peace of nations."*

Under Article 13, the members of the League are pledged to submit disputes that cannot be settled by ordinary diplomacy to arbitration, to "carry out in full good faith any award that may be rendered" and not to go to war with any member complying with the award.

Under Article 15, a dispute "likely to lead to a rupture" and not submitted to arbitration under Article 13, shall be submitted to the Council of the League. If the Council fails to settle the dispute, it shall recommend a settlement. If the recommendations are agreed to unanimously by the members of the Council (other than the representatives of the parties to the dispute), the members of the League agree not to go to war with any party complying with the recommendations. If unanimity is not achieved in the Council, the members of the League "reserve to themselves the right to take such action as they shall consider necessary for the maintenance of right and justice."

Under Article 16, any member going to war in disregard of its obligations under Articles 12, 13 or 15 (that is to say, refusing to accept arbitration or going to war with a Power that has accepted the recommendations unanimously agreed to in a report by the members of the Council—other than the parties to the dispute), shall "be deemed to have committed an act of war against all members of the League, which hereby undertake immediately to subject it to *the severance of all trade and financial relations, the prohibition of all intercourse between their nationals and the nationals of the covenant-breaking State, and the prevention of all financial, commercial or personal intercourse between the nationals of the covenant-breaking State and the nationals of any other State, whether a member of the League or not."*

Under the same article, the Council shall recommend *"what effective military, naval or air force the members of the League shall severally contribute to the armed forces to be used to protect the covenants of the League."*

Article 16, which is sometimes called the "sanctions article," is much too formidable, though not quite as formidable as it might appear at first sight. The unanimity required under Article 15 signifies a considerable weakening of the League's coercive powers. Besides, it is for each member of the Council to decide whether Article 16 has become applicable or not.

For years there was strong pressure from utopian pacifists to "stop the gaps" in the Covenant or, in other words, to convert it into a system by which any Power waging a war of aggression would automatically find itself at war with the League. The "Geneva Protocol" was a typical pacifist product. It was actually adopted by the League Council in 1929, but was, fortunately, never ratified by the Powers. The credit for wrecking it was chiefly England's (it was subjected to destructive analysis by the *Manchester Guardian* in a series of articles published on the 26th, 27th, 28th, 29th January 1925). It provided for compulsory arbitration and amplified and tightened up the coercive clauses of the Covenant. Had it been adopted, the power, not only to make war, but *also to conclude peace,* would have been taken out of the hands of the King, out of the hands of Parliament, and conferred upon an international jury which would inevitably have been a packed jury. Indeed, *every* international body with coercive powers is bound to have the character of a packed jury— the League Council had never been quite without this character, although its coercive powers are limited. *All* schemes of international coercion are open to this objection, which is a fundamental one.

The "Geneva Protocol" was attractive to France and her satellites because it would have placed the armed forces of England at their disposal in case of German attack.

In the Far Eastern dispute that began in 1931, the utopian pacifists demanded that "sanctions" be applied to Japan—a demand equivalent to one of war with Japan (it has been said that there are three kinds of English pacifists—those who want war with Japan, those who want war with Italy, and those who want war with Germany). England was in a dilemma. The Singapore base had been badly neglected and no other European Great Power was willing to co-operate, while the extent to which the United States were willing was, to say the least, very uncertain indeed. English interests in the Far East were very vulnerable—it would have been impossible to defend Shanghai and Hongkong with a fleet operating from a base so distant and so inadequate as Singapore. Sir John Simon was not the most successful of British Foreign Secretaries, but he did his country a great service by worming a way out of the dilemma. It was never admitted that Japan was at war with China. She did not declare war, though she did indubitably wage war (wars are none the less wars for being called "punitive expeditions," "pacifications" and so on—or, for that matter, "sanctions"). Not to admit the existence of war—and a very terrible one—against a fellow-member of the League was extremely sophistical, but the circumstances justified the sophistry. The result was that Article 16 of the Covenant never came into operation. The fault lay in those clauses—especially 16—of the Covenant which imposed obligations that were incapable of fulfillment.

[14] Karl Barth, *The Epistle to the Romans* (English translation, p. 479).

[15] One can well imagine with what glee certain Powers would witness the downfall of England and the break-up of the Commonwealth, how they would snatch at the opulent spoil, the richest that ever existed (though, no doubt, they would afterwards fight amongst themselves for it).

NOTES TO CHAPTER VIII

[1] The United States are supreme in the American continent. In other continents their influence can only be decisive in coali-

tion with other Powers. Japan is an exclusively Asiatic Power, Russia a European and Asiatic Power. Italy is an almost exclusively Mediterranean Power. Germany is still an exclusively European Power. France is a European and African Great Power, with a considerable influence in the Far East. Only England, through the Commonwealth, is a Great Power in *all* continents and on *all* seas.

[2] *MK*, p. 742.

[3] Japan is no less dependent on overseas communications than England, but as there is no other great naval Power within striking distance, she enjoys the unchallengeable control of her home waters. A British fleet based on Singapore could exercise a strong pressure on her as a "fleet in being," and might be able to avert an attack on Hongkong, but could not challenge her command of the Yellow Sea. The loss of a naval battle would compel Italy to sue for peace, but her land frontier would at least enable her population to live, if her neighbors were neutral or on her side.

[4] The invasion of England was possible in the days of sail even without the destruction of the British fleet, as the landing of William of Orange showed (the "Protestant Wind" prevented Lord Dartmouth's fleet from intercepting him). Napoleon could seriously contemplate the invasion of England. Today, no landing is possible without the destruction of the British fleet. And if the fleet were to be destroyed, England would be forced to surrender unconditionally without a landing. To England, the command of the sea is not less but more important than ever.

[5] This doctrine is expounded in Ludendorff's book *Der totale Krieg* (an excellent English translation has been published under the title *The Nation at War*). The closing paragraph is an amusing example of the "Führerprinzip" and of Ludendorff's egocentricity: "A nation deserves only to have a great general when it places itself at his service, that is, in the service of the totalitarian war which is waged for its assistance. In this case, the great general and the nation are one and indivisible, otherwise the general is wasted on the nation."

[6] The popularity of utopian pacifism was shown by the Fulham by-election and by the "Peace Ballot." There seems to be little doubt that both helped to precipitate the Anglo-Italian conflict.

[7] Mussolini is much smaller than photographs usually make

him appear. Nor is his lower jaw as monumental as it appears in photographs (which are taken with the camera placed near and slightly below the Duce's jaw, so as to make that European landmark look as impressive as possible).

[8] Speech by Sir Samuel Hoare on the 11th September 1935 (italics my own).

[9] That is why the Treaty of Paris (or the "Kellogg Pact") must be regarded as a most noble and a *realistic* declaration. It was signed in 1928. It embodies the principle of so-called "Outlawry." The conception is that of Mr. Levinson, a Chicago lawyer, who, with the simplicity of true genius, and with immense patience and determination, persuaded his own country, England and France—the other Powers, 59 in all, following suit—to accept it. As a "one-man achievement" Mr. Levinson's is prodigious. Even if the Pact were a piece of humbug, the achievement of one man without power, without exceptional influence, and without ever resorting to demagogy or cheap advertisement, in getting his idea accepted by nearly all the world, would still be prodigious. And humbug is just what the Pact is not. Other pacts and alliances perpetuate war as an *institution*. "Outlawry" *de-institutionalizes* war. If the League of Nations is to survive, it must cease to be an instrument of war and become *exclusively* an instrument of peace and be based on the principle of "outlawry." "Outlawry" is, indeed, the tacit principle underlying the political relations between the members of the British Commonwealth and between the Commonwealth and the United States.

If the Nobel Committee were as discriminating in their political as they are in their scientific or literary judgment, Mr. Levinson would be a holder of the Nobel Peace Prize (Mr. Levinson's name is not even mentioned in the article on the Treaty of Paris in the *Encyclopaedia Britannica*).

[10] If Utopia, Ruritania, and Erewhon agree to limit their armaments at the same level, so that there is "armed parity" between them, and if, as the result of economic, political, or religious differences (or no differences at all), they begin to think in terms of war (one would expect communities of such an ideal nature to be engaged in permanent warlike plottings), and if Utopia concluded an alliance with Erewhon, then both Powers would have *rearmed* in relation to Ruritania.

If Ruritania were to defeat the combined forces of Utopia and Erewhon, and, without reducing her own armaments, compel them both to disarm, Ruritania would have achieved the equivalent of her own rearmament. But if, in an access of magnanimity, she were to disarm also, she would, in effect, be rearming them.

In the same way, if the victorious Powers had reduced their armaments to the German level, it would have been the equivalent of rearming Germany. Indeed, Germany would have been rearmed all the more formidably in relation to the other Powers, because her relative rearmament would be all the cheaper, and she would be better able to make a bid for offensive superiority than she has now been able to make, seeing that she would be starting from the same level as the other Powers.

[11] There is a legend which is kept alive by German propagandists and widely believed in England that the Treaty of Versailles contains a promise to disarm, that Germany carried out her disarmament on the strength of this promise and that the promise was then broken. Under Article 8 of the Covenant, the members of the League merely "recognize that the maintenance of peace requires the reduction of national armaments to the lowest point consistent with national safety and the enforcement by common action of international obligations." In so far as this article implies a promise, the promise was not broken—it was more than kept by England, for she reduced her "national armaments" far below the level required by "the maintenance of peace."

The disarmament clauses of the Treaty (Part V) are introduced with the words: "In order to render possible the initiation of a general limitation of the armaments of all nations, Germany undertakes strictly to observe the military, naval, and air clauses which here follow." There is no word here about disarmament or about a reduction of armaments, but only of limitation (which is a very different thing). In so far as prolonged and repeated efforts were made to "initiate" a "general limitation" of armaments, the implied promise was also kept.

[12] The most intractable antagonism in eastern Europe is the feud between the Czechs and Poles. Both are Slav nations, both have a common danger to face and a common interest in saving their independence from being destroyed by German neo-imperialism. The feud does not arise out of the ill-treatment of the Polish minority in Czechoslovakia, for that minority is *not* ill-treated (it is treated far better than the national minorities in Poland). The feud arises out of profound differences of char-

acter, temperament, and outlook. The tragedy of Czechoslovakia is that she is more civilized than any of her neighbors and therefore an object of incomprehension and distrust.

[13] The proposal to form an international so-called "anti-Fascist front" of the "democratic Powers" is constantly being made nowadays. The Powers usually designated as "Fascist" are Germany, Italy, and Japan; those designated as "democratic" are England, France, and Russia. Germany and Italy are neither more nor less "democratic" than Russia, and Japan is not Fascist. But apart from this, the folly of such a proposal lies, first, in its tendency to create three enemies, all of them Great Powers, and, second, to drive them together instead of dividing them.

[14] There can be no doubt that if the former allies of the Great War had not been interested in the preservation of Austrian independence, the National Socialist Revolution of 1933 would have spread to Austria and would have accomplished the "Anschluss" (though not, perhaps, without armed resistance from the Austrian Socialists) very much as the French Revolution spread to what is now Belgium. Belgium became an integral part of revolutionary France, just as Austria, according to Hitler's conception, is destined to become an integral part of the Third Realm. It was this special circumstance that made it impossible for revolutionary France to surrender Belgium, just as the Third Realm cannot forgo the "Anschluss." Had Napoleon been able to surrender Belgium, he might have been able to make peace with England. (Austria is almost "Italy's Belgium" and makes a permanent German-Italian understanding very doubtful. Italy would certainly defend the independence of Austria against Germany if she were strong enough.)

[15] There is some confusion of terminology over the Spanish civil war. The "Rebels" and their partisans object to being called "Rebels." I defy anyone to establish the ultimate responsibility for the civil war. Revolution and counter-revolution were working up towards an armed conflict. The supporters of the "Left" committed political murders and burnt churches, and the Government was unwilling, or unable, to suppress revolutionary excesses long before the rebellion broke out. But whatever else the Government may have been, it *was* the lawful Government of Spain and civil war *was* begun by a military rising against that Government. The term "Rebels" is therefore correct, though "Insurgents" will do as well. To call the Rebels "Patriots" or

"Nationalists" is misleading, for their opponents are no less "patriotic" or "nationalistic" than they are. The term "Loyalist" is correct in so far as it denotes those who remained "loyal" to the Government when it was attacked, though the anarcho-syndicalists would have preferred a very different Government. But the term is not quite satisfactory (though there does not seem to be a better one), in so far as it might imply disloyalty on the part of the Rebels. In every civil war there is a conflict of loyalties. The Rebels are not less loyal than the Loyalists in a general sense, only their loyalty is a different one. The loyalty on both sides to an idea—the Government is supported not so much because it was the legal Government when the Rebellion began, but because it represented an idea. The term "Republicans" sometimes used of the "Loyalists" is misleading because it implies that the Rebels are royalists, which only some of them are (the "Falangists" are certainly not). The word "Reds" is unsatisfactory because red is the color of the socialist and communist internationals and, although the Spanish Government is chiefly made up of socialists and communists, it is strongly national in feeling.

[16] During the summer of 1937 clandestine attacks were made on merchant shipping in the Mediterranean. There can be no doubt that the principal authors of this "piracy" were the Italians who conducted a secret submarine campaign against Loyalist Spain very much as Germany did against England during the Great War. "Piracy" in the Mediterranean was brought to an end by the Nyon Agreement which was signed in September 1937. The "piracy" of the Italians in the Mediterranean would, in so-called "normal" times, have been a *casus belli*. (The term "piracy" is used in international law to denote attacks by vessels of *unknown* nationality on merchant shipping—the question of the identity of the "pirates" in the Mediterranean was not pressed.)

[17] There is nothing to choose between the atrocities committed by one side and the other. There were *at least* forty thousand executions in Madrid alone. A truthful eye-witness's account of the massacres and terrorism in Madrid is given by Luis de Fonteriz in *Red Terror in Madrid*. Executions by the Rebels are truthfully described by Ruiz Vilaplana in *Do Fey* (which has appeared in English translation under the title of *Burgos Justice*).

But only a fraction of the horrors perpetrated in Spain behind the fronts has come to light. It is probable that in the first twelve months of the war more persons were massacred than were killed at the fronts or in bombardments or air-raids.

[18] Almost all contemporary verse on the Spanish civil war is a romantic glorification of war. One only has to compare Auden's *Spain* or Roy Campbell's *A Legionary Speaks,* for example, with the poetry of Wilfred Owen and Rosenberg to see how rich the younger poets of the Great War were, not only in poetic imagination, depth, and realism, but also in common humanity, compared with the younger poets of today.

[19] It was Italy and Germany who *began* intervention in Spain. Russia did not begin to send war materials for at least a month after the first Italian and German deliveries arrived (Italian airplanes with pilots arrived in Spanish Morocco for service with the Rebels in July 1936 when the war began).

NOTES TO CHAPTER IX

[1] "This Moloch (the modern State) which sees everything, does everything, controls everything, ruins everything.... Each of the functions of the State is a catastrophe.... Socialism is nothing but an extension, a multiplication, a completion of the State.... Down with the State and all its incarnations—the State of yesterday, to-day and to-morrow; the bourgeois State and the Socialist State." (Mussolini in the *Popolo d'Italia,* 6th April 1920).

[2] Even in its foreign, commercial, and financial transactions the Spanish Government were sound: "Amid its immense difficulties it [the Spanish Government] is making this effort [to pay its post-clearing credits] in order to clear the name of Spain from the stigma of default.... In existing circumstances even the small payments must involve considerable sacrifices for the Government, and the gesture deserves appreciation.... On the other hand, the insurgent [*i.e.* Rebel] authorities have not shown so much as a sign of their willingness to contribute towards the external liabilities of Spain.... It may well be asked why the Franco Government does not make at least a token payment as a gesture of goodwill and as an indication that it has the honour of Spain at heart.... All the rhetoric about 'confiscation' and 'repudiation' by the 'Reds' cannot eradicate the impression created in the minds of non-political bankers by the contrast between

the attitude of the two Governments." *(Financial News,* 6th January 1938.)

[3] A revolutionary movement has spread in Rebel territory and, while supporting General Franco in the field, opposes him at home. This is the *Falange,* which has a good deal in common with the National Socialist movement in its earlier stages (its membership, according to *The Times* of 14th January 1938, is about 3,000,000). It is a kind of "Red Nationalism." It has not been weakened by the efforts of the Rebel authorities to counteract it (it would seem that several of its leaders have been executed). Whether its political activities encumber the military effort of the Rebels is hard to say, but it raises very great doubts whether even if General Franco wins the war, he can win the peace.

Spain has been invaded by foreign troops of which by far the greater number are on the side of the Rebels. The distrust of foreigners (a distrust that goes with exquisite courtesy to the individual foreigner) among the Spaniards, who have endured more, perhaps, than most nations at the hands of foreigners (from the Moors to the Bourbons); the popular character of the revolution and the interest France and England have in a Spain that will be independent of any foreign Power (in "Spain for the Spaniards"), may well outweigh the inferiority of the Government in airplanes, in artillery and in the number of foreign auxiliaries.

[4] *MK,* p. 742.

[5] It is always very difficult to change the general course of a national policy. A national policy is rather like a river—its course and the strength of its current are chiefly determined by the configuration and the lie of the land, and by tributaries, rains, snows, and other intractable phenomena.

[6] Dryden, *Absalom and Achitophel,* pp. 173-4, cf. the preceding passage:

> "For close designs and crooked counsels fit,
> Sagacious, bold, and turbulent of wit,
> Restless, unfixed in principles and place,
> In power unpleased, impatient of disgrace...
>
> "A daring pilot in extremity,
> Pleased with the danger, when the winds went high,
> He sought the storms; but for a calm unfit,
> Would steer too nigh the sands to boast his wit."

(pp. 151-5, 159-162.)

[7] Leonid Krassin, the Russian Commissar of Foreign Trade, and Chairman of the Russian Trade Delegation in London, established a close contact with Italian politicians and business men at the Genoa Conference in 1922. Mrs. Krassin, in her life of her husband, wrote:

"The Fascist—like the Soviet—régime was based on the complete surrender and submission of the individual to the State. Signor Mussolini, therefore, understood perfectly well that the State controlled all Russia's foreign trade. Krassin had, moreover, a high opinion of Signor Mussolini, in whom he saw, as many Italians did, the man who saved his country from a fatal collapse." (*Leonid Krassin, His Life and Works*, pp. 244-5.)

[8] The Esthonian Communist insurrection broke out in 1924. Although Esthonia is a small country, remote from any possible foreign aid, and a neighbor of the Soviet Union, the Union was unwilling or unable to help the Esthonian Communists, who were mercilessly suppressed.

[9] The first well-established Power to have normal and friendly relations with Russia was Turkey after the defeat of the Greeks in 1921. But this did not in the least prevent the Turks from hanging all the Communists (with the Dancing Dervishes) they could capture.

The "International Column" was made up of men belonging to the "Left" in all countries, most of them being Communists. The story of the column is one of the epics of the war. The column was unsurpassed for "plain heroic magnitude of mind" and "celestial vigour."

[10] Georgia proclaimed her independence in May 1918. She was recognized as an independent State by the Russian Government in the spring of 1920. Georgia had a Socialist Government and was befriended by the Socialist and Trade Union International. Lord Curzon believed that she would be attacked by Russia—but that nothing could be done to defend her. Georgia was invaded by the Red Army in February 1921 after an internal rising arranged for by the Georgian Communist Party (Russia annexed Georgia very much as Germany annexed Austria, the Austrian Nazis playing the same part as the Georgian Communists). A period of sanguinary repression followed in which many Georgian workmen (officially termed "bandits" by the Russians) were executed. The Georgians made a last desperate attempt to

recover their independence in the insurrection of 1924, which was mercilessly crushed.

[11] "Retour de l'U.S.S.R."—"Seven friends and philosophers, Diogenes and Hermias, Eulalius and Priscian, Damascius, Isidore, and Simplicius, who dissented from the religion of their sovereign, embraced the resolution of seeking in a foreign land the freedom which was denied in their native country. They had heard, and they credulously believed, that the republic of Plato was realised in the despotic Government of Persia, and that a patriot king reigned over the happiest and most virtuous of nations. They were soon astonished by the natural discovery that Persia resembled the other countries of the globe; that Chosroes, who affected the name of a philosopher, was vain, cruel, and ambitious; that bigotry, and a spirit of intolerance, prevailed among the Magi; that the nobles were haughty, the courtiers servile, and the magistrates unjust; that the guilty sometimes escaped, and the innocent were often oppressed. The disappointment of the philosophers provoked them to overlook the real virtues of the Persians.... Their repentance was expressed by a precipitate return, and they loudly declared that they had rather die on the borders of the Empire than enjoy the wealth and favour of the barbarian." (Gibbon, *Decline and Fall of the Roman Empire*, ch. xl.)

[12] "The whole task involved in the practical organisation of the rising was conducted under the immediate leadership of the chairman of the Petrograd Soviet, Comrade Trotzsky. That the garrison passed over so rapidly to the side of the Soviets and that the work of the revolutionary soldiers' Committee was so audacious is something the Party owes principally and above all to Comrade Trotzsky." (Stalin in the *Pravda*, 6th November 1918.)

[13] These messages make up the so-called "Testament" of Lenin. It was mentioned by Stalin himself in his speech at the meeting of the Central Committee of the Russian Communist Party in October 1927 (the full text of the speech is given in the official *IPC*, 8th November 1927). The "Testament" was never published in Russia and there were complaints that it was being kept secret. In his speech Stalin replied that the question of secrecy had been discussed in the Central Committee. "It was," he continued, "proved and always proved again that no one kept anything secret or is keeping anything secret, that Lenin's 'Testament' was addressed to the 13th Congress of the Party, that this

'Testament' was read out at the Congress of the Party, that the Congress decided unanimously not to publish the 'Testament' because, amongst other reasons, Lenin himself had not wished or demanded that it be published."

Stalin then quoted the passage in which Lenin refers to him as being "too rough" (the Russian word is "grub," which conveys something more than discourteous and a little less than brutal—the German word "grob" renders it accurately), that this quality makes him "unbearable" as Secretary General, and that he ought to be replaced by someone else. Stalin replied to Lenin's warning advice with characteristic cunning and effrontery:

"Yes, comrade, I am rough with those who are rough and disloyal in destroying and disintegrating the Party. At the very first plenary meeting of the Central Committee after the 13th Congress of the Party, I asked the delegates of the Central Commiteee to relieve me of my duties of Secretary General. ... The delegates, Trotzsky, Kameneff, and Zinovieff amongst them, unanimously obliged Stalin to remain at his post. What could I do? Run away from my post? That is not the kind of man I am. I have never run away from my post. And I have no right to run away, for that would be desertion. As I have said before: I am not a free person, and when the Party gives me orders, I have to obey."

On the 30th December 1922, Lenin wrote that the Russian State (at the time) had been "borrowed from Tsarism," that it had "hardly even rubbed against the Soviet world," and that it was "a bourgeois mechanism." He feared that the Constitution of the Soviet Union would be "a scrap of paper" and "powerless to defend" the non-Russian affiliated Republics. He expressed misgivings over the nationalistic bent of Stalin—and also of the principal terrorist of the Union, Djerzinsky—who, like Stalin, was a non-Russian (vide Boris Souvarine, *Stalin—aperçu historique du Bolchévisme*, p. 289).

Lenin's worst fears were more than justified. Can it be that, in his last illness and in the presence of death, he realized, at last, that the Kingdom of Heaven is not round the corner—or even not of this world?

The "Testament" was summarized in the *Sotsialistichneski Vestnik* of the 24th July 1924. The full text was given in Max Eastman's *Since Lenin Died*, in Max Pfemfert's *Aktion* (xviii. 10, 12, December 1923), in the book by Souvarine mentioned above (published 1935), and in Trotzsky's *The Real Situation in Russia*.

[14] Estimates of the number of persons who perished in the famine of 1932-3 are conjectured, as the existence of the famine was officially denied. W. H. Chamberlain, an accurate, scrupulously honest observer, who toured the stricken regions, puts the total at five or six million (W. H. Chamberlain, *Russia's Iron Age*, p. 67.)

[15] Julian Huxley, *A Scientist among the Soviets*, p. 51.

[16] Especially Anthony Jenkinson and Giles Fletcher.

[17] Giles Fletcher, *The Government of Muscovia with the Manners and Fashions of the People of that Country*.

[18] The trials of Zinovieff, Kameneff, and other leading Communists in 1937 were widely accepted as genuine in western Europe because the method, and the system and the mentality that made such a method possible, are quite beyond the range of ordinary western European experience. Nor was it generally known that the trials were not the first of their kind. The "Ramzin Trial" (December 1930), and others that had gone before, were similar, in so far as not persons only, but reputations, and the opinions for which the persons stood, or rather the opinions foisted upon them, were the objects of "liquidation" (as it is so feelingly called). Russian "purges" combine heresy hunting with human rat hunting, so to speak, both the heresy and the rat-like attributes being construed, first, and persons then being found to fit them. The victims are sentenced to imprisonment or to death, and all opinions, tendencies, or even moods that are obnoxious to the Dictatorship are associated with them (as a rule falsely) and destroyed with them. Political persecution in Russia is analogous to the persecution of the Jews in Germany in so far as the victims are not guilty but have their guilt thrust upon them, though there is this difference, that whereas the Jews in Germany are being ruined or isolated or squeezed out of the country (a few being killed or physically maltreated), in Russia the victims are exterminated in vast numbers like vermin.

The whole question is one of some complexity and a volume would be needed to deal with it even in summary fashion. It is possible to indicate only a few aspects of it here.

"Sabotage" or "wrecking" is quite common in Russia and is committed, chiefly, by workmen. If they are found out they are shot (without a public trial, for a "proletarian"—god-like being! —*cannot* commit a crime in Russia; he is sinless), but the foreman or manager of the factory, or one or two "experts" who may not be in the least responsible, will often be compelled to "confess" a guilt that is not his and be sentenced to death in a public trial. He will be charged, amongst other things, with being an agent of "capitalism," of "Fascism," or "Trotskyism." In this way hatred of these three "-isms" will be kept alive, the Dictatorship will appear to be in danger, it will also appear to have triumphed over that danger (each trial being a sort of victory of the established system and of orthodoxy over treason and heresy). Russian political trials are not a function of justice but a function of dictatorial government.

Zinovieff was a monster of cruelty, but he was quite incapable of conspiring to overthrow the Communist Dictatorship by force. The assassination of Stalin would be as commendable as the assassination of any tyrant. Neither Zinovieff nor any of his alleged accomplices had the stuff of a Brutus or a Charlotte Corday in them—they were old and tired men, reduced to mental pulp by years of shadowing fear.

The main charges were not only false, not only fantastic. The deeds attributed to the prisoners *could not* have been committed.

It is quite easy to demonstrate the complete absurdity of the accusation. A glance through the published evidence will reveal example after example, such as the following (a few of many):

In 1934 (according to the evidence) there was an attempt to murder Molotoff. He was in a car and the chauffeur, Arnold, a witness in the trial, was to have driven the car into a deep gorge (in which case he would have perished with his victim). Shestoff, accused of organizing the attempt, declares that the detectives guarding Molotoff followed the car and held it back with their hands, just in time. Why was not Arnold arrested and tried then? Why did the detectives give evidence? A brave man, this Arnold, in any case!

Lifshits, Deputy People's Commissar for Railways, is accused of organizing *thousands* of railway accidents. I suspect that the total number of railway accidents in all Russia during, say, the last five years, is well under the number of those that, according to the evidence, were *deliberately* caused by the highest railway officials (unless the Russian railways are the most inefficient in the world—which perhaps they are). But how *can* the *manager* of a great railway system actually *cause* accident after accident over a *series* of years? Is it conceivable that even if he really planned to do so, he could carry out the plan—the plan of a lunatic—without the knowledge of the G.P.U., which has a closer network of spies than any other organization in the world (except, perhaps, the Gestapo)?

Although the methods with which the "confessions" were extorted are not known in detail, their general nature and their complete efficacy will be understood by anyone acquainted with terroristic systems and the terroristic atmosphere. All, except the very courageous, who are arrested in Russia are ready to confess *anything* or do *anything* the authorities want them to do. If there is any recalcitrance it is broken by a threat, often no more than hinted at, to wife or husband, parent, child or friend. And who in the world will *not* "confess" if the penalty for refusal be the liberty, or even the life, of a mother or a child? Or who, confronted with the extorted evidence of alleged accomplices, who, one after the other, will, if need be, appear as witnesses against him in a public trial, and himself menaced, or subjected to mental or physical torture and the destruction of those dear to him, will not do all he is asked to do, even if he cannot save his own life?

In any case, *only* those who are ready to "confess" are tried in public. For years, no "political" offender has been publicly tried in Russia who has not confessed. Men with strong nerves like Tomsky have *anticipated* arrest by committing suicide.

The Western world imagines there is a terror in Germany. And so there is—but the terror in Russia is incomparably worse. London, Paris, and New York are strongholds of freedom compared with Berlin—Berlin is a stronghold of freedom compared with Moscow.

The Germans are mere amateurs in terrorism. The Germans do not understand, or hardly understand, that while there are limits to physical pain, there are *no* limits to *mental* pain. The brutish physical torments such as those that leave a man who has had the appalling misfortune to fall into the hands of the German "Gestapo" a whimpering wreck, with his mind temporarily unhinged, are rare in Russia—there are other ways, slower perhaps (sometimes extending over years) but much subtler, much more effective, indeed, irresistible for all but exceptional men. The Germans are not psychologists—the Russians are (a German Dostoievski would be inconceivable).

The refined "sleepless" method is hardly known in Germany and, when applied at all, is applied amateurishly. But it is the *cruelest* of the methods employed in Russia. A prisoner is simply kept awake—he is watched all the time and, when he dozes off, he is roused and taken off to be cross-examined by relays of interrogators for hours on end. This method may be applied day after day, for a week or ten days—only those can stand it who can hold out until their reason breaks, until they are *unable* to confess (I have known strong men who stood it for more than a week in Polish prisons and then broke down altogether).

Russian public trials have another aspect. In countries where the spirit of freedom is still alive even under terroristic despotism —in Poland, in Germany, in the Balkans—a prisoner has the support of those outside the jail, those who feel *with* him. In England, where such things, to her eternal glory, do not exist, it is *impossible* even to *begin* to understand what a consolation, what a source of strength that support is—that there are those who will know, those who will see and hear (if there is a trial), those who will be fired and fortified by defiance of despotism, those who will care for wife and child (who will be revered—and not treated like lepers).

Who will care what happens to a Zinovieff—or, to take for an example, a man who was relatively human—a Kameneff? The mob that has been worked up by hints in the Press, at first, then by direct accusations (long before the trial has begun), and then by the venomous invective of the Public Prosecutor, the cringing, servile instrument of the terrorist Dictatorship, Vishinsky, until it becomes a *lynching* mob, and all over Russia there are big public meetings where the death penalty is *demanded* even before the "evidence" has been heard?

Burke, with his marvelous insight, has gone to the heart of the matter: "In such a popular persecution, individual sufferers are in a much more deplorable condition than in any other. Under a cruel prince they have the balmy compassion of mankind to assuage the smart of their wounds; they have the plaudits of the people to animate their generous constancy under their sufferings. But those who are subjected to wrong under multitudes are deprived of all external consolation. They seem deserted by mankind, overpowered by a conspiracy of their whole species." *(Reflections on the French Revolution.)*

In the year 1937 alone the executions in Russia have gone into thousands. Day by day the names have appeared in the Russian press—sometimes five or six, or ten, or more, in the Moscow newspapers, and similar numbers of other names of local victims in the provincial papers from the Baltic Sea to the Pacific, from the Arctic Zone to the Pamir Plateau. Perhaps there is something of more than a human judgment in the extermination of the "Old Guard," of those who made the revolution, by one of their number, Stalin, though it is pertinent to ask how it is that Stalin, almost alone, is not a traitor, a spy, a wrecker, a German or Japanese agent, a Fascist, a Trotskyite. (For example, and it could be multiplied—the Central Committee of the Russian Communist Party elected in 1920 had nineteen members. Three died long ago. Two have been lost in political obscurity. Three hold office now (Stalin, Kalinin, Andreyoff). Eleven are "counter-revolutionaries"—Bucharin, Kameneff, Preobrajenski, Radek, Rakowski, Rykoff, Serebriakoff, Smirnoff, Tomsky, Trotsky, Zinovieff.—The "Politbureau" elected in 1924 had seven members. One holds office now—Stalin. The other six have been shot, imprisoned, or exiled as "counter-revolutionaries"— Bucharin, Kameneff, Rykoff, Tomsky, Trotsky, Zinovieff.)

Many of these men lived for the revolution and grew old and worse in its service, often facing death, enduring imprisonment, exile, and every conceivable hardship. It *cannot* be true that, iniquitous as the actions of many of them were, they betrayed everything they ever lived for and that Stalin, who endured less than most, is the only one who is not a Judas. It *can* only be that Stalin is an Ivan the Terrible, a Richard III, or a Macbeth who has murdered, or at least condoned the murder of, his closest friends (in so far as such a man is capable of friendship) and associates.

But the Russian trials have another and a higher aspect. Coleridge, in one of his Notebooks, says that the condemnation of a bad man is more shocking than the condemnation of a virtuous one, and gives Strafford as an example (not that amongst the thousands who have been executed in Russia during the course of a single year there cannot have been many obscure, virtuous men).

Quite apart from the question of technical guilt or innocence, of whether the accused did or did not commit what they were charged with, they were innocent in the sense that before a terrorist tribunal *no man* is guilty. He may be guilty before God and before his own conscience, but *not* before a Vishinsky or a Stalin. Even a monster like Zinovieff is innocent before *such* a tribunal, no matter if all the charges brought against him were true—indeed, if they had been true, he would have done something to redeem a life of falsehood and cruelty by striking at a despotism more terrible than that of the Tsars against which he rebelled in earlier years.

[19] The execution of Tukhachevski Putna and several other commanders was largely the result of information supplied to the Russian Government by the Czech Government (the Czech secret service is, perhaps, the best informed of all about Russia). The Czechs are naturally anxious to avert what is—to them—the danger of a German-Russian "rapprochement," but they probably exaggerated the extent of the danger. That some Russian commanders were in favor of compounding with Germany and that they were in touch with German commanders (doubtless with the knowledge and approval of Hitler and Stalin) is not evidence of a treasonable conspiracy against the Russian State.

[20] *vide* the very interesting article "Soviet Policy in the Far East," by W. J. Oudendyk (*International Affairs,* xv., 1936). Mr. Oudendyk writes of Outer Mongolia that "the country is so entirely dominated by its foreign tutors, especially in its foreign relations, that to all intents and purposes it may be considered as forming part and parcel of the (Soviet) Union." Russian "G.P.U." troops with armored cars, artillery, and bombing planes have intervened in the internal affairs of Sinkiang. They helped in suppressing the Tungan revolt at Urumchi. "Russian troops were undoubtedly the main factor in the defeat of Ma Chungying" (the Tungan chief) (Sir Eric Teichman, *Journey to Turkistan*); *vide* also Georg Vasel, *My Russian Jailers in China,* for an account of Russian methods in Sinkiang. China is, therefore, being "carved up" by Russia as well as by Japan.

[21] If Holland and Belgium were to remain neutral in a war between England and Germany, they would form a screen which would make it difficult for the English air force to attack the main German industrial centers (especially Westphalia), while the German air force could raid the east coast and London from airdromes near Bremen.

[22] The task of the German agents in Palestine is to work up Pan-Islamic feeling against the Jews and the English. Money, propaganda, and arms are placed at their disposal. The German calculation is, that if unrest or disorder can be created, England will have to dispatch troops who will, therefore, be unavailable in Europe if she is at war with Germany (*vide* the letters exchanged by the German Ministers of War and of Propaganda on this subject and quoted in the *Manchester Guardian* of the 15th January 1938).

[23] "Yea, who ever knew conferences in so great oppositions to ripen kindly, and bring any fruit to perfection? For many come rather for faction than satisfaction, resolving to carry home the same opinions they brought with them." (Thomas Fuller, *Holy War*.)

[24] It is, of course, mainly a matter of opinion whether a people are insular in mind or not. All the peoples living under "totalitarian" Governments are condemned to insularity. The English are certainly much less insular now than they were before the war. They seem to me less insular than the French (though there is some truth in Voltaire's observation that "just as England is an island, so every Englishman is an island"). Perhaps the least insular person in the world is the educated Scandinavian.

[25] At the time of writing (February 1938), the so-called "reform of the League" (or rather of the Covenant) is *sur le tapis*. Any reform of the League is difficult because of the large number of members with conflicting interests. It would, of course, be best if the "sanctionist" articles (especially Article 16) were reformed out of existence. But the Covenant is so elastic and has so many loopholes (especially since it was amended in April 1921), that, with a certain amount of evasion and agility, it is possible for members of the League to refrain from applying "sanctions" if they wish to! The question of reform is, therefore, not one of very great urgency. Nevertheless, it is desirable that all clauses authorizing coercive measures should be removed from the Covenant some time or other.

[26] Cromwell, *Letters and Speeches,* iii. pp. 340-2.
[27] Rom. 1:25.
[28] Thucydides, cxliii. p. 4.
[29] 2 Chron. 15:6, 7.

INDEX

Abyssinian War, 197-9, 208, 214-5
Adoratsky, 15
Adigar, crisis of, 1911, 153
Alsace-Lorraine, 154
Anglo-French alliance, 205, 207, 237
Anti-Comintern Pact, 231, 236
Anti-German alliance, 164
Aryans, 59, 60-2, 68, 86, 167
Asia, effects of the Russian revolution on, 227-8
Athenians, 238-9
Austria, union with Germany, 101, 163, 167-9, 204

Baltic, 157
Baltic States, their independence, 164, 218
Bavarian Soviet Republic, 20
Berdyeaff, Nicolas, 11
Bessarabia, Russia and, 218
Biological science, 40-1
Bismarck, Prince von, 26, 120, 123, 153, 160-1
Bolshevism, 217
Bourgeoisie, 7, 8, 15-6, 18, 20, 28-33, 38, 66, 75, 82-3, 90, 96-8, 122
Brest-Litovsk treaty, 97, 148, 157, 159
British race, 86-7
Buchner, Ludwig, 152
Burchardt, Jakob, 84, 152, 154
Burke, Edmund, 268, 273, 294

Capitalism, difficulty of defining, 4; Hitler's and Lenin's objection to, 64-5, 90-1; its ultimate form, 5; Marxist attitude towards, 5-8, 20-1, 38-9, 43, 55, 176; Socialism an advanced form of, 63; the transition from capitalism to communism, 42-3
Chernoff, Victor, 73
Chiang Kai-shek, 215
Chiliasm or the expectation of the Millennium in this World, 14, 16-24, 45
China, and national unity, 229; Russian influence on, 227
Christian dogma, 8
Christianity. *See* Religion.
Civilization itself contains a menace of war, 179

Clarendon, Earl of, 81
Class antagonisms and class-war, 21, 24, 38-9, 48, 64, 78, 80-1, 88, 96
Classless state. *See* Kingdom of Heaven on Earth.
Coleridge, Samuel Taylor, 49, 267, 294
Collective man, his enthronement, 33, 150, 165
Colonies, Germany and, 61, 158, 230
Communism and Fascism are much alike, 5; difficulty of defining, 4-5; Hitler and the danger of, 109, 216; in Germany, 32, 109-10, 119, 137-46; its principal achievement in Russia, 217-8; the Communists' disruptive activities, 215-6
Communist International Congresses, 20-3
Communist Manifesto, 6-7, 18-20, 25
Cosmic process, 4
Cromwell, Oliver, 69, 81, 85
Czechoslovakia, dismemberment of, 164, 169
Czechs, 170

Danzig, 155
Defoe, Daniel, 85
Democracy must have teeth and claws, 137
Democratic republic, Lenin and, 96
Dialectical materialism, 3, 8, 14-16, 18, 34
Dictatorship always usurps the function of the State, 39
Disarmament, 202
Dorten, Dr., 130

Engels, Friedrich, and dialectical materialism, 8; and Marxism, 3, 15; and the classless state, 19; and the collective control of production, 78; and the Communist Manifesto, 6-7; and the State, 38; his belief in violent revolution, 104; his mental arrogance, 42; on religion, 51, 52; thought "the right of revolution the only 'real' and 'historical' right," 66
England, a general anti-German policy would be excessively dangerous,

INDEX

England—*Continued*
207; and disarmament, 202-3; and non-intervention in Spain, 210-1, 217; and sanctions, 187-8, 196, 198, 204-7; and European peace, 231-5; and the enforcement of world peace, 196-8; and the League of Nations, 236-238; and the German menace, 204, 206-7, 230-4, 237, 239; and the friendship of the United States, 195, 236-7; and the Italian problem, 207-8; English policy should be neither one of intervention nor of aloofness, 207-8; hated and envied by the militant imperialisms, 230; her downfall would be irretrievable, 229; her vulnerability exposes her to permanent defeat in war, 191-6; influence of British command of the sea, 192-3; is the only world power, 192, 195, 236; Lenin on Communism in, 97-8; rearmament, 204, 209, 230-1; revolution in, without violence, 25; Russian hatred of, now passive, 217, 228; the aim of British foreign policy, 234
Eschatology, 42, 45, 54, 61-2
Esthonia, 215
Europe, the unity and peace of, 232-4, 238
European War, Germany and, 164-6
Evil and the capitalist system, 37-9

Fall, the, 46
Far East, balance of power in, 228; Russian imperialism in, 228
Fascism and Communism are much alike, 5; Social Fascism, 141
Feudalism, difficulty of defining, 4
Finland, independence of, 218
France, Anglo-French Alliance, 204, 207, 237; Hitler and her destruction, 101, 159, 161, 229
Franco, General, 213
Freedom, Lenin's and Hitler's hatred of, 76-7
Führerprinzip, 138

Genius, German men of, 150, 152-3
Georgia, independence of, 218
German Communist Party, 32, 109-10, 138-46
German Independent Socialist Party, 139
German Officer Corps, 127-9, 132, 153

German Proletariat, Lenin on, 95
German race, 86-7
German Republic, and federal law, 130; Communist attacks on, and its collapse, 122, 136-46; its establishment, 124-7; political freedom in, 137
German revolutions (1918), 127-31, 136-8; counter-revolution of 1920, 131, 134; (1923) 128, 147-8
Germany, a Pan-German Empire, 158-60, 163-4, 169; and another European War, 164-6; and colonies, 61, 159, 231; and the Peace Treaty, 154-9; even against war there is little opposition, 171; German expansion in central and eastern Europe, 206-7; German-Italian relations, 213-14; her military defenses, 172-4; is strong enough to achieve the aims of her foreign policy without allies, 208; rearmament, its effects, 204, 208; reasons for her intervention in Spain, 213, 232; religion in, 59; terrorism in, 37-8, 107, 136, 170; the German menace to England, 230-4, 236-9; the German State is strong both in the multitude and devotion of its supporters, 170; there is a widespread desire for freedom, 171; there is no serious political opposition in, 171
Goebbels, Dr. Joseph, 119
Goering, General, 110
Goethe, Johann Wolfgang von, 150
Gorki, Maxim, 54
Governments and the will of the people, 170-1
Great War, 87-90, 180, 183, 193
"Greater Germany," 57-8, 67, 158
Grillparzer, Franz, 151
Groner, General, 130

Heaven on Earth, Kingdom of. *See* Kingdom.
Hegel, and the dialectical process, 2, 9; on the State, 38
Heine, Heinrich, 152
Herrick, Robert, quoted, 36
Hindenburg, Paul von, 127-9, 132, 143
History, Marxian and National Socialist conceptions of, 82; Marx, Lenin and Hitler were obsessed by, 84; objective, 80

INDEX

Hitler, Adolf, a genius for portentous platitudes, 49, 103; a man of the people, 63, 90; an advocate of ruthlessness, 69-73; an uncompromising extremist, 23; and a Pan-German Empire, 158-9, 163-4, 169; and a war of conquest against Russia, 160-4; and class privileges, 64; and injury to the vital interests of England, 211; and power, 84; and religion, 50-1, 55-63, 100-1, 104; and the danger of Communism, 109, 216; and the union with Austria, 167-70; and the unity of German-speaking people, 49, 60, 190-1; and world power, 192, 215; compared with Lenin, 49-50, 62-3; compelled Russia to make peace with the rest of the world, 216; denounced the leaders of the 1918 revolution, 74, 128; despises the Germans, 67-8, 76, 220; few great men can have been so completely without any sort of nobility, candor or refinement, 120; he is silent and hardly ever argues, 120; his appearance, 120; his aspirations as stated in *Mein Kampf*, 101-4; his attitude towards war, 49, 71-3; his authoritarian despotism, 27; his belief in terrorism, 72, 107; his book and speeches are truculent and full of vengeful malignance, 36; his fondness for executions, 72; his genius for fostering false legends about his opponents, 108-11; his hatred of pacifism, 76; his hatred of weakness and humility, 105; his hatred of the Jews, 6, 62-3, 67-8, 105-6, 110-21, 167-8; his hatred of the bourgeois, 75; his intolerance and his hatred of freedom, 76-7; his method of the "purge," 119-20; his outbursts are full of cheap hot-gospeling rhetoric, but may also reveal great political insight, 120; his practical achievement, 103; his servility, 143; his untruthfulness, 105, 108; his vituperative violence, 73-4; is a master of stagecraft, 119; is absolutely humorless, 94; is anti-capitalistic, 63-5, 90-1; is bloody-minded to a horrifying degree, 120; is first and last a revolutionary, 27, 101, 106; is incomparably the most powerful man in Germany, 103; is not a commanding intellect or a commanding character, 108; is rigid, static, intolerant, monomaniacal and unoriginal, 79; is the greatest demagogue of modern times, 50-1, 64-5, 108; is unhistorical and subjective, 80; is terribly sincere, 103; is without tolerance, pity or any generous emotion, 104; lives at high tension and is very emotional, 120; never had any scruples, 105; no one has ever been able to command such devotion from such multitudes, 119; often appears shallower and more stupid than he really is, 103; on falsehood and propaganda, 47-8; on Marx, 79; on readers of newspapers, 67; repudiates objectivity, 56; showed no mental development after he had reached early maturity, 78; the essential kinship of Hitler and Lenin, 77-9; the influence of Marxism on, 79; the prophet of racial war and racial consciousness, 48-9, 59-62, 66, 78-80, 85-91; to him the individual means nothing, 66-7; was obsessed by history, 84; what he thinks of the masses, 67-8

Hitler-Ludendorff Putsch, 106
Hoare, Sir Samuel, 200-2
Hohenzollerns, German working-class hatred of, 125
Holderlin, Johann C. F., 150
Hungarian Soviet Republic, 20
Huxley, Julian, quoted, 221

Ideals, 238
Ideology, 3, 75
India, Russian influence on, 227
International air force, 185
Internationalism, 228
Isolation policy, 206-7
Italy, cannot realize her aspirations without the help of Germany, 208, 213-4; economic sanctions against, 197-204, 213-4; England and the Italian problem, 208-9; France's need for an understanding with, 209-10; Italian-German relations, 213; Russian and Italian interests are not in conflict, 214-5

Japan, and the extinction of China as a great power, 229; coercion of, 196-7, 203

INDEX

Jenkinson, Anthony, quoted, 12
Jews, 85-7, 111; persecution of, 6, 63, 106, 110, 112-21, 151, 167-9, 201
Jutland, battle of, 193

Kant, Immanuel, 12
"Kappist" counter-revolution of 1920, 20, 132, 134
Kautsky, 73
Kingdom of Heaven on Earth, Marxism and, 3, 13-5, 17-8, 22, 34, 37, 42, 44, 54, 61, 95, 185, 219
Kropotkin, Prince Peter, 73

Labor, organized, the power of, 83-4; the freedom of, 85; its defeat under Marxism, 85
Laval, Pierre, 198
League of Nations, although it has failed to stop war, it exercises beneficent secondary functions, 235; and sanctions, 186, 197-200; England and the leadership of a true League, 236; no League can be a substitute for policy, 237; should have no coercive powers, 234-6; the defects of the Covenant, 235
Lenin, Vladimir, 17; an advocate of ruthlessness, 69-73; and a Russian universal kingdom, 226; and capitalism, 64-5; and class war and international war, 48-9, 80, 88; and power, 85; and religion, 50, 52-9, 100-1; and Russian unity, 218; and terrorism, 72; and the democratic republic, 96; and the Marxian Kingdom of Heaven, 15, 17-9, 28, 61, 94; compared with Hitler, 49-50, 63; did not recognize the use of reform, 27; had a shrewd human judgment, 219; his attacks on the German Republic and the Social Democrats, 139-40; his attitude towards war, 71; his belief in the nobility of violent revolution, 104; his belief in the proletariat, 95-8; his belief in world-wide Socialist revolution, 20-1, 24-7, 94-9; his complete incapacity for philosophical and scientific thought, 40, 42, 48; his gift for the lapidary phrase, 103; his hatred, 73, 94, 104-5, 216; his hatred of pacifism, 75; his hatred of Social Democracy, 74; his hatred of the bourgeois, 75; his intolerance and his hatred of freedom, 76-7; his optimism with regard to human nature, 37; his ruthlessness, 220-1; his talent for conning political slogans, 109; his writings, 12, 36, 94, 98-9, 141; is absolutely humorless, 94; is rigid, static, intolerant, monomaniacal and unoriginal, 79; is unhistorical and subjective, 80; on revolutionary movements, 3; on Stalin and Trotsky, 219-20; on the Marxian theory, 40-2; on the State, 38-40, 42, 219; on the transition from capitalism to communism, 42-3; showed no mental development after he had reached early maturity, 78; the essential kinship of Lenin and Hitler, 77-9; to him the individual means nothing, 66-7; was a great strategist, 94, 98-9; was shrewd politician, but was in no sense a thinker, 49; was obsessed by history, 84; was unscrupulous, 105
Levinson, Salmon O., 281
Liebknecht, Karl, 143
Lies and credibility, 47
"Little man," 29, 32-3
Lloyd George, David, 97
Lossky, Nikolai O., 11
Ludendorff, Eric von, 128-9, 132, 136, 143, 196
Luxembourg, Rosa, 143

Macaulay, Lord, 81
Mann, Thomas, 152
Marx, Karl, 3, 12, 23, 26, 40-3, 91-2; and power, 85; and religion, 51-2, 101; and revolution in England without violence, 24-5; and terrorism, 71; and the Communist Manifesto, 6-7; and the State, 219; his mental arrogance, 42; Hitler on, 79; is unhistorical and subjective, 80; the prophet of class-war and class-consciousness, 80; was a great writer and a great personality, 92-4; was obsessed by history, 84-5; was original, 79
Marxism, and Chiliasm or expectation of the Millennium in this world, 14, 16-24, 45; and dialectical materialism, 3, 8-9, 14-6, 18, 35; and economic science, 64-5; and opposites, 3-5, 14-5, 23; and reform, 23-4, 26, 28; and religion, 33, 50-6, 58, 61-2; and science, 8, 12, 40-1,

INDEX

47-8; and Secular Messianism, or the hope of Heaven on Earth, 3, 13-8, 21-3, 33, 37, 41, 44, 54, 61-2, 219; and so-called self-criticism, 12; and the collective mass, 149-50; and the Fall, 46; and the petite bourgeoisie, 28-32; and the revolution or the "final struggle," 21-32, 44, 46, 66, 104; and the "withering away" of the State, 16-18, 35, 38, 40, 42; claims to be the Truth, 41-2; compared with the National Socialism, 35-6; is a denial of all but pragmatic thought, 13; is a religion of the mind rather than of the emotions, 36; is a secular religion, 3, 34-5, 97; is always in practice tyrannical, 219; is eschatology without God, 42; is intolerant of doubt, 9, 12; is obsessed with class and class welfare, 78, 80, 82; its ruthlessness, 69-72; its truculent crudity, 68; lives on hatred, 111; Marxian ethical standards, 43; Marxian attitude towards capitalism, 5-7, 21, 38, 43-4, 54; Marxist attitude towards events, persons, situations, 7; Marxian attitude toward mankind, 68; Marxian conception of history is sectarian and dictatorial, 82; Marxian theory is not a theory but a myth or ideology, 3, 8, 14; philosophy has no existence in, 8-12; professes to be scientific and objective, but is anti-scientific and subjective, 77-8; the feud between rival Marxian sects, 9; what the Marxist means by the State, 39-40

Max of Baden, Prince, 125
Mediterranean, its freedom and security, 199, 202-5, 208-10, 213-4, 217, 229-30
Mein Kampf, 7, 19, 36, 57-9, 71-2, 78-9, 101, 105, 112, 114, 148, 158-9, 167; its importance in studying contemporary German affairs, 101-3
Melians, 238
Memel, 140
Michaelis, Georg, 144
Militant nationalism, 151-2, 226, 228
Millennium. *See* Chiliasm.
Milton, John, his love of freedom, 76-7
Mongolia, Outer, 228
More, Sir Thomas, 276

Mussolini, Benito, and injury to the vital interests of England, 211; and the Abyssinian campaign, 199, 204; and the Mediterranean, 207; and war, 214; his appearance, 198; his character, 100-1, 280; is a conscious actor, 119

National Bolshevism, 141, 143, 147
National Socialism, a kind of modern Islam, established on the foundation of German unity, 154; and a Pro-German Empire, 158, 163-4, 169; and anti-Semitism, 6, 110; and colonies, 60; and economic science, 64-5; and religion, 34, 50, 55-63; and the doctrine of race and nationhood, 46, 48, 60-3, 66, 78; and the Fall, 46; and the supremacy of party, 57; and the unity of German-speaking people, 60; compared with Marxism, 36; is above all warlike, 167; is anti-political, 166; its attitude towards mankind, 68; its conception of history is sectarian and dictatorial, 82; its hostility to the Parliamentary system, 144; its mythological character, 46; its ruthlessness, 69-73; its truculent crudity, 69; lives on hatred, 111; rejects sovereignty of the mind and enthrones brutish instinct, 36; the falsehood that it was oppressed, 109; the language of Communism and National Socialism is often identical, 143; the National Socialist movement for ardent militancy, organized strength and inner cohesion has never been surpassed, 119; the National Socialist Party, 58, 103; the revolution of 1933, 107, 127, 147-8, 152; why it has proved more powerful than Marxism, 36; would have been inconceivable without Marxism, 35
Nationalism, 151-2, 226, 228
Nationhood and National Socialism, 60-3, 66, 78
Newspaper readers, 67
Nietzsche, Friedrich, a profound thinker, 92; and Socialism, 34; loathed anti-Semitism, 151; on the popular leader of the Hitler type, 152; on the study of history, 85
Non-intervention, 209-10, 217
North Sea, command of, 230-1

INDEX

Opposites and Marxism, 4-6, 14-5, 23
Overbeck, Protestant theologian, 152
Owen, Wilfred, 184

Pacifism, Lenin's and Hitler's hatred, 75-6
Pan-German Empire, 158-60, 163-4, 169
Papen, Franz von, 123
Pares, Sir Bernard, quoted, 53
Parliamentary system in Germany, 144
Pascal, Blaise, 12
Pax Americana, 177, 238
Pax Britannica, 175, 177, 179, 196
Pax Europaica, 177-8, 232-3, 235
Peace, Communists' and National Socialists' attitude towards, 167; England's share in the enforcement of world peace, 196; maintenance of peace in Europe, 232-4; the love of, and attainment of, 175-87; the doctrine of sanctions, 185-90, 196
Persia, Russian influence on, 227
Philosophy and Marxism, 8-9, 11-12
Plato, 17, 83
Poland, a strong Poland essential to maintain the balance between Russia and Germany, 162; German eastward expansion, at the expense of Poland, 164; Russia and the eastern regions of, 218; the Poles are in a state of latent anarchy, 170; freed from German rule, 155-6, 159; in danger of being crushed between Germany and Russia, 161; their treatment of minorities, 172; the Polish "corridor," 155
Politicians and religion, 57-8
Portugal, German political influence in, 231
Poverty, Marxism and, 91-2
Power, its corruption, 84
Pragmatic sciences and Marxism, 12-13
Production, collective control of, 78
Proletarians, 16, 17-20, 22-3, 27, 37-8, 44, 48, 53, 61, 66, 79, 82-3, 95-8, 151
Protestantism, Hitler and, 56-59
Protocols, of the Elders of Zion, 113-6

Race and National Socialism, 46, 60-2, 66, 78, 85-91
Radek, Karl, 138, 142
Red Sea, 214
Reform, Marxism and, 23-4, 26-7

Reichstag, burning of, 110
Religion, and Marxism, 51-6, 58, 62; and National Socialism, 48, 55-62, 122-3. *See also* Secular religion
Revolution, Marxism and, 3, 19-32, 43-4, 46, 66, 104
Rhineland, occupation of, 140, 156; German reoccupation of, 172; separatist movement in, 131, 135
Right, National Socialist and Marxian ideas of, 66-7, 238
Roehm, Captain, 120
Roman Catholic Church, Hitler and, 56, 59
Rosenberg, Isaac, 184
Ruhr, the, 134, 140, 147-8, 156
Rumania, 164, 218
Russia, achievement of the "new Russia" examined, 218-29; and a universal kingdom, 226; and an Anglo-German war, 217; and the League of Nations, 33, 215; and the pragmatic sciences, 12; and the treaty of Brest-Litovsk, 157; apparent success of Marxism in, 34-5; appeal of Marxian Messianism in, 28; Communism has established social and national unity, 217-9; education in, 12-3; effects of the revolution throughout Asia, 227-9; German colonization of European Russia, 101, 163; German infringement upon, 169; her Far Eastern imperialism, 228; her hatred of England, 217, 228; her ruthless attacks on the German Republic, 137, 146; her tragic past, 222; Hitler and a war of conquest against, 159-64; industry, 223; nationalism in, 226, 229; opposition not tolerated in, 10; philosophy does not exist in, 11-2; political persecution in, 11; religion in, 53-4, 58-9, 225; revolution of 1917, 99, 154, 222; Russian and Italian interests not in conflict, 214-5; terrorism, 36-7; the Five-Year Plan, 221; what a genuine German-Russian understanding would do, 163; what she is and what she stands for is injurious to Western civilization, 226-7

Sakhalin, 158
Sanctions, 185-92, 195-206, 236
Scheidemann, Philipp, 126
Schlageter, revolutionary, 142

INDEX

Science and Marxism, 8, 12, 39-41, 46-7, 77; and National Socialism, 77-8
Secular Messianism. *See* Kingdom of Heaven on Earth
Secular religion, 3, 35-7, 51, 55-6, 59, 97, 100-1, 142, 150-1, 154, 165-7, 177, 211, 233, 239
Silesia, armed rebellion in, 140; Upper Silesia, 155-6
Sinkiang, 228
Sino-Japanese War, 141
Slavs, 156, 170, 172, 206
Social Democrats, and the class-war, 88; and religion, 122; and the German Republic, 124-7, 133-8; and the unity of Germany, 124-5, 133-4; and the working man, 122, 125; collapse of, 135-9, 147; Lenin's hatred of Social Democracy, 73-4; subjected to ruthless attacks by Russia, 138-46; their achievement and influence, 124-6; their attitude towards Marxism, 122-3
Social Fascism, 141
Socialism an advanced form of capitalism, 5, 63; would remove certain evils, but has evils of its own, 6
Solovieff's "Anti-Christ," 34
Sorel, Albert, 100
Spanish civil war, 202, 208-9, 214, 217, 232
Spinoza, Baruch, 12
Stalin, Josef V., 12, 108; and Russian unity, 218; and the British Empire, 33; and the stamping out of Trotskyism, 11; his servility, 143; Russia under his despotism, 81, 86, 160, 216, 219-20, 223-5
State, the, Engels and Lenin on, 37-9, 42-3, 218-9; Hegel on, 38; is necessary because of sin, 18, 38-9; Marxism and its "withering away," 16, 34, 38, 40, 43, 176, 219
Suez Canal, closing of, 199
Swift, Jonathan, 17, 245, 264, 275-6

Terrorism in Russia and Germany, 37, 70-1, 107-8, 136-7, 170; Lenin and Hitler's belief in, 72
Third International, 215-6
Third Realm, 123, 136, 139, 142, 147, 149-50, 152-5, 159, 163-5, 170, 206, 215, 231
Thomas of Aquinas, St., 12
Thucydides, 81-2, 254
Tolstoi, Count Leo, 54
Tooke, Horne, 49
Trade Union International, 139
Trade Unionism, 83-4
Trotsky, Leon, 220
Trotskyism, 9-11
Tseretelli, 73
Turkey, Russian influence on, 227

Ukraine, 157
United States, Anglo-American harmony, 195, 236-8
Universal spirit, 9

Versailles Treaty, 97, 128, 131-3, 136, 147-9, 154-9, 181

War, causes of, 180-3; Communists and National Socialists always warlike, 166-7; defensive and aggressive wars, 178-83; Germany and another European war, 164-6; Hitler and Lenin on class war and international war, 49, 71-2; Hitler regards territorial expansion impossible without war, 158; its prevention by the use of sanctions, 185-9, 197, 204; Mussolini and, 213-5; promotes national unity, 171-2; revulsion against, 184-5; should not be declared for a principle, 200; the German people and, 171; there is no good in war, 178
Weimar Republic, 26
Wessel, Horst, 142
"White race," 86
William II, Kaiser, 125-6, 132, 152-3
Wilson, President, 128
Wirth, Albrecht, 160
Women, communal ownership of, 7
Working class, and reforms, 25-6; in Germany, 171; Social Democrats and, 123-5
World Power, 191-2, 213-4, 236

Yugoslavs, 170

Zinovieff, Grigoryi, his abuse of Social Democracy, 139, 141